SAFE ON BOARD AGAIN

[FRONTISPIECE]

SEE PAGE 211.

UNDER DRAKE'S FLAG

A TALE OF THE SPANISH MAIN

G. A. HENTY

With Illustrations by
GORDON BROWN

DOVER PUBLICATIONS, INC.
MINEOLA, NEW YORK

Bibliographical Note

This Dover edition, first published in 2005, is an unabridged republication of the edition originally published by Charles Scribner's Sons, New York, in 1905.

International Standard Book Number: 0-486-44215-2

Manufactured in the United States of America
Dover Publications, Inc., 31 East 2nd Street, Mineola, N.Y. 11501

CONTENTS

ILLUSTRATIONS

CHAPTER I

The Wreck on the Devon Coast

It was a stormy morning in the month of May, 1572, and the fishermen of the little village of Westport, situate about five miles from Plymouth, clustered in the public-house of the place, and discussed, not the storm, for that was a common topic, but the fact that Master Francis Drake, whose ships lay now at Plymouth, was visiting the Squire of Treadwood, had passed through the village over night, and might go through it again to-day. There was not one of the hardy fishermen there but would gladly have joined Drake's expedition; for marvellous tales had been told of the great booty which he and other well-known captains had already obtained from the Dons on the Spanish Main. The number, however, who could go was limited, and even of these the seafaring men were but a small proportion; for in those days, although a certain number of sailors were required to trim the sails and navigate the ship, the strength of the company were the fighting men, who were soldiers by trade, and fought on board ship as if on land. Captain Drake was accompanied by many men of good Devon blood, for that county was then ahead of all England in its enterprise and its seamanship, and no captain of name or repute ever had any difficulty in getting together a band of adventurers from the sturdy population of her shores.

"I went over myself last week," said a finely-built young sailor, "and I prayed the captain on my knees to take me on board; but he said the tale had been full long ago, and that so many were the applicants that Master Drake and himself had sworn a great oath that they would take none beyond those already engaged."

"Aye! I would have gone myself," said a grizzly, weather-beaten old sailor, "if they would have had me. There was Will Trelawney, who went on such another expedition as this, and came back with more bags of Spanish dollars than he could carry. Truly they are a gold mine, these Western seas; but even better than getting gold is the thrashing of those haughty Spaniards, who seem to look upon themselves as gods, and on all others as fit only to clean their worships' boots."

"They cannot fight neither, can they?" asked a young sailor.

"They can fight, boy, and have fought as well as we could; but somehow they cannot stand against us in those seas. Whether it is that the curse of the poor natives whom they kill, enslave, and ill-treat in every way rises against them, and takes away their courage and their nerve, but certain is it that when our little craft lay alongside their big galleons, fight as they will, the battle is as good as over. Nothing less than four to one, at the very least, has any chance against our buccaneers."

"They ill-treat those that fall into their hands, do they not?"

"Ay do they!" said the old sailor. "They tear off their flesh with hot pincers, wrench out their nails, and play all sorts of devil's games, and then at last they burn what is left of them in the market-places. I have heard tell of fearsome tales, lad; but the Spaniards outwit themselves. Were our men to have fair treatment as prisoners of war, it may be that the Spaniards would often be able to hold their own against us; but the knowledge that if we are taken this horrible fate is certain to be ours, makes our men fight with a desperate fury, and never to give in as long as one is left. This it is that accounts for the wonderful victories which we have gained there. He would be a coward, indeed, who would not fight with thumb-screws and a bonfire behind him."

"It is said that the queen and her ministers favor, though not openly, these adventures."

"She cannot do it openly," said the old man, "for here in Europe we are at peace with Spain—worse luck."

"How is it, then, that if we are at peace here we can be at war in the Indian Seas?"

"That is more than I can tell thee, lad. I guess the queen's writ runs not so far as that, and while her majesty's commands must be obeyed, and the Spanish flag suffered to pass unchallenged on these seas, on the Spanish Main there are none to keep the peace, and the Don and the Englishman go at each other's throats as a thing of nature."

"The storm is rising, methinks. It is not often I have heard the wind howl more loudly. It is well that the adventurers have not yet started, it would be bad for any craft caught in the Channel to-day."

As he spoke he looked from the casement. Several people were seen hurrying toward the beach.

"Something is the matter, lads; maybe a ship is driving on the rocks even now."

Seizing their hats and cloaks, the party sallied out and hurried down to the shore. There they saw a large ship driving in before the wind into the bay. She was making every effort that seamanship could suggest to beat clear of the head, but the sailors saw at once that her case was hopeless.

"She will go on the Black Shoal, to a certainty," the old sailor said, "and then, may God have mercy on their souls."

"Can we do nothing to help them?" a woman standing near asked.

"No, no," the sailor said; "we could not launch a boat in the teeth of this tremendous sea. All we can do is to look out and throw a line to any who may be washed ashore on a spar when she goes to pieces."

Presently a group of men, whose dress belonged to the upper class, moved down through the street to the beach.

"Aye! there is Mr. Trevelyan," said the sailor, "and the gentleman beside him is Captain Drake himself."

The group moved on to where the fishermen were standing.

"Is there no hope," they asked, "of helping the ship?"

The seamen shook their heads.

"You will see for yourself, Master Drake, that no boat could live in such a sea as this."

"It could not put out from here," the captain said; "but if they could lower one from the ship, it might live until it got into the breakers."

"Aye, aye," said a sailor; "but there is no lowering a boat from a ship which has begun to beat on the Black Shoal."

"Another minute and she will strike," the old sailor said.

All gazed intently at the ship. The whole population of the village were now on the shore, and were eager to render any assistance, if it were possible. In another minute or two a general cry announced that the ship had struck. Rising high on a wave she came down with a force which caused her mainmast at once to go over the side, another lift on the next sea and then high and fast she was jammed on the rocks of the Black Shoal. The distance from shore was but small, not more than three hundred yards, and the shouts of the sailors on board could be heard in the storm.

"Why does not one of them jump over with a rope?" Captain Drake said, impatiently. "Are the men all cowards, or can none of them swim? It would be easy to swim from that ship to the shore, while it is next to impossible for any one to make his way out through these breakers. Is there no one who can reach her from here?" he said, looking round.

"No one among us, your honor," the old sailor said; "few here can keep themselves up in the water in a calm sea, but if man or boy could swim through that surf, it is the lad who is just coming down from behind us. The 'Otter,' as we call him, for he seems to be able to live in water as well as on land."

The lad of whom they were speaking was a bright-faced boy of some fifteen years of age. He was squarely built, and his dress differed a little from that of the fisher lads standing on the beach.

"Who is he?" asked Captain Drake.

"He is the son of the schoolmaster here, a learned man, and they do say one who was once wealthy. The lad himself would fain go to sea, but his father keeps him here. It is a pity, for he is a bold boy, and would make a fine sailor."

The "Otter," as he had been called, had now come down to the beach, and, with his hands shading his eyes from the spray, sheets of which the wind carried along with blinding force, he gazed at the ship and the sea with a steady intentness.

"I think I can get out to her," he said, to the fishermen.

"It is madness, boy," Captain Drake said. "There are few men, indeed, so far as I know, in these climes—I talk not of the heathens of the Western Islands—who could swim through a breaking sea like yonder."

"I think I can do it," the boy said, quietly. "I have been out in as heavy seas before, and if one does but choose one's time, and humor them a bit, the waves are not much to be feared after all. Get me the light line," he said to the sailors, "and I will be off at once." So saying he carelessly threw off his clothes. The fishermen brought a light line; one end they fastened round his shoulders, and with a cheerful good-by he ran down to the water's edge. The sea was breaking with tremendous violence, and the chance of the lad's getting out through the breakers appeared slight indeed. He watched, however, quietly for three or four minutes, when a wave larger than usual broke on the beach. Following it out he stood knee-deep till the next great wave advanced, then with a plunge he dived in beneath it. It seemed an age before he was again seen, and Captain Drake expressed his fear that his head must have been dashed against a rock beneath the water. But the men said, "He dives like a duck, sir, and has often frightened us by the time he keeps under water. You will see he will come up beyond the second line of waves."

It seemed an age to the watchers before a black spot appeared suddenly beyond the foaming line of breakers. There was a general shout of "There he is!" But they had scarce time to note the position of the swimmer when he again disappeared. Again and again he came up, each time rapidly decreasing the distance between himself and the shipwrecked vessel, and keeping his head above the waves for a few seconds only at each appearance.

The people in the vessel were watching the progress of the lad with attention and interest even greater than was manifested by those on shore, and as he approached the ship, which already showed signs of breaking up, a line was thrown to him. He caught it, but instead of holding on and being lifted to the ship, he fastened the light rope which he had brought out to it, and made signs to them to haul.

"Fasten a thicker rope to it," he shouted, "and they will haul it in from the shore." It would have been no easy matter to get on board the ship; so, having done his work, the lad turned to make his way back to the shore. A thick rope was fastened at once by those of the crew who still remained on the deck of the vessel to the lighter one, and those on shore began to pull it rapidly in, but ere the knotted joint reached the shore a cry from all gathered on the beach showed that the brave attempt of the "Otter" had been useless. A tremendous sea had struck the ship, and in a moment it broke up, and a number of floating fragments alone showed where a fine vessel had a few minutes before floated on the sea.

The lad paused in his course toward the shore, and, looking round, endeavored to face the driving wind and spray in hopes that he might see among the fragments of the wreck some one to whom his assistance might be of use. For a time he could see no signs of a human being among the floating masses of wreck, and indeed he was obliged to use great caution in keeping away from these, as a blow from any of the larger spars might have been fatal. Presently close to him he heard a short muffled bark, and looking round saw a large dog with a child in its mouth. The animal, which was of the mastiff breed, appeared already exhausted. The "Otter" looked hastily round, and seeing a piece of wreck of suitable size he seized it, and with some difficulty succeeded in bringing it close to the dog. Fortunately the spar was a portion of one of the yards, and still had a quantity of rope connected to it. He now took hold of the child's clothes, the dog readily yielding up the treasure he had carried, seeing that the new-comer was likely to afford better assistance than himself. In a few moments the child was fastened to the spar, and the "Otter" began steadily to push it toward the shore, the dog swimming alongside, evidently much relieved at getting rid of his burden. When he neared the line of breakers the lad waved his hand as a sign to them to prepare to rush forward and lend a hand when the spar approached. He then paddled forward quietly, and keeping just outside the line of the breakers waved to those on shore to throw, if possible, a rope. Several attempts were made to hurl a stone, fastened to the end of a light line, within his reach.

After many failures he at last caught the line. This he fastened to the spar, and signalled to those on shore to pull it in, then side by side with the dog he followed. Looking round behind him he watched a great breaker rolling in, and, as before, dived as it passed over his head, and rode forward on the swell toward the shore. Then there was a desperate struggle: at one moment his feet touched the ground, at another he was hauled back and tossed into the whirling sea; sometimes almost losing his consciousness, but ever keeping his head cool and striving steadily to make progress. Several times he was dashed against the beach with great force, and it was his knowledge that the only safe way of approaching shore through a heavy surf is to keep sideways to the waves, and allow them to roll one over and over, that he escaped death—for had he advanced straight toward the shore the force of the waves would have rolled him heels-over-head, and would almost certainly have broken his neck.

At last, just as consciousness was leaving him, and he thought that he could struggle no more, a hand grasped his arm. The fishermen, joining hand in hand, had gone down into the surf, and after many ineffectual efforts had at last seized him as a retiring wave was carrying him out again for the fifth time. With the consciousness of rescue all feeling left him, and it was some minutes before he recovered his senses. His first question was for the safety of the child on the spar, and he was glad to hear that it had come to shore without hurt. The dog, too, had been rolled up the beach, and seized before taken off again, but had broken one of its legs.

The "Otter" was soon on his feet again, and saying, "I must make my way home, they will be alarmed about me," was about to turn away when a group of gentlemen standing near advanced.

"You are a fine lad," one of them said to him. "A fine lad, and an honor to the south of Devonshire. My name is Francis Drake, and if there be aught that I can do for you, now or hereafter, I shall be glad indeed to do my utmost for so gallant a youth as yourself."

"Oh, sir!" the boy exclaimed, his cheek flushing with excitement. "If you are Master Francis Drake, will you let me join your ship for the voyage to the Indies?"

"Ah! my boy," the gentleman said, "you have asked the only thing, perhaps, which I should feel obliged to refuse you. Already we have more than our number, and to avoid the importunity of the many who wish to go, or of my powerful friends who desired to place sons or relations in my charge, I have been obliged to swear that I would take no other sailor in addition to those already shipped. You are, however, young," he said, as he marked the change in the boy's face, "and I promise you that if I come back, and again sail on an expedition like that on which I now start, that you shall be one of my crew. What is your name, lad? I hear them call you Otter, and truly the beast is no better swimmer than you are."

"My name, sir, is Ned Hearne; my father is the schoolmaster here."

"Will he consent, think you, to your taking to a seafaring life?"

"Methinks he will, sir, he knows that my heart is set upon it, for he hath often said if I loved my lessons with one-tenth of the love I bear for the sea, I should make a good scholar and be a credit to him."

"I will not forget you, lad. Trust me, and when you hear of my return, fail not to send a reminder, and to claim a place in my next adventure."

Ned Hearne, delighted at the assurance, ran off at full speed to the cottage where his father resided at the end of the village. The domine, who was an old man, wore the huge tortoise-shell rimmed spectacles of the time.

"Wet again," he said, as his son burst into the room in which he was sitting studying a Greek tome. "Truly thou earnest the name of which thou art so proud, Otter, hardly. What tempted thee to go into the water on a day like this?"

Ned briefly explained what had taken place. The story was no unusual one, for this was the third time that he had swum out to vessels on the rocks between Westport and Plymouth. Then he related to his father how Captain Francis Drake had spoken to him and praised him, and how he had promised that, on his next trip to the West Indies, he would take him with him.

"I would not have you count too much upon that," the domine said, dryly. "It is like, indeed, that he may never come back from this hare-brain adventure, and if he brings home his skin safe, he will, methinks, have had enough of burning in the sun and fighting the Spaniards."

"But hath he not already made two or three voyages thither, father?" the boy asked.

"That is true enough," said his father; "but from what I gather these were mere trips to spy out the land. This affair on which he starts now will be, I wot, a very different matter."

"How is it, father," the boy said, on the following morning, re-suming the conversation from the point which they were at when he went up to change his wet clothes the day before, "that when England is at peace with Spain, our sailors and the Spanish do fight bloodily in the West Indies?"

"That, my son, is a point upon which the Roman law telleth us nothing. I have in my shelves some very learned treatises on war, but in none do I find mention of a state of things in which two powers at peace at home, do fight desperately at the ex-treme end of the earth."

"But, father, do you think it not lawful to kill the Spaniard, and to take the treasures which he robbeth from the poor hea-then of the West?"

"I know not about lawful, my son, but I see no warrant what-soever for it; and as for heathen, indeed, it appears to me that the attacks upon him do touch very closely upon piracy upon the high seas. However, as the country in general appeareth to ap-prove of it, and as it is said that the queen's most gracious majesty doth gladly hear of the beating of the Spaniards in those seas, it becometh not me to question the rights of the case."

"At any rate, father, you would not object when the time comes for me to sail with Mr. Francis Drake?"

"No, my boy; thou hast never shown any aptitude whatever for learning. Thou canst read and write, but beyond that thy knowledge runneth not. Your mind seems to be set on the water, and when you are not in it you are on it, therefore it appears to me to be flying in the face of Providence to try to keep you on shore. Had your poor mother lived, it would have been a different thing. Her mind was set upon your becoming a clerk; but there, one might as well try to make a silk purse from the ear of a sow. But I tell you again, count not too much upon this promise, it may be years before Mr. Francis Drake may be in a position to keep it."

Had Ned Hearne watched for Captain Drake's second voyage, he would, indeed, as his father had said, have waited long. Three days after the conversation, however, a horseman from Plymouth rode into the little village, and inquired for the house of Master Hearne. Being directed thither, he rode up in haste to the gate.

"Here is a letter!" he cried, "for the son of the schoolmaster, who goes by the name of the 'Otter.'"

"I am he," Ned cried. "What is it, and who can have written to me?"

"It is a letter from His Honor the Worshipful Mr. Francis Drake."

Seizing the letter, Ned broke the seal, read a few lines, threw his cap into the air with a shout of joy, and rushed in to his father.

"Father," he said, "Captain Drake has written to acquaint me that one of the boys in his ship has been taken ill and cannot go, and that it has pleased him to appoint me to go in his place, and that I am to be at Plymouth in three days at the utmost, bringing with me what gear may require for the expedition."

The schoolmaster was a little taken aback at this sudden prospect of departure, but he had always been wholly indulgent to his son, and it was not in his nature to refuse to allow him to avail himself of an opportunity which appeared to be an excellent one. The danger of these expeditions was no doubt very great, but the spoils were in proportion, and there was not a boy or man of the seafaring population of Devon who would not gladly have gone with the adventurous captains.

CHAPTER II

Friends and Foes

Three days after the receipt of the letter, Ned Hearne stood with his bundle on the quay at Plymouth. Near him lay a large row-boat from the ships, waiting to take off the last comers. A little way behind, Captain Francis Drake and his brother, Captain John Drake, talked with the notable people of Plymouth, who had come down to bid them farewell, the more since this was a holiday, being Whitsun Eve, the 24th of May, and all in the town who could spare time had made their way down to the Hove to watch the departure of the expedition, for none could say how famous this might become, or how great deeds would be accomplished by the two little craft lying there. Each looker-on thought to himself that it might be that to the end of his life he should tell his children and his children's children with pride, "I saw Mr. Drake start for his great voyage."

Small indeed did the fleet appear in comparison to the work which it had to do. It was composed of but two vessels. The first, the *Pacha,* of seventy tons, carrying forty-seven men and boys, was commanded by Captain Francis Drake himself. By her side was the *Swanne,* of twenty-five tons, carrying twenty-six men and boys, and commanded by Captain John Drake. This was truly but a small affair to undertake so great a voyage. In those days the Spaniards were masters of the whole of South America and of the Isles of the West Indies. They had many very large towns full of troops, and great fleets armed to carry the treasure which was collected there, to Spain. It did seem almost like an act of madness that two vessels, which by the side of those of the Spaniards were mere cockle-shells, manned in all by less than eighty men, should attempt to enter a region where they would be regarded, and rightly, as enemies, and where the hand of every man would be against them.

Captain Drake and his men thought little of these things. The success which had attended their predecessors had inspired the English sailors with a belief in their own invincibility when opposed to the Spaniards. They looked to a certain extent upon their mission as a crusade. In those days England had a horror of Popery, and Spain was the mainstay and supporter of this religion. The escape which England had had of having Popery forced upon it during the reign of Mary, by her spouse, Philip of Spain, had been a narrow one, and even now it was by no means certain that Spain would not sooner or later endeavor to carry out the pretensions of the late queen's husband. Then, too, terrible tales had come of the sufferings of the Indians at the hands of the Spaniards, and it was certain that the English sailors who had fallen into the hands of Spain had been put to death with horrible cruelty. Thus, then, the English sailors regarded the Spaniards as the enemy of their country, as the enemy of their religion, and as the enemy of humanity. Besides which, it cannot be denied that they viewed them as rich men well worth plundering; and although, when it came to fighting, it is probable that hatred overbore the thought of gain, it is certain that the desire for gold was in itself the main incentive to those who sailed upon these expeditions.

Amid the cheers of the townsfolk the boats pushed off, Mr. Francis Drake and his brother waving their plumed hats to the burghers of Plymouth, and the sailors giving a hurrah as they bent to the oars. Ned Hearne, who had received a kind word of greeting from Mr. Drake, had taken his place in the bow of one of the boats, lost in admiration at the scene, and at the thought that he was one of this band of heroes who were going out to fight the Spaniards, and to return laden with countless treasure wrested from them. At the thought his eyes sparkled, his blood seemed to dance through his veins. The western main in those days was a name almost of enchantment. Such strange tales had been brought home by the voyagers who had navigated those seas, of the wonderful trees, the bright birds, the beauties of nature, the gold and silver, and the abundance of all precious things, that it was the dream of every youngster on the seaboard some day to penetrate to these charmed regions. A week since and the realization of the dream had appeared beyond his wildest hopes. Now, almost with the suddenness of a transformation scene, this had changed, and there was he on his way out to the *Swanne,* a part of the expedition itself. It was to the *Swanne* that he had been allotted, for it was on board that ship that the boy whose place he was to take had been seized with illness.

Although but twenty-five tons in burden, the *Swanne* made a far greater show than would be made by a craft of that size in the present day. The ships of the time lay but lightly on the water, while their hulls were carried up to a prodigious height, and it is not too much to say that the portion of the *Swanne* above water was fully as large as the hull which we see of a merchantman of four times her tonnage. Still, even so, it was but a tiny craft to cross the Atlantic, and former voyages had been generally made in larger ships. Mr. Francis Drake, however, knew what he was about. He considered that large ships required large crews to be left behind to defend them, that they drew more water and were less handy, and he resolved in this expedition he would do no small part of his work with pinnaces and row-boats, and of these he had three fine craft now lying in pieces in his hold, ready to fit together on arriving in the Indies. As they neared the ships the two boats separated, and Ned soon found himself alongside of the *Swanne.* A ladder hung at her side, and up this Ned followed his captain, for in those days the strict etiquette that the highest goes last had not been instituted.

"Master Holyoake," said Mr. John Drake, to a big and powerful-looking man standing near, "this is the new lad, whose skill in swimming and whose courage I told you of yesternight. He will, I doubt not, be found as willing as he is brave, and I trust that you will put him in the way of learning his business as a sailor. It is his first voyage; he comes on board a green hand, but I doubt not that ere the voyage be finished he will have become a smart young sailor."

"I will put him through," John Holyoake, sailing-master of the ship, replied, for in those days the sailing-master was the navigator of the ship, and the captain was as often as not a soldier, who knew nothing whatever about seamanship. The one sailed the ship, the other fought it; and the admirals were in those days more frequently known as generals, and held that position on shore. As Ned looked round the deck he thought that he had never seen a finer set of sailors. All were picked men, hardy and experienced, and for the most part young. Some had made previous voyages to the West Indies, but the greater portion were new to that country. They looked the men on whom a captain could rely to the last. Tall and stalwart, bronzed with the sun, and with a reckless and fearless expression about them which boded ill to any foes upon whom they might fall. Although Ned had never been to sea on a long voyage, he had sailed too often in the fishing-boats of his native village to have any qualm of sea-sickness, or to feel in any degree like a new hand. He was, therefore, at once assigned to a place and duty. An hour later the admiral, as Mr. Francis Drake was called, fired a gun, the two vessels hoisted their broad sails and turned their heads from shore, and the crews of both ships gave a parting cheer as they turned their faces to the south.

As Ned was not in the slightest degree either homesick or seasick, he at once fell to work, laughing and joking with the other boys, of whom there were three on board. He found that their duties consisted of bearing messages, of hauling any rope to which they were told to fix themselves, and in receiving, with as good a face as might be, the various orders, to say nothing of the various kicks, which might be bestowed upon them by all on board. At the same time their cheerful countenances showed that these things, which, when told, sounded a little terrible, were, in truth, in no way serious.

Ned was first shown where he was to sling his hammock, and how; where he was to get his food, and under whose orders he was specially to consider himself; the master for the present taking him under his own charge. For the next ten days, as the vessel sailed calmly along with a favoring wind, Ned had learned all the names of the ropes and sails, and their uses; could climb aloft, and do his share of the work of the ship; and if not yet a skilled sailor, was at least on the highroad to become one. The master was pleased at his willingness and eagerness to oblige, and he soon became a great favorite of his. Between the four boys on the ship a good feeling existed. All had been chosen as a special favor, upon the recommendation of one or other of those in authority. Each of them had made up his mind that one of these days he too would command an expedition to the West Indies. Each thought of the glory which he would attain; and although in the hearts of many of the elder men in the expedition the substantial benefits to be reaped stood higher than any ideas of glory or honor, to the lads, at least, pecuniary gain exercised no inducement whatever. They burned to see the strange country, and to gain some of the credit and glory which would, if the voyage was successful, attach to each member of the crew. All were full of fun, and took what came to them in the way of work so good-temperedly and cheerfully, that the men soon ceased to give them work for work's sake. They were, too, a strong and well-built group of boys. Ned was by a full year the youngest, and by night a head the shortest of them; but his broad shoulders and sturdy build, and the strength acquired by long practice in swimming and rowing, made him their equal.

There were, however, no quarrels among them, and their strength they agreed to use in alliance, if need be, should any of the crew make a dead set at one or other of them; for even in an expedition like this there must be some brutal as well as many brave men. There were assuredly two or three, at least, of those on board the *Swanne* who might well be called brutal. They were for the most part old hands, who had lived on board ship half their lives, had taken part in the slave traffic of Captain Hawkins, and in the buccaneering exploits of the earlier commanders. To them the voyage was one in which the lust of gold was the sole stimulant, and, accustomed to deeds of bloodshed, what feelings they ever had, had become utterly blunted, and they needed but the power, to become despotic and brutal masters.

The chief among these was Giles Taunton, the armorer. He was a swarthy ruffian, who hid beneath the guise of a jovial *bonhomie* a cruel and unfeeling nature. He was ever ready to cuff and beat the boys on the smallest provocation. They soon gathered together, in a sort of defensive league, against their common oppressors. All four were high-spirited lads; the other three, indeed, were sons of men of substance in Devon, whose fathers had lent funds to Captain Drake for the carrying out of his great enterprise. They, therefore, looked but ill on the kicks and curses which occasionally fell to their lot. One day they gathered together round the bowsprit, and talked over what they should do. Gerald Summers, the eldest of the party, proposed that they should go in a body to Captain Drake, and complain of the tyranny to which they were subject. After some talk, however, all agreed that such a course as this would lower them in the estimation of the men, and that it would be better to put up with the ill-treatment than to get the name of tell-tales.

Ned then said to the others: "It seems to me that if we do but hold together we need not be afraid of this big bully. If we all declare to each other, and swear that the first time he strikes one of us we will all set upon him, my faith on it we shall be able to master him, big as he is; we are all of good size, and in two years will think ourselves men; therefore it would be shame indeed if the four of us could not master one, however big and sturdy he may be.

After much consultation it was agreed that this course should be adopted, and the next day, as Reuben Gale was passing by Giles, he turned round and struck him on the head with a broom. The boy gave a long whistle, and in a moment, to the astonishment of the armorer, the other three lads rushed up and at once assailed him with fury. Astonished at such an attack, he struck out at them with many strange oaths. Gerald he knocked down, but Ned leaped on his back from behind, and the other two, closing with him, rolled him on to the deck; then despite of his efforts, they pummelled him until his face was swollen and bruised, and his eyes nearly closed.

Some of the men of his own sort, standing by, would fain have interfered; but the better disposed of the crew, who had seen with disgust the conduct of the armorer and his mates to the boys, held them back, and said that none should come between. Just as the boys drew off, and allowed the furious armorer to rise to his feet, Captain John Drake, attracted by the unusual noise, came from his cabin.

"What is this?" he asked.

"These young wild-cats have leapt upon me," said Giles Taunton, furiously, "and have beaten me nigh to death, but I will have my turn; they will see, and bitterly shall they have cause to regret what they have done."

"We have been driven almost weary of our lives, sir, with the foul and rough conduct of this man, and of some of his mates," Gerald said; "we did not like to come to tell you of it, and to gain the name of carry-tales; but we had resolved among ourselves at last that, whoever struck one of us, the whole should set upon him. To-day we have carried it out, and we have shown Giles Taunton that we are more than a match for one man at any rate."

"Four good-sized dogs, if they are well managed," said Captain John Drake, "will pull down a lion, and the best thing that the lion can do is to leave them alone. I am sorry to hear, Master Taunton, that you have chosen to ill-treat these lads, who are indeed the sons of worthy men, and are not the common kind of ship-boys. I am sure that my brother would not brook such conduct, and I warn you that if any complaint again on this head reaches me I shall lay it before him."

With angry mutterings the armorer went below.

"We have earned a bitter foe," Ned said to his friends, "and we had best keep our eyes well open. There is very little of the lion about Master Taunton. He is strong indeed; but if it be true that the lion has a noble heart, and fights his foes openly, methinks he resembles rather the tiger, who is most prone to leap suddenly upon his enemies."

"Yes, indeed, he looked dark enough," Gerald said, "as he went below; and if looks could have killed us, we should not be standing here alive at present."

"It is not force that we need fear now, but that he will do us some foul turn; at all events we are now forewarned, and if he plays us a scurvy trick it will be our own faults."

For several days the voyage went on quietly and without adventure. They passed at a distance the Portuguese Isle of Madeira, lying like a cloud on the sea. The weather now had become warm and very fair, a steady wind blew, and the two barks kept along at a good pace. All sorts of creatures strange to the boys were to be seen in the sea. Sometimes there was a spout of a distant whale. Thousands of flying-fish darted from the water, driven thence by the pursuit of their enemies beneath, while huge flocks of gulls and other birds hovered over the sea, chasing the flying-fish or pouncing down upon the shoals of small fry whose splashings whitened the surface of the water, as if a sandbank had laid below it.

Gradually as the time went on the heat increased. Many of the crew found themselves unable to sleep below, for in those days there was but little thought of ventilation. The boys were among these, for the heat and the confinement were to them especially irksome. One day the wind had fallen almost to a calm, and the small boat had been lowered to enable the carpenter to do some repair to the ship's side, where a seam leaked somewhat when the waves were high. When night came on and all was quiet Ned proposed to the others that they should slip down the rope over the stern into the boat which was towing behind, where they could sleep undisturbed by the tramp of the sentry or the call to pull at ropes and trim sails.

The idea was considered a capital one, and the boys slid down into the boat, where, taking up their quarters as comfortably as they could, they, after a short chat, curled themselves up and were soon sound asleep, intending to be on board again with the earliest gleam of morn.

When they awoke, however, it was with a start and a cry. The sun was already high, but there were no signs whatever of the ship; they floated alone in the mid-ocean. With blank amazement they looked at each other.

"This is a stroke of misfortune indeed," Gerald said. "We have lost the ship and I fear our lives as well. What do you say, 'Otter'?" for the lad's nickname had come on board ship with him and he was generally known by it.

"It seems to me," said Ned, "that our friend the armorer has done us this bad turn. I am sure that the rope was well tied, for I was the first who slipped down it, and I looked at the knot well before I went over the side and trusted my weight to it. He must have seen us, and as soon as he thought we were fairly asleep must have loosened the knot and cast us adrift. What on earth is to be done now?"

"I should think," Gerald said, "that it will not be long before the ship comes back for us. The boat is sure to be missed in the morning, for the carpenter will be wanting it to go over the side; we, too, will be missed, for the captain will be wanting his flagon of wine soon after the day has dawned."

"But think you," Tom Tressilis said, "that the captain will turn back on his voyage for us?"

"Of that I think there is no doubt," Gerald said; "that only question is as to the finding us, but I should say that of that there is little fear; the wind is light, the ship was not making fast through the water, and will not be more than fifty miles, at most, away when she turns on her heel and comes to look for us. I expect that Master Taunton knew well enough that we should be picked up again, but he guessed that the admiral would not be pleased at losing a day by our freak, and that the matter is not likely to improve the favor in which we may stand with him and his brother."

"It is going to be a terrible hot day," Ned said, "and with the sun above our heads and no shade, and not so much as a drop of water, the sooner we are picked up the more pleasant it will be, even if we all get a touch of the rope's-end for our exploit."

All day the boys watched anxiously. Once they saw the two vessels sailing backward on their track, but the current had drifted the boat, and the ships passed fully eight miles away to windward of them, and thus without seeing them. This caused the boys, courageous as they were, almost to despair.

"If," argued Gerald, "they pass us in the daylight, our chance

ALONE IN MID-OCEAN

SEE PAGE 18.

is small indeed that they will find us at night. They will doubt-less sail back till dusk and then judge that they have missed us or that we have in some way sunk, then putting their heads to the west they will continue their voyage. If we had oars or a sail we might make a shift to pull the boat into the track they are fol-lowing, which would give us a chance of being picked up when they again turn west, but as we have neither one nor the other we are helpless indeed."

"I do not think," Ned said, "that Captain John or his brother are the men to leave us without a great effort, and methinks that when they have sailed over the ground to the point where, at the utmost, we must have parted from them, they will lay by through the night and search back again to-morrow."

And so it proved.

On the morrow about mid-day the boys beheld one of the ships coming up nearly in a line behind them, while the other, some six miles away to leeward, was keeping abreast of her.

"They are quartering the ground like hounds," Gerald said, "and thanks to their care and thoughtfulness we are saved this time."

By the time that, three hours later, the ship, which was the *Pacha,* came alongside, the boys were suffering terribly from the heat and thirst; for thirty-six hours no drop of water had passed their lips and the sun had blazed down upon them with terrible force, therefore when the vessel hauled her course and laid by for a boat to be lowered to pick them up, their plight was so bad a one that Captain Francis, although sorely vexed at having lost near two days of his voyage, yet felt that they had been amply punished for their escapade.

CHAPTER III

On the Spanish Main

The four boys, upon gaining the *Pacha's* deck, were taken below, and after drink and food had been given them were called to the captain's cabin. He spoke to them gravely and inquired how it was that they had all got adrift together. They told him the circumstances, and said that they thought there was no chance of any mishap occurring; the knot was well fastened, the night was calm, and though they regretted much the pains and trouble which they had given and the delay to which they had put the fleet, yet it did not appear to them, they said frankly, that they had been so very much to blame, as they could hardly have believed that the boat would have broken afloat; and indeed, Ned said plainly, they believed that it was not the result of chance, but that an enemy had done them an evil turn.

"Why think you so?" Captain Drake said, sharply. "How can boys like you have an enemy?"

Gerald then detailed the account of their trouble with Master Taunton.

"He is a rough man," Captain Drake said, "and a violent man maybe, but he is useful and brave. However, I will have reason with him. Of course it is a mere suspicion, but I will speak to my brother."

When the boat had first come in sight the *Pacha* had made the signal to the *Swanne* that the boys were found, and that she was to keep her course, drawing gradually alongside.

Before dark the vessels were within hailing distance, and Captain Drake, lowering a boat, went himself on board the *Swanne* with the four lads. Captain John was at the top of the ladder and was about to rate them soundly. Captain Francis said, "Let us talk together, John, first"; and he repaired with him to his cabin, while the crew swarmed round the boys to gather an account of how they got adrift.

Then Captain John appeared at the door of his cabin and called for Master Taunton, who went in and remained for some time in converse with the two captains. Then he came out, looking surly and black, and Captain Francis soon after issued out with his brother, walked round the ship, said a few cheery words to all the crew, and with a parting laugh and word of advice to the boys to be more careful where they slept in future, descended the side and went off to his ship again.

Opinions were much mingled on board the *Swanne* as to whether the slipping of the knot had been the effect of accident or of an evil turn; however, the boys said little about it, and endeavored, so far as might be, to let it pass as an accident. They felt that the matter between themselves and Master Taunton had already gone too far for their safety and comfort. They doubted not that he had been reprimanded by the admiral as well as by Captain John, and that they had earned his hatred, which, although it might slumber for a while, was likely to show itself again when a chance might occur. Not wishing to inflame farther his fury against them, they abstained from giving such a complexion to their tale as might seem to cast a suspicion upon him. Nevertheless, there was a strong feeling amongst many of the crew that Master Taunton must have had a hand in the casting adrift of the boys, or that if he did not himself do it, it had been done by one of the party who always worked with him.

Whatever the feelings of Giles Taunton might be, he kept them to himself. He now never interfered with the boys by word or deed, working sullenly and quietly at his craft as armorer. The boys felt their lives much lightened thereby, and now thoroughly enjoyed the voyage. Although as boys it was not a part of their duty to go aloft, which was done by the regular sailors who were hired for the purpose, yet they spent no small part of their time when not engaged—and their duties truly were but nominal—in going aloft, sliding down the ropes, and learning to be thoroughly at home among the sails. Every day too there would be practices with arms.

It was of the utmost importance that each man should be able to use sword and axe with the greatest skill; and on board each ship those who were best skilled would exercise and give lessons to those who were less practised with their arms, and, using wooden clubs in place of boarding-axes, they would much belabor each other, to the amusement of the lookers-on. The boys were most assiduous at this kind of work. It was their highest ambition to become good swordsmen and to have a chance of distinguishing themselves against the Spaniards; and so they practised diligently with point and edge. The knowledge of single-stick and quarter-staff still lingered in the country parts of England. They had all already some skill with these, and picked up fast the use of the heavier and more manly arms.

It was the end of July before they sighted land. Great was the delight of all, for, cooped up in what were after all but narrow quarters, they longed for a sight of the green and beautiful forests of which they had heard so much. They were still far from the destination which the admiral had marked as his base of operations. They cruised along for days, with the land often in sight, but keeping for the most part a long distance out, for they feared that the knowledge of their coming might be carried by the natives to the Spaniards in the towns, and that such preparations might be made as would render their journey fruitless. Near, however, to some of the smaller islands which were known to be uninhabited by Spaniards the vessels went closely, and one day dropped anchor in a bay.

They observed some natives on the shore, but the white men had so bad a name, caused by the cruelty of the Spaniards, that these withdrew hastily from sight. The captain, however, had a boat lowered, which, pulling toward shore, and waving a white flag in token of amity, met with no resistance. There were on board some who could speak Spanish, and one of these shouted aloud to the Indians to have no fear for that they were friends, and haters of the Spaniards, whereupon the natives came out from the woods and greeted them.

They were a fine race of men, but gentle and timid in their demeanor. They were copper in color, and wore head-dresses of bright feathers, but the men had but little other clothing, of which indeed in such a climate there is but slight necessity. In exchange for some trifles from the ship they brought many baskets of fruits such as none of those who had fresh come from England had ever before seen.

Great was the joy on board ship, especially among the four boys, at the profusion of strange fruits, and they were seen seated together eating pine-apples, bananas, and many other things of which they knew not so much as the name, but which they found delicious indeed after so long a voyage upon salted food.

Then, sailing on, they dropped anchor in the bay which Captain Drake had himself christened during his last voyage Port Pheasant, for they had killed many of this kind of bird there. Here the admiral purposed waiting for a while to refresh the crews and to put the pinnaces together. Accordingly the anchors were put out, and all was made snug. A boat's crew was sent on shore to see that all was safe, for there was no saying where the Spaniards might be lurking. They returned with a great plate of lead which they had found fastened to a tree close to the water's edge. Upon it were these words: "Captain Drake, if it is your fortune to come into this part, make haste away, for the Spaniards which were with you here last year have betrayed the place and taken away all that you left here. I departed hence on this present 7th July, 1572. Your very loving friend, John Garrett."

"I would I had been here a few days earlier," Captain Drake said when he read this notice, "for John Garrett would assuredly have joined us, and his aid would have been no slight assistance in the matter in which we are about to engage. However, it will not do to despise his caution; therefore, lest we be attacked while on shore by the Spaniards we will even make a fort, and we shall be able to unload our stores and put our pinnaces together without fear of interruption."

The crew were now landed and set to work with hatchet and

bill to clear a plot of ground. Three-quarters of an acre was after three days' work cleared, and the trees were cast outwards and piled together in such form as to make a sort of wall 30 feet high round it. This hard work done, most of the crew were allowed a little liberty, the carpenters and experienced artificers being engaged in putting the three pinnaces together.

The boys, in pairs, for all could never obtain leave together, rambled in the woods, full of admiration for the beauties of nature. Huge butterflies flitted about upon the brilliant flowers, long trailing creepers, rich with blossom, hung on the trees. Here and there, as they passed along, snakes slipped away among the undergrowth, and these in truth the boys were as ready to leave alone as the reptiles were to avoid them, for they were told that it was certain death to be bitten by these creatures. Most of all the boys admired the little birds, which indeed it was hard for them to believe not to be butterflies, so small were they, so rapid their movements, and so brilliant their color.

On the 7th day from landing the pinnaces were finished, and the vessels being anchored near the shore, the crews went on board for the last time preparatory to making their start the next day. There was one tall and bright-faced sailor with whom the boys had struck up a great friendship. He had sailed before with Captain Drake, and as the evening was cool and there was naught to do they begged him to tell them of his former visits in the Caribbean Seas.

"My first," he said, "was the worst and might well have been my last. Captain John Hawkins was our captain, a bold man and a good sailor, but not gentle as well as brave, as is our good Captain Francis. Our fleet was a strong one. The admiral's ship, the *Jesus,* of Lubeck, was 700 tons. Then there were the smaller craft, the *Minion,* Captain Hampton, in which I myself sailed; the *William and John* of Captain Boulton; the *Judith* with Captain Francis Drake, and two little ships besides. We sailed later in the year, it was the 2d October, five years back, that is 1567. We started badly, for a storm struck us off Finisterre, the ships separated, and some boats were lost. We came together at Cape de Verde, and there we tried to get slaves, for it was part of the object of our voyage to buy slaves on the coast of Africa and sell them to the Spaniards here. It was a traffic for which I myself had but little mind, for though it be true that these black fellows are a pernicious race, given to murder and to fightings of all kinds among themselves, yet are they human beings, and it is, methinks, cruel to send them beyond the seas into slavery so far from their homes and people. But it was not for me, a simple mariner, to argue the question with our admirals and captains, and I have heard many worshipful merchants are engaged in the traffic.

"However that be, methinks that our good Captain Francis did likewise turn himself against this kind of traffic in human flesh, for although he has been three times since in these regions, he has never again taken a hand in it. With much to do at Cape de Verde, we succeeded in getting a hundred and fifty men, but not without much resistance from the natives, who shot their arrows at us and wounded many, and most of those who were wounded did die of lock-jaw, for the arrows had been smeared in some poisonous stuff. Then we went farther down the coast and took in two hundred more. Coasting still farther down to St. Jorge de Mina, we landed, and Captain Hawkins found that the negro king there was at war with an enemy a little farther inland. He besought our assistance and promised us plenty of slaves if we would go there and storm the place with him. Captain Hawkins agreed cheerfully enough, and set off with a portion of his crews to assist the king. The enemy fought well, and it was only after a very hard fight on our part and a loss of many men that we took the town. Methinks the two hundred and fifty slaves which we took there were dearly paid for, and there was much grumbling among the ships at the reckless way in which our admiral had risked our lives for meagre gain. It is true that these slaves would sell at a high price, yet none of us looked upon money gained in that way quite as we do upon treasure taken in fair fight. In the one case we traffic with the Spaniards, who are our natural enemies, and it is repugnant to a Christian man to hand over even these poor negroes to such wilful masters as these; in the other we are fighting for our queen and country. The Spaniards are the natural enemies of all good Protestants, and every ship we seize and every treasure-bag we capture does something to pare the nails of that fierce and haughty power.

"Having filled up our hold with the slaves which we had captured at St. Jorge de Mina, we turned our back upon the African coast and sailed to the West Indies. At Rio de Hacha, the first port at which we touched, the people did not wish to trade with us; but the admiral was not the man to allow people to indulge in fancies of this kind. We soon forced them to buy or to sell that which we chose and not what they had a fancy for. Sailing along we were caught in a storm, and in searching for the port of St. Juan d'Ulloa, where we hoped to refit, we captured three ships. In the port we found twelve other small craft, but these we released, and sent some of them to Mexico to ask that victuals and stores might be sent.

"The next day thirteen great ships appeared off the harbor. In them was the Viceroy of Mexico. We had then only the *Jesus*, the *Minion* of 100 tons, and the *Judith* of 50 tons, and this big fleet was large enough to have eaten us, but Captain Hawkins put a good face on it and sailed out to meet them, waiting at the mouth of the harbor. Here he told them haughtily that he should not allow their fleet to enter save on his terms. I doubt not that Hawkins would have been glad enough to have made off if he could have done so, for what with the sale of the slaves and the vessels we had captured, we had now £1,800,000 in silver and gold on board of the ships. The Spanish admiral accepted the terms which Captain Hawkins laid down and most solemnly swore to observe them.

"So with colors flying, both fleets sailed into the harbor together. It is true, however, that the man who places faith in a Spaniard is a fool, and so it proved to us. No sooner had they reached the port than they began to plot secretly among themselves how to fall upon us; even then, though they had thirteen big ships, the smallest of which was larger than the *Jesus*, they feared to attack us openly. Numbers of men were set to work by them on the shore secretly to get up batteries by which they might fire into us, while a great ship, having 500 men on board, was moored close alongside the *Minion*. I remember well talking the matter over with Jack Boscowan, who was boatswain on board, and we agreed that this time we had run into an ugly trap, and that we did not see our way out of it. Englishmen can, as all the world knows, lick the Spaniards when they are but as one to five, but when there are twenty of the Dons to one of us it is clear that the task is a hard one. What made it worse was that we were in harbor. At sea our quickness in handling our ships would have made us a match for the Spanish fleet, but at anchor and with the guns of the port commanding us we did not truly see how we were to get out of it.

"The fight began by the Spaniards letting their big ship drift alongside the *Minion*, when suddenly 500 men leapt out on our decks. We were beaten below in no time, for we were scarce prepared for so sudden an onslaught. There, however, we defended ourselves stoutly, firing into the hull of the ship alongside, and defending our ports and entrances from the Spaniards. For a while our case seemed desperate. The *Jesus* was hard at work too, and when she had sunk the ship of the Spanish admiral, she came up, and gave a broadside into the ship alongside of us. Her crew ran swiftly back to her, and we with much rejoicing poured on deck again and began to pay them hotly for their sudden attack upon us. It was a great fight, and one that would have done your heart good, to see the three English ships, two of them so small as to be little more than boats, surrounded by a whole fleet of Spaniards, while from on shore the guns of the forts played upon us. Had it not been for those forts, I verily believe that we should have destroyed the Spanish fleet. Already another large vessel had followed the example of their admiral's ship and had gone to the bottom. Over 540 of their sailors we had, as they have themselves admitted, slain outright.

"We were faring well, and had begun to hope that we might get to find our way out of the toils, when a cry came from the lookout, who said that the *Jesus* was hoisting signals of distress, and that he feared she was sinking. Close as she was lying to a battery, and surrounded by enemies, our bold captain did not hesitate a minute, but sailed the *Minion* through a crowd of enemies close to the *Jesus*. You should have heard the cheer that the two crews gave each other; it rose above all the noise of the battle, and would assuredly have done your heart good. The *Jesus* was sinking fast, and it was as much as they could do to tumble into the boats and to row hastily to our side. We should have saved them all, but the Spaniards, who dared not lay us aboard, and who were in no slight degree troubled by the bravery with which we had fought, set two of their great ships on fire, and launched them down upon us, preferring to lose two of their own ships for the sake of capturing or destroying our little bark. The sight of the ships coming down in flames shook the hearts of our men more than all the fury of the Spaniards had been able to do, and without waiting for orders they turned the ship's head for the mouth of the port.

"The admiral, who had just come on board, cursed and shouted when he saw what was being done; but the panic of the fireships got the better of the men, and we made off, firing broadsides at the Spaniards' fleet as we passed through them, and aided by the little *Judith,* which stuck to us through the whole of the fight. When we cooled down and came to think of it, we were in no slight degree ashamed of our desertion of our comrades in the *Jesus*. Fortunately the number so left behind was not large; but we knew that according to their custom the Spaniards would put all to death, and so indeed it afterwards turned out, many of them being despatched with horrible tortures.

"This terrible treatment of the prisoners caused, when it was known, great indignation, and although Queen Elizabeth did not declare war with Spain, from that time she gave every countenance she could to the adventurers who waged war on their own account against her.

"The *Minion* suffered severely, packed close as she was with all her own crew and a great part of that of the *Jesus*, vast numbers of whom were wounded. However, at length a hundred were at their own request landed and left to shift for themselves, preferring to run the risk of Indians, or even of Spaniards, to continue any longer amid the horrors on board the ship. I myself, boys, was not one of that number, and came back to England in her. Truly it was the worse voyage that I ever made, for though fortune was for a time good to us, and we collected much money, yet in the end we lost all, and hardly escaped with our lives. It has seemed to me that this bad fortune was sent as a punishment upon us for carrying off the negroes into slavery. Many others thought the same, and methinks that that was also the opinion of our present good admiral."

"Did you come out with him in his further voyages here?" Ned asked.

"I was with him in the *Dragon* two years ago when with the *Swanne* she came here. Last year I sailed with him in the *Swanne* alone."

"You did not have any very stirring adventures?"

"No, we were mainly bent on exploring, but for all that we carried off many prizes, and might, had we been pilgrims, have bought farms in Devonshire, and settled down on our share of the prize-money; but there, that is not the way with sailors. Quick come, quick go, and not one in a hundred that I have ever heard off, however much he may have taken as his share of prizes, has ever kept it or prospered greatly therefrom."

It was now evening and many of the men had betaken themselves to the water for a swim. The heat had been great all day, and as it was their last, they had been pressed at work to get the stores which had been landed, again on board ship, and to finish all up ready for the division of the party next day.

"I do not care for bathing here," Ned said, in reply to a sailor, who asked him why he too did not join in the sport. "I confess that I have a dread of those horrible sharks of which we have heard so much, and whose black fins we see from time to time."

"I should have thought," said the harsh, sneering voice of Giles Taunton, "that an Otter would have been a match for a shark. The swimmers of the South Isles, and indeed the natives here attack the sharks without fear, I should have thought that any one who prides himself, as you do, upon swimming, would have been equally willing to encounter them."

"I do not know that I do pride myself on my swimming, Giles Taunton," Ned said, composedly; "at any rate no one has ever heard me speak of such abilities as I may have in that way. As to the natives, they have seen each other fight with sharks, and know how the matter is gone about. If I were to be present a few times when such strife takes place, it may be that I should not shirk from joining in the sport; but knowing nothing whatever of the method pursued, or of the manner of attack, I should be worse than a fool were I to propose to venture my life in such a sport."

Many sailors who were standing round approved of what Ned said.

"Aye, aye, lad," one said, "no one would think of making his first jump across the spot where he might be dashed to pieces. Let a man learn to jump on level ground, and then when he knows his powers he may go across a deep chasm."

By this time a good many of the men were out of the water, when suddenly there arose the cry of, "Shark!" from the lookout on the poop. There was a great rush for the ship, and the excitement on board was nearly as great as that in the water. Ned quietly dropped off his jacket and his shoes, and seizing a short boarding pike, waited to see what would come of it. It chanced that his friends, the other boys, were farther out than the men, having with the ardor of youth engaged themselves in races, regardless of the admonition that had frequently been given them to keep near the ship, for the terror of these water beasts was very great.

The men all gained the ship in safety, but the shark, which had come up from a direction in which it would cut them off, was clearly likely to arrive before the boys could gain the side. At first it seemed indeed that their fate was sealed; but the shark, who in many respects resembles a cat with a mouse, and seems to prefer to trifle with its victim to the last, allowed them to get close to the ship, although by rapid swimming it could easily have seized them before. The nearest to it as it approached the ship was Tom Tressilis, who was not so good a swimmer as the others; but he had swum lustily and with good

heart, though his white face showed how great the effect of the
danger was upon him. He had not spoken a word since the shark
first made its appearance. As he struck despairingly to gain the
ship, from which the sailors were already casting him ropes, his
eye caught that of Ned, who cried to him cheerily,

"Keep up your spirits, Tom; I will be with you."

As the huge fish swept along at a distance of some four yards
from the side of the ship, and was already turning on its back,
opening its huge mouth to seize its victim, Ned dived head foremost from the ship on to him. So great was the force and impetus with which he struck the creature, that it was fairly driven
sideways from its course, missing by the nearest shave the leg of
Tom Tressilis. Ned himself was half stunned by the force with
which his head had struck the fish, for a shark is not so soft a
creature to jump against as he had imagined; however, he retained consciousness enough to grasp at the fin of the shark, to
which he held on for half a minute. By this time the shark was
recovering from the effects of the sudden blow, and Ned was
beginning to be able to reflect. In a moment he plunged the half
pike deep into the creature's stomach. Again and again he repeated the stroke, until the shark, rolling over in his agony and
striking furiously with his tail, shook Ned from his hold. He instantly dived beneath the water and came up at a short distance.
The shark was still striking the water furiously, the sailors on
board were throwing down upon him shot, pieces of iron, and
all sorts of missiles, and some of the best archers were hastily
bringing their bows to the side. The shark caught sight of his op-
ponent and instantly rushed at him. Ned again dived just before
the creature reached him, and rising under him inflicted some
more stabs with the pike; then he again swam off, for he was in
no slight fear that he might be struck by his friends on board
ship, of whose missiles indeed he was more in dread than of the
shark himself.

When he rose at a short distance from the shark he was again
prepared for a rush on the part of his enemy, but the great fish
had now had enough of it. He was still striking the water, but his
movements were becoming slower, for he was weakened by the

loss of blood from the stabs he had received from below, and from the arrows, many of which were now buried to the goose-quill in him. In a minute or two he gradually turned on one side and floated with his white belly in the air. A shout broke from the crew of the *Swanne* and also of the *Pacha,* who had been attracted to the side by the cries. When he saw that the battle was over, and that the enemy had been vanquished without loss of life or hurt to any, Ned speedily seized one of the ropes and climbed up the side of the ship, where he was, you may be sure, received with great cheering, and shouts of joy and approval.

"You are a fine lad," Captain John Drake said, "and your name of Otter has indeed been well bestowed. You have saved the life of your comrade; and I know that my old friend, Mr. Frank Tressilis, his father, will feel indebted indeed to you when he comes to learn how gallantly you risked your life to preserve that of his son."

Ned said that he saw no credit in the action, and that he was mightily glad to have had an opportunity of learning to do that which the negroes thought nothing of, for that it shamed him to think that these heathens would venture their lives boldly against sharks, while he, an English boy, although a good swimmer, and not he hoped wanting in courage, was yet afraid to encounter these fierce brutes.

This incident acted, as might be expected, as a fresh bond between the boys, and as it also secured for Ned the cordial goodwill of the sailors, they were in future free from any persecution at the hands of Master Taunton or of his fellows.

CHAPTER IV

An Unsuccessful Attack

It should have been said in its proper place, that upon the day after the arrival of the *Pacha* and *Swanne* in Pheasant Bay a barque named the *Isle of Wight,* commanded by James Rause, with thirty men on board, many of whom had sailed with Captain Drake upon his previous voyages, came into the port, and there was great greeting between the crews of the various ships. Captain Rause brought with him a Spanish caravel, captured the day before, and a shallop also, which he had taken at Cape Blanco. This was a welcome reinforcement, for the crews of the two ships were but small for the purpose which they had in hand, especially as it would be necessary to leave a party to take charge of the vessels. Captain Drake made some proposals to Captain Rause, which the latter accepted, and it was arranged that he and his crew would be for a time under the command of Captain Drake. When the division of the crews was made, it was decided that James Rause should remain in command of the four ships at Pheasant Bay, and that Captain Drake, with fifty-three of his own men and twenty of Rause's, should start in the three pinnaces and the shallop for Nombre de Dios.

The first point at which they stopped was the Isle of Pines, on the 22d of July; here they put in to water the boats, and, as the crews had been cramped from their stay therein, Captain Drake decided to give them a day on shore. Ned and Reuben Gale were of the party, the other two being, to their great discontent, left behind in the ship. After the barriques had been filled with water, the fires lit for cooking, and the labors of the day over, Ned and Reuben started for a ramble in the island, which was of a goodly extent. When they had proceeded some distance in the wood, picking fruit as they went, and looking at the butterflies and bright birds, they were suddenly seized and thrown upon the ground by some men, who sprang out from the underwood through which they had passed. They were too surprised at this sudden attack to utter even a cry, and, being safely gagged and bound, they were lifted by their captors and carried away into the interior of the island. After an hour's passage they were put down in the heart of a thick grove of trees, and, looking round, saw they were surrounded by a large number of natives. One of these, a person evidently in authority, spoke to them in a language which they did not understand. They shook their heads, and after several times attempting to make them comprehend, Ned caught the word Españolos.

To this he vehemently shook his head in denial, which caused quite an excitement among his hearers. One of the latter then said "English," to which Ned and his companion nodded. The news evidently filled the natives with great joy; the bands were taken off the boys, and the Indians endeavored by gestures to express the sorrow that they felt for having carried them off. It was clear that they had taken them for Spaniards, and that they had been watched as they wandered inland, and captured for the purpose of learning the objects and force of the expedition. Now, however, that their captors understood that the ships were English, with great signs of pleasure they started with them for the sea-shore. It had already darkened when they arrived there, and the crews of the boats jumped hastily to their feet at the sight of so many persons approaching. Ned, however, called to them just as they were about to betake themselves to their arms, and shouted that the natives were perfectly friendly and well-disposed. Captain Drake himself now advanced, and entered into conversation with the leader of the natives in Spanish. It seemed that they had met before, and that many indeed of the natives were acquainted with his person. These were a party of Simeroons, as they were then called, *i.e.*, of natives who had been made slaves by he Spaniards, and who had now fled. The afterwards came to be called Cameroons, and are mostly so spoken of in the books of English buccaneers. These men were greatly pleased at the arrival of Captain Drake and his boats, for their own had been destroyed, and they feared taking to the sea in such as they could build.

After much talk Captain Drake arranged to put them on shore, so that they would go on to the Isthmus of Darien, where there were more of them in the forests, and they promised to prepare these to assist Captain Drake when he should come there. The natives, some thirty in number, were soon packed in the boats, and were ready to cross to the mainland; and the party then going forward, entered the port of Nombre de Dios at three in the morning.

As they sailed in, being yet a good way from the city, they came upon a barque of some 60 tons. It was all unprepared for attack, and the boats got alongside, and the crews climbed on to the deck before their presence was discovered or dreamt of. No resistance whatever was offered by the Spaniards against the English, all were indeed asleep below. A search was made, and it was found that the ship was laden with Canary wine, a circumstance which gave great pleasure to the English, who looked forward to a long bout of good drinking. While they were searching the ship, they had paid but little attention to the Spanish crew. Presently, however, they heard the sound of oars at some little distance from the ship.

"What is that?" said Captain Drake.

Ned ran to the stern of the vessel.

"I think, sir," he said, "that one or two of the Spaniards have got off with their boat. I saw it towing to the stern when we boarded."

Captain Drake leant over the side, and at once gave orders to one of the boats whose crew had not boarded the vessel, and was lying alongside, to pursue and to strain every nerve to catch the boat before she came near the town. The sailors leapt to the oars, and pulled with a will, for they knew as well as their captain how serious a matter it would be were the town alarmed, and indeed that all their toil and pains would be thrown away, as it was only by surprise that so small a handful of men could possibly expect to take a large and important town like Nombre de Dios.

Fortunately the boat overtook the fugitives before they were within hailing distance of the town, and rapidly towed them back to the ship. All then took their places in the pinnaces, and pushed off without further delay. It was not yet light, and steered by one who knew the town well, they rowed up alongside a battery, which defended it, without the alarm being given. As they climbed up over the wall the sentry fired his piece, and the artillerymen, who, there having been some rumors of the arrival of Drake's fleet in those waters, were sleeping by the side of their guns, sprang to their feet and fled as the English leapt down into the battery.

There were six large guns in the place, and many small, and bombards.

"Now, my lads," Captain Drake said, "you must lose no time; in five minutes yonder artillerymen will have alarmed the whole town and we must be there before the Spaniards have managed to get their sleepy eyes open. Advance in three parties, and meet in the market-place; it is good that we should make as much show as possible. There can be no more concealment, and, therefore, we must endeavor to make the Spaniards believe that we are a far stronger force than in truth we are."

It was not until the three parties met in the market-place that any real resistance, on the part of the Spaniards, began, although windows had been opened, and shots fired here and there. The alarm-bells were now ringing, shouts and screams were heard through the town, and the whole population was becoming fairly aroused. As they entered the market-place, however, a heavy fire was opened with arquebuses and guns. The English had taken with them no fire-arms, but each man carried his bow and arrows, and with these they shot fast and hard at the Spaniards, and silenced their fire.

At this moment, however, it happened, sadly for the success of the enterprise, that a ball struck Captain Drake, and inflicted a serious wound.

Ned was standing near him, and observed him stagger.

"Are you hit, sir?" he asked, anxiously.

"Tush, my boy," he replied, "it is a scratch; say nothing of it. Now, forward to the Treasury. The town is in your hands, my lads; it only remains to you to sack as much treasure as you can carry; but remember, do not lose your discipline, and keep together. If we straggle we are lost. Now, light at once the torches which you have brought with you, and shout aloud to the inhabitants, you that can speak Spanish, that if any more resistance is offered, we will burn the whole town to the ground."

This threat mightily alarmed the inhabitants, and the firing ceased altogether, for as these were not regular soldiers, and knew that the object of the English attack was to plunder the public treasuries rather than private property, the townsmen readily deemed it to their interest to hold aloof rather than to bring upon their city and themselves so grievous a calamity as that threatened by the English.

In the advance, two or three Spaniards had fallen into the hands of the men, and these being threatened with instant death if they hesitated, at once led the way to the governor's house, where the silver, brought down on mules from Panama, was stored. A party were placed at the door of this building, and Captain Drake with the rest entered.

The governor had fled with his attendants. The house was richly furnished, full of silk hangings, of vessels of gold and silver, and of all kinds of beautiful things. These, however, attracted little attention from the English, although Ned and his young comrade marvelled much. Never had they seen in England anything approaching to the wealth and beauty of this furnishing. It seemed to them, indeed, as if they had entered one of the houses of the magicians and enchanters, of whom they had read in books during their childhood. Captain Drake, however, passed through these gorgeous rooms with scarce a glance, and, led by the Spaniards, descended some steps into a vast cellar.

A cry of astonishment and admiration burst from the whole party as they entered this treasury. Here, piled up twelve feet high, lay a mighty mass of bars of silver, carefully packed. This

SILVER ENOUGH TO MAKE US ALL RICH

SEE PAGE 41.

heap was no less than 70 feet long and 10 feet wide, and the bars each weighed from 35 to 40 pounds.

"My lads," Captain Drake said, "here is money enough to make us all rich for our lives; but we must leave it for the present and make for the Treasury House, which is as full of gold and of precious stones as this is of silver."

The men followed Captain Drake and his brother, feeling quite astonished and almost stupefied at the sight of this pile of silver; but they felt, moreover, the impossibility of their carrying off so vast a weight unless the town were completely in their hands.

This, indeed, was very far from being the case, for the whole town was now rising. The troops, who had at the first panic fled, were now being brought forward, and as the day lightened, the Spaniards, sorely ashamed that so small a body of men should have made themselves masters of so great and a rich a city, were plucking up heart and preparing to attack them. Ill was it then for the success of the adventure that Captain Francis had suffered so heavy a wound in the market-place. Up to this time he had kept bravely on, and none except Ned, all being full of the prospect of vast plunder, had noticed his pale face, or seen the blood which streamed down from him, and marked every footstep as he went; but nature could now do no more, and, with his body wellnigh drained of all its blood, he suddenly fell down fainting.

Great was the cry that rose from the men as they saw the admiral thus fall. Hastily gathering round him, they lifted his body from the ground, and shuddered at seeing how great a pool of blood was gathered where he had been standing. It seemed almost as if, with the fall of their captain, the courage which had animated these men, and would animate them again in fighting against ever so great odds, had for the moment deserted them. In spite of the orders of Captain John, that four or five should carry his brother to the boats, and that the rest should seize without delay the treasures of gold and diamonds in the Treasury, and carry off as great a weight as they might bear, none paid attention.

They gathered round the body of Captain Francis, and lifting him on their shoulders they hurried to the boats, careless of the promised treasures, and thinking only to escape and bear with them their beloved commander from the forces of the Spaniards, who, as they saw the party fall back, with great shouting fell upon them, shooting hotly. The swoon of the admiral had lasted but a few moments. As cordial was poured down his throat he opened his eyes, and seeing what the men were minded to do, protested with all his force against their retreat. His words, however, had no weight with them; and in spite of his resistance they carried him down to the battery, and there, placing him in a pinnace, the whole took to their boats and rowed on board ship.

Wonderful to relate, although many were wounded, but one man, and he Giles Taunton the armorer, was killed in this attack upon the great city, in which they only missed making themselves masters of one of the greatest treasures upon earth by the accident of their commander fainting at a critical moment, and to the men being seized by an unaccountable panic. Some of the crew had indeed carried off certain plunder, which they had snatched in passing through the governor's house, and in such short searches as they had been able to make in private dwellings; but the men in general had been so struck with amazement and sorrow at the sight of their general's wound, that although this wealth was virtually at their mercy, they put off with him without casting a thought upon what they were leaving behind.

The boats now rowed without pausing to the isle, which they called the Isle of Victuals, and there they stayed two days, nursing their wounds and supporting themselves with poultry, of which there was a great abundance found in the island, and with vegetables and fruits from the gardens. There was great joy among them when it was found that Captain Drake's wound, although severe enough, was yet not likely to imperil his life, and that it was loss of blood alone which had caused him to faint. At this news the men all took heart and rejoiced so exceedingly that a stranger would have supposed that they had attained some great victory, rather than have come out unsuccessful from an adventure which promised to make each man wealthy.

Upon the second day after their arrival at the Isle of Victuals they saw a boat rowing out from the direction of Nombre de Dios. As they knew that there was no fleet in that harbor which would venture to attack them, the English had no fear of the approaching boat, although, indeed, they wondered much what message could have been sent them. On board the boat was an hidalgo, or Spanish noble, who was rowed by four negroes. He said that he had come from the mainland to make inquiries as to the gallant men who had performed so great a feat, and that he cherished no malice whatever against them. He wished to know whether the Captain Drake who commanded them was the same who had been there before, and especially did he inquire whether the arrows used by the English were poisoned; for, he said, great fear and alarm reigned in the town, many believing that all who had been struck by the English shafts would certainly die.

Upon this head he was soon reassured, and the English were, indeed, mightily indignant at its being supposed that they would use such cowardly weapons as poisoned arrows.

Then the hidalgo inquired why the English had so suddenly retreated from the town when it was in their hands, and why they had abstained from carrying off the three hundred and sixty tons of silver which lay at the governor's house, and the still greater value of gold in the treasure-house. The gold, indeed, being far more valuable than the silver, insomuch as it was more portable. The answers to all these questions were freely given, for in those days there was a curious mixture of peace and war, of desperate violence and of great courtesy, between combatants; and whereas now, an enemy arriving with a view merely to obtain information would be roughly treated, in those days he was courteously entertained, and his questions as freely answered as if he had been a friend and ally.

When he heard of the wound of Captain Drake he expressed great sorrow, and after many compliments were exchanged he returned to Nombre de Dios, while the next day Captain Drake and the English rowed away to the Isle of Pines, where Captain Rause was remaining in charge of the ships. He was mightily glad to see them return, as were their comrades who had remained, for their long absence had caused great fear and anxiety, as it was thought that Captain Drake must have fallen into some ambuscade, and that ill had come to the party. Although there was some regret at the thought that the chance of gaining such vast booty had been missed, yet the joy at the safe return overpowered this feeling, and for a day or two the crews feasted merrily and held festival. Captain Rause then determined to continue the adventure no further, but to separate with his ship and men from Captain Drake. He was of opinion firmly that now the Spaniards had discovered their presence in the island, such measures of defence would be taken at every port as to place these beyond the hazard of attack by so small a body as those carried by the three ships. He, therefore, receiving full satisfaction for the use of his men and for guarding the ships, sailed away on the 7th of August, leaving the *Swanne* and the *Pacha* to proceed upon the adventure alone.

Captain Drake sent his brother and Ellis Hickson to examine the river Chagres, and on their return Captain Drake with his two ships and three pinnaces sailed for Carthagena, where he arrived on the 13th day of August. While on the voyage thither he captured two Spanish ships, each of 240 tons, with rich cargoes, neither of them striking so much as a blow in resistance. At evening he anchored between the Island of Cara and St. Bernardo, and the three pinnaces entered the harbor of Carthagena.

Lying at the entrance they found a frigate, which in those days meant a very small craft, not much larger than a rowing-boat. She had but one old man on board, who said that the rest of the company had gone ashore to fight a duel about a quarrel which they had had overnight. He said, too, what was much more important to the English, that an hour before nightfall a pinnace had passed him, and that the man who was steering had shouted out that the English were at hand, and that he had better up anchor and go into the port. He said, moreover, that when the pinnace reached Carthagena guns were fired, and he could see that all the shipping and hauled in under shelter of the castle.

This was bad news indeed, and there was much hard language among the sailors when they heard it. It was clear that the castle of Carthagena, if prepared, was not to be carried by some thirty or forty men, however gallant and determined they might be. There was, too, but little hope that the old man had spoken falsely, for they had themselves heard guns shortly before their arrival there. With much bitterness it was determined to abandon the plan of attack, and thus Carthagena as well as Nombre de Dios escaped from the hands of the English.

They did not, however, go out empty-handed, for they succeeded in capturing, by boarding, four pinnaces, each laden with cargo, and as they turned their heads to go out to sea, a great ship of Seville came sailing in. Her they laid alongside and captured easily, she having just arrived from Spain, having no thoughts of meeting a foe just as she reached her port of destination.

This lightened the hearts of the crew, and with their prizes in tow they sailed out in good spirits. The ship contained large stores of goods from Spain, with sherries, and merchandise of every kind. They went back to the Isle of Pines, their usual rendezvous, and on adding up the goods that they had taken from various prizes, found that even now they had made no bad thing of their voyage.

They were now much reduced in fighting strength by illness, and Captain Drake determined in his mind that the crews were no longer strong enough for the manning of two ships, and that it would be better to take to one alone. He knew, however, that even his authority would not suffice to persuade the sailors to abandon one of the vessels, for sailors have a great love for their ships. He therefore determined to do it by a sudden stroke, and that known only to himself and another. Therefore he called to him Thomas Moore, the carpenter of the *Swanne*, and taking him aside told him to make auger-holes in the bottom of that ship. Moore, who was a good sailor, made a great resistance to the orders, but upon the admiral assuring him that it was necessary for the success of the enterprise that one of the ships should be destroyed, he very reluctantly undertook the task.

Previous to this Captain Drake had ordered all the booty and a considerable portion of the stores of both ships to be hauled on shore, so that they might lose nothing of value to them.

The next morning Ned and his friends were sitting on the bulwark of the vessel, watching the fish playing about in the depths of the clear blue water.

"We seem to be lower in the water than usual," Ned said; "does not it seem to you that we are not so high above the sea as we are wont to be?"

The others agreed that the vessel had that appearance; but as it seemed clearly impossible that it should be so, especially when she was lighter than usual, they thought that they must be mistaken, and the subject was put aside. Half an hour later Captain Drake himself rowing alongside called to his brother, who came to the side.

"I am going to fish," he said; "are you disposed to come also?"

Captain John expressed his willingness to do so.

"I will wait for you," his brother said.

Captain John was turning to go into his cabin to get his cap and cloak, when Captain Francis cried out—

"Is not your ship very low in the water this morning?"

"The same as usual, I suppose," Captain John said, laughing; but looking over the side himself, he said, "Methinks she does lie deep in the water," and calling the carpenter he bade him sound the well. The latter, after doing so, cried out loudly that there were four feet of water in the ship. A great astonishment seized upon both officers and crew at this unexpected news. All hands were at once set to work, the pumps were rigged, and with buckets and all sorts of gear they strove manfully and hard to get rid of the water. It soon, however, became plain that it entered faster than they could pump it forth, and that the vessel must have sprung a bad leak. When it was clear that the *Swanne* could not be saved, the boats of the *Pacha* were brought alongside, and all the goods that remained in her were removed, together with the arms and ammunition. Then the crew, taking to the boats, lay by, until in a few minutes the *Swanne* sank, among the tears of many of her crew, who had made three voyages in her and loved her well.

It was not for a long time afterwards known that the loss of this ship was the effect of the orders of the admiral, who indeed acted with his usual wisdom in keeping the matter secret, for assuredly, although the men would have obeyed his orders, he would have lost much favor and popularity among them had the truth been at that time known. The next day the news was spread among the men that it was determined to fill the *Pacha* with all the stores that were on shore, and leaving a party there with her, to embark the crews in the pinnaces for service in the river Chagres and along the coast, until, at any rate, they could capture another ship to replace the *Swanne*. Next day they rowed on into the Gulf of Darien; there the ship was laid up in a good place, and they remained quiet for fifteen days, amusing and refreshing themselves. By this means they hoped to throw all the Spaniards off their guard, and to cause a report to be spread that they had left the island.

The Simeroons, living near, had been warned by those who had been landed from the Isle of Pines of their coming, and received them with good cheer, and promised all aid that could be required. Then the pinnaces were sent out to catch any passing ships which might be cruising along the coast.

It happened one day that two of them had set off in pursuit of a great ship which they saw passing in the distance. The wind was light, and they had little doubt that they should overhaul her. Ned, who was one of those who remained behind, was much angered at missing so good an enterprise, but some four hours afterwards another ship was seen to pass along. The remaining pinnace was at once manned, Captain John Drake taking the command, and with fourteen men she set out to take the Spanish galleon. Gallant as are the exploits which have been performed in modern times by British tars in their attacks upon slavers, yet in none of these cases does the disparity of force at all approach that which often existed between the English boats and the Spanish galleons; indeed, the only possible reason that can be given for the success of the English is the fear that their enemy entertained for them. Both the Spanish captains and crews had come to look upon them as utterly invincible, and they seemed, when attacked by the English buccaneers, altogether paralyzed.

As the boat rowed up toward the great ship, her size became gradually more apparent, and her deck could be seen crowded with men; even Ned, who was not greatly given to reflection, could not but feel a passing doubt as to the possibility of one small boat with fourteen men attacking a floating castle like this.

Presently the boom of a cannon from the forecastle of the vessel was heard, and a ball whizzed over their heads, then shot after shot was fired, and soon a rattle of small arms broke out, and the water all round was cut up by bullets and balls. The rough seamen cared little for this demonstration. With a cheer they bent their backs to the oars, and although some were wounded they rowed up to the side of the ship without hesitation or doubt. Then from above a shower of missiles were hurled upon them—darts, stones, hot water, and even boiling tar.

It would have gone hard with the English had not the Spanish carelessly left a port-hole open near the water-level; through this the English climbered, eager to get at their foe, and many of them raging with the pain caused by the boiling materials. As they rushed on to the deck, the Spaniards were ranged in two ranks on either side of the hatchway and fell upon them at once; but so great was the fury of the English, that, facing either way, with a roar like beasts springing on their prey, they fell with axe and sword upon the Spaniards.

It was the wild rage with which the English buccaneers fought that was the secret of their success. The Spaniards are a people given to ceremony, and even in matters of battle are somewhat formal and pedantic. The combat, then, between them and the English was one which presented no familiar conditions to their minds. These rough sailors, hardened by exposure, skilled in the use of arms, were no doubt formidable enough individually, but this alone would not have intimidated the Spaniards or have gone any great distance toward equalizing the tremendous odds between them. It was the fury with which they fought that was the secret of their success. It was as when a cat, furious with passion, flies at a dog many times larger and heavier than itself. The latter may be as brave in many matters as the cat, and ready to face a creature much larger even than itself under ordinary circumstances. It is the fury of the cat which appals and turns it into a very coward. Thus when the band of English fell upon the Spaniards in the galleon—who were some six times as numerous as themselves—naked to the waist, with hair streaming back, with all their faces wild with pain, brandishing their heavy axes, and with a shout rushed upon their foes drawn up in regular order, the latter after a moment or two of resistance began rapidly to fall back. Their officers in vain shouted to them to stand firm. In vain they taunted them with falling back before a handful of men. In vain even turned their swords against their own soldiers. It was useless. Those in front, unable indeed to retreat, were cut down by the heavy axes. Those behind recoiled, and after but a few minutes' fighting some began to leap down the hatchways, and although the fight continued for a short time, isolated groups here and there making resistance, the battle was virtually won in five minutes after the English appeared on deck.

The captain and his two principal officers were killed fighting bravely, and had their efforts been in any way backed by those of their men, they would have made short work of the assailants. Captain Drake's voice was heard high above the din as soon as the resistance ceased.

He ordered the prisoners to be all brought upon deck and disarmed, and at once forced into their own boats and obliged to row away from the vessel; for he knew that were his men once to begin to plunder and to fall upon the liquors, the Spaniards, even if unarmed, would be able to rise and overpower them.

No sooner was the last Spaniard out of the ship, than the men scattered to look for plunder. Ned was standing on the poop watching the boats rowing away, and thinking to himself that, so crowded were they, if a breeze were to spring up there would not be much chance of their reaching Nombre de Dios. Suddenly he heard below him a scream followed by a splash; looking over he saw the head of a woman appear above the water, and without hesitation dived at once from the side. For a moment the girl, for she was little more, struggled with him as if she would have sunk, but Ned, grasping her firmly, in a few strokes swam with her alongside the ship to the boat, and two or three sailors running down assisted him to pull her into it; then dripping wet she was taken to the deck, where the captain in kind tones assured her that she would receive the most courteous treatment, and that she need be under no fear whatever.

She was the daughter of a wealthy Spaniard at Nombre de Dios, and was now coming from Spain to join him; frightened by the noise of the fighting and by the terrible reputation of the English buccaneers, she had, when the sailors rushed into the cabin with loud shouts, been so alarmed that she had jumped form the stern windows into the sea.

Captain Drake assured her courteously that, rough as his men might be, they would, none of them, lay a finger upon a woman. He then hoisted a flag and fired a gun as a signal to the Spanish boats, which were yet within a quarter of a mile, to return. For a moment they rowed on, but a ball, sent skimming across their bows, was a hint which they could not disregard; for, full as they were of men, they could not have hoped to avoid the English pinnace should it have put off after them.

When the boats came alongside, some of those on board were ordered to ascend the side of the ship, and plenty of accommodation having been made, the young Spanish lady and her maid, who had remained in the cabin, descended into the largest boat; handed down by Captain Drake with a courtesy equal to that which a Spanish hidalgo himself would have shown.

Before she went, the young lady turned to Ned, who was standing near, and expressed to him her deep thanks for the manner in which he had leapt over for her. Ned himself could understand only a few words, for, although many of the sailors spoke Spanish, and sometimes used it among themselves, he had not yet made any great progress with it, although he had tried to pick up as many words and phrases as he could. The captain, however, translated the words to him, and he said to her in reply, that there was nothing for her to feel herself under any obligation to him for, for that any dog would have jumped out and done the business just as well.

The young lady, however, undid a bracelet of gold on her arm and insisted upon herself fastening it round Ned's wrist, an action which caused blushes of confusion to crimson his face. In a few minutes the Spanish boats were again off. The captain added to that in which the young lady was placed, some food, some bottles of liqueur, and other matters which might render her voyage easy and pleasant. He promised that the Spaniards, who had been transferred again to the ship, should be landed at the earliest opportunity.

The vessel was now searched regularly and was found to contain much treasure in goods, but as she was on her way from Europe she had, of course, none of the gold and silver which was the main object of their search. However, they consoled themselves with the thought that the ship which had been chased by their comrades earlier in the day was homewards-bound, and they hoped, therefore, that a rich cargo would there be secured. They were not mistaken, for when the ship sailed up to the rendezvous they found another alongside, and the cheers of their comrades told them that the prize had been a handsome one. They found that they had secured nearly half-a-million in gold and silver, and transferring the cargo of the one ship into the other, they set the first on fire and sailed back to the spot where their camp was formed on the isthmus.

Several other ships fell into their hands in this way, but after this they hindered no more vessels on their way from Europe. They had ample stores and, indeed, far more than enough to supply them with every luxury, for on board the *Pacha* the richest wines, the most delicate conserves, the richest garments of all kinds were already in such abundance as to become common to them all.

Down to the common sailor, all feasted on the best, and drank

wines that an emperor might have approved. Captain Drake, in
this way, gave his men when on shore much license, insisting,
however, that they should abstain from drunkenness. For, as he
said, not only would they be at the mercy of any small body of
the enemy which might find them, but drunkenness breeds
quarrels and disputes, and as between comrades would be fatal
indeed. Thus, although enough of good liquor was given to each
man to make him merry, none were allowed to drink beyond
this point.

The reason why the ships coming from Europe were allowed
to pass unmolested, was, that Drake wished not that each day
some fresh tale of capture should be brought to Panama by the
crews set free in the boats, for it was certain that the tale so told
would, at last, stir up such fear and indignation at the ravages
committed by so small a body, that the governors of the Spanish
towns would combine their forces and would march against
them with a veritable army. While only the ships starting from
Darien were overhauled and lightened of their contents the tale
was not brought back to Darien, for the crews were allowed to
sail on with their ships to Europe, as Drake had already more
vessels than he knew what to do with, and as for prisoners they
were to him quite useless. Captain John did, indeed, at one time
propose to him that he should take out of each ship all the principal men, so as to hold them as hostages in case of any misfortune happening to the English, but the admiral said to him, that
so great was the enmity and fear of them, that did they fall into
the hands of the Spaniards, these would not exchange them and
let them go even if as many kings were set free in return.

In all five vessels were seized and plundered while lying at
Darien. All was not, however, going well, for while they lay there
a terrible sickness broke out among them; whether this was
from the change of life or from any noxious thing which they
ate, or merely from the heat, none could say, but very shortly the
illness made great ravages among them. First died Charles Clift,
one of the quarter-masters; then one day when the pinnace in
which Ned always sailed returned, they were met with the sad
news that Captain John Drake was also dead. He had fallen,

however, not by the fever, but by the ball of the Spaniards. He had gone out with one of the pinnaces, and had engaged a great Spanish ship, but the latter had shot more straight and faster than usual, and the captain himself and Richard Allen, one of his men, had been slain in an unsuccessful attempt to capture the ship. His sad end was not the result of rashness on his part, for he, indeed, had told the men that the vessel carried many guns, and that it was too rash an enterprise. The sailors, however, had by this time become so accustomed to victory as to despise the Dons altogether, and insisted upon going forward.

It was with bitter lamentation and regret that they returned, bringing the body of the admiral's brother. They were now at the end of the year, and in this week no less than six of the company died, among whom was Joseph Drake, another of the admiral's brothers. These losses saddened the crew greatly, and even the treasures which they had amassed now seemed to them small and of little account. Even those who did not take the fever were much cast down, and Captain Drake determined without any further loss to attempt the expedition on which he had set his mind. On February 3d, being Shrove Tuesday, he started with eighteen English and thirteen Simeroons for Panama. He had now since he sailed lost no less than twenty-eight of the party which set out from Plymouth.

In a few days they reached Venta Cruz, but one of the men who had taken too much strong liquor made a noise, and the alarm being given, much of the treasure was carried out of the place before they could effect a landing. They followed, however, one of the treasure parties out of the town, and pursued them for some distance. On their way they came across another large convoy with gold; this they easily took, and having sent the Spaniards away, unloaded the mules and buried the gold, desiring to press on further.

As they went one of the chief Simeroons took the admiral apart from the road they were traversing, and led him to the foot of a lofty tree. Upon this steps had been cut, and the Indian told the admiral to ascend and see what he could observe from the top. Upon reaching the summit the admiral gave a shout of joy and astonishment. From that point he could see the Pacific Ocean, and by turning his head the Atlantic which they had just left.

This was a joyful moment for the great sailor, and when he descended, one by one most of the men climbed to the top of the tree to see the two oceans. Drake was the first Englishman who had seen this sight; to the Spaniards it was, of course, familiar; indeed Vasco Nuñez had stood upon the spot and had seen the Pacific, and taken possession of it in the name of Spain in the year 1513.

They now retraced their steps, for with the force at their disposal, Captain Drake thought it would be madness to cross the isthmus with any view of attacking the Spaniards on the other side. He had now accomplished his purpose, and had learned the nature and geography of the place, and proposed on some future occasion to return with a force sufficient to carry out the great enterprises on which he had set his mind. On their return they were sorely disappointed at finding that the Spaniards, having captured one of the party, had extorted from him the hiding-place of the gold, and had lifted and carried it off. They now prepared to reëmbark in their pinnace. Reaching the sea-shore, however, they were surprised and in some way dismayed at seeing seven Spanish vessels nearing the coast. The Spaniards had at last determined to make an effort, and had arrived at a time more unfortunate for the English than could have been supposed. The pinnace, after landing the party, had sailed away in order to prevent the Spaniards seizing upon those on board, and when Captain Drake reached the shore she was not in sight, having indeed hauled her wind and made off on the approach of the Spanish fleet. The situation seemed bad indeed, for it was certain that the Spaniards would land their troops and search the shore, and it was of the highest importance that the pinnace should be discovered first.

There was a counsel held, and the men were well-nigh despairing. Captain Drake, however, bade them keep up their courage, and pointed out to them the four lads, all of whom had escaped the effect of fever and disease, their constitution, no doubt, being strengthened by the fact that none of them indulged in too much liquor, indeed seldom touching any.

"Look," said Captain Drake, "at these four lads; their courage is unshaken, and they look cheerful and hopeful on all occasions. Take example from them and keep up your hopes. I propose to make a raft upon which I myself will embark, and by making out from this bay into the open sea, may succeed in catching sight of the pinnace and bringing it hither to your rescue."

The proposal seemed a desperate one, for it was far more likely that the Spaniards' ships would come along and descry the raft than that the latter should meet with the pinnace. However, there seemed no other resource. The materials for the raft were scanty and weak, and when Captain Francis with three companions got fairly out of the bay the raft sank so deeply in the water that they were completely standing in the sea.

For some hours they beat about, and then to their great joy they descried the pinnace in the distance making for land. The wind had now risen, and it was blowing hard, and their position on the raft was dangerous enough. They found that it would be impossible for them to keep at sea, and still more impossible to place themselves in the track of the pinnace, which was making for a bay behind a projecting headland. Painfully paddling the raft to the shore Captain Francis landed, and they made their way with much toil and fatigue over the hill which divided them from that bay, and toward morning got down to the pinnace, where they were received with much joy. Then they at once launched the boat and made for the spot where they had left their comrades. These received them as if risen from the dead, for they had all made up their minds that their admiral and his companions had been lost upon the frail raft on which they had embarked. They now put to sea, and had the good fortune to escape the ken of the Spaniards, who had sailed further up the coast. So thanking God for their escape they sailed back to the bay, where the *Pacha* and her prizes lay, and then all hands began to make great preparation for return home.

CHAPTER V

Cast Ashore

It was time indeed for the little band of adventurers to be turning their faces toward England. Their original strength of eighty men was reduced to fifty, and of these many were sick and weak. They had gained a vast store of wealth, although they had missed the plunder of Nombre de Dios and of Carthagena. Their doings had caused such consternation and alarm that it was certain that the Spaniards would erelong make a great and united effort to crush them, and fifty men, however valiant, could not battle with a fleet. The men were longing for home, looking forward to the delight of spending the great share of prize-money which would fall to each. The sudden death which had stricken many of their comrades had, too, cast a chill on the expedition, and made all long more eagerly to be away from those beautiful but deadly shores. When, therefore, on the day after the return of Captain Francis, the word was given to prepare for the homeward voyage, the most lively joy prevailed. The stores were embarked, the Simeroons, who had done them good service, dismissed with rich presents, and all embarked with much joy and thankfulness that their labors and dangers were overpast. They were, however, extremely shorthanded, and were scattered among the three or four prizes which were the best among the ships which they had taken. Ned and Gerald, being now able to give good assistance in case of need to the sailors, were put on board one of the prizes with four seamen. Captain Drake had determined to keep for a time the prizes with him, for as it might well be that they should meet upon their way a great Spanish fleet, he thought that by keeping together with the flag of St. George flying on all the ships the Spaniards would believe that the *Pacha* had been joined by ships from England, and so would assuredly let her and her consorts pass at large. At the last land at which they touched Captain Drake intended to dismiss all but one of the prizes, and to sail across the Atlantic with her and the *Pacha*.

This, however, was not to be.

One day, shortly after their departure, Ned said to Gerald, "I do not like the look of the sky; it reminds me of the sky that we had before that terrible hurricane when we were moored off the Isle of Pines; and with our scanty crew we should be in a mightily unfavorable position should the wind come on to blow." In that wise the sailors shared Ned's apprehensions, and in the speediest possible time all sail was lowered and the ship prepared to meet the gale. It was not long before the whole sky was covered with black clouds. Captain Drake signalled to the vessels that each was to do its best, and if separated was to rendezvous at the spot before agreed upon. Then all having been done that could be thought of, they waited the bursting of the storm.

It came at last, with the suddenness and almost the force of an explosion. A faint rumbling noise was first heard, a white line of foam was seen in the distance, and then with a roar and a crash the hurricane was upon them. The vessel reeled over so far under the blow that for a time all on board thought that she would capsize. The two sailors at the helm, however, held on sturdily, and at last her head drifted off on the wind, and she flew along before its force. The sea rose as if by magic; where for weeks scarcely a ripple had ruffled the surface of the water now great waves with crested tops tore along; the air was full of blinding foam swept from the tops of the waves; and it was difficult for those on board even to breathe when facing the force of the wind.

"This is tremendous," Ned shouted in Gerald's ears, "and as there seem to be islands all over these seas, if we go on at the rate we are doing now methinks that it will not be long before we land on one or another. We are, as I reckon, near Hispaniola, but there is no saying which way we may drift, for these storms are almost always changeable, and while we are running south at present, an hour hence we may be going in the opposite direction."

For twenty-four hours the storm continued with unabated fury. At times it seemed impossible that the vessel could live, so tremendous were the seas which struck and buffetted her. However, being light in the water and buoyant, she floated over it. During the next night the wind sensibly abated, and although still blowing with tremendous force, there was evidence to the accustomed eyes of the sailors that the storm was well-nigh blowing itself out. The sea, too, sensibly went down, although still tremendous, and all began to hope that they would weather the gale, when one of the sailors, who had crawled forward to the bow, shouted,

"Breakers ahead!"

It was now fortunately morning, although the darkness had been so intense since the storm began that the difference between night and day was faint indeed; still it was better, if danger were to be met with, that there should be as much light as possible. All hands looked out over the bows and saw before them a steep coast rising both to the right and left.

"It is all over with the ship," Gerald said to Ned, "and I do not think that there is a chance, even for you. The surf on those rocks is terrible."

"We must do our best," said Ned, "and trust in God. You keep close to me, Gerald, and when you want aid I will assist you as far as I can. You swim fairly, but scarce well enough, unaided, to get through that surf yonder."

The men, seeing that what appeared to be certain destruction stared them in the face, now shook hands all round, and then commending their souls to God, sat down and waited for the shock. When it came it was tremendous. The masts snapped at the board like rotten sticks, the vessel shivered from stem to stem, and drawing back for an instant was again cast down with terrible force and, as if struck by lightning, parted amidships, and then seemed to fall all to pieces like a house of cards.

Ned and Gerald were standing hand in hand when the vessel struck; and as she went to pieces and they were precipitated into the water Ned still kept close to his friend, swimming side by side with him. They soon neared the edge of the line where the waves broke upon the rocks. Then Ned shouted to Gerald to coast along outside the broken water, for that there was no landing there with life. For upwards of an hour they swam on outside the line of surf. The sea, although tremendously high, did not break till it touched a certain point, and the lads rose and fell over the great billows. They had stripped off the greater portion of their clothing before the ship struck, and in the warm water had no sensation of chill, and had nothing to fight against but fatigue. When they were in the hollow of the waves their position was easy enough, and they could make each other hear by shouting loudly. When, however, they were on the crest of one of the mountainous waves, it was a hard struggle for life. The wind blew with such fury, taking the top of the water off in sheets and scattering it in fine spray, that the boys were nearly drowned, although they kept their back to the wind and held their breath as if diving, except when necessary to make a gasp for air.

Gerald became weak and tired at the end of the hour, but Ned kept up his courage, and aided him by swimming by his side and letting Gerald put his hand upon his shoulder every time that they were in the hollows of the waves, so that he got a complete rest at these periods. At last Ned thought he saw a passage between two of the big rocks, through which it might be possible, he thought, that they might swim, and so avoid the certain death which seemed to await them at every other spot.

The passage was about 40 feet wide, and it was no easy matter to calculate upon striking this in so wild a sea. Side by side with Gerald Ned made for the spot, and at last swam to the edge of the surf, then a great wave came rolling in, and the boys, dizzy and confused, half smothered and choking, were hurled with tremendous force through the great rocks into comparatively calm water beyond. Ned now seized Gerald's hair, for his friend was nearly gone, and turning aside from the direct line of the entrance found himself speedily in calm water behind the line of rocks. A few minutes' further struggle and the two boys lay on the beach well-nigh insensible after their great exertions. After a while they recovered their strength, and with staggering feet made their way further inland.

"I owe you my life, Ned," Gerald said. "I never could have struggled ashore nor indeed keep myself up for half that time had it not been for your aid."

"I am glad to have been able to help you," Ned said, simply. "We may thank heaven that the storm had abated a little in its force before the vessel struck, for had it been blowing as it was yesterday we could not have swum five minutes. It was just the lowering of the wind that enabled us to swim without being drowned by the spray. It was bad enough as it was on the top of the waves, but yesterday it would have been impossible."

One of the first thoughts of the boys upon fairly recovering themselves was to kneel down and thank God for having preserved their lives, and then having rested for upwards of an hour to recover themselves, they made their way inland.

"Our dangers are by no means over, Gerald," Ned said. "If this island is, as I believe, a thickly cultivated one and in the hands of the Spaniards, it will go hard with us if they find us, after all the damage to their commerce which we have been inflicting for the last year."

Upon getting to some rising ground they saw to their surprise a large town lying on a bay in front of them; instinctively they paused at the sight, and both sat down so as to be out of view of any casual lookers-on.

"What are we to do, Ned?" Gerald said. "If we stay here we shall be starved. If we go into the town we shall have our throats cut. Which think you is the best?"

"I do not like either alternative," Ned said. "See, inland, there are many high mountains, and even close to the town there appear to be thickets and woods. There are houses here and there and no doubt plantations; it seems to me that if we get round to that side we may conceal ourselves, and it is hard in a country like this if we cannot at any rate find fruit enough to keep us for some time. And we had better wait till dark; our white shoulders will be seen at too far a distance by this light."

Creeping into a thicket, the lads lay down and were soon sound asleep, and it was night before they awoke and looked out. All signs of the storm had passed. The moon was shining calmly, the stars were brilliant and seemed to hang like lamps in the sky, an effect which is only seen in tropical climes. There were lights in the town, and these served as a sort of guide to them. Skirting along at the top of the basin in which the town lay they passed through cultivated estates, picking some ears of maize, thus satisfying their hunger, which was, when they started, ravenous, for during the storm they had been unable to open the hatchways and had been supported only by a little biscuit which happened to be in the caboose on deck.

Toward morning they chose a spot in a thick plantation of trees about a mile and a-half from the town, and here they agreed to wait for a while until they could come to some decision as to their course.

Three days passed without any change; each night they stole out and picked maize, pineapple, and melons in the plantations for their subsistence, and as morning returned, went back to their hiding-place. Close to it a road ran along to a noble house which stood in some grounds at about a quarter of a mile from their grove. Every morning they saw the owner of this house, apparently a man of distinction, riding toward the town, and they concluded that he was one of the great merchants of the place. One day he came accompanied by a young lady carried in a litter by four slaves. The boys, who were weary of their solitude, pressed to the edge of the thicket to obtain a clear view of this little procession which broke the monotony of their day.

"Gerald," Ned exclaimed, grasping him by the arm, "do you know, I believe that the lady is the girl I picked out of the water the day we took that ship three months ago."

"Do you think so?" Gerald said; "it is too far surely to see."

"I do not know for certain," Ned answered, "but methinks that I cannot be mistaken."

"Perhaps she would help us or intercede for us," Gerald suggested.

"Perhaps so," Ned said; "at any rate we will try. To-night we will make a move into the gardens of the house she came from and will hide there till we see her alone in the garden, then I will sally forth and see how she takes it."

Accordingly, that night after obtaining their supply of fruit the boys entered the inclosure. When morning broke there was speedily a stir, negroes and negresses went out to the fields, servants moved hither and thither in the veranda outside the house, gardeners came out and set to work at their vocations. It was evident that the owner or his family was fond of gardening, for everything was kept with beautiful order and regularity. Mixed with the cactus and other gaudy-flowering plants of Mexico and South America, were many European plants brought out and acclimatized. Here fountains threw up dancing waters in the air, cool shady paths and bowers afforded protection from the heat of the day, and so carefully was it clipped and kept that a fallen leaf would have destroyed its perfection.

The point which the boys had chosen was remote from the house, for it was of importance that there should be no witnesses of the meeting. Here, in a spacious arbor, were chairs, couches, and other signs that some of the family were in the habit of taking their seats there, and although the boys knew that it might be days before they succeeded in carrying out their object, yet they determined to wait and watch patiently however long it might be. Their success, however, surpassed their expectations; for it was but an hour or two after they had taken up their post, and soon after the sun had risen that they saw, walking along the path, the young lady whom they so desired to meet.

She was not alone, for a black girl walked a little behind her chatting constantly to her and carrying some books, a shawl, and various other articles. When they reached the arbor the attendant placed the things there, and then as she took her seat the young lady said to the girl, "Go in and fetch me my coffee here, say I shall not come in until breakfast time, and that if any orders are required they must come here for them."

"Will you want me to read to you?"

"No," the young lady said; "it is not hot. I shall take a turn round the garden first and then read to myself."

The black girl went off at a trot toward the house and the young lady strolled round and round that portion of the garden until her black attendant returned with a tray containing coffee, lemonade, and fruits. This she placed on the table, and then in answer to the "You need not wait" of the lady, again retired.

Now was the time for the boys, who had watched these operations with keen interest and anxiety. It was uncertain whether she would keep the black attendant by her side, and all depended upon that. As soon as she was alone Ned advanced from their hiding-place. The boys had agreed that it was better at first that he should approach alone, lest the sudden appearance of the two, especially as Gerald was nearly as tall as a man, might have caused alarm, and she might have flown away before she had identified Ned as the lad who had jumped into the water to save her.

Ned approached the arbor with hesitating steps, and felt that his appearance was indeed sorely against him. He had no covering to his head, had nothing on, indeed, but a pair of trousers. He was shoeless and stockingless, and presented the appearance of a beggar boy rather than the smart young sailor whom she had seen on board the ship.

The lady started up with a short exclamation on seeing a white ragged boy standing before her.

"Who are you?" she exclaimed, "and by what right do you enter these gardens? A white boy, and in rags, how comes this?"

"Our ship has been wrecked," Ned said, using his best Spanish. "Do you not remember me? I am the boy who picked you up when you fell overboard on the day when the English captured the ship you come out in, some four months ago."

"Are you, indeed?" the young lady said, in surprise. "Yes, and

NED INTRODUCES HIMSELF
SEE PAGE 63.

now that I look close at you I recognize your face. Poor boy, how have you got into a strait like this?"

Ned understood but little of what she said, as he only knew a few words in Spanish. It was with difficulty that he could understand it even when spoken slowly, while spoken as a native would do he scarce gathered a word. He saw, however, from her attitude that her meaning was kind, and that she was disposed to do what she could for him. He, therefore, in his broken Spanish, told her how a ship on which he and five of his comrades were embarked had been driven ashore in the hurricane, and all lost with the exception of another boy and himself.

"It is lucky, indeed," the girl said to herself, when he had finished, "that I found that my father had left Nombre de Dios and had come down to his house here, for, assuredly the people would have made short work of these poor lads had I not been here to aid them. But, after all, what can I do? My father would, I know, do anything for my sake, and I have told him how this lad jumped overboard to save my life, but there is one here greater than he, that terrible Inquisition. These boys are heretics, and it will be impossible to conceal, for any time, from the priests that they are here. Still, at any rate, for a time we might hide them, and in gratitude only I would do all in my power for them."

Ned watched her face as these thoughts passed through her mind. He saw at once that she was willing to do all in her power, but saw also that there were difficulties in the way.

"Poor boy," she said, looking at him kindly; "you must be hungry, indeed," and taking an ivory mallet she struck a gong which hung in the arbor, and made signs to Ned to retire for the present. The little black girl came running out.

"I have changed my mind," her mistress said. "Let my breakfast be sent out here to me instead of in-doors, and I am hungry; tell the cook to be sure and let it be a good one, and as soon as possible."

Much surprised by these orders the black girl again left her.

"My father has gone to town," she said, to the boys, when they joined her; "when he comes back I will ask him what can be done. It will not be easy to hide you, for these negroes chatter like so many parrots, and the news will spread all over the town that some English boys are here, and in that case they will take you away, and my father would be powerless as I to help you."

The black cook was indeed astonished at the demolition of the breakfast effected by her young mistress, but she put it down to the fact that she must have given a large portion of it to her dogs, of which one or more were generally her companions in the garden.

Fortunately on the present occasion the great bloodhound Zeres had gone down into the town with his master. Of this, however, the cook knew nothing, and muttered to herself somewhat angrily as she saw the empty dishes which were brought back to her, "that it was a sin to give to that creature a meal which was sufficient for five noblemen."

When Señor Sagasta returned to his beautiful villa in the afternoon, his daughter at once confided to him what had happened. He entered warmly into her scheme for the aid and protection of the lads, and expressed himself willing to do anything that she could suggest. "But," he said, "you know as well as I do that if the news gets about that two boys of Captain Drake's band are here, nothing will save them from the rage of the population; and indeed if the people and the military authorities were disposed to let them alone the Inquisition would be too strong for them and would claim its own, and against the Inquisition even governors are powerless. Therefore, if they are to stop, and stop they must, at least for a time, it must be done in perfect secrecy. There is no possibility of disguising two English boys to look like negroes. The only plan I can suggest is that they should have the gardener's hut. I can remove the man who lives there at present, and will send him up the country to look after my place there. Then you must take old David into our confidence. He and his wife Floey are perfectly faithful and can be trusted to the death. It is lucky that she is a cook, for she will be able to prepare food for them. The hut must be kept, of course, locked up at all times; but as it is close to the fence, and the window indeed looks into the garden, you can go there of a day and speak to them and take them books and lighten their captivity. When it gets dark I will go with you down the garden and will see these brave lads. In the meantime old David shall get some shirts and shoes and other necessaries for them. We have a plentiful store of things in the magazine, and he can rig them up there perfectly. I will at once get the gardener out of the house, and will give David instructions to carry the things there as soon as it is empty."

That evening after it was dark the boys, who had been anxiously listening for every movement, saw in the dim light the white figure of the girl advancing with her father beside her. When she came to the arbor, she raised her voice.

"Are you here?" she cried. "You can come out without fear." And as they advanced, "My father will do all in his power to protect the saviour of his daughter."

The merchant shook the hands of the boys with the stately ceremony of the Spaniard, and assured them that he was their servant indeed for their treatment of his daughter, and that his house and all that it contained was at their disposal.

Ned and Gerald understood little enough of what he was saying, but his manner and gestures were sufficient, and they thanked him heartily for his kindness. He now led the way along many winding paths till they reached a low fence forming the border of the garden, and distant a long way from the house. A light was already burning in it, and a black servant was at work within. There was a break in the fence, by which they passed through without difficulty, and on entering the hut they found everything prepared for them.

On a table stood a dainty supper, the rooms were swept, and fresh furniture had been placed in them. In these countries furniture is of the slightest kind. A hammock to swing in by day or sleep in by night, a couple of cane chairs, and a mat of beautifully woven straw for the floor. This is nearly all the furniture which is required in the tropics.

First the negro beckoned the boys into an inner room, and there, to their intense delight, they saw a large tub full of water, and two piles of clothes lying beside it.

Don Sagasta and his daughter, after a few more words, left them, assuring them that they would be safe from observation there, but that they must not stir out during the day, and must keep the door securely fastened, and must give no answer to any one who might come and knock or call, unless to themselves, to the black who was now with them, or his wife, who would accompany him perhaps the next evening. Donna Anna herself promised that she would come and see them the next morning, and that she hoped to find that they were comfortable.

When left alone the boys luxuriated in the bath, and then having put on fresh suits they felt clean and comfortable once again. The clothes were those used by the upper class of slaves employed as overseers. Don Sagasta had determined to get them some clothes of a superior class, but he felt that it was better that, so long as they were in hiding, they should be dressed in a costume which would, should any one perchance get a distant look at them, excite no curiosity or surprise.

The boys ate a hearty supper, and then throwing themselves into the swinging hammocks were soon fast asleep. They were up with dawn next morning, tidied up their room, and made all ready for the visit of Donna Anna. She soon appeared, having got rid of her little black maid as upon the morning before. She brought them a store of books, and among them a Spanish dictionary and grammar; she told them that she thought it would be of assistance to pass away their time, and be of the greatest use for them to learn to speak as much Spanish as possible, and that she was willing, when she could spare time unobserved, to teach them the language. Very gratefully the boys accepted her offer, and day by day for the next month the young lady came every morning, and for an hour taught them the meaning and pronunciation of the words, which during the day they learnt by heart. They found that the island upon which they had been cast ashore was Porto Rico, an island of considerable size not far from Hispañiola.

CHAPTER VI

In the Woods

In the evening Señor Sagasta visited the lads, and had long conversations with them. He promised them that upon the very first opportunity which should occur he would aid them to escape, but pointed out that at present there was no possibility of their getting away. "Captain Drake," he said, "has left the seas, and until he comes back again, or some other of your English filibusters, I see no chance of your escape. As soon as I hear of an English ship in these waters I will have a small boat, well fitted up with sails and all necessaries, conveyed to a creek on the coast. To this you shall be taken down, and make your way to the point where we hear that the vessel is accustomed to rendezvous."

This appeared to the boys to be the only possible plan, and they warmly expressed their gratitude to their host for his thoughtful kindness.

Another month passed, and then one evening Don Sagasta came to the hut with a certain anxiety in his face.

"Is there anything the matter?" Ned, who now began to speak Spanish with some fluency, asked.

"I am much disturbed. Since you have been here I am sure that no one has got a sight of you, and I can rely so implicitly upon David and Flora that I am sure the secret has not leaked out there. But from what I hear it seems that you must have been seen during the time that you were wrecked and before you came here. I hear in the town to-day that a rumor is current among the people that two white men were seen near the sea upon the day after the great storm. Some one else, too, seems to have said that he caught sight of two white men not far from this house just before daybreak two days afterwards. This report has, it seems, been going from mouth to mouth, and has at last reached the ears of the governor. The portions of a wreck which were driven ashore seem to confirm the story, and unfortunately the board with the name of the ship was washed ashore, and it is known to be that of one of those captured by Captain Drake. Putting the two things together it is supposed that misfortune overtook a portion of his fleet, and that two of his men managed to save their lives, and are now lurking somewhere about the neighborhood. I hear that the governor has ordered a strict search to be set on foot, and that a large reward is to be offered for the discovery of any signs of the fugitives."

The next day the boys heard that the persons to whom the story had been traced had been taken before the governor and strictly examined, and that he was fully convinced of the truth of the story. Three days afterwards Don Sagasta brought them a copy of a notice which had been placed in the market-place, offering a reward of 1000 dollars for any news which would lead to the capture of the English pirates, and announcing the severest punishment upon any who should dare to conceal or to assist them. Gerald at once said that rather than be a cause of anxiety to their kind host and his daughter they would give themselves up. This offer was, however, indignantly refused by Don Sagasta.

"No, no," he said; "this must not be. I might take you into the house, but I fear that with so many servants, some of whom are as bigotted as any of us whites, you would be sure to be discovered, and they would either reveal in confession or disclose to the authorities the fact of your concealment. The only plan which promises to offer safety that I can suggest is that you shall take to the mountains. There are many runaways there, and although sometimes they are hunted down and slain, yet they have caverns and other places of concealment where you might remain for years. I will speak to David about it at once."

David on being questioned said that there was an old native

woman living at a hut a little way off, who had the reputation of having the evil eye, and who was certainly acquainted with the doings of the runaways. If any slave wished to send a message to one of his friends who had taken to the hills, the old woman would for a present always convey, or get it conveyed, to the man for whom it was intended. He thought that it would be absolutely necessary that some such means should be taken of introducing the boys to the runaways, otherwise, hunted as these were, they would either fly when they saw two whites approaching, or would surround and destroy them.

Don Sagasta at once accepted the suggestion, and David was dispatched to the old woman with offers of a handsome present if she would give a guide to the boys to the mountains. David was instructed especially to tell her that they were English, and the natural enemies of the Spaniards, that they had done them much harm at sea, and that if caught by the Spaniards they would be killed. He returned an hour later with news that the old Indian woman had at once upon hearing these facts promised to get them passed up to the hiding-places of the natives.

"You think," Don Sagasta said, "that there is no fear of her mentioning the fact that she has seen my friends to any of the searchers?"

"Oh, no," David said; "she is as close as wax. Over and over again, when she has been suspected of assisting in the evasion of a slave, she has been beaten and put to torture, but nothing was ever extracted from her lips, and it is certain that she would die rather than reveal a secret."

Donna Anna was much moved when she said adieu to the lads. She regarded Ned as the preserver of her life, and both had during the two months of daily intercourse much endeared themselves to her. Don Sagasta brought to them a handsome pair of pistols each and a sword, and then giving them a basket of provisions and a purse containing money, which he thought might be useful even among runaway slaves, he and his daughter bade adieu to them, with many expressions of kindness and gratitude on both sides.

"Do not hesitate," Don Sagasta said, "to let me know if I can at any time do or send anything for you; should it be possible I will send a message to you by the old woman if any expedition on a grand scale is being got up against the runaways, and this may make your position more comfortable among them."

Under the guidance of David they then started for the Indian woman's hut, while Flora set to work to carry away and obliterate all signs from the hut of its late residents. After a few minutes' walking the boys arrived at the Indian hut. It was constructed simply of boughs of trees thickly worked together. On hearing their footsteps an old woman—the boys thought they had never seen any one so old—with long white hair, and a face wrinkled till it hardly seemed like the face of a human being, came to the door with a torch made of resinous wood held aloft. She peered under her hand at the boys, and said a few words to David, which he translated to the boys to be— "And these are English, the people of whom the Spaniards are as afraid as my people are of them? Two Spaniards can drive fifty Indians before them, but I hear that a dozen of these Englishmen can take a ship with a hundred Spaniards on board. It is wonderful; they look something like our oppressors, but they are fairer, and their eyes are blue, and they look honest, and have not that air of pride and arrogance which the Spaniard never lays aside. I have a boy here." And as she spoke an Indian boy of some thirteen years of age slipped out from behind her. "He will show them to the refuge-places of the last of my race. There they will be well received, for I have sent by him a message to their chiefs, and it may be that these lads, knowing the ways of white warfare, will be able to assist my countrymen, and to enable them to resist these dogs of Spaniards. The blessing of an old woman be upon you. I have seen many changes. I have seen my people possessors of this island, save a small settlement which they had even then the folly to allow the Spaniards to possess. I have seen them swept away by the oppressor; my husband tortured and killed, my brothers burned alive; all that I loved slain by the Spaniards. Now, it does my old eyes good to see two of the race who will in the future drive those dogs from these fair lands as they have driven my people."

So saying, she returned into the hut.

The boy prepared at once to start, and the lads, wringing the hand of the black who had been so kind to them, at once followed their guide into the darkness. For some hours they walked without intermission, sometimes going at a sling trot and then easing down again. Dark as was the night their guide trod the paths without hesitation or pause. The boys could scarce see the ground upon which they trod, but the eyes of the native were keener than theirs, and to him the way seemed as clear as in broad daylight.

After traversing for some miles a flat level country they began to mount, and for about two hours ascended a mountain thickly covered with forest. Then the guide stopped and motioned to them that he could now go no further, and must rest for the present. The boys were surprised at this sudden stop, for their guide had gone along so quickly and easily that he taxed to the utmost their powers of progression, while he himself never breathed any harder than when walking upon the level ground. They had, however, no means of interrogating him, for he spoke no language which they understood. Without a word the lad threw himself down at full length, an example which they followed without hesitation.

"I wonder," Ned said, "why he stopped."

"Because he is tired, I expect," Gerald replied, "or that he does not know the exact spot upon which he is likely to meet the band, and that he has taken us so far along the one path which was certain to lead in the right direction, but for the precise spot he must wait till morning."

It was not many minutes before the three lads were fast asleep, but with the first gleam of daylight the Indian boy awoke. Touching his companions he sprang to his feet, and without hesitation turned off to the right, and climbed an even steeper path than any which they had followed in the darkness. The trees grew thinner as they advanced, and they were soon climbing over bare rock. They saw now that they were near the extreme summit of one of the hills. The boy, as they passed through the trees, had gathered some dry sticks and a handful or two of green leaves. Upon reaching the top he placed these down upon the ground and looked toward the east. The sun would not be up for another half-hour yet. The boy at once began with steady earnestness to rub two pieces of stick together, according to their way of kindling a fire. It was a quarter of an hour before the sparks began to drop from the wood; these, with some very dry leaves and tiny chips of wood, the Indian boy rapidly blew into life, and then with a very small fire of dry wood he sat patiently watching the east. At the moment that the sun showed above the sea, he placed the little fire in the heart of the pile of wood which he had collected, threw the green leaves upon it, and blew vigorously until the whole caught fire, and a wreath of smoke ascended above them. For five minutes only he allowed the fire to burn, and then at once extinguished it carefully, knocking the fire from each individual brand. When the last curl of white smoke had ceased to ascend he stood up and eagerly looked round the country.

It was a glorious view. On the one hand the wood-clad hills sloped to the foot of the plain, covered with plantations, dotted here and there with the villages of the slaves and the white houses of the overseers. At a distance could be faintly seen the towers of a city, while beyond, the sea stretched like a blue wall, far as the eye could see. Inland the country was broken and mountainous, the hills being in all cases thickly covered with trees. From two points in the heart of these hills white smoke curled up as soon as the smoke of their fire died away. These, too, in a short time also ceased to rise, and the boys knew that they were signal-fires in response to that which their guide had made. The boy hesitated for a minute or two as to the direction which he should take.

As, however, one of the fires appeared a good deal nearer than the other, this probably decided him in its favor, and he started in a straight line toward the spot where the smoke had curled up. Another two hours' walking and they entered an open glade, where ten or twelve natives and two or three negroes were gathered. They were greatly surprised at seeing two white men, but the presence of the native guide apparently vouched for these visitors, and although one or two of the men sprang up and at a rapid pace proceeded in the direction from which the new-comers had arrived, the rest simply rose to their feet, and, grasping the spears, bows and arrows, and clubs which they carried, waited silently to hear what the Indian boy had to tell them.

He poured forth an animated strain of words for a few minutes, and the faces of the Indians lit up with pleasure. The one among them who appeared to be the chief of the party advanced at once to the boys and made every sign of welcome. One of the negroes also approached, and in broken Spanish asked them if they could speak in that language. The boys were able now to reply in the affirmative, and quickly supplemented the account of them which had been given by their guide, by their own description of the manner of their coming there.

The negro, after explaining to the rest what the boys had said, then assured them in the name of the chief that every welcome was theirs, and that they hailed among them as a happy incident the arrival of two of the famous race who were the deadly enemies of the Spaniards.

The boys on their part assured them that they would endeavor to repay the hospitality with which they were received, by their assistance should the Spaniards make any attacks upon the tribe during the time they were there, that the English everywhere were the friends of those who were oppressed by the Spaniards, and that their countrymen were moved with horror and indignation at the accounts which had reached them of the diabolical treatment to which the Indians were exposed.

The party now pressed still further into the forest, and turning up a ravine followed its windings for some distance, and then passing through an exceedingly narrow gorge reached a charming little valley in which were some rough huts, showing that the residence of at least a portion of the runaways had been reached.

Here for some time life passed uneventfully with the boys.

Their first care was to study sufficient of the language of the natives to enable them to hold converse with them, for it was clear to them that they might have to stop there for some considerable time. Their food consisted of roots, of wild fruit, and of yams, which the natives cultivated in small scattered plots of ground. Many birds, too, were brought in, the natives bringing them down with small darts. They were able to throw their light spears with extreme precision, and often pierced the larger kinds of birds, as they sat upon the boughs of trees, with these weapons before they could open their wings for flight. With bows and arrows, too, they were able to shoot with great accuracy, and the boys felt sure that, if properly led, they would be able to make a stout resistance to the Spaniards.

They heard several times during the first three weeks of their sojourn there, of raids made by small parties of the Spaniards, but in none of these cases were the searchers successful in finding traces of the fugitive slaves, nor did they come into the part of the wood in which was the village which served as headquarters of the negroes. At the end of three weeks the boys accompanied a party of their friends to other points at which the fugitives were gathered. Altogether they found that in that part of the island there were some hundreds of natives, with about forty or fifty runaway negroes. Through the latter the boys explained to the natives that they ought to build strong places to which, in case of necessity, they could retreat, and where they could offer a desperate resistance to the enemy. The extreme roughness of the ground, the deep ravines and precipices, were all favorable for defence, and although they could not hope to make a permanent resistance to a large armed force, yet they might easily resist small parties and then make good their retreat before large reinforcements could arrive. The negroes expressed their approval of the plans, but the Indians shook their heads over the proposition.

"These men have no courage," the blacks said, to the boys; "their heart is broken; they fly at the sound of a Spaniard's voice. What good do you expect from them? But if the Spaniards come, we fight. Our people are brave and we do not fear death.

If the Spaniards come we fight with you, and die rather than be taken back as slaves."

One morning, on rising, the boys heard some exclamations among their allies.

"What is it?" they asked. The negroes pointed to films of smoke rising from the summits of two hills at a short distance from each other.

"What is that a sign of?" they asked.

"It is a sign that the Spaniards are coming. No doubt in pursuit of a runaway; perhaps with those terrible dogs. The Spaniards could do nothing among these mountains without them. They follow their game through the thickest woods."

"But," said Ned, "why on earth do not the negroes take to the trees? Surely there could be no difficulty in getting from tree to tree by the branches for a certain distance so as to throw the hounds off the scent."

"Many do escape in that way," the negro said; "but the pursuit is often so hot, and the dogs so close upon the trail, that there is little time for manœuvres of this sort, beside which, many of the fugitives are half mad with fear. I know myself that the baying of those horrible dogs seems to freeze the blood, and in my case I only escaped by luckily striking a rivulet. Then my hopes rose again, and after following it for a time I had the happy thought of climbing into a tree which overhung it, and then dropping down at some little distance off, and so completely throwing the dogs off the trail."

"Why do they not shoot the dogs?" Ned asked; "I do not mean the men whom they are scenting, but their friends."

"We might shoot them," the negro said, "if they were allowed to run free, but here in the woods they are usually kept on the chain, so that their masters are close to them. Listen," he said, "do you not hear the distant baying?"

Listening attentively, however, the boys could hear nothing; their ears were not trained so well as those of the negro, and it was some minutes before they heard a distant faint sound of the deep bark of a dog. A few minutes later a negro, panting for breath, bathed in perspiration, and completely exhausted, staggered into the glade where they were standing; the other negroes gave a slight cry of alarm at the proximity of so dangerous a comrade.

"Save me," the man cried; "I am pursued."

"How many men are after you?" Ned asked.

The negro started in astonishment at seeing a white face and being questioned in Spanish. Seeing, however, that his comrades were on good terms with his questioner, he answered at once, "There are some twenty of them, with two dogs."

"Let us give them a sharp lesson," Ned said, to the negroes standing round. "We have made preparations, and it is time that we began to show our teeth. If they find that they cannot come with impunity into our woods, they will not be so anxious to pursue single men, and will leave us alone, except they bring all the force of the island against us."

The negroes looked doubtful as to the wisdom of taking the initiative, so great was their fear of the Spaniards. However, the cheerfulness with which the two English boys proposed resistance animated them, and with sharp whistles they called the whole of their comrades to the place.

Ned briefly explained their intentions. "There is no time to be lost; we must take our places on the upper ground of that narrow valley, and tell the man to run straight through; we have plenty of stones piled there, and may give the Spaniards a warmer reception than they expect. We could not have a better opportunity, for with such small numbers as they have, they certainly would not be able to attack us with any hope of success up so steep a hillside."

The valley which Ned indicated was not one of those which led in the direction of their stronghold, but it was a very steep gorge which they had remarked as being particularly well fitted for checking a pursuing party, and for that end had prepared piles of stones on the upper heights. The negroes, taking with them the sharpened poles which they used as spears, and their bows and arrows, started under Ned and Gerald to the indicated spot. Gerald had arranged to go with a party to one side of the gorge, Ned to the other, but they decided that it was better that they should keep together, the more to encourage the natives, and while a few negroes were sent to one side of the gorge, the main body under the two English lads kept together on the other.

The fugitive had already gone ahead with one of the negroes to show him the way.

Scarcely had they taken their places at the top of the gorge when the baying of the hounds, which had been increasing every minute in volume, became so loud that the Spaniards were clearly close at hand. In another three or four minutes there issued from the wood a party of some twenty men, leading two dogs by chains. The creatures struggled to get forward, and their eyes seemed almost starting out of their heads with their eagerness to reach the object of their pursuit. Their speed was, however, moderated by the fact that the band, who were all on horseback, had to pick their way through the great boulders. The wood itself was difficult for horsemen, but here and there were spaces, and they had been able to ride at a fair pace. On entering the mouth of the gorge, however, they were obliged to fall into an order of two abreast, and sometimes even to go in Indian file. Huge boulders strewed the bottom of the chasm, where indeed a stream in winter poured through. The sides were by no means perpendicular, but were exceedingly precipitous. When the Spaniards had fairly got into the gorge Ned gave the signal, and a shower of great stones came leaping down the sides of the rocks upon the astonished foes. Several were struck from their horses; many of the horses themselves were knocked down, and a scene of confusion at once took place. The Spaniards, however, were accustomed to fighting, and the person in command giving a few orders, led ten of his men up the rocks upon the side where the assailants were in strongest force, while the rest of the party seizing the horses' heads, drove the frightened animals back through the ravine to the mouth. The instant that the Spaniards commenced their ascent long habits of fear told upon some of the slaves, and these took to their heels at once. Many others stood more firmly, but were evidently wavering. Ned and Gerald, however, kept them at work hurling stones down, and more than one of the Spaniards was carried off his feet by these missiles; still they bravely ascended; then Ned taking a deliberate aim with his pistol, brought down one of the leaders, and this greatly surprised and checked the advance. The pistol shot was followed by that of Gerald, and the Spaniards wavered at this unexpected addition to the forces of the natives. Then Ned in English shouted,

"Now, my brave Britons, show these Spaniards you can fight as well on land as at sea."

The words were probably not understood by any of the Spaniards, but they knew that the language was not Spanish or Indian, and the thought that a number of English were there completely paralyzed them. They hesitated and then began slowly to fall back. This was all that was needed to encourage the negroes. With a shout these now advanced to the attack, shooting their arrows and hurling stones, and the retreat of the enemy was rapidly converted into a flight. Their blood once thoroughly up, the negroes were ready for anything. Throwing aside their bows and arrows they charged upon the Spaniards, and, in spite of the superior arms and gallant defence of the latter, many of them were beaten down and killed by the heavy clubs and pointed staves of the negroes; more, indeed, would have perished, and indeed all might have fallen, had not at this moment a formidable reinforcement of strength reached them. The men from below having got the horses fairly out of the gorge, left but two of their number with them and advanced to the assistance of their friends, bringing with them the two blood-hounds.

"Never fear the hounds," Ned shouted; "we can beat them to death as easily as if they were pigs. Keep a bold front and attack them, and I warrant you they are no more formidable than their masters."

Had these reinforcements arrived earlier they might have changed the fight, but the Spaniards who survived were anxious only to be off, and the negroes' blood was so thoroughly up, that under the leadership of the boys they were prepared to face even these terrible dogs. These threw themselves into the fray with all the ferocity of their savage nature. Springing at the

GERALD DISPOSES OF THE BLOODHOUND
SEE PAGE 82.

throats of two of the negroes, they brought them to the ground. One of the dogs was instantly disposed of by Gerald, who, placing his pistol to its ear, blew out its brains. Ned fell upon the other with his sword, and the negroes joining him speedily beat it down and slew it. The diversion, however, had enabled the Spaniards to get upon their horses, and they now galloped off at full speed among the trees.

CHAPTER VII

An Attack in Force

The negroes were delighted at the success of the conflict, as were the Indians who soon joined them. But ten of the Spaniards had escaped, the rest having fallen either in the gorge, killed by the rocks, or in the subsequent fight. Ned and Gerald, who were now looked upon as the leaders of the party, told the negroes to collect the arms of the fallen men, and to give a hasty burial to their bodies. The boys knew too well the savage nature of the war which raged between the black and the white to ask whether any of the Spaniards were only wounded. They knew that an instant death had awaited all who fell into the hands of their late slaves.

"Now," Ned said, "my friends, you must not suppose that your fighting is over. The Spaniards will take the news back to the town, and it is likely enough that we shall have a large force upon us in the course of a few days. I do not suspect that they will come before that time; indeed it may be far longer, for they know that it will require a very large force to search these woods and that now our blood is up it will be no trifle to overcome us in our stronghold. If we are to succeed at last, labor, discipline, and courage will all be required."

The negroes now besought the boys formally to take the command, and promised to obey their orders implicitly.

"Well," Ned said, "if you promise this we will lead you. My friend is older than I, and he shall be captain and I will be first lieutenant."

"No, no," Gerald said; "this must not be, Ned; I am the oldest, it is true, by a few months, but you are far more active and quick than I, and you have been the leader ever since we left the ship; I certainly will not take the command from you."

"Well, we will be joint-generals," Ned said, laughing, "and I do not think that our orders will clash."

He then explained to the negroes and natives the course which he thought that they ought to pursue. First, every point at which the enemy could be harassed should be provided with missiles. In the second place, all signs of footsteps and paths leading to their accustomed dwelling-places should be obliterated; thirdly, they should fight as little as possible, it being their object to fight when pursued and interfered with by small parties of Spaniards, but to avoid conflict with large bodies.

"Our object," he said, "is to live free and unmolested here; and if the Spanish find that when they come in large numbers they cannot overtake us, and that when they come in small ones they are defeated with loss, they will take to leaving us alone."

All agreed to this policy, and it was arranged that the women, children, and most feeble of the natives should retire to almost inaccessible hiding-places far in the mountains, and that the more active spirits with the negroes, and divided into five or six bands acting to some extent independently of each other, but yet in accordance with a general plan, should remain to oppose the passage of the enemy.

This, their first success over the Spaniards, caused a wild exultation among the negroes and natives, and Ned and Gerald were viewed as heroes. The lads took advantage of their popularity to impress upon the negroes the necessity of organizing themselves and undergoing certain drill and discipline; without it, as they told them, although occasionally they might succeed in driving back the Spaniards, yet in the long run they must be defeated. It was only by fighting with regularity like trained soldiers that they would make themselves respected by the Spaniards, and the latter, instead of viewing them as wild beasts to be hunted, would regard them with respect.

The negroes, fresh from a success gained by irregular means, were at first loath to undertake the trouble and pains which the boys desired, but the latter pointed out that it was not always that the enemy were to be caught napping, and that after such a check as had been put upon them the Spaniards would be sure to come in greater numbers, and to be far more cautious how they trusted themselves into places where they might be caught in a trap. The weapons thrown away or left upon the ground by the Spaniards were divided among the negroes, and these and the natives were now formed into companies, natives and negroes being mixed in each company, so that the latter might animate the former by their example. Four companies of forty men each were formed, and for the next fortnight incessant drill went on, by which time the forest fugitives began to have a fair notion of the rudimentary elements of drill. When the boys were not engaged upon this, in company with one of the native chiefs they examined the mountains, and at last fixed upon a place which should serve as the last stronghold, should they be driven to bay by the enemy.

It was three weeks before there were any signs of the Spaniards. At the end of that time a great smoke rising from the signal-hill proclaimed that a large body of the enemy were approaching the forest. This was expected, for two days before three negro runaways had taken shelter with them. The negroes had been armed with long pikes of tough wood sharpened in the fire and capable of inflicting fully as deadly a wound as those carried by the Spaniards. Each carried a club, the leaders being armed with the swords taken from the Spaniards, while there were also eight arquebuses which had been gained from the same source. All the natives bore bows and arrows, with which they were able to shoot with great accuracy. The negroes were not skilled with these weapons, but were more useful from their greater strength for hurling down rocks and missiles upon the Spaniards when below. A consultation had been previously held as to the course to be taken in case of the approach of the enemy. It was determined as far as possible to avoid fighting, to allow the Spaniards to tramp from place to place, and then to harass them by falling upon them in the night, disturbing their sleep, cutting down sentries, and harassing them until they were forced by pure exhaustion to leave the forest.

These tactics were admirably adapted to the nature of the contest; the only thing which threatened to render them nugatory was the presence of the fierce dogs of the Spaniards. Preparations had already been made for checking the bloodhounds in pursuit of fugitive slaves. In a narrow place in one of the valleys at the entrance of the forest a somewhat heavy gallery had been erected; this was made of wood heaped with great stones, and was so arranged that any animal running through it would push aside a stick which acted as a trigger; this would release a lever, and the heavy logs above would fall, crushing to death anything beneath it. A look-out was always placed to intercept any fugitive slaves who might enter the forest and to guide them through this trap, which was, of course, not set until after they had passed. This had been done in the case of the two negroes who had arrived the previous day, and the boys felt that any pursuit of them by blood-hounds would at once be cut short and the Spaniards left to their own devices. This anticipation proved correct; the scouts reported that they could hear in the distance the baying of the dogs, and that undoubtedly the enemy were proceeding on the track of the slaves.

The four companies were each told off to positions considerably apart from each other, while Ned and Gerald, with the cacique or chief of the Indians, one negro, and four or five fleet-footed young men, remained to watch the success of the trap. This was all that they had hoped; the Spaniards were seen coming up the glade, a troop two hundred strong. The leaders were on horseback, some fifteen in number, and after them marched the pikemen in steady array, having men moving at a distance on each flank to prevent surprise.

"This," said Ned, "is a regular military enterprise. The last was a mere pursuing party gathered at random. It will not be so easy to deal with cautious men like these."

Three hounds ran ahead of the leaders with their noses on the ground, giving now and then the deep bay peculiar to their kind. They reached the trap, and rushed into the gallery, which was some twelve feet in length and of sufficient height to enable a man on foot to march through.

The leaders on seeing the trap drew in their horses in doubt what this structure could mean, and shouted to the hounds to stop; but the latter having the scent strong in their nostrils ran on without pausing. As the last hound disappeared in the gallery a crash was heard, and the whole erection collapsed, crushing the hounds beneath it.

A cry of consternation and surprise burst from the Spaniards. The artifice was a new one, and showed that the fugitives were assisted by men with intellect far in advance of their own. The pursuit was summarily checked, for the guides of the Spaniards were now gone. The enemy paused, and a consultation took place among the leaders. It was apparently determined to pursue their way alone, taking every precaution in hopes that the natives would attack them as they had done the previous expedition, when they hoped to inflict a decisive blow upon them. That they would themselves be able to find the runaway negroes in the forest they had but small hope, but they thought it possible that these would again take the initiative.

First, under the guidance of one who had evidently been in the last expedition, they took their way to the valley where the fight had taken place. Here all was still. There were no signs of their foes; they found in the gorge a great cairn of stones with a wooden cross placed over it, and the words in Spanish cut upon it:

"Here lie the bodies of ten Spaniards who sought to attack harmless men in these woods; let their fate be a lesson to those who may follow their example."

This inscription caused great surprise among the Spaniards, who gathered round the mound and conversed earnestly upon it, looking round at the deep and silent woods, which might, for aught they knew, contain foes who had proved themselves formidable.

It was evident that the soldiers, brave as they were, yet felt misgivings as to the task upon which they had entered. They knew that two Englishmen, a portion of the body which under Drake had rendered themselves so feared, were leaders of these men, and so great was the respect in which the English were at that time held, that this alone vastly added to the difficulties and dangers which the Spaniards saw awaiting them. However, after a few minutes' consultation the party moved forward. It was now formed in two bodies about equally strong, one going a quarter of a mile ahead, the other following it.

"What have these men divided their forces for?" the negro asked Ned.

"It seems to me," he answered, "that they hope we shall fall upon the first body thinking that there are no more behind, and that the others, coming up in the midst of the fight, will take us by surprise; however, we will let them march. Send word to the company, which lies somewhat in the line which they have taken, of their approach, and let them at once retire. Tell them to make circuits in the hills, but to leave behind them sufficient traces for the Spaniards to follow. This will encourage them to keep on, and by nightfall they will be thoroughly tired out. Whenever they get in valleys or other places where advantage may be taken of them, two of the companies shall accompany them at a good distance on their flanks, and pour in volleys of arrows or roll stones down upon them. I will take command of one of these companies, Gerald of the other. Do you," he said to the negro, "follow with the last. Keep out of their reach, but occasionally after they have passed fire arrows among the rear-guard. Do you, cacique, make your way to the leading column. See that they choose the most difficult gorges, and give as far as possible the appearance of hurry to their flight so as to encourage the Spaniards to follow."

These tactics were faithfully carried out. All day the Spaniards followed, as they believed, close upon the footsteps of the flying foe, but from time to time from strong advantage spots arrows were rained upon them, great rocks thundered down, and wild yells rang through the forest. Before, however, they could ascend the slopes and get hand to hand with their enemy these had retreated, and all was as silent as the grave in the woods.

Perplexed, harassed, and somewhat awe-struck by these new and inexplicable tactics, and having lost many men by the arrows and stones of the enemy, the two troops gathered at nightfall in an open glade. Here a bivouac was formed, branches of the trees cut down, and the provisions which each had brought with him produced. A rivulet ran through the glade, and the weary troops were soon lying on the grass, a strong line of sentries having been placed round. Already the appearance of the troop was greatly changed from that of the body which had entered the wood. Then all were eager for the fray, confident in the extreme of their power to crush with ease these unarmed negroes and natives, who had hitherto, except on the last occasion, fled like hunted deer at their approach.

Now, however, this feeling was checked. They had learned that the enemy were well commanded and prepared, and that so far, while they themselves had lost several men, not a native had been so much as seen by them. At nightfall the air became alive with mysterious noises; cries as of animals, occasionally Indian whoops, shouts from one voice to another were heard all around. The Spaniards stood to their arms and gazed anxiously into the darkness.

Soon the shouts of the sentries told that flights of arrows were being discharged at them by invisible foes. Volley after volley were fired from the musketoons and arquebuses into the wood. These were answered by bursts of taunting laughter and mocking yells, while the rain of arrows continued.

The Spanish troops, whose position and figures could be seen by the blaze of the lighted fires, while a dense darkness reigned within the forest, began to suffer severely from the arrows of these unseen foes. Bodies fifty strong advanced into the dark forest to search out their enemies, but they searched in vain. The Indians, better accustomed to the darkness, and knowing the forest well, easily retreated as they advanced, and the Spaniards dared not venture far from their fires, for they feared being lost in the forest.

The officer commanding, an old and experienced soldier, soon ceased these useless sorties. Calling his men into the centre of the glade, he ordered them to stand in readiness to repel an assault, extinguished every fire, and allowed half the troop at once to lie down to endeavor to snatch some sleep. This, however, was impossible, for although the Indians did not venture upon an attack, the chorus of shouts and yells was so terrible and continuous and the flights of arrows at times fell so fast that not one of the troop ventured to close an eye. From time to time volleys were fired into the darkness, and once or twice a loud cry told that some at least of the balls had taken effect; but the opponents, sheltered each behind the trunk of a tree, suffered comparatively slightly, while many of the Spaniards were struck by their missiles.

Morning dawned upon a worn-out and dispirited band, but with daylight their hopes revived. Vigorous sorties were made into the wood, and though these discovered in a few places marks of blood where some of their enemies had fallen, and signs of a party being carried away, the woods were now as deserted as they had appeared to be on the previous evening when they first halted. There was a consultation among the leaders, and it was determined to abandon the pursuit of these invisible foes, as it was agreed that nothing short of a great effort by the whole available force of the island would be sufficient to cope with a foe whose tactics were so bewildering and formidable.

Upon their march out from the wood the troop was pursued with the same persistence with which it had been dogged on the preceding day; and when at length it emerged and the captain counted the numbers of his men, it was found that there were no less than thirty wounded, and that twenty had been left behind dead.

The dwellers of the wood were overjoyed with their success, and felt that a new existence had opened before them. Hitherto they had been fugitives only, and no thought of resistance to the Spaniards had ever entered their minds. They felt now that so long as they remained in the woods, and maintained their drill and discipline and persisted in the tactics which they had adopted, they could defy the Spaniards, unless, indeed, the latter came in overwhelming strength.

Some time elapsed before any fresh effort was made by the Spaniards. The affair caused intense excitement in the city, and it is difficult to say whether alarm or rage most predominated. It was felt that a great effort must be made to crush the men of the forest, for unless this were done a vast number of the negro slaves would escape and join them, and the movement would become more formidable every day. Upon the part of those in the forest great consultations took place; some of the negroes were for sending messages to the slaves to rise and join them, but Ned and Gerald strongly opposed this course. There were, as they pointed out, no means whatever in the forest for supporting a larger body of men than those gathered there. The tree-clad hills which constituted their stronghold were some thirty miles in diameter, and the supply of fruits, of roots, and of birds was sufficient for their wants, but it would be very different were their numbers largely increased. Then they would be forced to make raids upon the cultivated ground beyond, and here, however strong, they would be no match for the Spaniards, whose superior arms and discipline would be certain to give them victory. The Indians strongly supported the reasoning of the boys, and the negroes, when they fully understood the difficulties which would arise, finally acquiesced in their arguments.

Schemes were broached for making sallies from the forest at night and falling upon the plantations of the Spaniards. This offered greater chances of success, but the boys foresaw that all sorts of atrocities would be sure to take place, and that no quarter would be given to Spaniards of either age or sex. They therefore combated vigorously this proposal also; they pointed out that so long as they remained quiet in the forest, and were not joined by large numbers of fugitive negroes, the Spaniards might be content to let them remain unmolested; but upon the contrary, were they to adopt offensive tactics, not only would every Spaniard in the island take up arms against them, but if necessary they would send for help to the neighboring islands, and would assemble a force sufficient thoroughly to search the woods, and to annihilate them. The only case in which the boys considered that an attack upon the Spaniards would be lawful would be in the event of fresh expeditions being organized. In that case they were of opinion that it would be useful to destroy one or two large mansions and plantations as near as possible to the town, sending at the same time a message to the Spaniards that if they persisted in disturbing them in the forest, a similar fate would befall every Spanish plantation situated beyond the town.

It was not long before these tactics were called into play. One of the negroes had, as was their custom, gone down to the town to purchase such articles as were indispensable. Upon these occasions, as usual, he went down to the hut of the old woman who acted as their intermediary, and remained concealed there during the day while she went into the town to buy cotton for dresses and other things. This she could only do in small quantities at a time, using various shops for the purpose, returning each time with her parcel to the hut. The suspicion of the Spaniards had however been aroused, and orders had been given to watch her closely; the consequence was that, after purchasing a few articles, she was followed, and a band of soldiers surrounded the hut after she had entered. The fugitive was there found concealed, and he and the old woman were at once fastened in the hut; this was then set alight, and they were burned to death upon the spot.

When the news reached the mountains Ned at once determined upon a reprisal. The negroes and natives were alike ready to follow him, and the next night the whole party, a hundred and fifty strong, marched down from the forest. The object of their attack was a handsome palace belonging to the military governor of the island, situated at a short distance from the town.

Passing through the cultivated country noiselessly and without detection, they reached the mansion and surrounded it. There were here a guard of some thirty soldiers, and sentries were placed at the entrance. At the signal given by the blowing of a conch shell, the attack commenced on all sides. The sentries were at once shot down, and the negroes and their allies speedily penetrated into the building. The Spanish guard fought with great bravery, but they were overpowered by the infuriated negroes. Yells, shrieks, and shouts of all kinds resounded through the palace.

Before starting on their adventure Ned and Gerald had ex-
acted a solemn oath from each of the men who were to take part
in it, that on no account would he lift his hand against a defenceless person, and also that he spare everybody who surren-
dered. The negroes were greatly loath to take this promise, and
had Ned urged them to do so purely for the sake of humanity,
the oath would unquestionably have been refused, for in those
days of savage warfare there was little or no mercy shown on either side. It was only on the ground of expediency and the extreme necessity of not irritating the Spaniards beyond a certain
point that he succeeded in obtaining their promise.

In the principal room of the palace they found the governor
himself; his sword was in his hand, and he was prepared to defend his life to the last. The boys, however, rushed forward and
cried to him to throw his sword down as the only plan by which
his life could be saved. The brave officer refused, answering by
a vigorous thrust. In a moment the two lads had sprung upon
him, one from each side, and wrested his sword from his hand.
The negroes with yells of triumph were rushing upon him with
drawn swords, but the boys sternly motioned them back, keeping well in front of their prisoner.

"You have sworn," they said, "and the first man who breaks his
oath we will shoot through the head." Then turning to the governor they said, "Sir, you see what these men whom you have so
long hunted as wild beasts can do. Take warning from this, and
let all in the town know the determination to which we have arrived. If we are let alone we will let others alone. We promise
that no serious depredations of any kind shall be performed by
any of our party in the forest; but if we are molested, or if any of
our band who may fall into your hands are ill-treated, we swear
that for each drop of blood slain we will ravage a plantation and
destroy a house. On this occasion, as you see, the negroes have
abstained from shedding blood, but our influence over them
may not avail in future. Now that you see that we too can attack,
you may think fit to leave us alone. In case of serious interference with us, we will lay waste the land up to the houses of the
city, and destroy every plantation and hacienda."

Then they hurried the governor to a back entrance, gave him his sword again, and having seen him in safety fairly beyond the reach of any of their party who might be wandering about, dismissed him.

Returning to the palace they had to exert themselves to the utmost to prevail on the negroes to spare all who were there; indeed one man who refused to obey Ned's orders and to lower his club, he shot down at once. This vigorous act excited for a moment yells of indignation among the rest, but the firm bearing of the two young Englishmen, and the knowledge that they were acting as they themselves had given them leave to act, should any of the party break their oaths, subdued them into silence.

The palace was now stripped of all portable and useful articles. Ned would not permit anything to be carried away of a merely ornamental or valuable character, but only such as kitchen utensils, crockery, stoves, arms, hangings, and articles of a description that would be useful to them in their wild life in the forest. The quantity of arms taken was considerable, as, in addition to those belonging to the guard, there were a considerable number piled in the armory in readiness for any occasion when they might be required.

When all that could be useful to them was removed, lights were applied to the hangings and wooden latticework, and before they retired they saw the flames take sufficient possession of the building to ensure its destruction.

Many of the negroes had at first laden themselves with wine, but this Ned peremptorily refused to allow them to carry away. He knew that it was of the most supreme necessity that good-fellowship and amity should run between the members of the bands, and that were wine to be introduced quarrels might arise which would in the end prove fatal to all. He allowed, however, sufficient to be taken away to furnish a reasonable share for each man at the feast which it was only natural they would wish to hold in commemoration of their victory.

CHAPTER VIII

The Forest Fastness

It was with a feeling of triumph, indeed, that the negroes after gaining their own fastness looked back at the sky lighted by the distant conflagration. They had now for the first time inflicted such a lesson upon their oppressors as would make a deep mark. They felt themselves to be really free, and knew that they in their turn had struck terror into the hearts of the Spaniards. Retiring to the depths of the forest great fires were made, sheep, fowls, and other articles of provision which had been brought back were killed and prepared. Huge bonfires were lit, and the party, secure that for twenty-four hours at least the Spaniards could attempt no retributive measures, sat down to enjoy the banquet.

They had driven with them a few small bullocks and also some scores of sheep; these, however, were not destined for the spit. They were to be placed in the heart of their country, so that, unless disturbed by the Spaniards, they might prove a source of future sustenance to them. There was wild feasting that night, with dances and songs of triumph in the negro and native dialects, and Ned and Gerald were lauded and praised as the authors of the change which had taken place in the condition of the fugitives.

Even the stern severity of Ned's act was thoroughly approved, and it was agreed again that any one refusing to obey the orders of the white chiefs should forfeit his life.

The blow which the negroes had struck caused intense consternation throughout Hispañiola.

The younger and more warlike spirits were in favor of organizing an instant crusade, for sending to the other islands for more troops, for surrounding the forest country and for putting the last of the negroes to the sword. More peaceful counsels, however, prevailed, for it was felt that the whole open country was, as Ned had told the governor, at their mercy; that the damage which could be inflicted would be enormous, and the satisfaction of putting the fugitives to death, even if they were finally conquered, would be but a poor recompense for the blow which might be given to the prosperity and wealth of the island. All sorts of schemes were mooted by which the runaways could be beguiled into laying down their arms, but no practicable plan could be hit upon.

In the meantime, in the mountains, the bands improved in drill and discipline. They had now gained some confidence in themselves, and gave themselves up heartily to the work. Portions of land, too, were turned up, and yams and other fruits on a larger scale than had hitherto been attempted, were planted. A good supply of goats was obtained, huts were erected, and the lads determined that, at least as long as the Spaniards allowed it, their lives should be made as comfortable as possible. Fugitive slaves from time to time joined the party, but Ned strongly discouraged any increase at present from this cause. He was sure that, were the Spaniards to find that their runaways were sheltered there, and that a general desertion of their slaves might take place, they would be obliged in self-defence to root out this formidable organization in their midst. Therefore emissaries were sent out among the negroes stating that none would be received in the mountains save those who had previously asked permission, this being only accorded in cases where such extreme brutality and cruelty had been exercised by the masters as would wholly justify the flight of the slaves.

For some months a sort of truce was maintained between the Spaniards and this little army in the woods. The blacks observed the promises which Ned had made with great fidelity, the planters found that no depredations took place, and that the desertions among their slaves were no more numerous than before, and had it depended solely upon them no further measures would have been taken.

The case, however, was different among the military party in the island. To them the failure of the expedition into the forest and the burning of the governor's house were matters which seriously affected their pride. Defeat by English buccaneers they were accustomed to, and regarding the English at sea as a species of demon against whom human bravery availed little, they were slightly touched by it; but that they should be defied by a set of runaway slaves and of natives, whom they had formerly regarded with contempt, was a blow to their pride. Quietly, and without ostentation, troops were drafted into the island from the neighboring posts, until a formidable force had been gathered there. The foresters had now plenty of means of communication with the negroes, who regarded them as saviors to whom they could look for rescue and shelter in case of their masters' cruelty, and were always ready to send messengers up into the forest with news of every occurrence which took place under their observation. The grown-up slaves, of course, could not leave the plantation, but there were numbers of fleet-footed lads who, after nightfall, could be dispatched from the huts into the mountains and return before daylight, while, even should they remain until the next night, they would attract no attention by their absence.

Thus, then, Ned and Gerald learned that a formidable body of Spaniards were being collected quietly in the town, and every effort was made to meet the coming storm. The various gorges were blocked with high barricades; difficult parts of the mountain were, with great labor, scarped so as to render the advance of an armed force difficult in the extreme; great piles of stones were collected to roll down into the ravines, and provisions of yams, sweet potatoes, and other food were stored up.

The last stronghold had, after a great debate, been fixed upon at a point in the heart of one of the hills. This was singularly well adapted for defence; the hill itself was extremely precipitous on all sides, on one side it fell sheer down. A goat-track ran along the face of this precipice to a point where the hill fell back, forming a sort of semicircular arena on the very face of the precipice. This plateau was some two acres in extent. Here quantities of forage were heaped up in readiness for the food of such animals as might be driven in there. The track itself was, with great labor, widened, platforms of wood being placed at the narrow points, and steps were cut in the hill behind the plateau to enable them, should their stronghold be stormed, to escape at the last moment up to the hilltop above. In most places the cliff behind the plateau rose so steeply as to almost overhang the foot, and in these were many gaps and crevices in which a considerable number of people could take shelter so as to avoid stones and other missiles hurled down from above. At one point, in particular, the precipice overhung, and under this a strong erection of the trunks of trees was made. This was for the animals to be placed in; the heavy roof was amply sufficient to keep out any bullet shots, while from its position no masses of rock could be dropped upon it. It was not thought probable that the Spaniards would harass them much from above, for the ascent to the summit was everywhere extremely difficult, and the hillside was perfectly bare, and sloped so sharply upward from the edge of the precipitous cliff, that it would be a difficult and dangerous task to descend so as to fire down into the arena; and, although every precaution had been taken, it was felt that there was little fear of any attack from above.

At last all was in readiness as far as the efforts of those in the forest could avail. A message was then sent in to the governor to the effect that the men of the forest desired to know for what purpose so many soldiers were being assembled in the island, and that, on a given day, unless some of these were embarked and sent off they would consider that a war was being prepared against them, and that the agreement that the outlying settlements should be left intact was therefore invalid. As the boys had anticipated the Spaniards answered this missive by an instant movement forward, and some four hundred men were reported as moving out toward the hills. This the boys were prepared for, and simultaneously with the movement the whole band—divided into parties of six, each of which had its fixed destination and instructions, all being alike solemnly pledged to take no life in cold blood and to abstain from all unnecessary cruelties—started quickly from the forest.

That night the Spanish force halted near the edge of the forest, but at midnight a general consternation seized the camp when, from fifty different points, flames were seen suddenly to rise on the plain. Furious at this misfortune the general in command put his cavalry in motion and scoured the country, only to find, however, that the whole of the *haciendas* of the Spanish proprietors were in flames, and that fire had been applied to all the standing crops. Everywhere he heard the same tale, that those who had resisted had been killed, but that no harm had been inflicted upon defenceless persons.

This was so new a feature in troubles with the negroes that the Spaniards could not but be surprised and filled with admiration at conduct so different to that to which they were accustomed. The sight of the tremendous destruction of property, however, roused them to fury, and this was still further heightened when toward morning, a great burst of flame in the city proclaimed that the negroes had fallen upon the town while the greater portion of its defenders were withdrawn.

This was indeed a masterly stroke on the part of the boys. They knew that even deducting those who had set forth there would still be an amply sufficient force in the city to defeat and crush their band, but they thought that by a quick stroke they might succeed in inflicting a heavy blow upon them. Each of the bands, therefore, had instructions after doing its allotted share of incendiarism to make for the town, and to meet at a certain point outside it. Then quietly and noiselessly they had entered. One party fell upon the armory and another attacked with fury the governor's house; the guards there, were, as had happened with his residence in the country, cut down. Fire was applied in a dozen places, and before the astonished troops and inhabitants could rally from the different parts of the town, the negroes were again in the country, having fulfilled their object and carried off with them a large additional stock of arms.

Before the cavalry from the front could arrive they were again far in the country, and, making a long detour, gained their fastness, having struck a terrible blow, with the cost of themselves of only some eight or ten lives.

It was a singular sight, as they looked out in the morning from their hilltops; great masses of smoke extended over the whole country; for although most of the dwellings were by this time levelled to the ground—for, built of the lightest construction, they offered but little resistance to the flames—from the fields of maize and cane clouds of smoke were still rising as the conflagration spread, and at one stroke the whole agricultural wealth of the island was destroyed. The boys regretted that this should necessarily be the case, but they felt that it was now war to the knife between the Spaniards and them, and that such a defeat would be beneficial. This, indeed, was the case, for the commander drew back his troops to the town in order to make fresh arrangements before venturing upon an attack on foes who showed themselves possessed of such desperate determination.

Another six weeks elapsed, indeed, before a forward movement was again commenced, and in that time considerable acquisitions of force were obtained. Strong as the bands felt themselves, they could not but be alarmed at the thought of the tremendous storm gathering to burst over their heads. The women had long since been sent away to small native villages existing on the other side of the island and living at peace with their neighbors. Thither Ned also despatched several of the party whom he believed to be either wanting in courage, or whose constancy he somewhat doubted. A traitor now would be the destruction of the party, and it was certain that any negro deserting to the enemy and offering to act as their guide to the various strongholds of the defenders would receive immense rewards. Thus it was imperative that every man of whose fidelity and constancy the least doubt was entertained should be carefully sent out of the way of temptation.

All the band were, indeed, pledged by a most solemn oath,

and death by torture was the penalty awarded for any act of treachery.

The great portion of the force were now provided with European arms; the negroes had musketoons or arquebuses, the natives still retained the bow, while all had pikes and spears. They were undefended by protective armor, and in this respect the Spaniards had a great advantage in the fight; but, as the boys pointed out, this advantage was more than counterbalanced by the extra facility of movement on the part of the natives, who could scale rocks and climb hills absolutely inaccessible to their heavily armed and weighty opponents. The scouts who had been stationed on the lookout at the edge of the forest brought word that the Spaniards, nigh 1500 strong, had divided in six bodies, and were marching so as to enter the forest from six different and nearly equidistant points. Each band was accompanied by blood-hounds and a large number of other fierce dogs of the wolf-hound breed which the Spaniards had imported for the purpose of attacking negroes in their hiding-places. Of these animals the negroes had the greatest dread, and even the bravest, who were ready to match themselves against armed Spaniards, yet trembled at the thought of the encounter with these ferocious animals.

It was clear that no repetition of the tactics formerly pursued would be possible; for, if any attempt at night attacks were made the dogs would rush out and attack them, and not only prove formidable enemies themselves, but guide the Spaniards to the places where they were stationed. Ned and Gerald would fain have persuaded the natives that dogs, after all, however formidable they might appear, were easily mastered by well-armed men, and that any dog rushing to attack them would be pierced with spears and arrows, to say nothing of being shot by the arquebuses before he could seize any of them. The negroes, however, had known so many cases in which fugitives had been horribly torn, and, indeed, frequently killed by these ferocious animals, that the dread of them was too great for them to listen to the boys' explanations. The latter, seeing that it would be useless to attempt to overcome their fears on this ground, abstained from the attempt.

It had been agreed that, in the event of the Spaniards advancing from different quarters, one column only should be selected for a main attack; and that, while the others should be harassed by small parties who should cast down rocks upon them while passing through the gorges, and so inflict as much damage as possible, no attempt would be made to strike any serious blow upon them. The column selected for attack was naturally that whose path led through the points which had been most strongly prepared and fortified. This band mustered about three hundred, and was clearly too strong to be attacked in open fight by the forest bands. Gerald and Ned had already talked the matter over in every light, and decided that a purely defensive fight must be maintained, each place where preparations had been made being held to the last, and a rapid retreat beaten to the next barricade. The Spaniards advanced in heavy column; at a distance of a hundred yards on each side marched a body of fifty in compact mass, thereby sheltering the main body from any sudden attack. The first point at which the lads had determined to make a stand was the mouth of a gorge. Here steep rocks rose perpendicularly from the ground, running almost like a wall along that portion of the forest; in the midst of this was a cleft through which a little stream ran. It was here that the boys had made preparations; the point could not be turned without a long and difficult march along the face of the cliff, and on the summit of this sixty men divided into two parties, one on each side of the fissure, were stationed. The Spaniards advanced until they nearly reached the mouth of the ravine.

It must be remembered that, although the forest was very thick and the vegetation luxuriant, yet there were paths here and there made by the constant passing to and fro of the occupants of the wood. Their main direction acted as a guide to the Spaniards, and the hounds, by their sniffing and eagerness, acted as a guide to the advancing force. They paused when they saw opening before them this entrance to the rocky gorge. While they halted the increased eagerness of the dogs told them that they were now approaching the point where their foes were concealed, and the prospect of an attack on so strong a position was formidable even to such a body.

A small party of thirty men was told off to advance and reconnoitre the position. These were allowed to enter the gorge and to follow it for a distance of a hundred yards to a point where the sides were approached to their nearest point. Then, from a parapet of rock piled across the ravine came a volley of musketry, and simultaneously from the heights of either side great stones came crashing down. Such of the party as did not fall at the first discharge fired a volley at their invisible assailants and then hurried back to the main body.

It was now clear that fighting and that of a serious character was to be undertaken. The Spanish commander rapidly reconnoitred the position, and saw that here, at least, no flanking movement was possible. He therefore ordered his men to advance for a direct attack. Being more afraid of the stones from above than of the defenders in the ravine, the Spaniards prepared to advance in skirmishing order; in that way they would be able to creep up to the barricade of rocks with the least loss to themselves from the fire of its defenders, while the stones from above would prove far less dangerous than would be the case upon a solid column. With great determination the Spanish troops advanced to the attack; as they neared the mouth of the gorge, flights of arrows from above were poured down upon them, and these were answered by their own musketeers and bowmen, although the figures occasionally exposed above offered but a poor mark in comparison to that afforded by the column below. The men on the ridge were entirely natives, the boys having selected the negroes, on whose courage at close quarters they could more thoroughly rely, for the defence of the ravine. The firearms in those days could scarcely be termed arms of precision; the bell-mouth arquebuses could carry a large and heavy charge, but there was nothing like accuracy in their fire; and although a steady fire was kept up from the barricade, and many Spaniards fell, yet a larger number succeeded in making their way through the zone of fire by taking advantage of the rocks and bushes, and these gathered near the foot of the barricade.

The stones which came crashing from above did serious damage among them, but the real effect of these was more moral than physical. The sound of the great masses of stone plunging down the hillside, setting in motion numbers of small rocks as they came, tearing down the bushes and small trees, was exceedingly terrifying at first; but as block after block dashed down doing comparatively little harm, the Spaniards became accustomed to them, and keeping under the shelter of masses of rock to the last moment, prepared all their energies for the attack. The Spanish commander found that the greater portion of his troop were within striking distance, and he gave the command to those gathered near the barricade to spring forward to the attack.

The gorge at this point was some fifteen yards wide. The barricade across it was thirty feet in height. It was formed of blocks of stone of various sizes, intermingled with which were sharp stakes with their points projecting, lines of bushes and arms of trees piled outwards, and the whole was covered loosely with sharp prickly creepers cut from the trees and heaped there. A more difficult place to climb, even without its being defended from above, would be difficult to find. The covering of thorny creepers hid the rocks below, and at each step the soldiers put their feet into deep holes between the masses of rock and fell forward, lacerating themselves horribly with the thorns, or coming face downwards on one of the sharp-pointed stakes. But if without any resistance from above the feat of climbing this carefully prepared barricade was difficult, it was terrible when from the ridge above a storm of bullets swept down. It was only for a moment that the negroes exposed themselves in the act of firing. Behind, the barricade was as level and smooth as it was difficult upon the outer side. Great steps, some three feet wide, had been prepared of wood, so that the defenders could easily mount, and standing in lines relieve each other as they fired. The stones of the top series had been carefully chosen of a form so as to leave, between each, crevices through which the

THE BARRICADE
SEE PAGE 104.

defenders could fire while scarcely exposing themselves to the enemy. The Spaniards behind endeavored to cover the advance of their comrades by keeping up a heavy fire at the summit of the barricade, and several of the negroes were shot through the head in the act of firing. Their loss, however, was small in comparison to that of the assailants, who strove in vain to climb up the thorny ascent, their position being the more terrible inasmuch as the fire from the parties on the rocks above never ceased, and stones kept up a sort of bombardment on those in the ravine. Even the fierce dogs could with difficulty climb the thorn-covered barriers, and those who reached the top were instantly shot or stabbed.

At last, after suffering very considerable loss, the Spanish commander drew off his soldiers, and a wild yell of triumph rose from the negroes. The combat, however, had, as the boys were aware, scarcely begun, and they now waited to see what the next effort of the Spaniards would be. It was an hour before the latter again advanced to the attack. This time the troops were carrying large bundles of dried grass and rushes, and although again suffering heavily in the attack, they piled these at the foot of the barricade, and in another minute a flash of fire ran up the side; the smoke and flame for a time separated the defenders from their foes, and the fire ceased on both sides, although those above never relaxed their efforts to harass the assailants.

As the Spaniards had calculated, the flame of the great heap of straw communicated with the creepers and burnt them up in its fiery tongue, and when the flames abated the rocks lay open and uncovered.

The Spaniards now with renewed hopes advanced again to the attack, and this time were able, although with heavy loss, to make their way up the barricade. When they arrived within three or four feet of the top Ned gave the word, and a line of thirty powerful negroes, each armed with a long pike, suddenly arose, and with a yell threw themselves over the edge and dashed down upon the Spaniards; the latter struggling to ascend, with unsteady footing on the loose and uneven rocks, were unable for an instant to defend themselves against this assault.

The negroes, barefooted, had no difficulty on the surface which proved so fatal to the Spaniards, and like the crest of a wave they swept their opponents headlong down the face of the barricade. The heavily armed Spaniards fell over each other, those in front hurling those behind backwards in wild confusion, and the first line of negroes being succeeded by another armed with axes, who completed the work which the first line had begun, the slaughter for a minute was terrible.

For some thirty paces the negroes pursued their advantage, and then at a loud shout from Ned turned, and with a celerity equal to that of their advance the whole were back over the barricade before the Spaniards in the rear could awaken from their surprise, and scarcely a shot was fired as the dark figures bounded back into shelter.

This time the Spanish officer drew back his men sullenly; he felt that they had done all that could be expected of them; upwards of sixty men had fallen, it would be vain to ask them to make the assault again. He knew too that by waiting the other columns would be gradually approaching, and that on the morrow some method of getting in the enemy's rear would probably be discovered.

In the meantime he sent off fifty men on either flank to discover how far this rocky wall extended, while trumpeters under strong guards were sent up to the hilltops in the rear and sounded the call lustily; musketoons heavily charged so as to make as loud a report as possible were also fired to attract the attention of the other columns.

The boys were perfectly aware that they could not hope finally to defend this position. They had, however, given the Spaniards a very heavy lesson, and the success of the defence had immensely raised the spirit and courage of their men. The signal was therefore given for a retreat, and in half an hour both the Indians on the summit of the hill and the negroes behind the barricade had fallen back, leaving only some half-dozen to keep up the appearance of defence, and to bring back tidings of the doings of the enemy, while the rest hurried off to aid the detached parties to inflict heavy blows upon the other columns. It was found that these were steadily approaching, but had lost a good many men; the reinforcements enabled the natives to make a more determined resistance, and in one or two places the columns were effectually checked. The reports when night fell were that the Spaniards had altogether lost over two hundred men, but that all their columns had advanced a considerable distance toward the centre of the forest and had halted, each as they stood, and bivouacked, keeping up huge fires and careful watches.

It formed no part, however, of the boys' plan to attack them thus, and when morning dawned the whole of the defenders, each taking different paths, as far as possible, some even making great circuits so as to deceive the enemy, were directed to make for the central fortress. The intermediate positions, several of which were as strong as the barricade which they had so well defended, were abandoned, for the advance from other quarters rendered it impossible to hold these.

CHAPTER IX

Baffled

By mid-day all the defenders of the forest were assembled in the semicircular plateau on the face of the hill, and scouts having been placed near the entrance they awaited the coming of the enemy. So far as possible, every means had been taken to prevent the access to their place of retreat being discovered. A stream had been turned so as to run down a small ravine leading to its approach, trees which had been blown down by the wind had been previously brought from a considerable distance, and these were piled in careless confusion across the gorge so as to look as if they had fallen there, and give an idea that no one could have passed that way. For the next two days all was quiet. A scout upon the hilltop and others who were told off to watch the Spaniards reported that the woods below were being thoroughly searched, that the enemy were acting in the most methodical way, the columns being now in close connection with each other, the intermediate forest being searched foot by foot, and that all were converging toward the central mountains of the position. The dogs had proved valuable assistants, and these were tracking the paths used by them and steadily leading them toward the stronghold. That they would finally escape detection none of the defenders had much hope. The Spaniards would be sure that they must be somewhere within their line; and after the loss suffered and the immense preparations made it was certain that they would not retire until they had solved the mystery, and, if possible, annihilated the forest bands. On the fourth day after entering the wood the Spaniards came to the point where the barricade of trees had been erected.

So skilfully had this been constructed that they would have retired, believing that there was no path beyond this little gorge; however, the restlessness and anger of the dogs convinced them that there must be something behind. Slowly a passage was cut with axes through the virgin forest on either side, for the lesson they had received had checked their impetuosity. They came down at the side of the barricade, and thus having passed it, pressed forward in steady array until they came to the foot of the great cliff; here the dogs were not long before they pointed out to the assailants the narrow path, scarce visible, running along its face, and a shout of satisfaction from the Spaniards testified that they now felt certain that they had caught their enemies in a trap.

Parties were sent off to positions whence they could obtain a good view of the place, and these soon reported that the ledge continued to a great opening in the face of the precipice, that in some places logs had been fixed to widen the path, and that there was plenty of room on the plateau formed by the retirement of the hill face for a large body to have taken refuge. They also reported that the cliffs rose behind this amphitheatre almost, if not quite perpendicularly for a great height, and that still higher the bare rock fell away at so steep an angle that it would be difficult in the extreme to take up such a position from above as would enable them to keep up a musquetry fire or to hurl rocks upon the defenders of the amphitheatre.

When the reports were considered by the Spanish leader, he saw at once that this was not an enterprise to be undertaken rashly. Men were sent down to the plain below to reconnoitre, while others were despatched round the mountain to see whether the path extended across the whole face of the precipice, and also to discover, if possible, whether the recess was commanded from above. Both reports were unfavorable; from the valley the great natural strength of the position was manifest, for half a dozen men could defend such a path as this against a thousand by placing themselves behind an angle and shooting down all who turned the corner, while the men from above reported that the peak shelved so rapidly toward the top of the sheer precipice that it would be impossible to get near enough to the edge to see down into the amphitheatre. They reported, however, that stones and rocks set going would dash down below, and that points could be gained from which these missiles could be despatched on their errand.

A council of war was held, and it was determined in the first place to endeavor to force the position by direct attack. Some men of approved courage were chosen to lead the forlorn hope, a number of marksmen with arrows and firearms were placed in the valley to keep up a fire upon any who might show themselves on the path, while above, several hundreds of men were sent up with crowbars to loosen and hurl down rocks.

The defenders on their part were not idle. Two spots had been chosen in the pathway for the defence; at each of these the face of the cliff extended sharply out in an angle, and it was on the side of this angle next to the amphitheatre that the preparations were made. Here barricades of stones were heaped up on the path, which at this point was some three yards wide; six of the steadiest and most courageous negroes were placed here with muskets and pikes; two of them were to lie with their guns pointed at the protecting angle, so that the instant any one showed himself round the corner they could open fire upon him, the others were lying in readiness to assist or to relieve those on guard. Either Gerald or Ned remained with them always. A few stones were thrown up on the outside edge of the path to protect the defenders from the sides of those in the valley below, not indeed that the danger from this source was very great, for the face of the precipice was some eight hundred feet high, and the path ran along some four hundred from the bottom. With the clumsy arms in use in those days the fear of any one being struck from below was by no means great. A similar barricade was erected behind, and the negroes were, in case of extreme necessity, to fall back from their first position. At the second point an equal number of men were placed. Lastly, where the path ended at the amphitheatre, strong barricades had been erected in a sort of semicircle, so that any one, after having forced the first defences, would, as he showed himself at the entrance to the amphitheatre, be exposed to the fire of the whole of its defenders.

The position was so strong that Ned and Gerald had no fear whatever of its being forced. As the time approached when Ned expected an attack, the defenders of the farthest barricade were strengthened by a considerable number of the negroes lying down upon the path; for it was certain that for the first two or three assaults the Spaniards would push matters to the utmost, and that they would not be repulsed by the defenders without severe fighting.

So indeed it proved. Advancing with great caution along the narrow path which was sometimes seven or eight feet wide, sometimes narrowing to a few inches, the leaders of the party of attack made their way along until they turned the projecting point; then the guns of the two men on guard spoke out and the two leaders fell, shot through the body, over the precipice. Now that they knew the position of their enemy the Spaniards prepared for a rush; gathering themselves as closely as they could together, they pressed round the corner. Shot after shot rang out from the defenders as they turned it; but although many fell, the others pressed forward so numerously and bravely that they could be said fairly to have established themselves round the corner. The barricade now, however, faced them, and behind this were gathered the bravest of the negroes, led by the boys. The barricade, too, had been covered with thorny branches as had that which they had defended before, and the Spaniards, of whom only some ten or twelve could find fighting room round the corner, were shot down before they could make any impression whatever.

Bravely as they fought, it was impossible for men to maintain so unequal and difficult a fight as this, and after trying for an hour to storm the barricade, the Spaniards fell back, having lost over fifty of the best of their men.

In the meantime, with a thundering sound the rocks were rolling down from the summit of the mountain. The greater portion of them did not fall in the amphitheatre at all, but, from the impetus of their descent down the sloping rocks above, shot far

out beyond its edge. Others, however, crashed down on to the
little plateau; but all who were there were lying so close to the
face of the rock, that the missiles from above went far beyond
them. From below in the valley a constant fire was kept up, but
this was as innocuous as the bombardment from above; and
when the Spaniards fell back, only three of the defenders had
been in any way injured, and these were hit by the pistol balls
fired by the assailants of the barricade.

When the Spaniards retired, all except the men told off for
the posts at the barricades, fell back to the amphitheater. The
negroes and natives were both alike delighted with the success
of the defence, and were now perfectly confident of their ability to hold out as long as their provisions lasted. There was no
fear of want of water, for from the face of the hill a little stream
trickled out. Piles of yams, bananas, sweet potatoes, and other
tropical fruit had been collected, and a score of sheep, and with
care the boys calculated that for five weeks they could hold out.

The Spaniards were furious at the non-success of their enterprise, but after reconnoitring the position in every way, the commanders came to the conclusion that it was absolutely impreg-
nable, and that the only plan was to starve out the besieged. It
did not appear that there could be any other way of retreat, and
a small force could watch the path, as it would be as difficult for
the besieged to force their way back by it as for the besiegers to
find an entry.

The greater portion of the force was therefore marched
home, a guard of two hundred men being set to watch the point
where the path along the precipice started.

The incidents of the five weeks which elapsed after the siege
began were not important. It was soon found that the Spaniards
had abandoned the notion of attack; but the vigilance of the
defenders was never relaxed, for it was possible, that at any
moment the enemy, believing that they had been lulled into
carelessness, might renew their attack.

Twice, indeed, at nightfall the Spaniards advanced and crept
round the point of defence, but were each time received so
quickly by the fire of the defenders of the barricade, that they

were finally convinced that there was no hope whatever of catching them napping.

At the end of five weeks it was determined that the time had arrived when they should leave their fortress. The Spaniards had placed a guard of fifty men near the foot of the precipice, to prevent any attempt of the besieged to descend its face by means of ropes, but above no precautions had been taken, as it appeared impossible to any one looking at the face of the cliff from a distance that a human being could scale it. Thanks, however, to the pains which had been taken previously, the way was open. In most places, rough steps had been cut, in others where this was impossible, short stakes had been driven into crevices of the rock to form steps, and although the ascent was difficult, it was quite possible to lightly clad and active men. The time chosen for the attempt was just after dusk had fallen, when it was still light enough to see close at hand, but dark enough to prevent those in the valley observing what was passing. A young moon was already up, giving sufficient light to aid the enterprise. Some of the most active of the natives first ascended; these were provided with ropes which at every bend and turn of the ascent they lowered so as to give assistance to those mounting behind. The strictest silence was enforced, and the arms were all wrapped up so as to avoid noise should they strike the rock. One by one the men mounted in a steady stream; all were barefooted, for Ned and Gerald had imitated the example of the natives, and upon such a task as this the bare foot has an infinitely safer hold than one shod with leather. Although the cliff looked quite precipitous from a distance, in reality it sloped gently backwards, and the task was far less difficult than it appeared to be. The most dangerous part indeed was that which followed the arrival at the top. The mountain sloped so steeply back that it was like climbing the roof of a very steep house, and hand and foot were alike called into requisition to enable them to get forward; indeed to many it would have been impossible had not the leaders lowered their ropes down from above, affording an immense assistance to those following.

At last the whole body reached the top and descending upon the other side plunged into the forest. They directed their course to a valley ten miles distant, where considerable supplies of provisions had been stored up, and where some of their crops had been planted a few weeks before the arrival of the Spaniards. Here for two days they feasted, secure that a considerable time might elapse before the Spaniards discovered that they had vanished from the fortress. Then they prepared to put into execution the plan upon which they had resolved. They knew that in the town there would be no watch of any sort kept, for all believed them cooped up without a chance of escape. The four troops then, commanded as before, issued from the forest as the sun went down, and marched toward the town. It was soon after midnight when they entered the streets, and proceeding noiselessly through them advanced to the spot assigned to each. One was to attack the governor's house and to make him a prisoner, two others were to fall upon the barracks and to do as much harm as possible, while the fourth was to proceed to the government magazines of stores and munitions to fire these at a great many places.

This programme was carried out successfully. The guards at the governor's house were overpowered in an instant, and as it had been surrounded all the inmates were captured. Those of the men who defended themselves were cut down, but Gerald and Ned had insisted that no unnecessary slaughter should take place. The party attacking the barracks had no such instructions; it was legitimate for them to inflict as much loss as possible upon the soldiers, and when with terrible shouts the negroes broke in upon them, the Spaniards, taken by surprise, offered but a feeble resistance. Large numbers of them were cut down before they could rally or open fire upon their enemies. As soon as the resistance became serious, the negroes and Indians vanished as quickly as they had come. In the meantime the whole of the town was lit up by sheets of fire rising from the government magazines. The alarm-bells of the churches tolled out, the shouts of the frightened inhabitants mingled with the yells of the natives, and the report of firearms from all parts of the town, and the townspeople thought that a general sack and slaughter was at hand.

The negroes, however, entered no private house, but in an hour from their first appearance they had retired beyond the town and were making their way in a solid and well-ordered mass for the forest, bearing in their centre the governor and two of his sons.

The success of the enterprise had been complete. They were now, Ned thought, in a position, if not to dictate terms to the enemy, at least to secure for themselves an immunity from attacks. Day was breaking when they entered the hills, and an hour later one of the sons of the governor was sent to the party still besieging their former stronghold to inform them that the besieged had all escaped, had made a raid upon the city, and had carried off the governor, whose instructions to them was that they were to at once fall back to avoid being attacked by the negroes.

The officer commanding the besiegers was glad enough to call his men together and to retire unharmed from the forest, which now began to inspire an almost superstitious fear in the Spaniards, so unexpected and mysterious had been the defeats inflicted upon them there. The governor's son accompanied the troops back to the city, and was the bearer of a missive from Ned to the officer commanding the troops and to the inhabitants. Ned offered upon the part of the forest men, that if the Spaniards would consent to leave them unmolested in their forest, they upon their part would in the first place release the governor, and in the second, promise that no acts of violence or raids of any kind should be made beyond its boundaries. The question of fugitive slaves who might seek refuge among them was to be discussed at a meeting between the heads of each party, should the proposal be accepted. The governor sent a line on his part to say that he was well treated, that he authorized them to enter into any negotiations which they might think fit, adding, that in case they should decide to refuse the offer made them, no thought of his safety should be allowed for an instant to sway their notions.

It was two days before the messenger returned. Several stormy meetings had taken place in the town. The officers were for the most part anxious to renew the fighting. They were intensely mortified at the idea of the forces of Spain being compelled to treat upon something like even terms with a handful of escaped slaves, and would have again marched the troops into the forest and renewed the war. The townspeople, however, were strongly opposed to this. They had suffered immensely already by the destruction of the outlying plantations and haciendas, and the events of the attack upon the town showed that there was no little danger of the whole place being burnt to the ground. They were therefore eager in the extreme to make terms with this active and ubiquitous enemy. The troops, too, were by no means eager to attempt another entry into the forest. They had fared so ill heretofore, that they shrank from another encounter; for there was neither glory nor booty to be obtained, and warfare such as this was altogether unsuited to their habits. Their discipline was useless, and they were so bewildered by the tactics of their active foes, that there was a very strong feeling among them in favor of making terms. The council sat the whole day and finally the pacific party prevailed.

The deputation consisting of the officer commanding the troops, of the ecclesiastic of highest rank in the town, and of one of the principal merchants, proceeded to the forest. When they were seen by the lookout to be approaching, Ned and Gerald with the leading native and negro proceeded to meet them. The details were soon arranged upon the basis which had been suggested. The forest men were to enjoy their freedom unmolested. They were to be allowed to cultivate land on the edge of the forest, and it was forbidden to any Spaniard to enter their limits without previously applying for a pass. They on their part promised to abstain from all aggression in any shape. The question of runaways was then discussed. This was by far the most difficult part of the negotiations. The Spaniards urged that they could not tolerate that an asylum should be offered to all who chose to desert from the plantations. The boys saw the justice of this, and finally it was arranged that the case of every slave who made for the forest should be investigated, that the owners should themselves come to lay a formal complaint of their case, that the slave should reply, and each might produce witnesses. The negro was to be given up unless he could prove that he had been treated with gross cruelty, in which case he was to be allowed protection in the forest.

These preliminaries settled, a short document embodying them was drawn up in duplicate, and these treaties were signed by the three Spaniards who formed the deputation and by the governor on the one side, and by the four representatives of the forest men on the other.

Thus ended the first successful resistance to Spanish power among the islands of the western seas.

The governor and his son then left for the city, and the forest men retired to what was now their country. Ned and Gerald impressed upon their allies the importance of observing strictly the conditions of peace, and at the same time of continuing their exercises in arms and maintaining their discipline. They pointed out to them that a treaty of this kind, extorted as it were from one, and that the strongest of the contracting powers, was certain not to have long duration. The Spaniards would smart at the humiliation which had in their opinion befallen them, and although the fugitive clause might for some time act favorably, it was sure sooner or later to be a bone of contention. They impressed upon them also that although they might, as had been shown, achieve successes for a time, yet that in the long run the power of the Spaniards must prevail, and that nothing short of extermination awaited them; therefore he urged the strictest adherence to the treaty, and at the same time a preparedness for the recommencement of hostilities.

Some months passed without incident, and the relations between the little community in the mountains and the Spaniards became more pacific. The latter found that the natives if left alone did them no damage. Bad masters learned that a course of ill treatment of their slaves was certain to be followed by their flight, and upon the bad treatment being proved, these found shelter among the mountains. Upon the other hand, the owners who treated their slaves with kindness and forbearance found that if these took to the mountains in a fit of restlessness, a shelter there was refused them.

Upon the edge of the forest patches of plantation ground made their appearance, and the treaty was upon the whole well observed on both sides.

It was about a year after they had taken to the hills that news reached the boys that an English ship had come into those waters. It was brought them across at an island by some Simeroons who had been where the English ship anchored. They said that it was commanded by Master John Oxenford. The boys knew him, as he had been on board Captain Francis Drake's ship during the last expedition, and they determined to make an effort to join him. He had, however, left the island before the natives started with the news, and they made an arrangement with them to convey them across to that place, when it should be learned that the vessel was returning or was again there.

It was not long before they were filled with grief at the news that reached them, although they felt not a little thankful that they had not been able to join Captain Oxenford when he first reached the islands.

This adventurous seaman had, after the return to England of Captain Francis Drake's expedition, waited for some time on shore, and then, fretting under forced inactivity,—for Captain Drake had for the time abandoned any project which he had entertained of a return to the Spanish seas, and had engaged in a war in Ireland,—determined to equip an expedition of his own with the assistance of several of those who had sailed in the last voyage with him, and of some Devonshire gentlemen who thought that a large booty might be made out of the venture.

He equipped a sloop of 140 tons burden and sailed for Darien. When he arrived at this isthmus he laid up his ship and marched inland, guided by Indians. After travelling twelve leagues among the mountains, he came to a small river running down into the Pacific. Here he and his comrades built a boat, launched it in the stream, and dropped down into the bay of Panama; then he rowed to the Isle of Pearls, and there captured a small barque from Quito with sixty pounds of gold. This raised the spirits of the adventurers, and six days later they took another barque with a hundred and sixty pounds of silver. They then set off in quest of pearls. They searched for a few days, but did not find them in proportion to their expectations; they therefore determined to return, and reëntered the mouth of the river they had descended. Here they loosed the prizes they had taken and let them go.

The delay at Pearl Island was a mistake and a misfortune. Captain Oxenford should have known that the Spanish authorities of the mainland would, when they heard that a single boat's load of Englishmen was ravaging their commerce, make a great effort to capture him, and his attack should have been swift and determined, and his retreat made without a halt. The fortnight which had been allowed to slip away caused his ruin. The news of their presence speedily arrived at Panama. Captain Ortuga was dispatched with four barques in search of them, and falling in with the liberated prizes learned the course that the English had taken. The river had three branches, and the Spaniard would have been much puzzled to know which to ascend, but the carelessness of the adventurers gave him a clue, for as he lay with his boats wondering which river he should ascend, he saw floating on the water large quantities of feathers. These were sufficient indications of a camp on the banks, and he at once followed that branch of the stream.

In four days he came upon the boat, which was hauled upon the sand, with only six men with her. They were lying asleep on the bank, and the coming of the Spaniards took them completely by surprise, and one of them was killed before he could make his escape into the woods. The rest got off. The Spaniards left twenty men to guard the boat, and with eighty others went up the country. Half a league away they found some huts, and in these the treasures of gold and silver which the English had captured were discovered.

Satisfied with having recovered these, Captain Ortuga was about to return to the river with his men when Oxenford with the English and two hundred Simeroons attacked them. The

Spaniards fought bravely, and the Simeroons would not stand against their fire. The English struggled desperately, eleven of these were killed, and the Simeroons took to their heels. Oxenford and a few of his companions escaped and made their way back toward the spot where they had left their ship. News of what was going on had, however, been sent across from Panama to Nombre de Dios, and four barques from that port had put out, and had found and taken Oxenford's ship. A band of a hundred and fifty men scoured the mountains, and into the hands of these Captain Oxenford and his companions fell. All of them were executed on the spot except Oxenford, the master, the pilot, and five boys. These were taken to Panama, where the three men were executed, the lives of the five boys being spared.

This news was a sore blow to the lads, who had hoped much to be able to reach the ship and to return to England in her. The delay, however, was not long, for a few weeks afterwards came the news that another English ship was in those waters. A party of Simeroons offered to take Ned and Gerald thither in their boat, and they determined to avail themselves of the offer.

Great was the lamentation among the community in the forest when the news that their leaders were about to leave became known. The simple Indians assembled around them, and wept and used every entreaty and prayer to change their resolution. However, the boys pointed out to them that they had already been absent near three years from home, and that, as the settlers were now able to defend themselves, and had earned the respect of the Spaniards, they would, if they continued their present course of avoiding giving any cause of complaint to the whites, no doubt be allowed to live in peace. They had, too, now learned the tactics that should be pursued in case of difficulty, and by adhering to these, the boys assured them that they might rely upon tiring out the Spaniards. Some of the negroes were in favor of retaining the English leaders by force, but this was objected to by the majority. Many of the Indians possessed gold which had been the property of their ancestors before the arrival of the Spaniards, and some of these treasures were now dug up and the boys were presented with a great store of pretty ornaments and other workmanship of the natives. Much rough gold was also placed on board their canoe, and a great portion of the dwellers of the hills marched down at night with them to the point of embarkation, a lonely creek far from the settlement of the Spaniards, to bid them farewell.

The boys themselves were affected by the sorrow of their friends, and by the confidence which these had placed in them, and they promised that should they return to those parts they would assuredly pay a visit to them again in the hills. Before leaving they had seen that two of the worthiest and wisest of the natives were chosen as leaders, and to these all the rest had sworn an oath, promising to obey their orders in all respects. They had constantly acted with the boys, and had, indeed, been their chief advisers in the matters internal to the tribe, and the lads had little doubt that for some time at least things would go well in the mountains; as to the ultimate power of the refugees to maintain their independence, this must, they felt, depend upon events beyond them. If the Spaniards were left at peace and undisturbed by English adventurers or other troubles, there was little doubt, sooner or later, they would destroy the whole of the natives of this island, as they had destroyed them in almost every place where they had come in contact with them. However, the boys had the satisfaction of knowing that they had been the means of at least prolonging the existence of this band, and of putting off the evil day, perhaps for years to come.

The Simeroons paddled out from the creek, and hoisting the sail the boat merrily danced over the water, and the boys felt their spirits rise at the hope of seeing their countrymen and hearing their native tongue again after eighteen months passed absolutely separate from all civilized communion. After two days' sailing and paddling they reached the bay where the natives had reported the English ship to be lying, and here, to their great delight, they found the *Maria*, Captain Cliff, lying at anchor.

Ned and Gerald, when they explained who they were, were received with great joy and amazement. The story of their loss had been told in England, and the captain, who came from the neighborhood where Gerald's father dwelt, reported that the family had long mourned him as dead. He himself was bent, not upon a buccaneering voyage, although, no doubt, if a rich ship had fallen into his hands he would have made no scruple in taking it, but his object was to trade with the natives, and to gather a store of such goods as the islands furnished in exchange for those of English make. He had, too, fetched slaves from the western coast of Africa, and had disposed of them to much advantage, and the ship was now about to proceed on her way home, each man's share of the profits of the expedition amounting to a sum which quite answered his expectations.

It was two months later, before the boys, to their great delight, again saw the hills behind Plymouth. None who had seen them embark in the *Swanne* would have recognized in the stalwart young fellows who now stepped ashore on the hove the lads who then set sail. Nearly three years had passed; the sun of the tropics had burned their faces almost to a mahogany color; their habit of command among the natives had given them an air and bearing beyond their years; and though Ned was but eighteen, and Gerald a little older, they carried themselves like men of mature years.

It had been, indeed, no slight burden that they had endured. The fighting which had formed the first epoch of their stay in the island, serious as it had been, had been less wearing to them than the constant care and anxiety of the subsequent quiet time. The arrival of each fugitive slave was a source of fresh danger, and it had often needed all their authority to prevent the younger and wilder spirits of their little community from indulging in raids upon the crops of the Spaniards.

Once in Plymouth, the lads said good-bye to each other, promising to meet again in a few days. Each then proceeded to his home. Ned, indeed, found that he had a home no longer; for on reaching the village he found that his father had died a few months after his departure and a new pedagogue had taken his place and occupied the little cottage.

The shock was a great one although hardly unexpected, for

his father's health had not been strong, and the thought that he would not be alive when he returned had often saddened Ned's mind during his absence. He found, however, no lack of welcome in the village. There were many of his school friends still there, and these looked with astonishment and admiration on the bronzed, military-looking man, and could scarce believe that he was their playmate the "Otter." Here Ned tarried a few days, and then, according to his promise to Gerald, started for the part of the country where he lived, and received a most cordial welcome from the father and family of his friend.

CHAPTER X
Southward Ho!

Upon making inquiries Ned Hearne found that Captain Drake had, upon the return of his expedition, set aside the shares of the prize-money of Gerald Summers, himself, and the men who were lost in the wreck of the prize, in hopes that they would some day return to claim them. Upon the evidence given by Gerald and himself of the death of the others, their shares were paid by the bankers at Plymouth who had charge of them to their families, while Ned and Gerald received their portions.

Owing to the great mortality which had taken place among the crews each of the lads received a sum of nearly a thousand pounds, the total capture amounting to a value of over a million of money. As boys, they each received the half of a man's share; the officers of course had received larger shares, and the merchants who had lent money to get up the expedition, gained large profits.

Ned thought at first of embarking his money in the purchase of a share in a trading vessel, and of taking to that service; but hearing that Captain Drake intended to fit out another expedition, he decided to wait for that event, and to make one more voyage to the Spanish Main before determining on his future course. Having therefore his time on his hands he accepted the invitation of the parents of his three boy friends, Tom Tressilis, Gerald Summers, and Reuben Gall. He was most warmly welcomed, for both Tom and Gerald declared that they owed their lives to him. He spent several weeks at each of their homes, and then returned to Plymouth, where he put himself into the hands

of a retired master mariner to learn navigation and other matters connected with his profession, and occupied his spare time
in studying the usual branches of a gentleman's education.

It was some months before Captain Francis returned form
Ireland, but when he did so he at once began his preparations
for his next voyage. The expedition was to be on a larger scale
than that in which he had formerly embarked, for he had
formed the resolve to sail round Cape Horn, to coast along
north to the Spanish settlements upon the great ocean he had
seen from the tree-top in the Isthmus of Darien; and then, if all
went well, to sail still further north, double the northern coasts
of America, and to find some short way by which English ships
might reach the Pacific. These projects were, however, known
to but few, as it was considered of the utmost importance to prevent them from being noised abroad, lest they might come to
the ears of the Spaniards, and so put them upon their guard.

In spite of the great losses of men upon the former expedition, the number of volunteers who came forward directly
Captain Drake's intention to sail again to the Indies was known,
was greatly in excess of the requirements. All, however, who had
sailed upon the last voyage, and were willing again to venture,
were enrolled, and Captain Drake expressed a lively pleasure at
meeting Ned Hearne and Gerald Summers, whom he had given
up as lost. The expenses of the expedition were defrayed partly
from the funds of Captain Drake and his officers, partly by
moneys subscribed by merchants and others who took shares in
the speculation. These were termed adventurers. Ned embarked five hundred pounds of his prize-money in the venture,
as did each of his three friends. He was now nineteen, and a
broad, strongly-built young fellow. His friends were all somewhat older, and all four were entered by Captain Francis as
men, and ranked as "gentlemen adventurers," and would therefore receive their full share of prize-money.

On the 12th of November, 1577, the fleet sailed out of
Plymouth Sound amid the salutes of the guns of the fort there.
It consisted of five ships: the *Pelican*, of 100 tons, the flag-ship,
commanded by Captain-general Francis Drake; the *Elizabeth*,

80 tons, Captain John Winter; the *Marigold,* a barque of 30 tons, Captain John Thomas; the *Swan,* a flyboat of 50 tons, Captain John Chester; and the *Christopher,* a pinnace of 15 tons, Captain Thomas Moore.

The voyage began unfortunately, for meeting a head-wind they were forced to put into Falmouth, where a tempest ill-treated them sorely. Some of the ships had to cut away their masts, and the whole were obliged to put back into Plymouth to refit, entering the harbor in a very different state to that in which they had left it a fortnight before. Every exertion was made, and after a few days' delay the fleet again set sail.

They carried an abundance of stores of all kinds, together with large quantities of fancy articles as presents for the savage people whom they might meet in their voyaging. The second start was more prosperous than the first, and after touching at various points on the west coast of Africa they shaped their way to the mouth of the La Plata, sailing through the Cape de Verde Islands, where their appearance caused no slight consternation among the Portuguese. However, as they had more important objects in view they did not stop to molest any of the principal towns, only landing at quiet bays to procure a fresh supply of water, and to obtain fruit and vegetables, which in those days, when ships only carried salt provisions, were absolutely necessary to preserve the crews in health. All were charmed with the beauty and fertility of these islands, which were veritable gardens of tropical fruits, and they left these seas with regret.

The fleet reached the La Plata in safety, but made no long stay there, for the extreme shallowness of the water and the frequency and abundance of the shoals in the river made the admiral fear for the safety of his ships; and accordingly, after a few days' rest, the anchors were weighed and the fleet proceeded down the coast. For some time they sailed without adventure, save that once or twice in the storms they encountered, one or other of the ships were separated from the rest. After several weeks' sailing they put into the Bay of St. Julian on the coast of Patagonia. Here the crews landed to obtain water. Soon the natives came down to meet them. These were tall active men, but

A Race for Life
See page 129.

yet far from being the giants which the Spaniards had represented them, few of them being taller than a tall Englishman. They were dressed in the scantiest clothing—the men wearing a short apron made of skin, with another skin as a mantle over one shoulder, the women wearing a kind of petticoat made of soft skin. The men carried bows and arrows and spears, and were painted strangely—one half the head and body being painted white, the other black. Their demeanor was perfectly friendly, and Captain Drake, fearing no harm, walked some distance inland, and many of those not engaged in getting water into the boats also strolled away from the shore. Among those who rambled farthest were Ned and Tom Tressilis, together with another gentleman adventurer named Arbuckle. When they left Captain Francis, the armorer, who had brought a bow on shore with him, was showing the natives how much farther our English bow could carry than the native weapon.

Wondering what the country was like beyond the hills, the little party ascended the slope. Just as they reached the top they heard a shout. Looking back they saw that all was confusion.

The string of the armorer's bow had snapped, and the natives, knowing nothing of guns, believed that the party were now unarmed. As the armorer was restringing his bow one of the natives shot an arrow at him, and he fell mortally wounded. One standing near now raised his arquebuse, but before he could fire he too was pierced by two arrows and fell dead. The admiral himself caught up the arquebuse and shot the man who had first fired.

The little party on the hill had been struck with amazement and consternation at the sudden outburst, and were recalled to a sense of their danger by the whiz of an arrow, which struck Master Arbuckle in the heart, and at the same moment a dozen of the savages made their appearance from among the trees below them. Seeing the deadliness of their aim, and that he and Tom would be shot down at once before they could get to close quarters, Ned turned to fly.

"Quick, Tom, for your life!"

Fortunately they stood on the very top of the ascent, so that a single bound backward took them out of sight and range of their enemies. There was a wood a few hundred yards inland, apparently of great extent, and toward this the lads ran at the top of their speed. The savages had to climb the hill, and when they reached its crest the fugitives were out of bow-shot range.

A yell broke from them as they saw the lads, but these had made the best use of their time and reached the wood some two hundred yards ahead of their pursuers. Ned dashed into the undergrowth and tore his way through it, Tom close at his heels. Sometimes they came to open spaces, and here each time Ned changed the direction of their flight, choosing spots where they could take to the underwood without showing any sign, such as broken boughs, of their entrance.

After an hour's running the yells and shouts, which had at first seemed close behind, gradually lessened, and were now but faintly heard. Then, utterly exhausted, the lads threw themselves on the ground.

In a few minutes, however, Ned rose again.

"Come, Tom," he said, "we must keep on. These fellows will trace us with the sagacity of dogs; but, clever as they may be, it takes time to follow a track. We must keep on now. When it gets dark, which will be in another hour or so, they will be able to follow us no longer, and we can then take it easily."

"Do as you think best, Ned; you are accustomed to this kind of thing."

Without another word they started off at a run again, keeping as nearly as they could a straight course, for Ned's experience in forest life enabled him to do this when one unused to woodcraft would have lost all idea of direction. The fact, however, that the mosses grew on the side of the trees looking east was guide enough for him, for he knew that the warm breezes from the sea would attract them, while the colder inland winds would have an opposite effect. Just as it was getting dark they emerged from the wood, and could see stretching far before them an undulating and almost treeless country.

"Fortunately there has been no rain for some time, and the ground is as hard as iron," Ned said. "On the damp soil under the trees they will track our steps, but we shall leave no marks here; and in the morning, when they trace us to this spot, they will be at fault."

So saying, he struck off across the country. For some hours they walked, the moon being high and enabling them to make their way without difficulty. At last they came upon a clump of bushes, and here Ned proposed a halt. Tom was perfectly ready, for they had now walked and run for many hours, and both were thoroughly fatigued; for after so long a voyage in a small ship they were out of condition for a long journey on foot.

"The first thing to do is to light a fire," Ned said; "for it is bitterly cold."

"But how do you mean to light it?"

"I have flint and steel in my pouch," Ned said, "and a flash of powder for priming my pistols in my sash here. It is a pity, indeed, we did not put our pistols into our belts when we came ashore. But even if I had not had the flint and steel I could have made a fire by rubbing two dead sticks together. You forget I have lived among savages for a year."

"You don't think that it is dangerous to light a fire?"

"Not in the least. It was dark when we left the wood, and they must have halted on our track far back among the trees to follow it up by daylight; besides, we have walked five hours since then, and must be twenty miles away, and we have crossed five or six hills. Find a few dead sticks and I will pull a handful or two of dried grass; we will soon have a fire."

Ned made a little pile of dried grass, scooped out a slight depression at the top, and placed a dead leaf in it; on this he poured a few grains of powder, added a few blades of dried grass, and then set to work with his flint and steel. After a blow or two a spark fell into the powder; it blazed up, igniting the blades of grass and the leaf, and in a minute the little pile was in a blaze. Dried twigs and then larger sticks were added, and soon a bright fire burned up.

"Throw on some of the green bush," Ned said; "we do not want a blaze, for although we have thrown out the fellows in pursuit of us there may be others about."

"And now, Ned," Tom said, after sitting for some time gazing into the red fire, "what on earth are we to do next?"

"That is a question more easily asked than answered," Ned said, cheerfully; "we have saved our skins for the present, now we have got to think out what is the best course to pursue."

"I don't see any way to get back to the ship," Tom said, after a long pause; "do you?"

"No," Ned replied, "I don't, Tom. These savages know that they have cut us off, and will be on the watch, you may be sure. They shoot so straight with those little bows and arrows of theirs that we should be killed without the least chance of ever getting to close quarters. Besides, the admiral will doubtless believe that we have been slain, and will sail away. We may be sure that he beat off the fellows who were attacking him, but they will all take to the woods, and he would never be able to get any distance among the trees; besides, he would give up all hope of finding us there. As to our getting back through the wood, swarming with savages, it seems to me hopeless."

"Then whatever is to become of us?" Tom asked hopelessly.

"Well, the lookout is not bright," Ned said, thoughtfully, "but there is a chance for us. We may keep ourselves by killing wild animals, and by pushing inland we may come upon some people less treacherous and bloody than those savages by the seashore. If so, we might hunt and live with them."

Tom groaned. "I am not sure that I would not rather be killed at once than go on living like a savage."

"The life is not such a bad one," Ned said; "I tried it once, and although the negroes and Indians of Porto Rico were certainly a very different people to these savages, still the life led on these great plains and hills, abounding with game, is more lively than being cooped up in a wood as I was then. Besides, I don't mean that we should be here always. I propose that we try and cross the continent. It is not so very wide here, and we are nearly in a line with Lima. The admiral meant to go on there, and expects a rich booty. He may be months before he gets round the Horn, and if we could manage to be there when he arrives we should be rescued. If not, and I own that I have not much hope of it, we could at least go down to Lima some time or other. I can talk Spanish now very fairly, and we shall have such a lot of adventures to tell that, even if they do not take us for Spanish sailors, as we can try to feign, they will not be likely to put us to death. They would do so if we were taken in arms as buccaneers, but coming in peaceably we might be kindly treated. At any rate, if we get on well with the Indians we shall have the choice of making, some day or other, for the Spanish settlements on the west coast; but that is all in the distance. The first thing will be to get our living somehow, the second to get further inland, the third to make friends with the first band of natives we meet. And now the best thing to do is to go off to sleep. I shall not be many minutes, I can tell you."

Strange as was the situation, and many the perils that threatened them, both were in a few minutes fast asleep.

The sun was rising above the hills when with a start they awoke and at once sprang to their feet, and instinctively looked round in search of approaching danger. All was, however, quiet. Some herds of deer grazed in the distance, but no other living creature was visible. Then they turned their eyes upon each other and burst into a simultaneous shout of laughter. Their clothes were torn literally into rags by the bushes through which they had forced their way, while their faces were scratched and stained with blood from the same cause.

"The first thing to be done," Ned said, when the laugh was over, "is to look for a couple of long springly saplings and to make bows and arrows. Of course they will not carry far, but we might knock down any small game we come across."

Both lads were good shots with a bow, for in those days, although firearms were coming in, all Englishmen were still trained in the use of the bow.

"But what about strings?" Tom asked.

"I will cut four thin strips from my belt," Ned said. "Each pair tied together will make a string for a five-foot bow, and will be fully strong enough for any weapon we shall be able to make."

After an hour's walk they came to a small grove of trees growing in a hollow. These were of several species, and trying the branches they found one kind which was at once strong and flexible. With their hangers, or short swords, they cut down a small sapling of some four inches in diameter, split it up, pared each half down, and manufactured two bows, which were rough, indeed, but sufficiently strong to send an arrow a considerable distance. They then made each a dozen shafts, pointed and notched them. Without feathers or metal points these could not fly straight to any distance, but they had no thought of long-range shooting.

"Now," Ned said, "we will go back to that bare space of rock we passed a hundred yards back; there were dozens of little lizards running about there, it will be hard if we cannot knock some over."

"Are they good to eat?" Tom asked.

"I have no doubt they are," Ned said; "as a rule everything is more or less good to eat; some things may be nicer than others, but hardly anything is poisonous. I have eaten snakes over and over again, and very good they are. I have been keeping a look-out for them ever since we started this morning."

When they reached the rock the lizards all darted off to their cracks and crevices, but Ned and Tom lay down with their bows bent and arrows in place, and waited quietly. Ere long the lizards popped up their heads again and began to move about, and the lads now let fly their arrows. Sometimes they hit, sometimes missed, and each shot was followed by the disappearance of the lizards, but with patience they found by the end of an hour that they had shot a dozen, which was sufficient for an ample meal for them.

"How will you cook them, Ned?"

"Skin them as if they were eels, and then roast them on a stick."

"I am more thirsty than hungry," Tom said.

"Yes, and from the look of the country water must be scarce. However, as long as we can shoot lizards and birds we can drink their blood."

The fire was soon lighted, and the lizards cooked; they tasted like little birds, their flesh being tender and sweet.

"Now we had better be proceeding," Ned said, when they had finished their meal. "We have an unknown country to explore, and if we ever get across we shall have materials for yarns for the rest of our lives."

"Well, Ned, I must say you are a capital fellow to get into a scrape with. You got Gerald and me out of one, and if any one could get through this I am sure you could do so. Gerald told me that he always relied upon you, and found you always right; you may be sure that I will do the same. So I appoint you captain-general of this expedition, and promise to obey all orders un-questioningly."

"Well, my first order is," Ned said, laughing, "that we each make a good pike. The wood we made our bows from will do capitally, and we can harden the points in the fire. We may meet some wild beasts, and a good strong six-foot pike would be bet-ter than our swords."

Two hours' work completed the new weapons, and with their bows slung at their backs, and using their pikes as walking staves, they again set out on their journey across the continent.

CHAPTER XI

The Marvel of Fire

"What are those—natives?" exclaimed Tom, suddenly. Ned looked steadily at them for some time.

"No, I think they are great birds; the ostrich abounds in these plains; no doubt they are ostriches."

"I suppose it is of no use our chasing them?"

"Not a bit. They can run faster than a horse can gallop."

During the day's walk they saw vast number of deer of various kinds, but as they were sure that these would not allow them to approach they did not alter their course, which was, as nearly as they could calculate by the sun, due west. The sun was warm during the day, but all the higher hill-tops were covered with snow. "If the worse comes to the worst," Ned said, "we must go up and get some snow. We can make a big ball of it and bring it down with us in one of our sashes. But I should think there must be some stream somewhere about. The snow must melt; besides, these great herds of deer must drink somewhere."

Late in the afternoon they came on the crest of a ridge.

"There," Ned said, pointing to a valley in which were a number of trees, "we shall find water there, or I am mistaken."

An hour's tramp brought them to the valley. Through this a stream ran between steep banks. They followed it for half a mile and then came to a spot where the banks sloped away. Here the ground was trampled with many feet, and the edge of the stream was trodden into mud.

"Hurrah, Tom! here is meat and drink, too. It is hard if we do not kill something or other here. Look at that clump of bushes where the bank rises. If we hide there the deer will almost touch us as they pass to water, and we are sure to be able to shoot them even with these bows and arrows. But first of all for a drink. Then we will cross the stream and make a camping-ground under the trees opposite."

The stream was but waist deep, but very cold, for it was composed of snow-water.

"Shall we light a fire, Ned; it might frighten the deer?"

"No, I think it will attract them," Ned said; "they are most inquisitive creatures, and are always attracted by anything strange."

A fire was soon lighted, and after it got quite dark they piled up dry wood upon it, recrossed the river, and took their places in the bushes.

An hour passed, and then they heard a deep sound. In a minute or two the leading ranks of a great herd of deer appeared on the rise, and stood looking wonderingly at the fire. For some little time they halted, and then, pushed forward by those behind and urged by their own curiosity, they advanced step by step with their eyes fixed on the strange sight. So crowded were they that as they advanced they seemed a compact mass, those outside coming along close to the bushes in which the boys lay. Silently these raised their bows, bent them to the full strain, and each launched an arrow. The deer were not five feet from them, and two stags fell pierced through and through. They leaped to their feet again, but the boys had dashed out with their swords in hand, and in an instant had cut them down.

There was a wild rush on the part of the herd, a sound of feet almost like thunder, and then the boys stood alone by the side of the two deer they had killed. They were small, the two together not weighing more than a good-sized sheep. The boys lifted them on their shoulders rejoicing, and waded across the stream. One they hung up to the branch of a tree, the other they skinned and cut up, and were soon busy roasting pieces of its flesh over the fire.

They had just finished an abundant meal when they heard a

roar at a short distance which brought them to their feet in a moment. Ned seized his pike and faced the direction from which the sound had come.

"Throw on fresh sticks, Tom; all animals fear fire."

A bright blaze soon lit up the wood.

"Now, Tom, do you climb the tree; I will give you the pieces of meat up, and then do you lift the other stag to a higher branch. I don't suppose the brute can climb, but he may be able to do so; at any rate we will sleep in the tree, and keep watch and ward."

As soon as Tom had followed these instructions Ned handed him up the bows and arrows and spears, and then clambered up beside him. As the fire again burned low an animal was seen to approach cautiously.

"A lion!" whispered Tom.

"I don't think that he is as big as a lion," Ned said, "but he certainly looks like one. A female, I suppose, as it has got no mane."

Of course the lads did not know, nor indeed did any one else at that time, that the lion is not a native of America; the animal before them was what is now called the South American lion, or puma.

The creature walked round and round the fire snuffing, and then with an angry roar raised itself on its hind legs and scratched at the trunk of the tree. Several times it repeated this performance, and then, with another roar, walked away into the darkness.

"Thank goodness it can't climb!" Ned said; "I expect with our spears and swords we could have beaten it back if it had tried, still it is just as well not to have had to do it; besides, now we can both go to sleep. Let us get well up the tree, so that if anything that can climb should come, it will fall to at the deer to begin with; that will be certain to wake us."

They soon made themselves as comfortable as they could in crutches of the tree, tied themselves with their sashes to a bough to prevent a fall, and were soon asleep.

The next day they rested in the wood, made fresh bow-strings from the twisted gut of the deer, cut the skins up into long strips, thereby obtaining a hundred feet of strong cord, which Ned thought might be useful for snares. Here, too, they shot several birds, which they roasted, and from whose feathers, tied on with a threadlike fibre, they further improved their arrows. They collected a good many pieces of fibre for further use, for, as Tom said, when they got on to rock again they would be sure to find some splinters of stone which they could fasten to the arrows for points, and would be then able to do good execution even at a distance.

They cut a number of strips of flesh off the deer and hung them in the smoke of the fire, by which means they calculated that they could keep for some days, and could be eaten without being cooked, which might be an advantage, as they feared that the odor of cooking might attract the attention of wandering Indians.

The following morning they again started, keeping their backs as before to the sun.

"Look at these creatures," Tom said suddenly, as a herd of animals dashed by at a short distance; "they do not look like deer."

"No, they look more like sheep or goats, but they have much longer legs. I wonder what they can be!"

During the day's journey they came across no water, and by the end of the tramp were much exhausted.

"We will not make a fire to-night," Ned said; "we must be careful of our powder. I don't want to be driven to use sticks for getting fire; it is a long and tedious business. We will be up at daybreak to-morrow, and will push on till we find water. We will content ourselves for to-night with a bit of this smoked venison."

They found it dry work eating this without water, and soon desisted, gathered some grass to make a bed, and were asleep a short time after it became dark. They were now in an open district, not having seen a tree since they started in the morning, and they had, therefore, less fear of being disturbed by wild beasts. They had indeed talked of keeping watch by turns, but without a fire they felt that this would be dull work, and would moreover be of little avail, as in the darkness the stealthy tread of a lion would not be heard, and they would therefore be attacked as suddenly as if no watch had been kept. If he should announce his coming by a roar both would be sure to awake quickly enough. So lying down close together with their spears at hand, they were soon asleep, with the happy carelessness of danger peculiar to youth.

With the first streak of daybreak they were up and on their way. Until midday they came upon no water, their only excitement being the killing of an armadillo. Then they saw a few bushes in a hollow, and making toward it found a small pool of water. After a hearty drink, leaves and sticks were collected, a fire made, and slices of the smoked deer's meat were soon broiling over it.

"This is jolly," Tom said. "I should not mind how long I tramped if we could always find water."

"And have venison to eat with it," Ned added, laughing. "We have got a stock to last a week, that is a comfort, and this armadillo will do for supper and breakfast. But I don't think we need fear starvation, for these plains swarm with animals, and it is hard if we can't manage to kill one occasionally somehow or other."

"How far do you think it is across to the other coast?"

"I have not an idea," Ned said. "I don't suppose any Englishman knows, although the Spaniards can of course tell pretty closely. We know that after rounding Cape Horn they sail up the coast northwest, or in that direction, so that we have got the base of a triangle to cross; but beyond that I have no idea whatever. Hallo!"

Simultaneously the two lads caught up their spears and leaped to their feet. Well might they be alarmed, for close by were a party of some twenty Indians who had, quietly and unperceived, come down upon them. They were standing immovable, and their attitude did not betoken hostility. Their eyes were fixed upon them, but their expression betrayed wonder rather than enmity.

"Lay down your spear again, Tom;" Ned said, "let us receive them as friends."

Dropping their spears the lads advanced a pace or two holding out their hands in token of amity. Then slowly, step by step, the Indians advanced.

"They look almost frightened," Ned said. "What can they be staring so fixedly at?"

"It is the fire!" Ned exclaimed; "it is the fire! I do believe they have never seen a fire before."

It was so, as Sir Francis Drake afterwards discovered when landing on the coast, the Patagonian Indians at that time were wholly unacquainted with fire. When the Indians came down they looked from the fire to the boys, and perceived for the first time that they were creatures of another color from themselves. Then simultaneously they threw themselves on their faces.

"They believe that we are gods or superior beings of some kind," Ned said; "they have clearly never heard of the Spaniards. What good fortune for us! Now let us reassure them."

So saying he stooped over the prostrate Indians, patted them on the head and shoulders, and after some trouble he succeeded in getting them to rise. Then he motioned them to sit down round the fire, put on some more meat, and when this was cooked, offered a piece to each, Tom and himself setting the example of eating it.

The astonishment of the natives was great. Many of them, with a cry, dropped the meat on finding it hot, and an excited talk went on between them. Presently, however, the man who appeared to be the chief set the example of carefully tasting a piece. He gave an exclamation of satisfaction, and soon all were engaged upon the food.

When they had finished Ned threw some more sticks on the fire, and as these burst into flames and then consumed away, the amazement of the natives was intense. Ned then made signs to them to pull up some bushes and cast on the fire. They all set to work with energy, and soon a huge pile was raised on the fire. At first great volumes of white smoke only poured up, then the leaves crackled, and presently a tongue of flame shot up, rising higher and higher till a great bonfire blazed away far above their heads. This completed the wonder and awe of the natives, who again prostrated themselves with every symptom of worship

"THEY HAVE NEVER SEEN A FIRE BEFORE," SAID NED.
SEE PAGE 141.

before the boys. These again raised them, and by signs intimated their intention of accompanying them.

With lively demonstrations of gladness and welcome the
Indians turned to go, pointing to the west as the place where
their abode lay.

"We may as well leave our bows and arrows," Ned said. "Their
bows are so immensely superior to ours that it will make us sink
in their estimation if they see that our workmanship is so inferior to their own."

The Indians, who were all very tall, splendidly made men,
stepped out so rapidly that the lads had the greatest difficulty in
keeping up with them, and were sometimes obliged to break
into a half trot, seeing which the chief said a word to his followers, and they then proceeded at a more reasonable rate. It was
late in the evening before they reached the village, which lay in
a wooded hollow at the foot of some lofty hills. The natives gave
a loud cry, which at once brought out the entire population, who
ran up and gazed, astonished at the new-comers. The chief said
a few words, when with every mark of awe and surprise all prostrated themselves as the men had before done.

The village was composed of huts made of sticks closely inter-
twined, and covered with the skins of animals. The chief led
them to a large one, evidently his own, and invited them to
enter. They found that it was also lined with skins, and others
were laid upon the floor. A pile of skins served as a mat and bed.
The chief made signs that he placed this at their disposal, and
soon left them to themselves. In a short time he again drew
aside the skin which hung across the entrance, and a squaw advanced, evidently in deep terror, bearing some raw meat. Ned
received it graciously, and then said to Tom, "Now we will light
a fire and astonish them again."

So saying, the boys went outside, picked up a dry stick or two,
and motioned to the Indians who were gathered round that they
needed more. The whole population at once scattered through
the grove, and soon a huge pile of dead wood was collected. The
boys now made a little heap of dried leaves, placed a few grains
of powder in a hollow at the top, and the flint and steel being

put into requisition, the flame soon leaped up amid a cry of astonishment and awe from the women and children; wood was now laid on, and soon a great fire was blazing. The men gathered round and sat down, and the women and children gradually approached and took their places behind them. The evening was cold, and as the natives felt the grateful heat, fresh exclamations of pleasure broke from them, and gradually a complete babel of tongues broke out. Then the noise was hushed, and a silence of expectation and attention reigned as the lads cut off slices of the meat, and spitting them on pieces of green wood, held them over the fire. Tom made signs to the chief and those sitting round to fetch meat and follow their example; some of the Indian women brought meat, and the men with sharp stone knives cut off pieces and stuck them on green sticks as they had seen the boys do. Then very cautiously they approached the fire, shrinking back and exhibiting signs of alarm at the fierce heat it threw out as they approached near to it.

The boys, however, reassured them, and they presently set to work. When the meat was roasted it was cut up and distributed in little bits to the crowd behind, all of whom were eager to taste this wonderful preparation. It was evident by the exclamations of satisfaction that the new viand was an immense success, and fresh supplies of meat were soon over the fire.

An incident now occurred which threatened to mar the harmony of the proceedings. A stick breaking, some of the red-hot embers scattered round. One rolled close to Ned's leg, and the lad, with a quick snatch, caught it up and threw it back upon the fire. Seeing this, a native near grasped a glowing fragment which had fallen near him, but dropped it with a shriek of astonishment and pain.

All leaped to their feet as the man danced in his agony. Some ran away in terror, others instinctively made for their weapons, all gesticulated and yelled. Ned at once went to the man and patted him assuringly. Then he got him to open his hand, which was really severely burned. Then he got a piece of soft fat and rubbed it gently upon the sore, and then made signs that he wanted something to bandage it with. A woman brought some large fresh leaves which were evidently good for hurts, and another a soft thong of deer hide. The hand was soon bandaged up, and although the man must still have been in severe pain he again took his seat, this time at a certain distance from the fire.

This incident greatly increased the awe with which the boys were viewed, as not only had they the power of producing this new and astonishing element, but they could, unhurt, take up pieces of wood turned red by it, which inflicted terrible agony on others.

Before leaving the fire and retiring to their tent, the boys made signs to the chief that it was necessary that some one should be appointed to throw on fresh wood from time to time to keep the fire alight. This was hardly needed, as the whole population were far too excited to think of retiring to bed. After the lads had left they gathered round the fire, and each took delight in throwing on pieces of wood and in watching them consume, and several times, when they woke during the night, the boys saw by the bright light streaming in through the slits in the deer skin, that the bonfire was never allowed to wane.

In the morning fresh meat was brought to the boys, together with raw yams and other vegetables. There were now other marvels to be shown. Ned had learned when with the negroes how to cook in calabashes, and he now got a gourd from the natives, cut it in half, scooped its contents out, and then filled it with water. From the stream he then got a number of stones, and put them into the fire until they became intensely hot. Then with two sticks he raked them out and dropped them into the water. The natives yelled with astonishment as they saw the water fizz and bubble as the stones were thrown in. More were added until the water boiled. Then the yams, cut into pieces, were dropped in, more hot stones added to keep the water boiling, and when cooked, the yams were taken out. When sufficiently cooled, the boys distributed the pieces among the chiefs, and again the signs of satisfaction showed that cooked vegetables were appreciated. Other yams were then cut up and laid among the hot embers to bake.

After this the boys took a few half-burned sticks, carried them to another spot, added fresh fuel and made another fire, and then signed to the natives to do the same. In a short time a dozen fires were blazing, and the whole population were engaged in grilling venison, and in boiling and baking yams. The boys were both good trenchermen, but they were astounded at the quantity of food which the Patagonians disposed of.

By night time the entire stock of meat in the village was exhausted, and the chief motioned to the boys that in the morning he should go out with a party to lay in a great stock of venison. To this they made signs that they would accompany the expedition. While the feasting had been going on, the lads had wandered away with two of the Indian bows and arrows. The bows were much shorter than those to which they were accustomed, and required far less strength to pull. The wood of which the bows were formed was tough and good, and as the boys had both the handiness of sailors and, like all lads of that period, had some knowledge of bow-making, they returned to the camp and obtained two more of the strongest bows in the possession of the natives. They then set to work with their knives, and each taking two bows, cut them up, fitted and spliced them together.

The originals were but four feet long, the new ones six. The halves of one bow formed the two ends, the middle being made of the other bow doubled. The pieces were spliced together with deers' sinews, and when, after some hours' work, they were completed, the boys found that they were as strong and tough as the best of their homemade bows, and required all their strength to draw them to the ear. The arrows were now too short, but upon making signs to the natives that they wanted wood for arrows, a stock of dried wood, carefully prepared, was at once given them, and of these they made some arrows of the regulation cloth-yard length. The feathers, fastened on with the sinews of some small animals, were stripped from the Indian arrows, and fastened on, as were the sharp-pointed stones which formed their heads, and on making a trial the lads found that they could shoot as far and as straight as with their own familiar weapons.

"We can reckon on killing a stag, if he will stand still, at a hundred and fifty yards," Ned said, "or running, at a hundred; don't you think so?"

"Well, six times out of seven we ought to at any rate," Tom replied, "or our Devonshire archership has deserted us."

When they heard, therefore, that there was to be a hunt upon the following day they felt that they had another surprise for the natives, whose short bows and arrows were of little use at a greater distance than fifty yards, although up to that distance deadly weapons in their hands.

CHAPTER XII

Across a Continent

The work upon which the boys were engaged passed unnoticed by the Indians, who were too much absorbed by the enjoyment of the new discovery to pay any attention to other matters. The bows and arrows had been given to them, as anything else in camp for which they had a fancy would have been given, but beyond that none had observed what was being done. There were then many exclamations of astonishment among them when Ned and Tom issued from their hut in the morning to join the hunting party, carrying their new weapons. The bows were of course unstrung, and Ned handed his to the chief, who viewed it with great curiosity. It was passed from hand to hand and then returned to the chief. One or two of the Indians said something, and the chief tried its strength. He shook his head. Ned signed to him to string it, but the chief tried in vain, as did several of the strongest of the Indians. Indeed, no man, however powerful, could string an old English bow unless trained to its use.

When the Indians had given up the attempt as hopeless, the two lads strung their bows without the slightest difficulty to the intense surprise of the natives. These again took the bows, but failed to bend them even to the length of their own little arrows. The lads then took out their newly-made shafts and took aim at a young tree of a foot diameter, standing at about two hundred yards distance, and both sent their arrows quivering into the trunk.

The Indians gave a perfect yell of astonishment.

"It is not much of a mark," Tom said; "Hugh Willoughby of our village could hit a white glove at that distance every time, and the fingers of a glove five times out of six; it is the length of the shots, not the accuracy, which astounds these fellows. However, it is good enough to keep up our superiority."

The party now started on their hunt. There was but little difficulty in finding game, for numerous herds could be seen grazing; the task was to get within shot. The boys watched anxiously to see the course which the Indians would adopt. First ascertaining which way the wind was blowing, the chief, with ten others, accompanied by the boys, set off to make a circuit so as to approach one of the herds up wind. When they had reached the point desired all went down upon their bellies and crawled like snakes until they reached a clump of low bushes a quarter of a mile from the herd. Then they lay quiet, waiting for their comrades, whose turn it now was to set. These also making a circuit, but in the opposite direction, placed themselves half a mile to windward of the deer in a long line. Then they advanced toward the herd, making no effort to conceal themselves.

Scarcely had they risen to their feet than the herd winded them. For a minute or two they stood motionless, watching the distant figures, and then turning, bounded away. The chief uttered an exclamation of disgust, for it was evident at once that from the direction that they were taking the herd would not pass, as he hoped, close by the bushes. The lads, however, were well satisfied, for the line would take them within a hundred and fifty yards. As in a closely-packed body they came along Ned and Tom rose suddenly to their feet, drew their bows to their ears, and launched their arrows. Each had, according to the custom of English archers, stuck two arrows into the ground by the spot where they would stand up, and these they also discharged before the herd was out of shot. With fair shooting it was impossible to miss so large a mark, and five of the little deer rolled over, pierced through by the arrows, while another, hit in a less vital spot, carried off the weapon.

The Indians raised a cry of joy and surprise at shooting which to them appeared marvellous indeed, and when the others came

up showed them with marks of astonishment the distance at
which the animals had fallen from the bush from which the arrows had been aimed. Two more beats were made. These were
more successful, the herds passing close to the places of concealment, and upon each occasion ten stags fell. This was considered sufficient.

The animals were not all of one kind. One herd was composed of deer far larger than, and as heavy as good sized sheep,
while the others were considerably smaller, and the party had as
much as their united efforts—except those of Ned and Tom,
whose offer to assist was peremptorily declined—could drag
back to the village, where the feasting was at once renewed.

The lads, when the natives had skinned the deer, took some
of the smaller and finer skins, intending to dry them, but the natives, seeing their intention, brought them a number of the
same kind, which were already well cured and beautifully sup-
ple. Fashioning needles from small pieces of bone, with sinews
for thread, and using their own tattered clothes as patterns, the
two lads set to work, and by the following evening had manufactured doublets and trunks of deer-skin, which were a vast
improvement upon their late ragged apparel, and had at a short
distance the appearance of being made of a bright brownish-
yellow cloth.

By this time the Indians had become quite accustomed to
them. The men, and sometimes even the women, came to the
hut and sat down and tried to talk with them. The boys did their
best to learn, asking the name of every article and repeating it
until they had thoroughly learned it, the Indians applauding like
children when they attained the right pronunciation.

The next morning they saw a young Indian starting alone with
his bow and arrow. Anxious to see how he was going to proceed
by himself the boys asked if they might accompany him. He
assented and together they started off. After an hour's walking
they arrived at an eminence from which an extensive view could
be obtained. Here their companion motioned to them to lie
down and watch his proceedings. They did so, and saw him
make a wide circuit and work up toward the herd of deer.

"They will be off long before he can get within bow-shot," Tom said; "look, they are getting fidgety already, they scent danger, and he is four hundred yards away. They will be off in a minute. Look, what on earth is he doing?"

The Indian was lying on his back, his body being almost concealed by the grass, which was a foot high. In the air he waved his legs to and fro, twisting and twining them. The boys could not help laughing at the curious appearance of the two black objects waving slowly about. The herd of deer stood staring stupidly at the spectacle. Then, as if moved by a common impulse of curiosity, they began slowly to approach in order to investigate more closely this singular phenomenon. Frequently they stopped, but only to continue their advance, which was made with a sort of circling movement, as if to see the object from all sides. Nearer and nearer they approached, until the leaders were not more than fifty yards away, when the native leaped to his feet and discharged his arrows with such rapidity and accuracy that two of the animals fell before they could dart away out of range. The lads soon joined the native, and expressed their approval of his skill. Then while he threw one carcass over his shoulder they divided the weight of the other between them, and so accompanied him into camp.

The next day Ned and Tom, walking to an eminence near the camp, saw in the distance some ostriches feeding. Returning to the huts they found the young hunter whom they had accompanied on the preceding day, and beckoned to him to accompany them. When they reached the spot from which the ostriches were visible they motioned to him to come out and shoot them. He at once nodded.

As they were about to follow him back to camp for their bows and arrows, he shook his head and signed to them to stay where they were, and going off by himself returned with his bow and arrow, and, to the surprise of the boys, the skin of an ostrich.

To show the lads what he intended to do he put on the skin, sticking one arm up the long neck, his black legs alone showing. He now imitated the motions of the bird, now stalking along, now picking up bits of grass, and this with such an admirable imitation of nature that Ned and Tom shouted with laughter. The three then set off together, taking a line which hid them from the view of the ostriches. The Indian at last led them to a small eminence and signed to them to ascend this, and there to lie down and watch the result. On arriving at their post they found themselves about a quarter of a mile from the group of great birds.

It seemed a long time before they could see any signs of the native, who had to make a long detour so as to approach the birds up wind. About a hundred and fifty yards from the spot where they were feeding was a clump of bushes, and presently the lads suddenly beheld an ostrich feeding quietly beside this clump.

"There was no bird near those bushes two minutes ago," Tom said, "it must be the Indian."

Very quietly and by degrees the ostrich approached the group. When within four yards of them, the ostrich, as if by magic, vanished, and an Indian stood in his place. In another moment his bow twanged and the ostrich next to him fell over, pierced through with an arrow; while the rest of the flock scattered over the plain at an immense speed. Ned and Tom now rose to their feet and ran down the slope to the Indian, who was standing by the dead bird. He pulled out the tail feathers and handed them to them, cut off the head and legs, opened and cleaned the body, and then putting it on his shoulder started again for the camp.

For another week they remained in the Indian village, and in that time picked up a good many native words. They then determined that they must be starting on their westward journey. They therefore called upon the chief and explained to him by signs eked out with a few words, that they must leave him and go toward the setting sun. The grief of the chief was great, as was that of the tribe when he communicated the tidings to them. There was great talking among the groups round the fire that night, and Ned saw that some question was being debated at great length. The next morning the chief and several of the leading men came into their hut, and the chief made a speech accompanied with great gesticulation. The lads gathered that he was imploring them not to leave them, and pointing out that there would be hostile Indians on the road who would attack them. Then the chief led them to the fires and signed that if they went out the tribe would be cold again, and would be unable to cook their food.

Already, indeed, on one occasion after a great feast the tribe had slept so soundly that all the fires were out before morning, and Ned had been obliged to have recourse to his flint and steel. After this two fires had been kept constantly burning night and day; others were lighted for cooking, but these were tended constantly, and Ned saw that there was little chance of their ever going out together so long as the tribe remained in the village.

Now, however, he proceeded to show them how to carry fire with them. Taking one blazing stick and starting out as for a journey he showed that the fire gradually went out. Then he returned to the fire and took two large pieces, and started, keeping them so crossed that the parts on fire were always in contact. In this way, as he showed them, fire could be kept in for a very long time; and that if two brands were taken from each fire there would be little difficulty in keeping fire perpetually.

Finally, he showed them how in case of losing fire in spite of all these precautions, it could be recovered by means of friction. He took two pieces of dried wood; one being very hard grained and the other much softer. Of the former he cut a stick of about a foot long and an inch round, and pointed at both ends. In the other he made a small hole. Then he unstrung one end of a bowstring, twisted it once round the stick, and strung it again. Then he put one point of the stick in the hole in the other piece of wood, which he laid upon the ground. Round the hole he crumbled into dust some dry fungus. On the upper end of the short stick he placed a flat stone, which he bade one of the natives press with moderate force. Now working the bow rapidly backwards and forwards the stick was spun round and round like a drill. The Indians, who were unable to make out what Ned was doing, watched these proceedings with great attention. When a little smoke began to curl up from the heated wood they understood at once, and shouted with wonder. In a few minutes sparks began to fly from the stick, and as these fell on the dried fungus they rapidly spread. Tom knelt down and blew gently upon them, adding a few dried leaves, and in another minute a bright flame sprang up.

The natives were delighted; they had new means of making fire, and could in future enjoy warmth and cooked food, and their gratitude to the lads was unbounded. Hitherto they had feared that when these strange white beings departed they would lose their fires, and return to their former cheerless existence, when the long winter evenings had to be spent in cold and darkness. That evening the chief intimated to his visitors that he and a portion of the men of the tribe would accompany them for some distance, the women remaining behind with the rest of the fighting men as their guard. This decision pleased the young men much, for they could not hope to go far without meeting other tribes, and although, as had been found in the present instance, the gift of fire would be sure to propititate the Indians, it was probable that they might be attacked on the march and killed without having an opportunity of explanation. Their friends, however, would have the power of at once explaining to all comers the valuable benefits which they could bestow.

During the time that they had been staying in the village they had further improved their bows by taking them to pieces, fitting the parts more accurately together, and gluing them with glue prepared by boiling down sinews of animals in a gourd. Then rebinding them with fine sinews, they found that they were in all respects equal to their English weapons. They had now no fear as to their power of maintaining themselves with food on the way, and felt that, even when their new friends should leave them, they would have a fair chance of defending themselves against attack, as their bows would carry more than thrice as far as those of the natives.

The following morning the start was made. The chief and twenty picked warriors accompanied them, together with six young Indians, two of whom carried lighted brands; the others dragged light sleighs, upon which were piled skins and long poles for making tents at night, for the temperature was exceedingly cold after sundown. The whole village turned out to see the party off, and shouts of farewell and good wishes rang in the air.

For the first three days no adventures were met with. The party had no difficulty in killing game sufficient for their needs, and at night they halted at streams or pools. Ned observed, however, that at the last halting-place the chief, who had hitherto taken no precaution at night, gave some orders to his followers, four of whom, when the rest laid down to rest, glided off in different directions into the darkness.

Ned pointed to them inquiringly, and the chief intimated that they were now entering the hunting-grounds of another tribe. The following day the band kept closely together. A vigilant look-out on the plains was kept up, and no straggling was allowed. They had sufficient meat left over from their their spoils of the day before to last for the day, and no hunting was necessary.

The next evening, just as they had retired to rest, one of the scouts came in and reported that he heard sounds around which betokened the presence of man. The calls of animals were heard on the plain, and a herd of deer which had evidently been disturbed, had darted past at full speed.

The chief now ordered great quantities of dried wood to be thrown into the fire, and a vast blaze soon shot up high, illuminating a circle of a hundred yards in diameter. Advancing to the edge of this circle the chief held out his arms to show that he was unarmed, and then shouted at the top of his voice to the effect that he invited all within hearing to come forward in peace. The strange appearance that they saw was a boon given to the Indian people by two great white beings who were in his camp, and that by its aid there would be no more cold.

Three times he shouted out these words, and then retired to the fire and sat down. Presently from the circle of darkness a number of figures appeared, approaching timidly and with an awe-struck air until within a short distance of the fire.

Then the chief again rose and bade them welcome. There were some fifty or sixty of them, but Ned and his friend had no fear of any treachery, for they were evidently under the spell of a sense of amazement greater than that which had been excited among those they first met, and this because they first saw this wonder by night.

When the new-comers had taken their seats the chief explained to them the qualities of their new discovery. That it made them warm and comfortable their own feelings told them; and on the morrow, when they had meat, he would show them how great were its effects. Then he told them of the dancing water, and how it softened and made delicious the vegetables placed in it. At his command one of his followers took two brands, carried them to a distance, and soon lighted another fire.

During the narrative the faces of the Indians lighted up with joy, and they cast glances of reverence and gratitude toward the young white men. These finding that amity was now established retired to sleep to the little skin tents which had been raised for them, while the Indians remained sitting round the fire engrossed with its wonders.

The young men slept late next morning, knowing that no move could be made that day. When they came out of the tents they found that the natives had lost no time. Before daybreak hunting parties had gone out, and a store of game was piled near the fire, or rather fires, for a dozen were now burning, and the strangers were being initiated in the art of cooking by their hosts.

Two days were spent here, and then after much talk the tribe at which they had now arrived arranged to escort and pass the boys on to their neighbors, while the first party returned to their village. Ned and Tom were consulted before this matter was settled, and approved of it. It was better that they should be passed on from tribe to tribe than that they should be escorted all the way by a guard who would be as strange as themselves to the country, and who would naturally be longing to return to their homes and families.

For some weeks the life led by the travellers resembled that which has been described. Sometimes they waited for a few days at villages where great festivities were held in their honor. The news of their coming in many cases preceded them, and they and their convoy were often met at the stream, or other mark which formed the acknowledged boundary between the hunting-grounds, by large bodies eager to receive and welcome them.

They had by this time made considerable progress in the language, knew all the names of common objects, and could make themselves understood in simple matters. The language of savage people is always simple; their range of ideas is narrow; their vocabulary very limited, and consequently easily mastered. Ned knew that at any time they might come across people in a state of active warfare with each other, and that his life might depend upon the ability to make himself understood, consequently he lost no opportunity of picking up the language. On the march Tom and he, instead of walking and talking together, each went with a group of natives and kept up a conversation, eked out with signs, with them, and consequently they made very considerable progress with the language.

CHAPTER XIII

Through the Cordilleras

After three months of steady travel, the country, which had become more and more hilly as they advanced toward the west, assumed a different character. The hills became mountains, and it was clear that they were arriving at a great range running north and south. They had for some time left the broad plains behind them, and game was very scarce. The Indians had of late been more and more disinclined to go far to the west, and the tribe with whom they were now travelling told them that they could go no farther. They signified that beyond the mountains dwelt many tribes with whom they were unacquainted, but who were fierce and warlike. One of the party, who had once crossed, said that the people there had fires like those which the white men had taught them to make.

"You see, Tom," Ned said, "they must have been in contact with the Spaniards, or at least with tribes who have learned something from the Spaniards. In that case our supernatural power will be at an end, and our color will be against us, as they will regard us as Spaniards, and so as enemies. At any rate we must push on and take our chance."

From the Indians they learned that the track lay up a valley before them, and that after a day's walking they would have to begin the ascent. Another day's journey would take them to a neck between two peaks, and the passage of this would occupy at least a day. The native described the cold as great here even in summer, and that in winter it was terrible. Once across the neck the descent on the other side began.

"There can be no snow in the pass now, Tom; it is late in

158

December, and the hottest time of the year; and although we must be a very great height above the sea, for we have been rising ever since we left the coast, we are not so very far south, and I cannot believe the snow can now lie in the pass. Let us take a good stock of dried meat, a skin for water—we can fill it at the head of the valley—and make our way forward. I do not think the sea can lie very far on the other side of this range of mountains, but at any rate we must wait no longer. Captain Drake may have passed already, but we may still be in time."

The next morning they bade adieu to their companions, with whom they had been travelling for a fortnight. These, glad again to turn their faces homeward, set off at once, and the lads, shouldering their packs, started up the valley. The scenery was grand in the extreme, and Ned and Tom greatly enjoyed it. Sometimes the sides approached in perpendicular precipices, leaving barely room for the little stream to find its way between their feet; at others it was half a mile wide. When the rocks were not precipitous the sides were clothed with a luxuriant foliage, among which the birds maintained a concert of call and song. So sheltered were they that, high as it was above the sea, the heat was very oppressive, and when they reached the head of the valley late in the afternoon they were glad indeed of a bathe in a pool of the stream.

Choosing a spot of ground near the stream, the lads soon made a fire, put their pieces of venison down to roast, and prepared for a quiet evening.

"It seems strange to be alone again, Tom, after so many months with those Indians, who were ever on the watch for every movement and word, as if they were inspired. It is six months now since we left the western coast, and one almost seems to forget that one is English. We have picked up something of half a dozen Indian dialects; we can use their weapons almost as well as they can themselves; and as to our skins, they are as brown as that of the darkest of them. The difficulty will be to persuade the people on the other side that we are whites."

"How far do you think the sea lies on the other side of this range of giant mountains?" Tom asked.

"I have no idea," Ned replied, "and I do not suppose that any one else has. The Spaniards keep all matters connected with this coast a mystery; but I believe that the sea cannot be many days' march beyond the mountains."

For an hour or two they chatted quietly, their thoughts naturally turning again to England and the scenes of their boyhood.

"Will it be necessary to watch, think you?" Tom asked.

"I think it would be safer, Tom; one never knows. I believe that we are now beyond the range of the natives of the Pampas. They evidently have a fear of approaching the hills; but that only shows that the natives from the other side come down over here. I believe that they were, when the Spaniards landed, peaceable people, quiet and gentle. So at least they are described. But those who take to the mountains must be either escaped slaves, or fugitives from the cruelty of the Spaniards, and even the gentlest man, when driven to desperation, becomes savage and cruel. To these men our white skins would be like a red rag to a bull. They can never have heard of any white people save the Spaniards, and we need expect little mercy if we fall into their hands. I think we had better watch, turn about; I will take the first watch, for I am not at all sleepy, and my thoughts seem busy tonight with home."

Tom was soon fast asleep, and Ned sat quietly watching the embers of the fire, occasionally throwing on fresh sticks, until he deemed that nearly half the night was gone. Then he aroused his companion and lay down himself, and was soon fast asleep.

The gray light was just beginning to break when he was aroused by a sudden yell, accompanied by a cry from Tom. He leaped to his feet just in time to see a crowd of natives rush upon himself and his comrade, discharging as they did so numbers of small arrows, several of which pierced him as he rose to his feet. Before they could grasp their bows or any other weapons the natives were upon them. Blows were showered down with heavy clubs, and although the lads made a desperate resistance they were beaten to the ground in a short time. The natives at once twisted strong thongs round their limbs, and then dragging them from the fire, sat down themselves and proceeded to roast the remains of the boys' deer-meat.

"This is bad business, indeed, Tom," Ned said. "These men doubtless take us for Spaniards. They certainly must belong to the other side of the mountains, for their appearance and language are altogether different to those of the people we have been staying with. These men are much smaller, slighter, and fairer. Runaways though no doubt they are, they seem to have more care about their persons, and to be more civilized in their appearance and weapons, than the savages of the plains."

"What do you think they will do with us, Ned?"

"I have no doubt in the world, Tom, that their intention is either to put us to death with some horrible torture, or to roast us. The Spaniards have taught them these things if they did not know them before, and in point of atrocities nothing can possibly exceed those which the Spaniards have inflicted upon them and their fathers."

Whatever were the intentions of the Indians it was soon evident that there would be some delay in carrying them out. After they had finished their meal they rose from the fire. Some amused themselves by making arrows from the straight reeds that grew by the stream. Others wandered listlessly about. Some threw themselves upon the ground and slept, while others coming up to the boys, poured torrents of invective upon them, among which they could distinguish in Spanish the words "dog" and "Spaniard," varying their abuse by violent kicks. As, however, these were given by the naked feet, they did not seriously inconvenience the boys.

"What can they be waiting for?" Tom said. "Why don't they do something if they are going to do it?"

"I expect," Ned answered, "that they are waiting for some chief, or for the arrival of some other band, and that we are to be kept for a grand exhibition."

So it proved. Three days passed, and upon the fourth another band, smaller in numbers, joined them. Upon the evening of that day the lads saw that their fate was about to be brought to a crisis. The fire was made up with huge bundles of wood; the natives took their seats around it with gravity and order; and the boys were led forward by four natives armed with spears. Then began

what was a regular trial. The boys, although they could not understand a word of the language, could yet follow the speeches of the
excited orators. One after another arose and told the tale of the
treatment that he had experienced. One showed the wheals
which covered his back. Another held up his arm from which the
hand had been lopped. A third pointed to the places where his
ears once had been. Another showed the sear of a hot iron on his
arms and legs. Some went through a pantomime which told its
tale of an attack upon some solitary hut, the slaughter of the old
and infirm, and the dragging away of the men and women into
slavery. Others spoke of long periods of labor in a bent position in
a mine under the cruel whip of the task-master. All had their tale
of barbarity and cruelty to recite, and as each speaker contributed
his quota the anger and excitement of the rest rose.

"Poor devils!" Ned said; "no wonder that they are savage
against us. See what they have suffered at the hands of the white
men. If we had gone through as much, you may be sure that we
should spare none. Our only chance is to make them understand
that we are not Spanish, and that, I fear, is beyond all hope."

This speedily proved to be the case. Two or three of the natives who spoke a few words of Spanish came to them, calling
them Spanish dogs. Ned shook his head and said, "Not
Spanish." For all reply the natives pointed to the uncovered portions of their body, pulled back the skins which covered their
arms, and pointing to the white flesh, laughed incredulously.

"White men are Spaniards, and Spaniards are white men,"
Tom groaned, "and that we shall have to die for the cruelty
which the Spaniards have perpetrated is clear enough."

"Well, Tom, we have had more good fortune than we could
have expected. We might have been killed on the day when we
landed, and we have spent six jolly months in wandering together as hunters on the plain. If we must die, let us behave like
Englishmen and Christians. It may be that our lives have not
been as good as they should have been; but so far as we know,
we have both done our duty, and it may be that, as we die for the
faults of others, it may come to be considered as a balance
against our own faults."

"We must hope so, Ned. I think we have both done, I won't say our best, but as well as could be expected in so rough a life. We have followed the exhortations of the good chaplain and have never joined in the riotous ways of the sailors in general. We must trust that the good God will forgive us our sins, and strengthen us to go though this last trial."

While they had been speaking the natives had made an end of their deliberation. Tom was now conducted by two natives with spears to a tree and was securely fastened. Ned, under the guard of the other two, was left by the fire. The tree was situated at a distance of some twenty yards from it, and the natives mostly took their place near the fire. Some scattered among the bushes and presently reappeared bearing bundles of dry wood. These were laid in order round the tree at such a distance that the flames would not touch the prisoner, but the heat would gradually roast him to death.

As Ned observed the preparations for the execution of his friend the sweat stood in great drops on his forehead, and he would have given anything to be able to rush to his assistance and to die with him. Had his hands been free he would, without hesitation, have snatched up a bow and sent an arrow into Tom's heart to release him from the lingering death which awaited him, and he would then have stabbed himself with a spear. But while his hands were sufficiently free to move a little, the fastenings were too tight to admit of his carrying out any plan of that sort.

Suddenly an idea struck him, and he began nervously to tug at his fastenings. The natives when they seized them had bound them without examining their clothes. It was improbable that men in savage attire could have about them any articles worth appropriating. The knives, indeed, which hung from their belts had been cut off; but these were the only articles which had been touched. Just as a man approached the fire, and, seizing a brand, stooped forward to light the pyre, Ned succeeded in freeing his hands sufficiently to seize the object which he sought. This was his powder-flask, which was wrapped in the folds of the cloth round his waist. With little difficulty he succeeded in freeing it, and, moving a step closer to the fire, he cast it into the midst of it at the very moment the man with the lighted brand was approaching Tom. Then he stepped back as far as he could from the fire.

The natives on guard over him, not understanding the movement, and thinking he meditated flight, closed around him.

An instant later there was a tremendous explosion. The red hot embers were flaming in all directions, and both Ned and the savages who stood by him were, with many others, struck to the ground. As soon as he was able Ned struggled up again.

Not a native was in sight. A terrific yell had broken from them at the explosion, which sounded to them like one of the cannons of the Spanish oppressors, and smarting with the wounds simultaneously made by the hot brands, each, without a moment's thought, had taken to his heels. Tom gave a shout of exultation as Ned rose. The latter at once stooped and with difficulty picked up one of the still blazing brands and hurried toward the tree.

"If these fellows will remain away for a couple of minutes, Tom, you shall be free," he said, "and I don't think they will get over their scare as quickly as that."

So saying, he applied the end of the burning brand to the dry withes with which Tom was bound to the tree. These at once took fire and flared up, and the bands fell to the ground.

"Now, Tom, do me the same service."

This was quickly rendered, and the lads stood free.

"Now let us get our weapons."

A short search revealed to them their bows laid carefully aside, while the ground was scattered with the arms which the natives in their panic had dropped.

"Pick them all up, Tom, and toss them on the fire. We will take the sting out of the snake, in case it tries to attack us again."

In a minute or two a score of bows, spears, and other weapons were thrown on the fire, and the boys then, leaving the place which had so nearly proved fatal to them, took their way up the mountain side.

It was a long pull, the more so that they had the food, water, and large skins for protection from the night air to carry. Steadily as they kept on, with only an occasional halt for breath, it was late before they emerged from the forest and stood upon a plateau between two lofty hills. This was bare and treeless, and the keen wind made them shiver as they met it.

"We will creep among the trees, Tom, and be off at daybreak to-morrow. However long the journey, we must get across the pass before we sleep, for the cold there would be terrible." A little way down the crest it was so warm that they needed no fire, while a hundred feet higher, exposed to the wind from the snow-covered peaks, the cold was intense. They kept careful watch, but the night passed quietly. The next morning they were on foot as soon as the voices of the birds proclaimed the approach of day. As they emerged from the shelter of the trees they threw their deer-skins round them to act as cloaks, and stepped out at their best pace. The dawn of day was yet faint in the east, the stars burning bright as lamps overhead in the clear thin air, and the cold was so great that it almost stopped their breathing. Half an hour later the scene had changed altogether. The sun had risen, and the air felt warm. The many peaks on either side glistened in the flood of bright light. The walking was easy indeed after the climb of the previous day, and their burdens were much lightened by their consumption of food and water. The pass was of irregular width, sometimes but a hundred yards, sometimes fully a mile across. Long habit and practice with the Indians had immensely improved their walking powers, and with long elastic strides they put mile after mile behind them. Long before the sun was at its highest a little stream ran beside them, and they saw by the course of its waters that they had passed the highest part of the pass through the Cordilleras.

Three hours later they suddenly emerged from a part where the hills approached nearer on either side than they had done during the day's walk, and a mighty landscape opened before and below them. The boys gave simultaneously a loud shout of joy, and then dropped on their knees in thanks to God, for far away in the distance was a dark level blue line, and they knew the ocean was before them.

"How far off should you say it was, Ned," Tom asked, when they had recovered a little from their first outburst of joy.

"A long way off," Ned said; "I suppose we must be fifteen thousand feet above it, and even in this transparent air it looks an immense distance away. I should say it must be a hundred miles."

"That's nothing!" Tom said; "we could do it in two days, in three easily."

"Yes, supposing we had no interruption and a straight road," Ned said. "But we must not count our chickens yet. This vast forest which we see contains tribes of natives bitterly hostile to the white man, maddened by the cruelties of the Spaniards, who enslave them and treat them worse than dogs. Even when we reach the sea we may be a hundred or two hundred miles from a large Spanish town, and however great the distance, we must accomplish it, as it is only at large towns that Captain Drake is likely to touch."

"Well, let us be moving," Tom said; "I am strong for some hours' walking yet, and every day will take us nearer to the sea."

"We need not carry our deer-skins any farther," Ned said, throwing his down. "We shall be sweltering under the heat to-morrow below there."

Even before they halted for the night the vegetation had assumed a tropical character, for they had already descended some five thousand feet.

"I wish we could contrive to make a fire to-night," Ned said.

"Why?" Tom asked; "I am bathed in perspiration now."

"We shall not want it for heat, but the chances are that there are wild beasts of all sorts in this forest."

Ned's premises turned out correct, for scarcely had night fallen when they heard deep roarings, and lost no time in ascending a tree, and making themselves fast there, before they went to sleep.

In the morning they proceeded upon their journey. After walking a couple of hours Ned laid his arm upon Tom's shoulder. "Hush!" he whispered; "look there."

Through the trees, at a short distance off, could be seen a

stag. He was standing gazing intently at a tree, and did not appear to have heard their approach.

"What can he be up to?" Tom whispered. "He must have heard us."

"He seems paralyzed," Ned said. "Don't you see how he is trembling? There must be some wild beast in the tree."

Both gazed attentively at the tree, but could see nothing to account for the attitude of the deer.

"Wild beast or no," Ned said, "he will do for our dinner."

So saying, he unslung his bow, and fitted an arrow; there was a sharp twang, and the deer rolled over, struck to the heart. There was no movement in the tree, but Ned placed another arrow in place; Tom had done the same.

They stood silent for a few minutes, but all was still.

"Keep your eyes on the tree and advance slowly," Ned said. "Have your sword ready in case of need. I cannot help thinking there is something there, though what it is I can't make out."

Slowly, and with the greatest caution, they approached the tree. All was perfectly still.

"No beast big enough to hurt us can be up there," Ned said at last; "none of the branches are thick enough to hide him. Now for the stag."

Ned bent over the carcass of the deer, which lay a few feet only from the tree. Then suddenly there was a rapid movement among the creepers which embraced the trunk, something swept between Ned and Tom, knocking the latter to the ground, while a cry of alarm and astonishment rose from Ned.

Confused and surprised Tom sprang to his feet, instinctively drawing his sword as he did so. For a moment he stood paralyzed with horror. A gigantic snake had wound its coils round Ned's body. Its head towered above his, while its eyes flashed menacingly, and its tongue vibrated with a hissing sound as it gazed at Tom; its tail was wound round the trunk of the tree.

Ned was powerless, for his arms were pinioned to his side by the coils of the reptile. It was but a moment that Tom stood appalled. He knew that at any instant by the tightening of its folds the great boa could crush every bone of Ned's body; while

A MOMENT OF PERIL
SEE PAGE 167.

the very closeness of its embrace rendered it impossible for him to strike at it for fear of injuring its captive. There was not an instant to be lost. Already the coils were tightening, and a hoarse cry broke from Ned. With a rapid spring Tom leaped beyond his friend, and with a blow, delivered with all his strength, severed the portion of the tail coiled round the tree from the rest of the body.

Unknowingly he had taken the only course to save Ned's life. Had he, as his first impulse had been, struck at the head as it raised itself above that of Ned, the convulsion of the rest of the body would probably have crushed the life out of him; but by cutting off the tail he separated the body from the tree which formed the fulcrum upon which it acted.

As swiftly as they had inclosed him the coils fell from Ned a writhing mass upon the ground, and a second blow from Tom's sword severed the head from the body. Even now the folds writhed and twisted like an injured worm; but Tom struck and struck until the fragments lay, with only a slight quivering motion in them, on the ground.

Then Tom throwing down his cutlass, raised Ned, who, upon being released from the embrace of the boa, had fallen senseless. Alarmed as Tom was at his comrade's insensibility, he yet felt that it was the shock and the revulsion of feeling which caused it, and not any serious injury which he had received. No bones had been heard to crack, and although the compression had been severe, Tom did not think that any serious injury had been inflicted.

He dashed some water from the skins over Ned's face, rubbed his hands, spoke to him in a loud voice, and ere long had the satisfaction of seeing him open his eyes.

"Thank God!" Tom exclaimed, fervently. "There, don't move, Ned, take it quietly, it's all right now. There, drink a little water."

He poured a few drops down Ned's throat, and the latter, whose eyes had before had a dazed and wondering expression, suddenly sat up and strove to draw his sword. "Gently, Ned, gently; the snake is dead, chopped up into pieces. It was a near shave, Ned."

CHAPTER XIV

On the Pacific Coast

"A close shave indeed," Ned said, raising himself with difficulty from the ground. "Another moment and I think my ribs would have given in. It seemed as if all the blood in my body had rushed in my head."

"Do you feel badly hurt?" Tom asked, anxiously.

"No," Ned said, feeling himself all over. "Horribly bruised, but nothing broken. To think of our not seeing that monstrous boa! I don't think," he continued, "that I can walk any farther to-day. I feel shaken all over."

"Then we will camp where we are," Tom said, cheerfully. "We have got a stag, and he will last us for some days, if necessary. There is plenty of fruit to be picked in the forest, and on this mountain side we are sure to be able to find water within a short distance."

Lighting a fire, the deer was soon cut up, and the lads prepared to spend a quiet day, which was all the more welcome inasmuch as for the last three weeks they had travelled without intermission.

The next day Ned declared himself well enough to proceed on his journey; but his friend persuaded him to stop for another day.

Late in the evening Ned exclaimed, "What is that, Tom, behind that tree?"

Tom seized his bow and leaped to his feet.

"I see nothing," he said.

"It was either a native or a gigantic monkey. I saw him quite plainly glide along behind the tree."

Tom advanced cautiously, but on reaching the tree he found nothing.

"You are sure you were not mistaken?" he asked.

"Quite certain," Ned said. "We have seen enough of Indians by this time to know them. We must be on the lookout to-night. The natives on this side are not like those beyond the mountains. They have been so horribly ill-treated by the Spaniards that they must hate any white face, and would kill us without hesitation if they got a chance. We shall have difficulty with the Spaniards when we fall into their hands, but they will at least be more reasonable than these savages."

All night they kept up their fire and sat up by turns on watch. Several times they thought that they heard slight movements among the fallen leaves and twigs; but these might have been caused by any prowling beast. Once or twice they fancied that they detected forms moving cautiously just beyond the range of the firelight, but they could not be certain that it was so.

Just as morning was breaking Ned sprang to his feet.

"Wake up, Tom!" he exclaimed; "we are attacked"; and as he spoke an arrow quivered in the tree just over his head.

They had already discussed whether it would be better to remain, if attacked, in the light of the fire or to retreat into the shadow, and concluding that the eyes of the natives would be more accustomed to see in darkness than their own, they had determined to stay by the fire, throwing themselves down on their faces, and to keep the natives at bay beyond the circle of the light of the flames till daylight. They had in readiness heaped a great pile of brushwood, and this they now threw upon the fire, making a high pyramid of flame which lit the wood around for a circle of sixty yards. As the light leaped up Ned discharged an arrow at a native whom he saw within the circle of light, and a shrill cry proclaimed that it had reached its mark. There was silence for a while in the dark forest, and each moment that passed the daylight became stronger and stronger.

"In ten minutes we shall be able to move on," Ned said, "and in the daylight I think that the longer range of our bows will enable us to keep them off. The question is how many of them are there."

A very short time sufficed to show that the number of the savages was large, for shrill cries were heard answering each other in the circle around them, and numbers of black figures could be seen hanging about the trees in the distance.

"I don't like the look of things, Ned," Tom said. "It is all very well; we may shoot a good many before they reach us, and in the open no doubt we might keep them off. But by taking advantage of the trees they will be able to get within range of their weapons, and at short distances they are just as effective as are our bows.

As soon as it was broad daylight the lads started through the forest, keeping up a running fight with the natives.

"It is clear," Tom said, "we cannot stand this much longer. We must take to a tree."

They were on the point of climbing when Ned exclaimed, "Listen! I can hear the sound of bells."

Listening intently they could make out the sound of little bells such as are carried by horses or mules.

"It must be a train to one of the mines. If we can reach that we shall be safe."

Laying aside all further thought of fighting, the boys now ran at headlong pace in the direction of the sounds. The natives, who were far fleeter of foot, gained fast upon them, and the arrows were flying round them, and several had inflicted slight wounds, when they heard ahead of them the cry of "Soldiers on guard. The natives are at hand; fire in the bushes."

The boys threw themselves upon their faces as from the thickets ahead a volley of musketry was heard.

"Load again," was the order, in Spanish. "These black rascals must be strong indeed to advance to attack us with so much noise."

Crawling forward cautiously, Ned exclaimed in Spanish, "Do not fire, senors; we are two Spaniards who have been carried away from the settlements, and have for long been prisoners among the natives."

A cry of surprise was heard, and then the Spaniard in command called them to advance fearlessly. This they did. Fortunately they had long before settled upon the story that they would tell when they arrived among the Spaniards. To have owned themselves Englishmen, and as belonging to the dreaded buccaneers would have been to ensure their imprisonment, if not execution. The imperfection of Ned's Spanish, and the fact that Tom was quite ignorant of the language, rendered it difficult for them to pass as Spaniards. But they thought that by giving out that they had been carried away in childhood—Tom at an earlier age than Ned—their ignorance of the language would be accounted for.

It had been a struggle with both of them to decide upon telling an untruth. This is a point upon which differences of opinion must always arise. Some will assert that under no circumstances can a falsehood be justified. Others will say that to deceive an enemy in war or to save life, deceit is justifiable, especially when that deceit injures no one. It was only after very great hesitation that the boys had overcome their natural instincts and teaching, and agreed to conceal their nationality under false colors. Ned, indeed, held out for a long time; but Tom had cited many examples from ancient and modern history, showing that people of all nations had, to deceive an enemy, adopted such a course, and that to throw away their lives rather than tell a falsehood which could hurt no one would be an act of folly. Both, however, determined that should it become necessary to keep up their character as Spaniards by pretending to be true Catholics, they would disclose the truth.

The first sight of the young men struck the captain of the Spanish escort with astonishment. Bronzed to the darkest brown by the sun of the plains and by the hardships they had undergone, dressed in the skins of animals, and carrying weapons altogether uncouth and savage to the Spanish eye, he found it difficult to believe that these figures were those of his countrymen. His first question, however, concerned the savages who had, as he supposed, attacked his escort. A few words from Ned, however, explained the circumstances, and that the yells he had heard had been uttered by the Indians pursuing them, and had no reference whatever to the convoy. This consisted of some two hundred mules, laden with provisions and implements on its way to the mines. Guarded by a hundred soldiers were a large number of natives, who, fastened together as slaves, were on their way up to work for their cruel taskmasters.

When the curiosity of the captain concerning the natives was allayed, he asked Ned where he and his comrade had sprung from. Ned assured him that the story was a very long one and that at a convenient opportunity he would enter into all details. In the first place he asked that civilized clothes might be given to them, for, as he said, they looked and felt at present rather as wild men of the woods than as subjects of the king of Spain.

"You speak a very strange Spanish," the captain said.

"I only wonder," Ned replied, "that I speak in Spanish at all. I was but a child when I was carried away, and since that time I have scarcely spoken a word of my native tongue. When I reached the village to which my captors conveyed me I found my companion here, who was, as I could see, a Spaniard, but who must have been carried off as an infant, as he even then could speak no Spanish whatever. He has learned now from me a few words; but beyond that is wholly ignorant."

"This is a strange story, indeed," the captain said. "Where was it that your parents lived?"

"I know not the place," Ned said. "But it was far to the rising sun across on the other ocean."

As it seemed perfectly possible that the boys might have been carried away as children from the settlements near Vera Cruz, the captain accepted the story without the slightest doubt and at once gave a warm welcome to the lads, who had, as he supposed, escaped after so many weary years of captivity.

"I am going up now," he said, "to the mines, and there must remain on duty for a fortnight, when I shall return in charge of treasure. It will be dangerous, indeed, for you to attempt to find your way to the coast without escort. Therefore you had better come on with me and return under my protection to the coast."

"We should be glad of a stay with you in the mountains," Ned said. "We feel so ignorant of everything European that we should be glad to learn from you a little of the ways of our countrymen before we venture down among them. What is the nearest town on the coast?"

"Arica," the captain said, "is the port from which we have come. It is distant a hundred and thirty miles from here, and we have had ten days' hard journeying through the forest."

For the next fortnight the lads remained at the mines. These were worked by the Spaniards entirely by slave labor. Nominal wages were indeed given to the unfortunates who labored there. But they were as much slaves as if they had been sold. The Spaniards, indeed, treated the whole of the natives in the provinces occupied by them as creatures to be used mercilessly for labor, and as having no more feeling than the lower animals. The number of these unfortunates who perished in the mines from hard work and cruel treatment is beyond all calculation. But it may be said that of the enormous treasures drawn by Spain from her South American possessions during the early days of her occupation, every doubloon was watered with blood. The boys, who had for nearly six months lived among the Indians and had seen their many fine qualities, were horrified at the sights which they witnessed; and several times had the greatest difficulty to restrain their feelings of indignation and horror. They agreed, however, that it would be worse than useless to give vent to such opinions. It would only draw upon them the suspicion of the Spaniards, and would set the authorities at the mine and the captain of the escort against them, and might prejudice the first report that would be sent down to Arica concerning them.

During the first few days of their stay the boys acted their parts with much internal amusement. The pretended to be absolutely ignorant of civilized feeding, seized the meat raw and tore it with their fingers; sat upon the ground in preference to chairs; and in every way behaved as persons altogether ignorant of civilization. Gradually, however, they permitted themselves to be taught, and delighted their entertainers by their docility and willingness. The Spaniards were indeed somewhat surprised by

the whiteness of their skin where sheltered from the sun, and by
the lightness of their hair and eyes. The boys could hear many
comments upon them, and wondering remarks why they should
be so much fairer than their countrymen in general. As, however, it was clearly useless to ask them, none of the Spaniards
thought of doing so.

The end of the fortnight arrived, and under the charge of the
escort the lads set out, together with twenty mules laden with
silver for the coast. They had no longer any fear of the attacks of
the natives, or any trouble connected with their food supply, an
ample stock of provisions being carried upon spare mules. They
themselves were mounted, and greatly enjoyed the journey
through the magnificent forests. They were, indeed, a little un-
easy as to the examination which they were sure to have to
undergo at Arica, and which was likely to be very much more severe and searching than that to which the good-natured captain
had subjected them. They longed to ask him whether any news
had been heard of the arrival of an English squadron upon the
western coast. But it was impossible to do this without giving
rise to suspicion, and they had the consolation at least of having
heard no single word concerning their countrymen uttered in
the conversations at the mine. Had Captain Francis Drake and
his companions arrived upon the coast, it was almost certain that
their presence there would be the all-absorbing topic among the
Spanish colonists.

Upon their arrival at Arica the boys were conducted at once
to the governor—a stern and haughty-looking Spaniard, who
received the account given by the captain with an air of incredulity.

"This is a strange tale indeed," he said, "and passes all probability. Why should these children have been kidnapped on the
eastern coast and brought across the continent. It is more likely
that they belong to this side. However, they could not be male-
factors who have escaped into the forest, for their age forbids
any idea of that kind. They must have been stolen. But I do not
recall any such event as the carrying off of the sons of Spaniards
here for many years back. However, this can be inquired into

when they learn to speak our language well. In the meantime they had better be assigned quarters in the barracks. Let them be instructed in military exercises and in our language."

"And," said an ecclesiastic, who was sitting at the table, "in our holy religion, for methinks, stolen away as they were in their youth, they can be no better than pagans."

Tom had difficulty in repressing a desire to glance at Ned as these words were spoken. But the eyes of the governor were fixed so intently upon them that he feared to exhibit any emotion whatever. He resolved mentally, however, that his progress in Spanish should be exceedingly small, and that many months should elapse before he could possibly receive even rudimentary instruction in religious matters.

The life in the barracks at Arica resembled pretty closely that which they had led so long on board ship. The soldiers received them with good feeling and *camaraderie,* and they were soon completely at home with them. They practised drill, the use of the pike and rapier, taking very great care in all these exercises to betray exceeding clumsiness. With the bow alone they were able to show how expert they were. Indeed the Spaniards were in no slight degree astonished by the extraordinary power and accuracy of their shooting. This Ned accounted for to them by the long practice that he had had among the Indians, declaring that among the tribes beyond the mountains he was by no means an exceptionally good shot—which, indeed, was true enough at short distances, for at these the Indians could shoot with marvellous dexterity.

"By San Josef!" exclaimed one of the Spanish officers, after watching the boys shooting at a target two hundred yards distant with their powerful bows, "it reminds me of the way that those accursed English archers draw their bows and send their arrows singing through the air. In faith, too, these men with their blue eyes and their light hair remind one of these heretic dogs."

"Who are these English?" Ned asked, carelessly. "I have heard of no such tribe. Do they live near the seacoast, or among the mountains?"

"They are no tribe, but a white people like ourselves," the

captain said. "Of course you will not have heard of them. And, fortunately, you are not likely ever to see them on this coast; but if you had remained where you were born, on the other side, you would have heard little else talked of than the doings of these pirates and scoundrels, who scour the seas, defy the authority of his sacred majesty, carry off our treasures under our noses, burn our towns, and keep the whole coast in an uproar."

"But," said Ned, in assumed astonishment, "how is it that so great a monarch as the King of Spain and Emperor of the Indies does not annihilate these ferocious sea robbers? Surely so mighty a king could have no difficulty in overcoming them."

"They live in an island," the officer said, "and are half fish, half men."

"What monsters!" Ned exclaimed. "Half fish and half men! How then do they walk?"

"Not really; but in their habits. They are born sailors, and are so ferocious and bloodthirsty that at sea they overcome even the soldiers of Spain, who are known," he said, drawing himself up, "to be the bravest in the world. On land, however, we should teach them a very different lesson; but on the sea it must be owned that, somehow, we are less valiant than on shore."

Every day a priest came down to the barracks, and for an hour endeavored to instil the elements of his religion into the minds of the now civilized wild men. Ned, although progressing rapidly in other branches of his Spanish education, appeared abnormally dull to the explanations of the good father, while Tom's small stock of Spanish was quite insufficient to enable him to comprehend more than a word here and there.

So matters might have remained for months had not an event occurred which disclosed the true nationality of the lads.

One day the ordinarily placid blue sky was overclouded. The wind rose rapidly, and in a few hours a tremendous storm was blowing on the coast. Most of the vessels in the harbor succeeded in running into shelter. But later in the day a cry arose that a ship had just rounded the point of the bay, and that she would not be able to make the port. The whole population speedily gathered upon the mole, and the vessel, a small one employed in the coasting trade, was seen struggling with the waves, which were rapidly bearing her toward a reef lying a quarter of a mile from the shore. The sea was at this time running with tremendous force. The wind was howling in a fierce gale, and when the vessel struck upon the rocks, and her masts at once went by the board, all hope of safety for the crew appeared at an end.

"Cannot a boat be launched," said Ned, to the soldiers standing round, "to effect the rescue of these poor fellows in that wreck?"

"Impossible!" they all said; "no boat could live in that sea."

After chatting for a time Tom and Ned drew a little apart from the rest of the crowd, and watched the ill-fated vessel.

"It is a rough sea, certainly," Ned said; "but it is all nonsense to say that a boat could not live. Come along, Tom. Let us push that shallop down. There is a sheltered spot behind that rock where we may launch her, and methinks that our arms can row her out to yonder ship."

Throwing off their doublets, the young men put their shoulders to the boat and soon forced it into the water. Then, taking their seats and putting out the oars, they rowed round the corner of the sheltering rock, and breasted the sea which was rolling in. A cry of astonishment broke from the crowd on the mole as the boat made its appearance, and the astonishment was heightened when it was declared by the soldiers that the two men on board were the wild men of the wood, as they were familiarly called among themselves.

It was a long struggle before the boys reached the wreck, and it needed all their strength and seamanship to avoid being swamped by the tremendous seas. At last, however, they neared it, and catching a line thrown to them by the sailors, brought the boat up under the lee of the ship, and as the captain, the four men who composed his crew, and a passenger, leaped one by one from the ship into the sea, they dragged them on board the boat, and then turned her head to shore.

CHAPTER XV

The Prison of the Inquisition

A mong the spectators on the mole were the governor and other principal officers of Arica. "It seems almost like a miracle from heaven," the priest, who was standing next the governor, exclaimed.

The governor was scowling angrily at the boat.

"If there be a miracle," he said, "good father, it is that our eyes have been blinded so long. Think you for a moment that two lads who have been brought up among the Indians from their childhood could manage a boat in such a sea as this? Why, if their story were true they could neither of them ever have handled an oar, and these are sailors, skilful and daring beyond the common, and have ventured a feat that none of our people here on shore were willing to undertake. How they got here I know not; but assuredly they are English sailors. This will account for their blue eyes and light hair, which have so puzzled us, and for that ignorance of Spanish which they so craftily accounted for."

Although the assembled mass of people on the beach had not arrived at the conclusions to which the governor had jumped, they were filled with astonishment and admiration at the daring deed which had been accomplished, and when the boat was safely brought round behind the shelter of the rock, and its occupants landed on the shore, loud cheers broke from the crowd, and the lads received a perfect ovation, their comrades of the barracks being especially enthusiastic. Presently the crowd were severed by two soldiers who made their way through it, and approaching Ned and Tom, said:

"We have the orders of the governor to bring you to him."

The lads supposed that the governor desired to thank them for saving the lives of the shipwrecked men, for in the excitement of the rescue the thought that they had exposed themselves by their knowledge of seamanship had never crossed their minds. The crowd followed tumultuously, expecting to hear a flattering tribute paid to the young men who had behaved so well. But the aspect of the governor, as, surrounded by his officers, he stood in one of the batteries on the mole, excited a vague feeling of astonishment and surprise.

"You are two English seamen," he said, when the lads approached. "It is useless lying any longer. Your knowledge of seamanship and your appearance alike convict you."

For an instant the boys were too surprised to reply, and then Tom said, boldly, "We are, sir. We have done no wrong to any man, and we are not ashamed now to say we are Englishmen. Under the same circumstances, I doubt not that any Spaniard would have similarly tried to escape recognition. But as chance has betrayed us, any further concealment were unnecessary."

"Take them to the guard-house," the governor said, "and keep a close watch over them; later, I will interrogate them myself in the palace."

The feelings of the crowd on hearing this unexpected colloquy were very mixed. In many, the admiration which the boys' conduct had excited swallowed up all other feeling. But among the less enthusiastic minds a vague distrust and terror was at once excited by the news that English sailors were among them. No Englishman had ever been seen on that coast, and they had inflicted such terrible losses on the West Indian Islands and on the neighboring coast, that it is no matter for surprise that their first appearance on the western shores of South America was deemed an omen of terrible import.

The news rapidly spread from mouth to mouth, and a large crowd followed in the rear of the little party, and assembled around the governor's house. The sailors who had been rescued had many friends in the port, and these took up the cause of the boys, and shouted that men who had done so gallant a deed should be pardoned, whatever their offence. Perhaps, on the whole, this party were in the majority. But the sinister whisper that circulated among the crowd, that they were spies who had been landed from English ships on the coast, gradually cooled even the most enthusiastic of their partisans, and what at one time appeared likely to become a formidable popular movement, gradually calmed down and the crowd dispersed.

When brought before the governor the boys affected no more concealment; but the only point upon which they refused to give information was respecting the ships on which they had sailed, and the time at which they had been left upon the eastern coast of America. Without absolutely affirming the fact, they led to the belief that they had passed some years since they left their vessels.

The governor presently gazed sharply upon them and demanded, "Are you the two whites who headed the negro revolt in Porto Rico, and did so much damage to our possessions in that island?"

Ned would have hesitated as to the answer, but Tom at once said firmly, "We are not those two white men, sir, but we know them well; and they were two gallant and loyal Englishmen who, as we know, did much to restrain the atrocities of the Indians. We saw them when they regained their ships."

It was lucky, indeed, that the governor did not put the question separately instead of saying, "Were you two the leaders?" for in that case Ned would have been forced to acknowledge that he was one of them.

The outspokenness of Tom's answer allayed the governor's suspicions. A great portion of his questioning was directed to discovering whether they really had crossed the continent, for he, as well as the populace outside, had at first conceived the idea that they might have been landed on the coast as spies. The fact, however, that they were captured far up among the Cordilleras, their dress and their appearance, and their knowledge of the native tongues—which he tested by bringing in some natives, who entered into conversation with them—convinced him that all this portion of their story was true. As he had no fear of their escaping he said that at present he should not treat them as prisoners, and that their gallant conduct in rowing out to save the lives of Spaniards in danger entitled them to every good treatment; but that he must report their case to the authorities at Lima, who would of course decide upon it. The priest, however, urged upon the governor that he should continue his instructions to them in the Catholic religion; and the governor then pointed out to Ned, who alone was able to converse fluently in Spanish, that they had now been so long separated from their countrymen that they might with advantage to themselves become naturalized as Spaniards, in which case he would push their fortunes to the utmost, and with his report in their favor they might rise to positions of credit and honor; whereas, if they insisted upon maintaining their nationality as Englishmen, it was but too probable that the authorities at Lima would consider it necessary to send them as prisoners to Spain. He said, however, that he would not press them for an answer at once.

Greatly rejoiced at finding that they were not at present to be thrown into prison, but were to be allowed to continue their independent life in the barracks, the lads took their departure from the governor's house, and were most cordially received by their comrades. For a short time everything went smoothly. The suspicion that they were spies had now passed away, and the remembrance of their courageous action made them popular among all classes in the town. A cloud, however, began to gather slowly round them. Now that they had declared their nationality, they felt that they could no longer even pretend that it was likely that they might be induced to forsake their religion, and they accordingly refused positively to submit any longer to the teaching of the priests. Arguments were spent upon them in vain, and after resorting to these, threats were not obscurely uttered. They were told, and with truth, that only two or three months before six persons had been burned alive at Lima for defying the authority of the Church, and that if they persisted in their heretical opinions a similar fate might fall upon them.

English boys are accustomed to think with feelings of unmit-

igated horror and indignation of the days of the Inquisition, and
in times like these, when a general toleration of religious opinion prevails, it appears to us almost incredible that men should
have put others to death in the name of religion. But it is only
by placing ourselves in the position of the persecutors of the
middle ages that we can see that what appears to us cruelty and
barbarity of the worst kind was really the result of a zeal in its
way as earnest, if not as praiseworthy, as that which now impels
missionaries to go with their lives in their hands to regions
where little but a martyr's grave can be expected. Nowadays we
believe—at least all right-minded man believe—that there is
good in all creeds, and that it would be rash indeed to condemn
men who act up to the best of their lights, even though those
lights may not be our own. In the middle ages there was no idea
of tolerance such as this. Men believed fiercely and earnestly
that any deviation from the creed to which they themselves belonged meant an eternity of unhappiness. Such being the case,
the more earnestly religious a man was, the more he desired to
save those around him from this fate. The inquisitors and those
who supported them cannot be charged with wanton cruelty.
They killed partly to save those who defied the power of the
Church, and partly to prevent the spread of their doctrines.
Their belief was that it was better that one man should die,
even by the death of fire, than that hundreds should stray from
the pale of the Church, and so incur the loss of eternal happi-
ness. In the Indies, where the priests in many cases showed a
devotion and heroic qualities equal to anything which has ever
been displayed by missionaries in any part of the world, persecution was yet hotter than it ever was in civilized Europe.
These men believed firmly that it was their bounden duty at
any cost to force the natives to become Christians; and however
we may think that they were mistaken and wrong, however we
may abhor the acts of cruelty which they committed, it would
be a mistake indeed to suppose that these were perpetrated
from mere lightness of heart and wanton bloodthirstiness. The
laws of those days were in all countries brutally severe. In
England, in the reign of Henry VIII, the loss of an ear was the

punishment inflicted upon a man who begged. The second time he offended his other ear was cut off. A third repetition of the offence, and he was sold into slavery; and if he ran away from his master he was liable to be put to death by the first person who met him. The theft of any article above the value of three shillings was punishable by death, and a similar code of punishment prevailed for all kinds of offences. Human life was then held in such slight regard that we must remember that, terrible as the doings of the Inquisition were, they were not so utterly foreign to the age in which they were perpetrated as would appear to us living in these days of moderate punishment and general humanity.

By the boys, however, brought up in England, which at that time was bitterly and even fiercely anti-catholic—a state of things which naturally followed the doings in the reign of Queen Mary, and the threatening aspect maintained by Spain toward this country—popery was held in utter abhorrence, and the Inquisition was the bug-bear with which mothers frightened their children when disobedient. The thought, therefore, of falling into the hands of this dreaded tribunal was very terrible to the boys. They debated between themselves whether it would not be better for them to leave Arica at once secretly, to make for the mountains, and to take up their lot for life among the natives of the plains, who had so hospitably received them. They had, indeed, almost arrived at the conclusion that this would be their best plan of procedure.

They lingered, however, in the hope, daily becoming fainter, of the arrival of Drake's fleet, but it seemed that by this time it must have failed in its object of doubling the Horn. Nearly six months had elapsed since they had been left on the eastern coast, and according to their calculation of distance two months should have amply sufficed to enable them to make the circuit of Southern America. They could not tell that the fleet had been delayed by extraordinary accidents. When off the Cape they had met with storms which continued from the 7th of September to the 28th of October without intermission, and which the old chronicler of the expedition describes as being "more violent and of longer continuance than anything since Noah's flood." They had to waste much time, owing to the fact that Captain Winter with one of the ships had, missing his consorts in the storm, sailed back to England, that two other ships were lost, and that Captain Drake with his flagship, which alone remained, had spent much time in searching for his consorts in every inlet and island.

Among those saved in the boat from the Spanish ship was a young gentleman of rank and fortune, and owner of large estates near Lima, who had come down upon some business. He took a great affection for the young Englishmen, and came each day to visit them, there being no let or hindrance on the part of the governor. This gentleman assured them that he possessed great influence at Lima, and that although he doubted not that the military authorities would treat them with all courtesy after the manner in which they had risked their lives to save subjects of his majesty, yet that, should it be otherwise, he would move heaven and earth in their favor. "There is but one thing I dread," he said, and a cloud came over his handsome face.

"You need hardly say what it is," Ned said, gravely. "You mean, of course, the Inquisition."

The Spaniard signified his assent by a silent movement of the head.

"We dare not speak above our breath of that dreaded tribunal," he said. "The very walls appear to have ears, and it is better to face a tiger in his den than to say aught against the Inquisition. There are many Spaniards who, like myself, loath and abhor it; but we are powerless. Their agents are everywhere, and one knows not in whom he dare confide. Even in our families there are spies, and this tyranny, which is carried on in the name of religion, is past all supporting. But even should the 'holy office' lay its hands upon you, keep up heart. Be assured that I will risk all that I am worth, and my life to boot, to save you from it."

"Would you advise us to fly?" Ned said. "We can without doubt escape from here, for we are but lightly guarded, and the governor, I am sure, is friendly toward us."

"Whither would you fly?" asked the young Spaniard.

"We would cross the mountains to the plains, and join the Indians there."

"It would be a wretched life," the Spaniard said, "and would cut you off from all kindred and friends. I can give you no advice. To me, I confess, death would be preferable, even in its worst forms. But to you, fond of exercise, and able to cause yourself to be respected and feared by the wild Indians of the Pampas, it might be different. However, you need not decide yet. I trust that even should the worst befall you, I may be able at the last moment to give you the opportunity of choosing that life in preference to death in the dungeons of the Inquisition."

It was about ten days from the date of the governor's writing that a ship came in from Lima, and the same evening the governor came in to them with a grave face. He was attended by two officials dressed in the deepest black.

"Senors," he said, "it is my duty, in the first place, to inform you that the governor of Lima, acting upon the report which I sent him of the bravery which you manifested in the matter of the wreck here, has agreed to withdraw all question against you touching your past connection with the English freebooters, and to allow you freedom, without let or hindrance, and to further your passage to such place as opportunity may afford, and where you may be able to meet with a ship from your own country. That is all I have to say to you."

Then the men in black stepped forward and said, "We arrest you in the name of the holy Inquisition on the charge of heresy."

The young men glanced at the governor, believing that he was sufficiently their friend to give them a sign if resistance would be of any avail. He replied to the unspoken question by an almost imperceptible shake of the head, and it was well that the boys abandoned the idea, for the door opened and a guard of six men, armed to the teeth, although in plain dark clothes, entered. These were the alguazils of the holy office, the birds of night whose appearance was dreaded even by the most bigoted Spaniards, and at whose approach mothers clasped their children closer to their breast, and men crossed themselves at the thought that their passage boded death to some unhappy victim. For it must be remembered that the Inquisition, framed at first only for the discovery and punishment of heresy, later became an instrument of private vengeance. Men denounced wives of whom they wished to be rid, wives husbands, no relations of kin were sufficient to ensure safety. The evidence, sometimes true, was more often manufactured by malice and hate, until at last even the most earnest and sincere Catholics trembled when they thought that at any moment they might be denounced and flung into the dungeons of the Inquisition.

Brave as the lads were, they could not avoid a thrill of horror at the presence of the familiars of this dreaded body. They were, however, cheered by the thought of the promises of the young Spaniard, in whose honesty and honor they had great faith; and with a few words of adieu to the governor, and thanks to him for what he had done in their behalf, they followed the officers of the Inquisition along the streets of Arica, and suffered themselves to be placed on board the boat which lay alongside the mole.

Although it was late in the evening, their passage was not unobserved. Many of the soldiers recognized in the two men marching, surrounded by the black guard of the Inquisition, their late comrades, and, confident in their numbers, these did not hesitate to lift their voices in loud protest against this seizure of men who had behaved so gallantly. In the darkness, too, they feared not that their faces would be recognized, and their curses and threats rose loud in the air. People looking out from their doors to hear the cause of the uproar were variously affected. Some joined in the movement of the soldiers; but more shrank back with dread into their houses rather than be compromised with so dreaded a body. The threats, however, did not proceed to open violence, and as the young men themselves gave no sign of attempting an effort for freedom, their comrades contented themselves with many shouts of good wishes, mingled with curses upon their captors, and the lads were embarked without the alguazils having to use the swords which they had drawn in readiness for the expected fray.

"You are witness, senor officer," Ned said, "that we came without resistance, and that, had we chosen, we could with the assistance of the soldiers have easily broken from the hold of your men. We are willing, however, to proceed with you to Lima, where we doubt not that the justice of our judges will result in our acquittal. No one can blame us that we are of the religion of our fathers. Had we been born Catholics and then relapsed into heresy, it would have been reasonable for you to have considered our case; but as we but hold the religion which we have been taught, and known indeed of no other, we see not how in any man's eyes blame can rest upon us."

"I take note," the officer said, "of the docility with which you have remained in our hands, and will so far testify in your favor. Touching the other matter, it is beyond my jurisdiction."

The vessel in which the boys were embarked was a slow one, and two days after leaving Arica they saw a small sailing craft pass them at no great distance, sailing far more rapidly than they themselves were going. The boys gave no thought to this occurrence until they arrived at the harbor of Lima. A large number of ships were here anchored, and after the solitude of the sea which they had endured during their voyage from England, this collection of fine galleons greatly pleased the boys, who had never seen so large a number of ships collected together, there being nigh forty sail then in harbor.

As the officers of the Inquisition scarcely ever pass through the streets in the daytime, owing to the known hostility of the mass of the population, no attempt at a landing was made until nightfall. The officer in charge was, however, surprised, upon reaching the landing-place, to find a large crowd assembled, who saluted his party with hisses and groans, and loud cries of "shame!" Those behind pressed forward, and those in front were forced into the ranks of the alguazils, and it seemed at one time as if the prisoners would be separated from their guards. A man in a rough peasant's dress was forced in contact with Ned, and said hastily in a low voice to him, "Keep up your heart; when preparations are made I will act."

Ned recognized the voice of the young Spanish gentleman

whom he had left at Arica, and guessed immediately that he had taken passage in the swift-sailing caravel, in order to be able to reach Lima before the vessel containing the prisoners.

Ned had in confidence, in his talks with him, informed him that he still hoped, although his hopes had now fallen almost to zero from the long tarrying of the fleet, that the English admiral would arrive, and that he should be able to go on board and so rejoin his countrymen. This expectation, indeed, it was which had prevented Ned and Tom making their escape when they could have done so and taking to the mountains, for it was certain that some time at least would elapse before stringent measures would be taken against them. Another effort would without doubt be made to persuade them to abandon their religion, and every day might bring with it the arrival of the English vessels.

The young men were conducted to a dark and sombre building which bore the appearance of a vast monastery. The interior was even more dismal in its appearance than the walls without. A solitary figure met them at the doorway; their guards entered, and the gates were closed behind. The officer in charge handed to the new-comer a paper, and the latter, receiving it, said, "I accept the charge of the prisoners, and your duties are at an end concerning them."

Motioning them to follow, he led them through some long dark corridors into a room much better furnished and provided than they had expected. Here, placing a lamp upon the table and pointing to two manchets of bread and a vessel of water which stood on the table, and to two truckle-beds in the corner of the room, he left them without a word. Ned had already agreed with his companion that they would not, when once within the building, say a word to each other which they would not have heard by their jailors, for they were well aware that these buildings were furnished with listening places, and that every word which prisoners said would be overheard and used against them. They comforted themselves, therefore, with general observations as to their voyage, and to the room in which they now were, and to the hopes which they entertained that their judges would take a favorable view of their conduct. Then with a sincere prayer to God to spare them through the dangers and trials which they might have to undergo, they lay down for the night, and, such is the elasticity and strength of youth, they were, in spite of the terrible position in which they were placed, in a few minutes fast asleep.

The next day the door of the apartment opened and two attendants, dressed in black from head to foot and bearing white wands, entered, and motioned to them to follow them. Through more long corridors and passages they went until they stopped at some thick curtains overhanging a door. These were drawn aside, the door behind them was opened, other curtains hanging on the inside were separated, and they entered a large apartment lighted artificially by lamps from above. At a table at the end of the room were seated three men, also in black. They were writing, and for some time did not look up from their work. The attendants stood motionless by the side of the lads, who, in spite of their courage, could not but shudder at the grim silence of this secret tribunal. At last the chief inquisitor laid down his pen, and lifting his eyes toward them said, "Your names are Edward Hearne and Thomas Tressilis. You are English sailors, who, having crossed from the other side of the continent, made your way to Arica, where you did, as I am told, a brave action in saving the lives of some Spanish sailors."

Tom assented gravely to the address.

"You are accused," the inquisitor went on, "of being steeped in the errors of heresy, and of refusing to listen to the ministrations of the holy father who tried to instruct you in the doctrines of the true Church. What have you to say to this?"

"It is true, sir," Ned said, "every word. We were born Protestants, and were brought up in that Church. Had we been born in Spain we should no doubt have been true members of your Church. But it is hard that men once ingrained in a faith should change it for another. It were like asking a tiger to become a leopard. We are unlearned men, and in no way skilled in the exercises of theology. We accepted what we were taught, and would fain die in the same belief. Doubtless your priests could give us arguments which we should be unable to refute, whatever might be done by learned men of our Church, and we would pray you to suffer us to hold to the creed in which we have been reared."

"It is impossible," the inquisitor said, "that we should permit you to go on straightway in the way of damnation. Your bodies are as nothing to the welfare of your souls, and to save the one it were indeed for your good that the other were tormented. We will not, however, press you now to recant your errors. You shall be attended by a minister of the true religion, who will point out to you the error of your courses, and in three days we shall expect an answer from you. If you embrace the faith of the Holy Church you may, if you choose to remain here, rise to posts of honor and wealth, for we have heard good things of your courage and prudence. If, however, you remain stubborn, we shall find means to compel you to do that which we would fain that you should do of your free-will; and if you still defy at once the kindness and the chastisement of the Church, you will receive that doom which awaits all who defy its authority."

The attendants now touched the lads on the arm in token that the audience was over, and led them back to the room in which they had first been confined. When left alone the boys examined this closely, although seeming to be looking without motive at the walls. The windows were placed high up from the ground, far beyond their reach, and were thickly barred. The door was of massive oak, and the room, although in appearance but an ordinary apartment, was truly a dungeon as safe and as difficult to break out of as if far below the surface of the earth. Later on when an attendant came in with the bread and water, which formed the substance of each meal, as he placed it on the table he said in a low muttered whisper, "Hope always. Friends are working." This intimation greatly raised the spirits of the prisoners, as they felt that their friend the Spaniard had already succeeded in corrupting some at least of the familiars of the Inquisition, and that no means would be spared to secure their escape should the worst occur.

For three days they were visited for many hours daily by a

priest, who endeavored to explain to Ned the points of difference between the two religions, and to convince him of the errors of that of England. Ned, however, although but a poor theologist, gave answer to all his arguments, that he could in no way reply to the reasonings of the priest, but that he was, nevertheless, convinced of their error, and sure that a divine of his Church would have found replies to difficulties to which he could see no outlet. The priest strove earnestly with him, but at the end of the third day he retired exasperated, saying angrily that he now left them to other hands.

CHAPTER XVI

The Rescue

The next day they were again brought before the tribunal, and the grand inquisitor, without this time entering into any length of speech, informed them briefly that he gave them another three days, and that if, at the end of the third day, their obstinacy did not yield, he would use the means at his disposal, and he pointed to various instruments hanging on the walls or ranged on the table. Of these, although the lads were ignorant of their uses, they entertained no doubt whatever, that they were the instruments of torture of which they had heard,— thumbscrews, iron gags, the boot, the rack, and other devilish inventions. They made no reply to the address, and were taken away this time down several winding-stairs to a black and noxious dungeon far below the general level of the earth. No ray of light entered this cell. The walls were damp with moisture. In the corner the boys discovered by the sense of feeling a small pile of rotten straw which had, without doubt, formed the bed of some other unfortunate who had before tenanted the prison. Here, at least, they had no fear of being overheard; but as the ingenuity of the inquisitors was well known they agreed to say no word of the hopes they still cherished, but to talk of other matters purely personal to themselves. Here, an hour after hour passed, they strengthened each other in their resolution by an agreement that no torture should wring from them a recantation of their faith, and by many prayers for strength and support from above.

Once a day the door opened and an attendant brought in

bread and water, which he placed in silence on the ground. The second day, as he did so, he placed a bundle by the side of the bread, and, whispering, "Be prudent: use these only as the last resource: friends are preparing to help you," retired as noise-lessly as usual. When left in darkness again the lads seized upon the parcel. It was large and heavy, and, to their great delight, they found that it contained two daggers and two brace of heavy pistols.

"I wonder," Ned said, in a whisper to Tom, "that our friend does not contrive to get us passed through the prison. But I sup-pose that he finds that only one or two, perhaps, of the atten-dants are corruptible, and that our jailer, although he might free us from this cell, could not pass us through the corridors and out of the building."

"Let us see," Tom said, "if we can make our way into any cell which may adjoin this. If is is empty we might perchance make our escape."

All night the boys labored with their daggers, having first tapped the wall all round to hear if any difference of sound gave an intimation that a hollow space was behind. They could not perceive this, but fancying that upon the one side there was some very slight difference, they attempted to remove the stones there. All through the night and next day they continued their labor, and succeeded with great difficulty in removing two of the stones of the wall. Behind these, however, was a mass of rubble, formed of cement so hard that the daggers failed to make any impression whatever upon it, and after laboring through the whole day they were forced to abandon the design and replace the stones as they had before been, filling up the interstices with the mortar which they had dug out, so that no trace of the task upon which they were employed should remain.

That night when the door opened, two figures, as before, pre-sented themselves, and they knew that their summons before the dreaded court was at hand. With their daggers and pistols concealed within their vests they followed their guides; each with a grasp of his hand assuring the other of his steadfastness

NED AND TOM BECOME MASTERS OF THE SITUATION

SEE PAGE 198.

and faith. They had resolved that, sooner than submit to torture, which would cripple them for life, they would fight to the last and die resisting.

This time they found in the audience hall, in addition to the three judges, four men clothed also in black, but evidently of an inferior order. These were standing ranged along by the wall, in readiness to obey the orders of the judges. Their attendants fell back to the door, and the prisoners remained standing alone in the centre of the room.

"Acting in all kindness," the judge said, "we have given you ample time to retract and to consider your position, and we now call upon you to consent formally to abandon your accursed heresies, and to embrace the offer which the Holy Church kindly makes to you, or to endure the pains which it will be necessary that we should inflict, in order to soften your hardness of heart."

"We are perfectly resolved," Ned said, "to maintain the religion of our fathers. As Englishmen we protest against this outrage. When your countrymen fall into our hands no man dreams of endeavoring to compel them to abandon their faith. They are treated as honorable prisoners; and if any outrage be attempted upon our bodies, sooner or later, be assured, the news of it will come to the ears of our English captains; and for every drop of blood of ours shed, a Spanish life will answer."

"You are insolent," the inquisitor said, coldly. "It is rash to threaten men in whose power you are. These walls reveal no secrets, and though the town were full of your English pirates, yet would your doom be accomplished without a possibility of rescue, and without your fate ever becoming known beyond these four walls. Bethink you," he said, "before you compel me to use the means at my disposal; for men have spoken as bravely and as obstinately as you, but they have changed their minds when they felt their bones cracking under the torture. We would fain abstain from injuring figures as manly as yours; but, if needs be, we will so reduce them to wrecks that you will envy the veriest cripple who crawls for alms on the steps of the cathedral here."

The boys remained silent, and the inquisitor, with an air of

angry impatience, motioned to the men ranged along by the wall
to seize their prisoners.

The lads saw that the time for action was come. Each produced his pistol from his breast, the one levelling his at the head
of the grand inquisitor, while the other faced the foremost of
those advancing toward them.

"One step nearer," Ned said, "and the two of you are dead
men."

A silence as of death fell in the chamber. The judges were too
astonished even to rise from their seats, and the familiars
paused in their advance.

"You see," Ned said, to the grand inquisitor, "that you are not
masters of the situation. One touch upon my trigger and the
death with which you threaten me is yours. Now, write, as I
order you, a pass by which we may be allowed to quit these accursed walls without molestation."

Without hesitation the judge wrote on a piece of paper the required order.

"Now," Ned said, "you must come with us, for I put no faith
whatever in your promises, for I know the ways of your kind,
that promises made to heretics are not considered sacred. You
are yourself my best safeguard, for be assured that the slightest
interruption to us upon our way, and I draw my trigger and send
you to that eternity to which you have despatched so many vic-
tims."

The judge rose to his feet, and Ned could see that, quiet as he
appeared, he was trembling with passion. Tom had at the first
alarm retreated to the door so as to prevent the escape of the
attendants stationed there, or of any of the others, to give the
alarm. He now opened it, and Ned was about to pass out with
the inquisitor when, glancing round, he saw that one of the
other judges had disappeared, doubtless by some door placed
behind the arras at the end of the room.

"Treachery is intended," he muttered, to the inquisitor; "but
remember that you will be the first victim."

Slowly Ned passed along the corridors, the inquisitor between the two Englishmen, the attendants following in a group

behind, uncertain what course to pursue, and without orders from their superior, when at last they came to a door. This was locked, and Ned ordered the inquisitor to have it opened.

"I have not the keys," he said; "they are in the hands of the attendant whose duty it is to attend to this portion of the building."

"Call them," Ned said, impatiently.

The inquisitor struck on the closed door with his hands and called aloud, but no answer was returned.

"Bid these men behind you force it in," Ned said.

The men advanced, but as they did so a small side door in the passage, behind Ned, opened noiselessly, and suddenly a thick blanket was thrown over his head, while an arm struck up the hand which had the pistol. He drew the trigger, however, and the grand inquisitor with a groan sank to the ground. At the same instant a number of men rushed through the door and threw themselves upon the lads, and were joined by the attendants standing behind. A desperate struggle ensued. Tom shot the first two men who sprang upon him, and for some minutes the lads maintained a desperate struggle. Again and again the crowd of their assailants pulled one or other of them to the ground; but it was not until their strength was utterly exhausted by their struggles that both were secured and bound hand and foot. Then at the order of one of the other judges, who, now that all danger was over, appeared upon the scene, they were lifted bodily carried back to their dungeon, and cast upon the ground.

Panting and breathless, the lads lay for some time too exhausted to speak.

"I am afraid that I missed that rascally chief inquisitor," Ned said; "did you notice, Tom?"

"I scarcely saw, for at the same moment I was struck from behind; but I fancy that he fell when your pistol exploded."

"In that case," Ned said, "we may have a respite for a day or two. He will feel inclined to be present at the ceremony of torturing, himself. On one thing I am determined. We will not be taken by the men in black and submit to having our limbs wrenched without an effort. I should think that if we snatch up some of the iron instruments lying about, we can manage to make such a resistance that they will have to kill us before we are overcome. If I could kill myself I certainly would do so. I do not think I am a coward, Tom, but I confess that the sight of those horrible instruments makes my blood run cold."

"I feel with you, Ned; death itself were nothing; but to be torn limb from limb is something horrible."

The day passed without any visit being paid to them. No food was brought in, and they were left as if forgotten by their jailers. Thus they were unable to tell the hour, and as it was perfectly dark it was by guesswork that they at last lay down to sleep on the damp stones.

Presently they were awoke by the tramp of numerous footsteps. Then there was a tremendous battering at the door.

"What on earth are they doing!" Ned exclaimed. "Have they lost the key, and are they going to break open the door and finish with us now? Get ready; we will make a fight at once, and try and end it."

Presently the door gave way before the heavy blows which were struck upon it, and to the astonishment of the lads a band of Indians, naked to the waist and holding torches, burst into the cell.

"Here they are!" exclaimed one of them in Spanish. "Quick! there is not a moment to be lost. Follow us"; and, stooping down, he cut the cords which bound them.

Bewildered and confused with the sudden light, and by the unexpected irruption, the boys followed the speaker, and, closely surrounded by the Indians, made their way down the passages and out into the courtyard. There was no resistance or interference. The familiars had, apparently, fled at the sudden attack upon the jail, and no one appeared to bar their exit. The great gates of the court-yard stood uninjured, but the postern door had been battered in. Another body of natives, armed with spears and bows and arrows, were standing round the entrance; and a good many of the people of the neighborhood, roused by the sudden tumult, were standing at the doors. These looked on apparently with mere curiosity, and with no desire to interfere

with what was going on. Indeed, the Inquisition was never popular with the great body of the Spaniards, over whom its secret
proceedings and terrible cruelties hung like a dark cloud, as
none could ever say that they might not be the objects of de-
nunciation.

It was clear that the Indians were acting upon a fixed plan, for
the moment that those from within the prison sallied out, all
formed in a compact body, and at a brisk slinging trot started
down the street, the lads being kept well in the centre, so as to
conceal them from the gaze of the public. Not a word was spoken till they had issued from the town. For another quarter of a
mile their hurried march continued, and then, without a word,
the whole of the escort, with the exception of one man, turned
up a cross-road and vanished into the darkness.

"Heaven be praised that I have saved you, senors!" said the
Indian, who remained. "Do you not recognize me? I am Don
Estevan, whose life you saved at Arica. I feared that I might be
too late to find you unharmed; but it required time to get the
necessary force together. You recognized me, of course, on the
pier when you landed. The instant I heard of your arrest I
chartered a swift-sailing country craft, and arrived here the
day before you. I was the bearer of a letter, signed by many of
the soldiers in garrison at Arica, to their comrades here, saying
how bravely you had behaved, and that you had become good
comrades in the regiment, and urging them to do anything in
their power to save you from the Inquisition. This I thought
might be useful, as they would be sure to be called out in case
of an attack upon the Inquisition, and I prayed them to be as
slow as possible in their movements, in case of any sudden
alarm. This will account for the fact that none of them arrived
upon the spot before we had finished our business just now.
But there is not a moment to delay. I have horses two miles
away in readiness, and we must make for there. They will be
sure to put on bloodhounds in pursuit, and we may have to
ride for it."

The boys briefly expressed their intense gratitude to their
preserver for his efforts in their behalf, Ned adding, "I fear, Don

Estevan, that your generous deed of tonight will involve you in fearful danger."

"I have taken every precaution," the young Spaniard said. "I did not charter the vessel in my own name, and came up in disguise. All my friends believe me to be still at Arica, and no one, so far as I know, has recognized me here. I was obliged to go to my estate, which lies a hundred miles up the country. There I armed my peons and vaqueros, and a number of Indians who were living near, to whom I have always shown kindness. None of them knew that it was the dungeon of the Inquisition which they were to attack, but believed that it was merely a prison they were about to force, for the power of superstition is very great in this country, and although a great many of the men may lead wild and godless lives, they tremble at the thought of lifting their hands against that mysterious and awful body, the Inquisition. News travels slowly indeed in this country, and it is not likely that the fact that the prison of the Inquisition has been broken open will ever reach the men on my estate. The priest of the village is a worthy man, and he has, I know, no sympathy with bigotry and cruelty. Consequently, if any of them should in their confession tell him that they have been engaged in breaking a prison, he will perchance guess what prison it was, and may imagine that I had a hand in it. But I feel sure that the knowledge so gained would go no further. I might, had I chosen, have had the horses brought to the point where we separated from my men. But in that case the hounds might have followed upon the main body, and so some clue would have been gained as to the direction from which they came. As it is, they will follow us up at any rate until we take horses. We will make our track visible for some distance, so that the pursuit may be carried on. Before it is over they will have lost all track of the rest of their assailants, and will not indeed be able to trace the direction in which they went. They, too, have horses at a short distance, and will speedily regain the estate."

"How did you know in which cell we were confined?"

"Through the jailer. The man who attended you was once employed by my father. I met him the day I arrived from Arica, and bribed him to convey the arms to you with which I thought that, should they bring you to trial and torture before I could collect my force, you might make a resistance, for I judged that you would rather die than suffer mutilation and agony. When you disclosed your arms to-day he slipped at once from the building, as he knew that he would be suspected. Changing his clothes in a house near, he mounted his horse and rode to meet us, conveying the news that the crisis had arrived. How it ended he could not tell; but he hoped that some delay might occur in resuming proceedings against you."

By this time they had reached their horses, which were tied in a clump of trees at a short distance from the road.

"They are fine animals," Don Estevan said, "and we may reckon upon showing our heels to any of those who pursue us; for I can assure you that the chase is likely to be a hot one."

"Whither do you intend to go?"

"I am thinking of making for Arica. Before we reach that town you can, if you choose, strike to the hills and join the natives beyond, as you proposed when at Arica; or, should you prefer it, you can, in disguises, enter Arica and remain there for a time until all possibility of your friends appearing before that place be at an end. My absence will not have been noticed, for I mentioned to friends there that I was going into the interior to investigate a mine, of whose existence I had heard from some Indians. When I return, therefore, I shall say that the mine was not sufficiently promising in appearance for me to care about asking for a concession from the government. I shall, of course, pretend to be extremely vexed at the time that has been wasted, and I do not see that any suspicion can fall upon me as having been concerned in the affair at Lima. We will walk our horses at a slow pace, in order to save them as far as possible, and to ascertain whether our pursuers have correctly followed our steps. When we once hear them we can then put on our best speed; and as they will not know that we are but a short distance ahead, they will go at a moderate pace. Besides, the speed of bloodhounds when tracking is by no means great."

An hour later they heard a faint sound in the distance.

Instinctively they checked their horses, and again in the darkness of the night the deep distant bay of a hound was heard.

"Just as I thought!" Don Estevan exclaimed. "They have got the bloodhounds, and I should think, by the sound, that they must have just reached the spot where we mounted. The hounds will be puzzled now; but the sagacity of these creatures is so great that I am by no means sure that they will be unable to follow us by the track of the horses. Now let us set spur."

For the next four or five hours they proceeded at a steady gallop toward the south. The country was flat, the road sandy, but even, and the cool night air was exhilarating indeed after the confinement in the dark and noisome dungeon at Lima. So rejoiced were the boys with their newly-recovered freedom that it was with difficulty they restrained themselves from bursting into shouts of joy. But they were anxious that no sounds should be heard by the villagers of the little hamlets lying along the road. The sound of the horses' hoofs on the sandy track would scarcely arouse a sleeping man; and the fact that their tracks would be plainly visible in the sand when daylight came caused them no concern, as, so far, they had made no effort to deceive their pursuers.

Soon after daylight arrived they found themselves upon a stream which ran down from the mountains and crossed the road.

"Now," Don Estevan said, "it is time to begin to throw them off our track. They will believe that the party consist solely of Indians, and our turning east will seem as if we intended to take refuge in the mountains. Let us then strike up the river for awhile, land at a spot where the horses' hoofs will be clearly visible, and then pursue a course to the southeast, taking us nearer and nearer to the hills. Three leagues hence is another stream. This we will enter, and they will make sure that we have pursued our former tactics—that we have followed it up and again struck for the hills. Instead of doing this we will follow it down for a mile or two, and quit it at some spot where the bank is firm, and will leave no marks of our footsteps. Then we will strike across the country and regain the road some seven or eight leagues further south."

The plan appeared a capital one, and was followed out as arranged. Late in the evening they were again in the vicinity of the southern road. In their wallets was a plentiful supply of provisions, and they had filled their water bottles at the last stream which they had crossed. Entering a grove of trees, they unsaddled their horses and allowed them to crop the foliage and shrubs, while they threw themselves down upon the soft earth, stiff and wearied with their long journey.

"We will travel by night always," Don Estevan said. "I do not think that any suspicion whatever will arise that we have again struck south; but should any inquiry be made, it is as well that no one along the road shall have seen three mounted men."

For another two days they journeyed as proposed by night, resting by day in quiet places, and, so far as they knew, without having been seen by any of the scattered population. It was in the middle of the third night, as they were cantering slowly along, that they heard the tread of a horse at full gallop approaching from the south.

"You had better withdraw from the road," Don Estevan said, "so that but one horseman will be met. I will stop the rider and hear why he gallops so fast. It may be that news has preceded us, and it is as well to gather what intelligence we can."

The boys withdrew from the road, Don Estevan proceeding ahead. They heard the sound of the galloping hoofs pause as their rider met the Spaniard. There was a talk for a few minutes, and then the horseman again rode forward at full speed. Don Estevan paused for a little while to allow him to get beyond earshot, and then rejoined his companions.

"I have great news," he said, "and it is for you to decide whether it will alter your plans of proceeding. The man whom I have just met is a messenger despatched by the governor of Arica to Lima to warn the governor there that an English ship, under the noted freebooter Francis Drake, has put into that harbor, and has started again, sailing for the north, after exacting certain contributions, but otherwise refraining from injuring the town."

The boys gave a shout of joy, for they had begun to fear that the expedition must have met with some disaster in doubling Cape Horn, and been compelled to return.

"What will you do?" the Spaniard asked.

"Return to Lima!" the boys exclaimed, simultaneously. "We shall be there before the admiral can arrive, and can then rejoin our comrades."

"That will indeed be your best plan," Don Estevan said; "but you must be disguised thoroughly. However, you are not likely to be so closely investigated as you otherwise would be at Lima; for you may be sure that when the messenger arrives there the town will be in such a ferment of excitement at the approach of your countrymen that our little affair will for the time be entirely forgotten."

"I trust," Ned said, "that we shall be able to do something to render your security more perfect; for, if I mistake not, when the admiral hears of the doings of the officials of the Inquisition, how many people they have burned to death lately at Lima, and what frightful cruelties they have perpetrated in that ghastly prison, he will burn the place to the ground and hang up the judges, in which case we may be sure that no further inquiry will ever be thought of concerning the attack on the prison. What do you advise us to do, senor, for it is clear that your best course is to return to Arica direct?"

"I cannot think of doing that," the generous young Spaniard replied. "A few days' longer absence will pass unnoticed, especially as people will have plenty of other matters to think and talk about. I do not see how you can possibly obtain disguises without my assistance, and as our pursuers will long since have been thrown off our track and will probably have given up the search and have returned to Lima, convinced that we already have crossed the mountains and are beyond their reach, I think that there is little danger in my nearing the city. Come, let us turn our horses' heads at once."

In a few minutes they were returning by the route they had

hitherto travelled. They were already dressed as young Spaniards. The disguises had been brought by their rescuer, and assumed at the first halt. He himself had also washed the paint from his face and hands, and had assumed European garb, in order that any inquiry about three mounted Indians might be baffled.

"There is now," he said, "no longer any occasion for us to ride by night. We are journeying north, and any inquiries which may ever be set on foot will certainly point only to men going south, and whereas our Indian disguises might have been suspected, I am now in my proper character and my passing through can excite no rumor or comment."

Don Estevan had, indeed, assumed the garb of a Spanish proprietor of rank, while the boys were dressed as vaqueros; and as they passed through villages in the daytime kept their horses half a length behind that of their leader. They avoided on their ride back putting up at any of their *posadas* or village inns on the road, sleeping as before in the woods. Their marches were long but were performed at a much slower rate of speed, as they were certain that they would reach Lima long before the admiral's ship, even should he not pause at any place on the way.

It was upon the sixth day after their rescue from prison that they again approached Lima. After much consultation they had agreed to continue in their Spanish dresses, taking only the precaution of somewhat staining their faces and hands to give them the color natural to men who spend their lives on the plains. Don Estevan himself determined to enter the city with them after nightfall, and to take them to the house of a trusty friend, where they should lie concealed until the news arrived that the English ship was off the port. He himself would at once mount his horse and retrace his steps to Arica.

The programme was carried out successfully. No one glanced at the hidalgo as with his vaqueros he rode through the streets of Lima. There were no lights in those days save those which hung before shrines by the roadside, or occasionally a dim oil lamp suspended before the portico of some mansion of importance.

The friend to whom Don Estevan assigned them was a young man of his own age, a cousin, and one, like himself, liberal in his opinions, free from bigotry, and hating the cruelties perpetrated in the name of religion by the Inquisition. He heard with surprise the narrative which Don Estevan related, for the latter had not visited him during his short stay in the city, and was supposed still to be at Arica. Great was his astonishment indeed when he found that the attack upon the prison of the Inquisition, which had caused such intense excitement in the city, had been planned and executed by his cousin; and his expressions of approval of the deed were warm and frequent. He assured the boys that he would do everything in his power to make them comfortable until the arrival of the English ship. A discussion took place as to whether it was better that they should appear as friends of his who had come in from their country estate, or whether they should continue their disguise as vaqueros. There were objections to either plan. In the first place, the attendants in waiting would detect the shortcomings in Ned's Spanish, and would be astonished at the silence of his companion. Upon the other hand, it would seem strange that they should be kept apart from the servitors of the house. Finally, it was agreed that they should appear as man of rank, but that Tom should feign sickness and therefore keep his room; Ned for the most part remaining shut up with him and taking his meals there. This course was followed out, and when the arrangement was complete they took a hearty leave of the noble young Spaniard, who at once remounted his horse and started on his weary ride back again to Arica.

CHAPTER XVII

The "Golden Hind"

The lads were all anxiety to know what course had been determined upon with reference to the arrival of the English vessel. They were told that a large fleet was assembled in the harbor, but that great dissension existed among the authorities as to whether resistance should be offered or not.

"Surely," Ned said, "they will never allow one vessel to enter a harbor thronged with shipping, and with a strong garrison on shore ready to take part in the defence?"

Their host flushed a little, and said, "You English must form but a poor opinion of Spanish courage. On shore, however, we have proved on the battlefields of the continent that we can hold our own against all comers. But I own to you that your sea-dogs have caused such a panic among our sailors of the western isles that they are looked upon as invincible, and our men appear to be paralyzed at the very name of the English buccaneers."

"Why we are particularly anxious to know," Ned said, "is, that if resistance is to be offered, it is clear that we must be ready to embark in a canoe and to join the ship before she arrives off the harbor, as otherwise, if she is beaten off we may have no opportunity whatever of regaining her."

"I think," the Spaniard said, "that when the time comes it is probable that no resistance may be offered, and that the valor of those who, so long as the ship is at a distance, are anxious to fight, will evaporate very rapidly. The citizens, too, are for the most part opposed to resistance, for they argue that if the

English conquer they are likely to lay the town in ruins; whereas if unopposed they may content themselves with certain exactions upon the richer citizens, as has been their custom in the west."

During the days that elapsed, many arguments took place between the Spaniard and Ned as to the lawfulness of the war which the English buccaneers carried on with the colonies of a nation at peace with their own, the Spaniard saying that they approached very nearly to the verge of piracy. Ned had never given the subject much consideration before. He had done as others did, and had regarded the Spaniards as lawful prey, their cruelty toward the natives forming, in the eyes of the English sailors, a justification for any treatment which they might inflict upon them. He was, however, forced to confess, that now the other side was presented to him, the conduct of his countrymen was really indefensible, and he blushed as he thought of the various acts of sacrilege in churches and other deeds of plunder in which he had taken part. He assured his friend that in the future neither he nor his companion would ever share in such deeds again.

It was upon the evening of the 15th of February, two days after their return to Lima, that their host entered with the news that a ship was seen in the distance approaching the port, and that it was the general opinion of the mariners that she was the dreaded English pirate. He had already made arrangements that a small boat should be lying at one end of the mole. He told them that he could not venture to engage rowers, as the fact of the escape of two white men from the town might be noticed and inquiries made. The boys assured him, however, that they were perfectly able to row themselves, and that the smaller the number in the boat, the less chances there would be of their being received by a random shot from their friends.

It was just nightfall when the English ship entered the harbor, where thirty Spanish vessels were lying all prepared for defence. The *Golden Hind* entered the port and dropped her anchor in the midst, and the quiet resolution and confidence which this act betrayed struck such a panic into the minds of the Spanish captains, that not one dared be the first to fire a gun at the intruder. Half an hour after the *Golden Hind* came to anchor a boat was seen approaching and was met by the hail, "Who goes there?"

The joyful shout of "Friends, your comrades, Ned Hearne and Tom Tressilis," was received by a cry of incredulity and astonishment by those on board the English vessel. Two minutes later the lads were on deck receiving the hearty embraces and congratulations of all the messmates, Reuben Gale and Gerald Summers being almost beside themselves with joy at the return to them of the comrades they believed to be so long ago dead. The admiral himself was greatly moved at seeing them; for their gallantry during the preceding voyage, and their eager zeal to do all in their power for the expedition, had greatly raised them in his affections.

They were soon seated in the cabin, which was thronged by as many of the officers and gentlemen adventurers as could find room there. A brief narrative was given of their adventures since leaving the fleet upon the other side of the continent, and loud were the expressions of surprise and approval at the manner in which they had gone through the various dangers and difficulties which they had encountered, Tom insisting generously that the credit was entirely due to the sagacity and coolness of his friend. When the story of the scene in the dungeons of the Inquisition was told, and Captain Drake was informed that large numbers of persons had been burned alive in Lima by the Inquisition, he was filled with fury, and at once despatched two boat-loads of men, armed to the teeth, to the shore, with orders to burn down the prison, to release any prisoners found there and to offer them a safe passage to Europe, and also to hang all officials who might be found within the walls. Ned acted as guide. The streets of Lima were deserted as the news of the landing of a party from the English ship spread through the town; shops were closed and windows barred, and it was as through a city of the dead that the band passed rapidly along until they reached the prison of the Inquisition. Here the doors were broken down, and the English sailors entered the ghastly prison. The cells were found to be tenanted only by natives, most of them men who had been captured in the hills and who had refused to accept the Catholic religion. These were all loosed and allowed to depart in freedom for the mountains, taking with them a store of such provisions for the way as could be found within the walls. The sight of the torture-room roused the fury of the sailors to the utmost pitch, and breaking into the part wherein dwelt the principal inquisitors, these were seized and hung from their windows. The contents of the various rooms were then heaped together, a light applied, and in a few minutes a glow of flame told the people of Lima that the dreaded prison of the Inquisition was no more.

The party then returned through the streets to the ship, and took part in the further operations commanded by the admiral. Proceeding from vessel to vessel, they took out all goods which they fancied, and which were either valuable, or might be useful to them in their further voyaging. They hewed down the masts of all the largest ships, and cutting their cables allowed them to drift on shore. No more astonishing scene was ever witnessed than that of thirty ships, backed by a garrison and considerable population on shore, allowing themselves to be thus despoiled and wrecked by the crew of one, and this a vessel inferior in size and in the numerical strength of her crew to many of those within the harbor.

The next day a party landed and stripped many of the churches of their valuables, and also levied a contribution upon the principal inhabitants. Ned and Tom, not thinking it worth while at this time to enter into a controversy with the comrades to whom they had been so recently restored as to the legality of their acts, simply declined to make part of the party who landed, alleging that they had had enough of the shore of the South American continent for the rest of their lives.

The 15th of February, the date upon which the *Golden Hind* arrived at the port of Lima, was indeed one to be remembered throughout the lives of the rescued seamen. Their future had appeared well-nigh hopeless. On the one side the dungeon of the Inquisition and probably a death by fire. On the other, a life passed in the midst of savages, away from all possibility of ever rejoining their friends or returning to their country. Now they were once again among those delighted to see them, and proudly trod the decks of the *Golden Hind* as gentlemen adventurers, having a good share in the booty as well as in the honor which would accrue to all on board. So far, indeed, the plunder had been but small. Upon their way down to the Cape they had gleaned nothing, and since rounding it they had only touched at Valparaiso, where they had taken all that they required in the way of wines, stores, and provisions of all kinds, besides much gold and, it is sad to say, the rich plunder of the churches, including golden crosses, silver chalices, and altar-cloths.

Nowadays it gives one a positive shock to hear of English sailors rifling churches; but in those rough times acts of sacrilege of this kind awakened but little reprobation.

The following day they hove the anchor and sailed northwards. In the port they had obtained news that, on the evening before they arrived, a ship laden with much treasure from Panama had appeared, but receiving news of the approach of the English, had again set sail. All determined that, if possible, the treasures on board the *Cacafuego* should pass into the hold of the *Golden Hind.* Spreading all sail, they pressed northward. On the 20th of February they touched at the port of Paita, but did not find her there. On the 24th they passed the port of Guayaquil, and on the 28th crossed the line. On the 1st of March a sail was descried ahead, and, sailing toward her, they found that she was indeed the vessel of which they were in search, and of which they had heard not only at Lima, but from a ship which they took at Paita, laden with wine; and from another, on board of which they found eighty pounds weight in gold, in Guayaquil. The *Cacafuego* had no thought that the solitary ship which was seen approaching was that of Captain Drake; but taking her for a Spaniard, made no effort to fly. When, upon her coming close and hailing her to surrender they discovered their mistake, the captain made a bold fight. Hastily loading his carronades, he poured a volley into the *Golden Hind,*

and did not surrender his ship until one of his masts had fallen
by the board and he himself was wounded. Then, finding further resistance useless, he hauled down his flag.

The booty taken was even greater than had been expected. Of
gold and silver alone there was on board her to the value
£750,000, equal to a vastly larger sum in these days; besides immense quantities of precious stones, silver vessels, and other
valuables. For six days they lay alongside the *Cacafuego,* transferring her cargo to the *Golden Hind;* and at parting Captain
Drake was considerate enough to give the captain a letter to
Captain Winter, or any of the other captains of the fleet, should
they come north and meet her, begging that she should be allowed to pass without interruption; or that should they have
need of any of the few articles left on board her, they would pay
double the value. He also, in exchange for the valuables transferred, was good enough to bestow upon the master a little linen
and some other commodites.

As it was now certain that the whole coast would be thoroughly alarmed, and the Governor-general at Panama would be
prepared with a powerful fleet to resist the *Golden Hind* should
she stir in that direction, Captain Francis determined to sail
boldly out to sea and then to shape his course so as to strike the
coast again far north of the Spanish possessions. His object in
thus undertaking a voyage which would seem likely to yield but
little profit was, that he hoped he might find a passage round the
north of America, and so not only shorten his own return journey home, but open a most valuable country for trade for his
own countrymen.

On the 7th of March, before putting out to sea, he touched at
the Island of Cano, off the coast of Nicaragua. Here they had an
alarm which startled even the boldest. As they lay at anchor they
felt the shock of a terrible earthquake, which almost brought
down the masts of the ship, and for a moment all thought that
she had been struck by some hostile machine, or had fallen
down on a rock. The pumps were manned, and it was happily
found that she made no water. Here they made their last prize
on the American coast—a ship which had come across from

China. She was laden with linen, China silk, and China dishes. Among the spoil is enumerated a falcon made of gold, with a great emerald set in his breast. It was not until the 15th of April that they again touched the land, and landed at Guatulco, whence, after a stay of a few hours, they departed; "not forgetting," the chronicler says, "to take with them a certain pot of about a bushel in bigness, full of royals of plate, together with a chain of gold, and some other jewels which we entreated a gentleman Spaniard to leave behind him as he was flying out of town." They then steered out to sea, and did not see the land again until, after sailing 1400 leagues, they came, on June 3d, in sight of land in 42° north latitude.

Before going further, the adventures of the fleet must be briefly related from the day, being the 21st of June, when the attack was made upon them by the Patagonians and the boys were driven into the wood. Captain Francis and those of the crew on shore with him soon beat off the natives, inflicting some loss upon them. These took to the woods, in which they could not be followed, and Captain Francis, mourning for the loss of his three adventurers, and of the gunner killed by his side, and despairing of ever recovering the bodies of those who were, as he believed, cut off and murdered, embarked on board ship and sailed down the coast. A few days later he put in to another bay, and there remained some time.

Here a strange scene was enacted, which has cast a shadow over the reputation of the great sea captain. Calling his officers together, he accused one of them, Captain Doughty, of treachery. He alleged that the plots against him were commenced before leaving Plymouth, and yet, as he had promoted Captain Doughty to the command of one of the ships when upon the voyage, it is difficult to understand how he can at that time have believed that he was unfaithful. Nor, again, does it appear in what way his treachery could have injured the admiral, for as all the officers and crew were devoted to him, Captain Doughty might have tried in vain to lead them aside from his authority. He professed indeed the highest regard for the man he accused, and spoke to the captains of the great good-will and inward affection, even more then brotherly, which he held toward him. And yet he averred that it was absolutely necessary that Captain Doughty should be put upon his trial.

Captain Doughty, it is said, stricken with remorse at his conduct, acknowledged himself to have deserved death, for that he had conspired not only for the overthrow of the expedition, but for the death of the admiral, who was not a stranger, but a dear and true friend to him, and he besought the assembly to take justice into their hands in order to save him from committing suicide.

The forty officers and gentlemen who formed the court, after examining the proofs, judged that "he had deserved death, and that it stood by no means with their safety to let him live, and therefore they remitted the matter thereof, with the rest of the circumstances, to the general." The Captain Drake offered to the prisoner either that he should be executed there and then, or that he should be left alone when the fleet sailed away, or that he should be sent back to England, there to answer his deeds before the lords of her majesty's council. Captain Doughty asked for twenty-four hours to consider his decision, and then announced his preference for instant execution, saying that death were better than being left alone in this savage land, and that the dishonor of being sent back to England would be greater than he could survive.

The next day Mr. Francis Fletcher, the pastor and preacher of the fleet, held a solemn service. The general and the condemned man received the sacrament together, after which they dined "also at the same table together as cheerful in sobriety as ever in their lives they had done aforetime, each cheering the other up and taking their leave by drinking each to other, as if some journey only had been in hand." After dinner, Captain Doughty came forth, kneeled down at the block, and was at once beheaded by the provost-marshal.

Such is the story of this curious affair as told by the chroniclers. But it must be remembered that these were favorable to Captain Drake, and it certainly seems extraordinary that upon such a voyage as this Captain Doughty could not have been deprived of his command and reduced to the rank of a simple adventurer, in which he could, one would think, have done no harm whatever to the expedition.

At the island where this execution took place the fleet abode two months, resting the crews, wooding, watering, and trimming the ships, and bringing the fleet into a more compact compass; destroying the *Mary*, a Portuguese prize, and arranging the whole of the crews in three ships, so that they might the more easily keep together. On August the 17th they set sail, and on the 20th reached the entrance to the Straits, Cape Virgins. Here the admiral caused his fleet, in homage to the Queen, to strike their foresails, acknowledging her to have the full interest and honor in the enterprise, and further, in remembrance of his honored patron, Sir Christopher Hatton, he changed the name of the ship in which he himself sailed from the *Pelican* to *Golden Hind,* this animal forming part of the chancellor's armorial bearings.

They now entered the narrow Straits of Magellan, which are in many places no wider than a river; and in the night passed a burning mountain, which caused no little surprise to those who had never beheld anything of the kind. Here all were astonished by the sight of huge numbers of penguins, which were then for the first time discovered by Englishmen. These strange birds, with their long bodies, short necks, and absence of wings, greatly astonished them, and were so tame that in the course of an hour or two they killed no less then three thousand of them, and found them to be excellent food. One of these islands the admiral christened St. George. Sailing on for some days they came to a bay in which they found many natives, who came out in a canoe, whose beauty and form were considered by all to be far superior to anything that they had hitherto beheld, which was the more singular, inasmuch as these people were of a very low type. However, they appear in those days to have been more advanced in civilization than their descendants now are.

On the 6th of September they entered the South Sea, Drake having been the fourth commander who had sailed through the Straits. The first passage was made by Magellan in 1520, the second by Loyasa in 1526, the third by Juan de Ladrilleros from the Pacific side. In this voyage the English commander had far better weather than had been experienced by his predecessors, accomplishing in a fortnight a voyage which had taken them some months. His good fortune, however, here deserted them, for upon the very day after they entered the South Sea a contrary wind fell upon them, and increased to a powerful hurricane. This augmented rather than decreased in force, and on the night of September the 30th the *Marigold*, Captain John Thomas, was separated from the rest of the fleet, and was never heard of after. Until the 7th of October they did not again see land, being driven far to the south. They then discovered an island, and entering a harbor came to anchor. The shelter, however, was a poor one, and the gale blew so furiously that in the night the *Elizabeth* was blown from her anchors and lost sight of the *Golden Hind*. It is a question whether this event was not partly caused by the captain, Winter, who certainly behaved as if he had the fixed intention of returning to England. He never made any serious effort to rejoin the *Golden Hind*, but after remaining for some little time in those quarters he sailed for England, reaching home in safety some months afterwards.

They christened the bay "The Parting of Friends," and the *Golden Hind* was driven down again into 55° south latitude. Fresh gales fell upon them, and, as has been said, it was not till October the 28th, after fifty-two days of almost unexampled bad weather, that the sky cleared, and they were able to renew their journey. They searched the islands in all directions for their missing friends, and in remembrance of them the admiral gave them the name of the Elizabethedes.

Hoping that Captain Winter had sailed north, the *Golden Hind*'s head was turned in that direction, with great hope that they might meet her in latitude 30°, which had been before appointed as a place of rendezvous should the fleet happen to be separated. Touching at many points, they inquired everywhere of the natives, but could hear no word of any ship having been seen before. At the island of Mocha they had a misadventure. The island was thickly inhabited by many Indians, whom the cruel conduct of the Spaniards had driven from the mainland. With these people the admiral hoped to have traffic, and the day after his landing they brought down fruit and vegetables and two fat sheep, receiving in return many little presents. They seemed to be well content, and the next morning early, all being ready for a general traffic, the admiral repaired to the shore again with two-thirds of his men with water-barrels to fill up the ship. As they were peaceably engaged in this task the natives, to the number of five hundred, suddenly sprang from an ambush, and with their arrows shot very grievously at the English. The general himself was struck in the face, under his right eye and close by his nose. Nine other persons of the party were all wounded grievously. The rest gained the boats, and all put off. None of the wounded died, which, considering that there was no surgeon on board the ship, was looked upon by the mariners as a special miracle in their favor. There was a great talk of returning to shore to punish the men who had so treacherously attacked them. But the admiral, seeing that many of the men were hurt, and believing that the attack had been the result of the cruel treatment bestowed upon the natives by the Spaniards, with whom they had naturally confounded our men, determined to leave them alone, and the same night sailed north, seeking some convenient spot where the men could land and obtain a supply of fresh provisions.

Such a place they found at Philip's Bay, in latitude 32°. Here they came to an anchor; and an Indian, described as a comely personage of a goodly stature, his apparel being a white garment reaching scarcely to his knees, came on board in a canoe. His arms and legs were naked; his hair upon his head very long, and without a beard; of very gentle, mild, and humble nature, and tractable to learn the use of everything. He was courteously entertained, and, receiving gifts, returned to the shore, where his companions, being much pleased with his reception, at once did all that they could for the fleet, and brought down provisions and other things desired. The natives also offered to guide them to a better harbor, where, the people being more numerous, they could obtain a greater store of the things desired. The offer was accepted, and on the 4th of December, piloted by him, they came to a harbor in such a place as was wished for.

This was the Spanish harbor of Valparaiso, and here, indeed, they found all that they desired, and that without payment. The Spaniards, having no idea of the English being in the vicinity, received them with all honor, but as soon as the mistake was discovered they fled, and the town fell in to their hands. In a ship in the harbor called the *Grand Captain,* 1800 jars of wine and a large quantity of gold were found. The churches were plundered of their ornaments and relics, and the storehouses of the city laid under contribution of all things desired.

Sailing again on the 19th of December, they touched to the southward of the town of Coquimbo, where fourteen of them landed. The Spaniards here, however, appeared to be bolder than their comrades in other towns, for a hundred of them, all well mounted, with three hundred natives, came up against them. This force being described, the English retreated, first from the mainland to a rock within the sea, and thence to their boat. One man, however, Richard Minnioy, refused to retire before the Spaniards, and remained defying the advancing body until they arrived. He, of course, fell a victim to his obstinacy, and the Spaniards, having beheaded the body, placed it against a post, and used it as a target for the Indians. At nightfall they left it, and the English returned to shore in their boat and buried it. The next day, finding a convenient place, they remained for a month refitting the ships and resting the crews, obtaining an abundance of fish and other provisions such as they required, fresh water, however, being absent.

Sailing along, they came to Iquique, and landing here they lighted upon a Spaniard who lay asleep, and had lying by him thirteen bars of silver. Thinking it cruel to awaken him, they removed the money and allowed him to take his sleep out in security. Continuing their search for water, they landed again, and near the shore met a Spaniard with an Indian boy driving eight "Peruvian sheep," as the chronicler calls them, these being of course, the llamas, which were used as beasts of burden. Each sheep bore two leather bags, in each of which was fifty pounds' weight of refined silver. The chronicler says, "We could not endure to see a gentleman Spaniard turned carrier so, and therefore, without entreaty, we offered our services, and became drivers, only his directions were not so perfect that we could keep the way which he intended, for almost as soon as he was parted from us we, with our new kind of carriages, were come unto our boats."

Beyond this Cape lay certain Indian towns, and with the natives of these, who came out on frail rafts, they trafficked knives, beads, and glasses, for dried fish. Here they saw more of the llamas, which are described at great length by the historians of the expedition, who considered, and rightly, that they were extraordinary and most useful animals. If, however, this assertion, that upon one of their backs "did sit at one time three well-grown and tall men and one boy" be true, they must have been considerably larger in those days than at present. It was but a few days later that they arrived at Arica, at which place also they gleaned considerable booty, and thence proceeded to Lima, which they reached seven days after leaving Arica.

After their long voyage out to sea they again bore north, and reached the land at the Bay of San Francisco. Here they complained bitterly of the cold, which is not a little singular, inasmuch as the time of the year was June, a period at which the heat at San Francisco is at present excessive. It must be assumed, therefore, that some altogether exceptional season prevailed during this portion of the voyage. Here they were well north of the Spanish possessions, and fell among a people who knew nothing of the white man. A native in a canoe speedily came out to the ship as soon as she cast anchor, and, standing at a long distance, made delivery of a very prolix oration, with many gestures and signs, moving his hand, turning and twisting his head and body, and ending with a great show of reverence and submission. He returned to shore. Again, and for a third time, he came out and went through the same ceremony; after which he brought a little basket of rushes filled with an herb which is called there tambac, which he threw into the boat. Then he again returned to shore. The people came out, many of them in boats, but would not approach the vessel; and upon the third day the vessel, having received a leak at sea, was brought to anchor nearer the shore, and preparations were made to land her stores.

CHAPTER XVIII

San Francisco Bay

After his experience of the treachery of the natives, the admiral determined to build a fort to protect the party on shore. The people, seeing these preparations, appeared in large numbers and approached, but their attitude expressed astonishment rather than hostility. They then, laying down their arms, gathered round the little party of white men; but as they brought their women with them, the admiral concluded that no hostility was intended, and allowed them freely to mix with the whites. Their attitude and deportment showed that they looked upon them as gods, paying worship in the most abject manner. In order to show them that his men were but human, the admiral ordered them to eat and drink, that the people might observe that they were but men as they. Even this failed to convince them, and during the whole time that they remained there they were treated as being creatures of celestial origin.

Two days later the natives returned in great numbers. A leader at their head again delivered a long and tedious oration, "to which," according to the chronicler, "these people appear to be much addicted." This oration was delivered with strange and violent gestures, the speaker's voice being extended to the uttermost strength of nature, and his words falling so thick, one in the neck of another, that he could hardly fetch his breath again. When he had concluded, the people bowed to the earth, giving a long cry of "Oh," which appears to have answered to our "Amen." Then the men came forward, and the women went through a number of exercises, which appear to have shocked and appalled our seamen. "As if they had been desperate, they used violence against themselves, crying and shrieking piteously, tearing their flesh with their nails from their cheeks in a monstrous manner, the blood streaming down over their bodies. Then, holding their hands above their heads so that they might not save their bodies from harm, they would with fury cast themselves upon the ground, never respecting whether it were clean or soft, but dash themselves in this manner on hard stones, knobby hillocks, stocks of wood, and prickly bushes, or whatever else were in their way, iterating the same course again and again some nine or ten times each, others holding out for fifteen or sixteen times, till their strength failed them." The admiral, horrified by this cruel exhibition of reverence, ordered his men to fall to prayers, and signified to them that the God whom we did serve did not approve of such measures as they had taken.

Three days later, the king himself came down, and the ceremonies were repeated. The king then offered to the admiral the monarchy of that land, and perceiving that this would please them, and having in mind the honor and glory of her majesty, Captain Francis accepted the crown, and with many ceremonies was installed king of that country, taking possession of the land in the name of the Queen. It is not a little singular that this, one of the richest and most valuable portion of the United States, should thus have become by right alike of discovery and of free gift of the people, a possession of England.

For some days the people continued their cruel exercises upon themselves, and so fixed were they in their idolatry that, even when forcibly prevented acting this way, they would, immediately they were released, set to with even redoubled fury to cut and injure themselves. After a time their worship took a new form. All the people of the country having wounds, shrunken limbs, or diseases of any kind were brought down to be cured, and the people were much grieved that an instantaneous cure could not be effected, but that our men proceeded by the application of lotions, plasters, and unguents to benefit those who had anticipated immediate remedy.

Altogether, the account given by the voyagers of the people of this part of America is most favorable. They appear to have been of a tractable, free, and loving nature, without guile or treachery. They were finely built men, and one of them could carry easily uphill and down a weight which two or three Englishmen could scarcely lift. They were swift at running, and could catch a fish in the sea if it were in water within their depth. When the ship was repaired, the admiral, with many of his officers, made a journey into the interior, and found that it was a goodly country with a very fruitful soil. There were many thousands of large and fair deer grazing in herds. This country was christened by the admiral, Albion, partly from the color of its cliffs, partly in remembrance of his country. On the shore a monument was set up, and on it a plate of brass was affixed engraved with the Queen's name, the date of the arrival of the ship and of the free giving up of the province and kingdom into her majesty's hand, and a piece of current English money was fastened beneath a hole made in the brass plate, so that it might remain as a proof that the English had taken possession of this land to which the Spaniards had never approached.

As the stores were being taken on board again, and the natives saw the preparations for embarkation, the joy with which the arrival of these white beings had been received was changed into sorrow, and all the people went about mourning and crying. For many days this continued, and the parting when the ship set sail on the 23d of July was a very sorrowful one, the people climbing to the top of the hills so as to keep the ship in sight as long as they could, and making great fires and burning thereon sacrifices to the departing gods.

The admiral had now made up his mind to abandon the search for a passage round the north of America. The cold had become even greater while they remained in the bay. The natives themselves were wrapped in black cloths and huddled together for warmth, and those in the ship suffered exceedingly. Moreover, the shores of the country trended far more to the west than had been expected, and the admiral concluded that far to the north the shores of America and Asia must unite. He thought, too, that in that country must be very lofty mountains covered with snow, for so alone could he account for the exceeding coldness of the wind. Believing, therefore, that no passage could be made in that way, and seeing that the ship had already gone through heavy tempests, and the men, although still of good heart yet were longing for a return home after their great labors, he steered to the west, making the Moluccas his aim.

During the voyage from Lima, along the coast of South America, the boys had met with no special adventures. Upon the day after they came on board ship Ned and Tom were called by the admiral into his cabin, and there recounted to him at great length all the adventures that they had gone through. He wondered greatly at their recital, and commended them exceedingly for the prudence and courage which they had shown. The account of the strange places never before trodden by the foot of white men which they had seen, he ordered his secretary to write down at full length, that it might be delivered to her gracious majesty, together with the record of the voyage of the *Golden Hind,* and he predicted that the Queen would take great pleasure in this record of the first journey across the continent.

"As to you," he said, turning to Ned, "you seem to be fated to get into adventures, and to find your way out of them. I have not forgotten the strange passage in the Island of Puerta Rico, and I predict that if you go on as you have begun you will come to great things."

Warmly, also, did he praise Ned's companion on the journey; but the latter modestly ascribed all the success which had attended their journey to the knowledge of native life which Ned had gained among the negroes, and to his courage and prudence.

"Nevertheless," said the admiral, "there is praise due also to you, for you have known when to subordinate yourself to one younger in years, although older in experience. This virtue is rare and very commendable, and I doubt not that had you not so freely given up your own wishes and inclinations to those of your comrade, you might both have perished miserably."

He further expressed his high opinion of Ned's bravery and discretion by giving him a command in the ship as third officer, finding, on inquiry, that he had learned how to take the altitude of the sun and to do other things necessary for the discovery of the position of the ship. These signs of good-will on the part of the admiral caused, as might have been expected, some jealousy among a considerable portion of the equipage. Many, indeed, were glad at the position which Ned had gained by his enterprise and courage. Others, however, grumbled, and said that it was hard that those who had done their duty on board the ship should be passed over in favor of mere youngsters who had been wandering on their own account on land. Ned himself felt that there was some reason for this jealousy upon the part of those who had borne the burden of all the great labors which those on board the *Golden Hind* had undergone, and he spoke to the admiral and expressed his willingness, nay more, his desire, to remain as a private gentleman and adventurer on board the ship. This, however, Capital Francis would not hear of.

"Merit has to be rewarded," he said, "wheresoever it is found. These men have done their duty. All indeed on board the ship have wrought nobly for their own safety and for the honor of her majesty the Queen. But you have gone beyond this, and have by your journey across the continent brought fame and credit to the country. It is right that men who discover strange lands into which, some day, the power of Christianity and civilization may enter, should receive honor and credit of their countrymen. Of those who seek to do these things many perish, and those who survive should be held in honor."

Most of all delighted at the success and honor which had befallen Ned, were his three friends. Two of them even considered that they owed their lives to him. All regarded him as their leader as well as their comrade. But Reuben Gale grumbled much that he had had no share in the adventures which had befallen his three friends.

"You have all three strange histories to tell. You have seen wonderful things and have journeyed and fought with wild men and Spaniards; while I with equal good-will have never had the chance of doing more than join in the taking of Spanish caravels, where the resistance was so poor that children might have done the business."

Ned laughed, and promised him that the next adventure he got into he would, if possible, have him as his comrade.

"We have a long voyage yet," he said. "We have not gone much more than a third of the circumference of the world, and before we reach England strange things may happen yet. We left Plymouth with a noble fleet of six ships. Now there remains but one, and fifty-eight men. At the same rate we shall be reduced to a cock boat, and four men, before we reach England. So keep up your heart, there is plenty of time before us."

So great was the confidence which they felt in Ned that Reuben was cheered with this promise, although he knew, in his heart, that these adventures fell upon Ned not from any effort of his own, but by the effect of accident, or, as we may say, Providence.

The young men liked not their stay in San Francisco Bay. Those who were best-looking and youngest were especially chosen out by the women as object of their adoration, and the lads were horrified at the way in which these poor creatures beat and tore themselves and grovelled upon the ground; and so, being sick at heart at these mummeries, and at receiving a worship fit only for the Creator of the world, they remained on board ship as much as possible during the time that they tarried there.

Except for a group of islands which they passed the day after sailing west, the *Golden Hind* saw no more land from the 23d of July until September the 30th, sixty-eight days in all, when they fell in sight of some islands lying about eight degrees to the northward of the line. As soon as the ship was seen a great number of canoes came out, having in them some four, some six, some fourteen, or even twenty men paddling rapidly and bringing cocoas, fish, and fruits. The beauty and workmanship of these canoes astonished the voyagers. They were made out of one tree of great length, hollowed with fire and axe, and being so smooth, both without and within, that they shone like polished wood. The bow and stern were alike in shape, rising high and falling inwards almost in a semicircle, and being covered with white and glistening shells for ornament. These canoes had upon either side outriggers,—that is, pieces of cane extending six or seven feet beyond the side, and to which were fixed spars of very light wood, so that the boat could in nowise overturn. These people evinced no fear of the English, and it was clear that, although they might not themselves have seen a ship before, the presence of the Portuguese in these seas was known to the islanders, and the manner of their vessels.

The nature of these people was very different from that of the gentle savages on the western coast of America. They did not trade honestly as these had done, but obtained as much as they could, and then pushed off from the side of the ship without handing up the goods which they had bargained to give, and behaved so rascally that the admiral, seeing that their intentions were altogether evil, ordered a gun to be fired, not with the intent of hurting any, but of frightening them. The roar of the cannon was followed by the instant disappearance of every native from the fleet of canoes, amid the laughter of those on board ship. For a long time none could be seen, each as he came above water keeping on the further side of his canoe, and then paddling with it astern, so that the ship, as she floated on, left them gradually behind. When they thought that they were in safety they again took their places in the canoes, and finding that none were hurt, again paddled alongside the ship and made pretence to barter. Some of them indeed came on board with their wares, but while pretending to be engaged in honest trade they stole the daggers and knives from the men's girdles, and pillaged whatever they could lay their hands upon. The admiral, being wroth at this conduct, had some of these men seized and flogged, and then driving the rest into their canoes, hoisted sail and went onwards, christening the place the "Island of Thieves," so as to deter all passengers hereafter from ever visiting it.

Passing through many other islands they made for Tidore, the principal place in the Moluccas. But as they passed the Island of Motir, which was then called Ternate, a deputy, or viceroy, of the king of that island came off to the ship in a great canoe, and entreated the admiral to anchor at that island, and not at Tidore, assuring him in the name of the king that he would be wondrous glad to see him, and to do all that the admiral could require. He himself promised to return to the king at once, who would get all in readiness; whereas if they went on to Tidore, where the Portuguese held sway, they would find in them deceit and treachery. On these persuasions Captain Drake resolved to run into Ternate, where next morning he came to anchor.

The admiral then sent a party, consisting of Ned and three other adventurers, to the king, bearing the present of a velvet cloak, as a testimony of his desire for friendship and good-will, with the message that he should require no other thing at his hands but that he might be allowed by traffic and exchange of merchandise to obtain provisions, of which, after his long voyage across the seas, he had now but small store. As the boat rowed to shore it was met by a large canoe coming out with a message from the king, that he had heard from his viceroy how great was the nobleness of the captain, and of the Queen whom he served, and that he, who was the enemy of the Portuguese, whom he had expelled from his dominions, would gladly agree to aid him and to enter into treaties by which all ships of his nation might come to Ternate, and trade for such things as they required, all other white men being excluded. On arriving at the shore the deputation were met by many personages. They were dressed in white cloths of Indian manufacture, and the party marvelled much at the difference between their stately manners and ways and those of the people whom they had lately left. Accompanied by these personages, and with great honor, they were conducted to the interior of the island, where, in a house surprisingly large for a people so far removed from civilization, and which, indeed, they afterwards learned had been built by the Portuguese, they found the king, who received them with much honor. He was a tall and stout man, with much dignity in his manner. It was clear that his authority among his people was very great, for even the nobles and councillors whom he had sent to greet them bowed to the dust in his presence.

Ned had consulted with his comrades on the way, and had

agreed that, as the messengers of the admiral, and therefore in some way as the representatives of the Queen, it was their duty to comport themselves as equal, at least, in dignity to this island monarch. Therefore while all the people knelt in the dust in humility, they walked straight to his majesty and held out their hands in English fashion. His majesty was in no whit offended at this, and indeed by his manner strove to express his respect. A certain amount of conversation was carried on with him, for in the island were an Italian and a Spaniard, who, having been made prisoners by the Portuguese, had escaped to Ternate. These men, acting as interpreters, conveyed to the king the messages sent by the admiral, and in return informed Ned that the king was in all ways most anxious to express his pleasure to the admiral, and that on the morrow he would himself visit him on board ship. He also, as a pledge, delivered his own signet-ring to Ned to carry on board.

Having returned on board ship with these messages, they waited for the morrow, when three large canoes put off from the shore. In these were the greatest personages on the island. They sat in the canoes in accordance with their rank, the old men in the stern. Next to these were divers others, also attired in white, but with differences in the way in which the clothes were worn. These also had their places under the awning of reeds. The rest of the men were soldiers, who stood ranged on each side. On the outside of these again sat the rowers. These canoes must have in some way resembled the old Roman triremes, for it is said that "there were three galleries on either side of the canoe, one being builded above the other, and in each of these galleries were an equal number of benches, whereon did sit the rowers, about the number of fourscore in each canoe." In the forepart of each canoe sat two men, one holding a drum and the other a piece of brass, whereon both at once struck, marking the time for each stroke. The rowers on their part ended each stroke with a song, giving warning to those on the prow to strike again; and so, rowing evenly, they came across the sea at great speed. Each of these canoes carried a small cannon of about a yard in length. All the men, except the rowers, had swords, daggers, and

shields, lances, bows, and arrows, and some had guns. These canoes came up to the ship and rowed round her in solemn procession, to the great admiration of all on board, who had never
beheld a sight like this. But the admiral said that the vessels re-
minded him of the descriptions which he had read of the great
barges of Venice. As they rowed they did homage to the admiral, the greatest personages beginning, first standing up and
bowing their bodies to the ground, the others following in order
of rank. Then a messenger came on board, signifying that they
had come before the king, who had sent them to conduct our
ship into a better anchorage, and desiring that a rope might be
given them out that they might, as their king commanded, tow
the ship to the place assigned.

Very shortly the king himself came out, having with him in his
canoe six grave and ancient fathers, and did himself at once
make a reverent kind of obeisance. He was received in the best
manner possible. The great guns thundered, and as these had
been filled with a large quantity of small shot, they tore up the
water in the distance, and made a fine show for these people.
The trumpets also, and other instruments of music, sounded
loudly, whereat the king was much delighted, and requested
that the music might come into a boat. The musicians, at
Captain Francis' orders, so did, and laying alongside the king's
canoe, were towed behind the ship by the rowers in the three
first canoes.

The king and many others came on board and were bounti-
fully entertained, many presents being given to them. When the
anchorage was reached the king asked leave to go on shore,
promising that next day he would again come on board and in
the meantime send such victuals as were requested. Accordingly, at night and the next morning large quantities of hens,
sugar-canes, rice, figos—which are supposed to have been plan-
tains—cocoas, and sago were sent on board. Also some cloves
for traffic; but of these the admiral did not buy many, as he did
not wish the ship to be crowded with goods.

At the time appointed, all things being set in readiness, the admiral looked for the king's return, but he failed to keep his promise, to the great discontent and doubt on the part of the crew. The king's brother came off to invite Captain Drake to land and visit him; but this brother, who seemed to be an honest gentleman himself, whispered a few words in confidence to the admiral, warning him that it would be better that he should not go on shore. With his free consent the admiral retained this nobleman as a pledge, and then although, in consequence of the king's bad faith, he resolved not to land himself, he sent many of his officers, who were conducted with great honor to the large and fair house inhabited by the king, where at least a thousand people were gathered.

The king was seated in a great chair of state, and many compliments were exchanged between him and the English. The king was now attired in his full state, having from the waist to the ground a robe of cloth of gold, with many rings of plated gold on his head, making a show something like a crown. On his neck he had a chain of perfect gold, the links very large. On his left hand were a diamond, an emerald, a ruby, and a turquoise, and on his right hand many beautiful gems. Thus it will be seen that the king of these islands was a potentate of no mean grandeur. Most of the furniture and decorations of the court were obtained from the Portuguese during the time that they inhabited the island. Had they not followed the tyrannous ways of their people they might have remained there in fair comfort; but, desiring to obtain the entire authority, they had killed the late king. This cruelty, however, had brought about a different end to that which they had expected, for the people, headed by the king's eldest son, had risen against them in great force, had killed many, and had driven the rest from the island, placing the king's son upon the throne, who had become the deadly enemy of the Portuguese, and was now preparing an expedition to drive them from Tidore. The religion of these people was that of the Mussulmans, and the rigor with which they fasted—it being, at the time of the English visit, one of their festivals—greatly astonished those who saw them, for during the whole time they would eat nothing between morning and night; but the appetite with which they devoured many meals throughout the night almost equally astonished the British.

While the *Golden Hind* lay in the harbor of Ternate they received a visit from a Chinese gentleman of high station, and who was assuredly the first Chinaman who ever came in contact with one of our race. His reason for being at the Moluccas was singular. He had been a man of great rank in his own country, but was accused of a capital crime of which, though innocent, he was unable to free himself. He then implored the emperor to allow him to leave the country, placing he proof of his innocence in the hands of Providence; it being a bargain that if he could bring back to the emperor strange and wonderful tidings of things new to him, such as he had never heard of, he should be restored to his place and honors, and held to be acquitted of that crime. If such news could not be gained by him he was to remain in exile and to be accounted guilty of that of which he was accused. Coming on board, he very earnestly entreated the admiral to give him the account of his adventures from the time of leaving his country. This Captain Drake willingly did, and the Chinaman in great delight exclaimed that this was fully sufficient for him to bear back to the emperor. He gave a very warm and pressing invitation to Sir Francis to bring the ship to China, where he assured him of a welcome at the hands of the emperor. Had Captain Drake been able to accede to this proposition it is probable that our dealings with the East on a large scale might have begun some centuries earlier than they did; but the *Golden Hind* was much battered by the voyage she had gone through, being, indeed, not a new ship when she started. The crew, too, were all longing to get home, and the treasure which had been gathered from the Spaniards was ample for all their desires. The admiral, therefore, although truly he longed to see this country, and to open relations between it and the Queen, was yet forced to decline the invitation, and so to depart on his westward voyage.

The *Golden Hind* now made slow progress through the water, her bottom being foul with weeds and other things which had attached themselves to it during its long voyage. The captain therefore determined to enter the first harbor in an uninhabited island that he came to, for at none of the places at which he had hitherto touched had he ventured to take this step. However friendly the inhabitants might have appeared, some causes of quarrel might have arisen, and with the ship hauled up and bent over it might have fallen into the hands of the natives, and so been destroyed, and all return to England cut off from him. Five days after leaving Ternate he found such a place, and fetching up in a small harbor the whole party landed, pitched tents, and entrenched themselves. Then they took the casks and water-vessels ashore and thoroughly repaired them, trimmed the ship, and scraped her bottom, and so put her in a state to perform the rest of the voyage.

Greatly here were the crew astonished by the first sight of fire-flies, creatures which were new to them all. This island swarmed with crayfish of a size sufficient to satisfy four hungry men at dinner. These creatures never went into the sea, but kept themselves on land, digging holes in the roots of the trees, and there lodging numbers together. Strangely enough, too, these crayfish, when they found themselves cut off from their natural retreats, climbed up trees, and there concealed themselves in the branches.

On December the 12th they again set sail, being now among the Celebes, where they found the water shoal and coasting very dangerous. The wind, too, was high and contrary, and their difficulties greater than anything they had found. On January the 9th the wind, however, came aft, and they appeared to have found a passage out of these dangers, sailing then at full speed. They were, at the first watch at night, filled with consternation at a crash, followed by silence, and the vessel was found to have run high upon a reef of which the surface had presented no indication. Not since the *Golden Hind* had left England had her strait been as sore as this. The force with which she had run upon the reef seemed to have carried her beyond all hope of extrication. All considered that death was at hand, for they hardly hoped that the ship could hold long together. The admiral at once, to still the confusion which reigned, ordered all to prayers, and the whole, kneeling on the deck, prayed for mercy, preparing themselves for imminent death. Presently, having finished praying, the admiral addressed them in a consoling speech, and then, their courage being much raised, all bestirred themselves to regard the position. The pumps were first tried and the ship freed of water, and to their great joy they found that the leakage was no greater than before, and that the rocks had not penetrated through the planks. This appeared to all on board to be an absolute miracle wrought in their favor, for it seemed impossible to them that, running at so high a rate of speed, the vessel could have failed to break herself against the rocks. It is probable that, in fact, the ship had struck upon a newly-formed coral reef, and that the coral—which, when first made, is not very hard—had crashed to pieces under the shock, and so she lay in safety upon the bed of pounded fragments.

CHAPTER XIX

South Sea Idols

When order and tranquillity were perfectly restored the admiral ordered a boat to be lowered and soundings to be taken, intending to put out the anchors ahead, and to get her off by working upon them with the windlass. It was found, however, that under the forefoot of the vessel the water deepened so rapidly that at a distance of a few fathoms no soundings could be obtained. This plan, therefore, was abandoned. The prospect seemed dark indeed. The ship's boats would, at most, only carry half the men on board, and if the ship had to be abandoned the whole of her treasures must be lost, as well as many lives.

"There is an island far away to the south," the admiral said. "If the worst come, we must seek refuge on that. It will be well to send a boat to examine it, and see what capabilities it offers for the purpose. Then if the weather holds fair we can make several trips, and land our men, and a portion at least of our valuables."

"Will you let me go, sir, with my three friends?" Ned asked. "The canoe which we took from our last halting-place will carry the four of us, and as she paddles swiftly we may be back before many hours."

"The idea is a good one," Captain Drake said. "Make for the island. It is, I should say, fifteen miles off. When you have reached it see if there be water, fuel, and other necessaries, and whether the landing be good. If you should come upon any natives, parley with them. Take a few articles as presents, and explain to them, if they will come out here with their canoes and aid to bring the things ashore we will give them presents which will make them wealthy beyond their grandest dreams. Be careful, my boys. I know that you will be brave if necessary; but care and caution are the great things, and remember that our safety depends upon yours."

The young men speedily lowered the canoe under the shelter of the lee side of the ship, took some beads, calicoes, and other articles, and then, seating themselves in the boat, paddled rapidly away. At first they felt a little awkward in using the paddles, in which they had had no practice whatever. But being powerful men, and accustomed to the use of oars, they soon fell into regular stroke, and the light boat danced rapidly over the waters. The distance was further than Captain Drake had imagined, the clearness of the air making the land appear nearer than it really was; and it was only after three hours of hard work that they neared it. It turned out to be an island of about a mile in length so far as they could judge. A reef of coral ran round it. The centre of the island was somewhat elevated, and was covered with cocoanut-trees; and it was this alone which had enabled it to be seen from so great a distance from the deck of the *Golden Hind.* Paddling round the reef, they came to an opening, and entering this found themselves in perfectly smooth water, and were soon on the shore.

"Our best way to look for water," Ned said, "will be to follow the beach all round the island. If there is any stream we must then come upon it. We had better take our arms, and haul up the canoe."

Ned, although the youngest of the party, being an officer of the ship, was naturally in command.

"It will be hard," Reuben said, "if we do not meet with some adventure. This is the first time that I have been out with you, Ned. The others have had their share, and it will be hard upon me if, when I got home, I have not some tale to tell my friends."

"I hope that it will not be so," Ned said, "for more than storytelling depends upon our success. I fear the *Golden Hind* is fixed fast, and that all the fruits of our expedition are lost, even if our lives be saved. Everything depends upon the report we may make when we return, and anything that should occur to delay us or to prevent our bearing back tidings of this place to the admiral, would be bad fortune indeed."

"I don't mean," Reuben said, "anything that would prevent our returning. But we might do something, and yet return safely."

A walk round the island showed no signs of water, nor although they searched for some hours, walking backwards and forwards across it, could they find any sign of a pool. It was clear that there were no fresh-water springs on the island, and that the vegetation depended entirely upon the rain that fell in the regular season. But they discovered from the top of the island another and much larger one lying still again some fifteen miles to the south. After much deliberation they determined to make for this, as it was of importance that they should have some news of a place to which the goods could be transported, to carry back to the ship. This island was much higher, and there appeared every probability that water and all they required would be found there. Accordingly, taking their places in the canoe, they again paddled out through the entrance to the reef, and steered their course for their new discovery. This was a large island, measuring at least, as they judged from the view of the one side, twenty miles round. The shores were steep, and they rowed for some time before they succeeded in finding a place where a landing could be effected. Then a deep bay suddenly opened out, and into this they rowed.

Scarcely had they fairly entered it when from some bushes near the shore two large war-canoes, crowded with natives, shot out and made toward them. The lads at first grasped their muskets, but Ned said, "Let the arms be. We are here to make peace with the natives, and must take our chance."

They stood up in the canoe, holding up their arms in token of amity. The canoes came alongside at racing pace, the natives uttering yells of joy. The canoe had evidently been seen approaching the island, and preparations had been made to seize it immediately on its arrival. Ned held up in his hands the beads and pieces of cloth. But the natives were too excited for pause or negotiation. In an instant the boys were seized and placed on board the canoes, two in each. They were tenderly handled, and were clearly objects of veneration rather than of hostility. The moment that they were on board the contents of the canoe were transferred to the large boat, and it was then cast adrift, and the two war-boats at full speed made out through the passage. Ned endeavored in vain to attract the attention of the leaders of the savages to his gestures, and to explain to them that there was a vessel from which he had come at a short distance off, and that if they would accompany him thither they would obtain large quantities of the beads and cloth which he showed them. The natives, however, were too much excited to pay any attention to his efforts, and with a sigh of despair he sat down by the side of Reuben, who was in the same boat with him, as the canoes on emerging from the bay turned their heads to the southwest and paddled steadily and rapidly away from the island.

"Whither can they be going to take us?" Reuben said.

"They must belong to some other island," Ned answered, "and be a war party which has come on plundering purposes here. What a misfortune! What terribly bad luck! They have clearly never seen white men before, and regard us as superior beings, and so far as we are concerned it is probable that our lives are safe. But what will the admiral think when night comes on and we do not return? What will become of our comrades?"

And at the thought of their messmates left without help in so perilous a position Ned fairly broke down and cried.

For some hours the natives continued their course without intermission, and gradually an island, which had at first seemed like a low cloud on the horizon, loomed up nearer and nearer, and at last, just as night fell, they landed upon its shores. Here in a bay, a village of huts constructed of the boughs of trees had been raised, and the arrival of the war-canoes was greeted with wild and prolonged cries by the women and children. All prostrated themselves in wonder and astonishment when the white men in their strange attire were brought on shore, and Ned saw that his suspicions were correct, and that they were regarded by their captors as gods. Further proof was given of this when they were escorted to a large shed composed of a roof of thatch supported on four up right posts which stood in the centre of the village. Under this were placed some of the hideous effigies which the South Sea Islanders worship, and which are affixed to the prow of their boats, and may be seen in the British Museum, and in other places where collections of Indian curiosities are exhibited. These effigies were carved in the shape of human beings, with enormous goggle eyes, splashes of bright paint, and strange and immense headdresses of brilliant colors. Here the lads were motioned to sit down, and the natives brought them offerings of cocoas and other fruits.

The boys could hardly help laughing at their strange position, surrounded by these hideous idols.

"You wanted an adventure, Reuben, and you have got one indeed," Ned said. "You are translated into a heathen god, and, if you ever get home, will have your story to tell, which will astonish the quiet firesides in Devonshire."

"Ought we not to refuse to accept this horrid worship?" Gerald said.

"I think not," Ned replied. "It can do no harm, and we are at least better than these wooden idols. So long at least as we are taken for gods our lives are safe. But I would not say as much if they once became convinced, by our actions, that we are men like themselves."

"But we cannot sit here all our lives among these idols," Reuben said.

"I agree with you there, Reuben; but patience does wonders, and I am not troubled in the least about ourselves. Sooner or later a way of escape will present itself, and when it does, be assured that we will use it. Patience is all that we require now. It is of our poor shipmates that I am thinking."

As night fell great bonfires were lighted. The natives indulged in wild dances round them, and feasting and festivities were kept up all through the night. Four watches were stationed, one at each post of the temple, and the boys saw that for the present, at least, all thought of escape was out of the question. And therefore, stretching themselves at full length on the sand they were speedily asleep.

For some days the position remained unchanged. The boys were well fed and cared for. Offerings of fruit, fish, and other eatables were duly presented. A perfumed wood which, according to the native ideas, personified incense, was burned in large quantities round the temple, and nearly choked the boys with its smoke.

Upon the fifth day it was clear that some expedition was being prepared. Four large war-canoes were dragged down and placed in the water, and the great idols which stood in the bow of each were removed and carried up to the temple, and placed there in position. Then the boys were motioned to come down to the beach.

"I do believe," said Tom, bursting into a shout of laughter, "that they are going to put us in the bows of their canoes in place of their old gods."

The others joined in the laughter, for to act as the figure-head of a canoe was indeed a comical, if an unpleasant situation. When they reached the boats the boys saw that their suspicions were correct, and that the natives were preparing to lash them to the lofty prows which rose some twelve feet above the water, in a sweep inwards.

"This will never do," Tom said, "if we are fastened like that our weight will cut us horribly. Let us show them how to do it."

Whereupon, with great gravity he took a large piece of flat wood, and motioned to the savages to lash this in front of the bow of one of the boats at a height of three feet above the water, so as to afford a little platform upon which he could stand. The natives at once perceived the drift of what he was doing, and were delighted that their new deities should evince such readiness to fall in with their plans. The additions were made at once to the four canoes; but while this was being done, some of the leading chiefs, with every mark of deference, approached the boys with colored paints, and motioned to them that they would permit them to deck them in this way. Again the boys indulged in a hearty laugh, and stripping off their upper garments, to the immense admiration of the natives, they themselves applied paint in rings, zigzags, and other forms to their white shirts, painted a large saucer-like circle round the eyes with vermilion, so as to give themselves something the appearance of the great idols, and having thus transmogrified themselves, each gravely took his place upon his perch, where, leaning back against the prow behind them, they were by no means uncomfortable.

"If these fellows are going, as I expect, upon a war expedition," Ned shouted to his friends, as the boats, keeping regularly abreast, rowed off form the island amidst a perfect chaos of sounds, of yells, beatings of rough drums made of skins stretched across hollow trunks of trees, and of the blowing of conch shells, "our position will be an unpleasant one. But we must trust to circumstances to do the best. At any rate we must wish that our friends conquer, for the next party, if we fall into their hands, might take it into their heads that we are devils instead of gods, and it might fare worse with us."

It was manifest, as soon as they started, that the object of the expedition was not the island upon which they had been captured, but one lying away to the south. It was a row of several hours before they approached it. As they did so they saw columns of smoke rise from several points of the shore, and knew that their coming there was observed by the islanders. Presently six canoes, equally large with their own and crowded with men, were observed pulling out, and yells of defiance came across the water.

"It is clear," Tom said, "that this island is stronger than our own, and that it is only on the strength of our miraculous presence that the islanders expect to conquer their foes, for they would never, with four canoes, venture to attack a place of superior force, unless they deemed that their victory was certain."

With wild yells, which were answered boldly from their own canoes, the enemy approached, and the combat began with a general discharge of arrows. Then the canoes rowed into each other, and a general and desperate hand-to-hand combat commenced. The enthusiasm with which the inmates of the boys' canoes were animated at first gave them the superiority, and they not only beat back the attacks of their foes, but leaping into their enemy's boats succeeded in clearing two of them of their occupants. Numbers, however, told, and the enemy were, with very heavy clubs and spears, pointed with sharp shells, gradually forcing the adventurers back, when Ned saw that a little supernatural interference was desirable to bring matters straight again. Giving the word to his friends, he stood up on his perch, and swinging himself round, alighted in the boat, giving as he did so a loud British cheer, which was answered by that of his comrades. Then with his arms erect he began to move along the benches of the canoe toward the conflict which was raging on either side. The sudden interference of the four deities at the head of the boat was received with a yell of terror by the natives who were attacking them, which was increased when the boys, each seizing a club from the hands of a native, jumped into the enemy's canoes and began to lay about them with all their strength. This was, however, required but for a moment. The sight of so terrible and unexampled an apparition appalled the islanders, who, springing overboard with yells of despair, swam rapidly toward land, leaving their boats in the hands of the victors. These indulged in wild yells of triumph, knelt before their good geniuses, and then, taking their places, paddled toward the shore. Before they had reached it, however, the defeated savages had landed, and running up to their village had borne the news of the terrible apparitions which had taken part against them. The conquerors on reaching the village found it deserted; plundered it of a few valuables; carried down all their enemy's gods in triumph into the canoes; and then, having fired the huts, started again with the ten canoes toward their own island.

Their triumphant arrival at the village was received with frantic excitement and enthusiasm. The sight of six canoes towed in by the four belonging to the place was greeted with something of the same feeling which in Nelson's time Portsmouth more than once experienced upon a English vessel arriving with two captured French frigates of size superior to herself. And when the warriors informed their relatives of the interposition of the white gods in their favor the latter rose to an even higher estimation in public opinion than before. They were escorted to their shrine with wild dancing and gesticulation, and great heaps

of fruit, fish, and other luxuries were offered to them, in token
of the gratitude of the people. But this was not all. A few hours
later a solemn council was held on the sea-shore, and after a
time a great hurrying to and fro was visible in the village. Then,
to the sound of their wild music, with dancing, brandishing of
spears, and the emission of many wild yells, the whole population moved up toward the shrine.

"What can they be going to do now?" Tom said. "Some fresh
piece of homage, I should guess. I do wish they would leave us
alone. It is annoying enough to be treated as a god, without
being disturbed by these constant worshippings."

When the crowd arrived before the shed they separated, and
in the midst were discovered four girls. On their heads were
wreaths of flowers, and their necks and arms were loaded with
necklaces and shells and other ornaments.

"Don't laugh, you fellows," said Ned. "I do believe that they
have brought us four wives in token of their gratitude."

The lads had the greatest difficulty in restraining themselves
from marring the effect of the solemnity by ill-timed laughter.
But they put a great restraint upon themselves, and listened
gravely while the chief made them a long harangue, and pointed
to the four damsels, who, elated at the honor of being selected,
but somewhat shy at being the centre of the public gaze, evidently understood that the village had chosen them to be the
wives of the gods. Although the boys could not understand the
words of the speaker, there was no question as to his meaning,
and they consulted together as to the best steps to be taken
under the circumstances.

"We must temporize," said Tom. "It would never do for them
to consider themselves slighted."

After a short consultation they again took their places in a
solemn row in front of the shed. Reuben, who was the tallest
and most imposing of the set, and who was evidently considered
by the villagers to be the leading deity, then addressed a long
harangue to the chief and villagers. He beckoned to the four
girls who timidly advanced, and one knelt at the feet of each of
the whites. Then Reuben motioned that a hut must be built

close to the shrine, and pointing to the sun, he traced its way across the sky, and made a mark upon the ground. This he repeated fourteen times, signifying that the girls must be shut up in the hut and guarded safely for that time, after which the nuptials would take place.

"You are quite sure, Ned," he said, pausing and turning round to his friend, "that we shall be able to make our attempt to escape before the end of the fourteen days, because it would be fearful indeed if we were to fail, and to find ourselves compelled to marry these four heathen women."

"We will certainly try before the fourteen days are up, Reuben; but with what success, of course we cannot say. But if we lay our plans well we ought to manage to get off."

The villagers readily understood the harangue of Reuben, and without delay the whole scattered into the wood, and returning with bundles of palm leaves and some strong posts, at once began to erect the hut. Fires were lighted as the evening came on, and before they ceased their labor the hut was finished. During this time the girls had remained sitting patiently in front of the shrine. The lads now offered them their hands and escorted them with grave ceremony to the hut. The palm leaves which did service as a door were placed before it, and the boys proceeded to dance one after the other in solemn order fourteen times round the hut. They then signified to the natives that provisions, fruit, and water must be daily brought for the use of their future wives; and having made another harangue, thanking the natives for their exertions and signifying future protection and benefits, they retired under the shelter of the shed, and the village subsided to its ordinary state of tranquillity.

"There are two difficulties in the way of making our escape," Ned said. "In the first place it is useless to think of leaving this island until we have a sufficient stock of provisions and water to put in a canoe to last us until we can get back to Ternate. Did we put into any island on the way our position might be ten times as bad as it now is. Here at least we are well treated and honored, and, did we choose, could no doubt live here in a sort of heathen comfort for the rest of our lives, just as many white sailors on the western isles have turned natives, and given up all thought of ever returning to their own country. The *Golden Hind* was four days on her journey from Ternate to the place where she refitted; another two to the spot where she went on the reef. The wind was very light, and her speed was not above five knots an hour. We should be able to paddle back in the course of ten days, and must take provisions sufficient for that time. The first point, of course, will be to find whether the old ship is still on the reef. If she is not there she may have succeeded in getting off, or she may have gone to pieces. I trust, however, that the admiral, who is full of resource, has managed to get her off in safety. He will no doubt have spent a day or two in looking for us; but finding no signs of us in the island to which we were sent, or in the other lying in sight to the southward, he will have shaped his way for the Cape. The first difficulty then is to procure sufficient provisions; the next is to make our escape unseen. The four natives who night and day watch at the corners of this shed mean it as a great honor no doubt; but, like many other honors, it is an unpleasant one. Our only plan will be to seize and gag them suddenly, each pouncing upon one. Then there is the fear that the natives, who are, I must say, the most restless sleepers I ever saw, may in their wanderings up to look at us find that we have gone before we are fairly beyond reach of pursuit, for one of their great canoes will travel at least two feet to our one. Hitherto we have only taken such provisions from the piles they have offered us as were sufficient for our day's wants, and left the rest for them to take away again next morning. In future we had best each day abstract a considerable quantity, and place it conspicuously in the centre of this shed. The people will perhaps wonder, but will probably conclude that we are laying it by to make a great feast upon our wedding day. As to water, we must do with the calabashes which they bring the day before, and with the milk which the cocoas contain, and which is to the full as quenching as water. With a good number of cocoas we ought to be able to shift for some days without other food, and there is indeed an abundance of juice in many of the other fruits which they offer us."

This programme was carried out. Every morning the lads danced in solemn procession round the hut, lessening their rounds by one each day. Daily the heap of fruit, dried fish, and vegetables under the shed increased, and the natives, who believed that their new deities were intent upon the thoughts of marriage, had no suspicion whatever of any desire on their part to escape.

Having settled how to prevent their escape being detected before morning, they accustomed themselves to go to sleep with the cloths, woven of the fibre of the palm with which the natives had supplied them, pulled over their heads.

Seven days after the fight with the other islanders the lads judged that the pile of provisions was sufficiently large for their purpose, and determined upon making the attempt that night. A canoe of about the size that they desired, which had been used during the day for fishing, lay on the shore close to the water's edge. They waited until the village was fairly hushed in sleep. An hour later they believed that the four guards or worshippers, for it struck them that their attendants partook partly of both characters, were beginning to feel drowsy, and each of the boys having furnished himself with a rope of twisted cocoanut fibre, stole quietly up to one of these men. To place their hands over their mouths, to seize and throw them upon their faces, was but the work of a moment, and was accomplished without the least noise, the natives being paralyzed by the sudden and unexpected assault. A piece of wood was shoved into the mouth of each as a gag, and secured by a string passing round the back of the head and holding it in its place. Their arms and legs were tied, and they were set up against the posts in the same position they had before occupied. Four of the great effigies were then taken from their places and laid down upon the ground and covered over with the mats, so that to any casual observer they presented exactly the same appearance as the boys sleeping there. Then, loading themselves with provisions, the boys stole backwards and forwards quietly to the boat. Once they had to pause, as a sleepless native came out from his hut, walked up to the shrine, and

bowed himself repeatedly before the supposed deities.
Fortunately he perceived nothing suspicious, and did not notice the constrained attitude of the four guardians. When he
retired the boys continued their work, and soon had the whole
of the store of cocoas and other provisions in the canoe, together with some calabashes of water. Then with some difficulty they launched the boat, and taking their places, paddled
quietly away from the island.

Once fairly beyond the bay they laid themselves to their work,
and the light boat sped rapidly across the waters. In order that
they might be sure of striking the point where they had left the
ship they made first for the island where they had been captured, and when day broke were close beside it. They then
shaped their course northwards, and after two hours' paddling
were in sight of the low island which they had first visited. By
noon they reached the spot where, as they judged, the *Golden
Hind* had gone on the reef; but no sign whatever of her was to
be discovered. By the position in which the island they had left
lay, they were sure that, although they might be two or three
miles out in their direction, they must be within sight of the vessel were she still remaining as they had left her. There had been
no great storm since she had grounded, and it was unlikely,
therefore, that she could have gone entirely to pieces. This afforded them great ground for hope that she had beaten off the
reef and proceeded on her voyage. Hitherto they had been
buoyed up with the expectation of again meeting their friends,
but they now felt a truly unselfish pleasure at the thought that
their comrades and admiral had escaped the peril which threatened the downfall of their hopes, and the termination of an
enterprise fairly and successfully carried out so far.

There was nothing now for them but to make for Ternate.
They found no difficulty whatever in doing without water, their
thirst being amply quenched by the milk of the cocoas and the
juice of the guavas and other fruits. They paddled for two days
longer, working steadily all day and far into the night, and passed
one or two islands. In the course of the next day's passage they
went within a short distance of another, and were horrified at

seeing from the narrow bay a large war-canoe put out and make rapidly toward them.

They had already talked over what would be their best course in such a contingency, and proceeded at once to put their plans into execution. They had, at starting, taken with them a supply of the paints used in their decoration, and with these they proceeded to touch up the coloring on their faces and white shirts, and on the strange ornaments which had been affixed to their heads. Two of them now took their place, one at the stern and the other at the bow of the canoe. The other two stood up and paddled very quietly and slowly along, and as the canoe approached rapidly the four broke into a song—one of the old Devonshire catches which they had often sung together on board ship. The war-canoe as it approached gradually ceased paddling. The aspect of this small boat paddling quietly along and taking no heed of their presence filled its occupants with surprise. But when the way on their canoe drifted them close to it, and they were enabled to see the strange character of the freight, a panic of astonishment and alarm seized them. That a boat, navigated by four gods, should be seen proceeding calmly along the ocean alone was a sight for which Indian legend gave them no precedent whatever, and after gazing for a while in superstitious dread at the strange spectacle they turned their boat's head and paddled rapidly back to shore.

For an hour or two the boys continued their course in the same leisurely manner; but when once convinced that they were out of sight of their late visitors they again sat down, and the four stretched themselves to their work. On the evening of that day there was a heavy mist upon the water. The stars were with difficulty seen through it, and the lads were all convinced that a change of weather was at hand. Before nightfall had set in, an island had been seen at a short distance to the north, and they decided at once to make for this, as if caught in mid-ocean by a storm they had little hope of weathering it in a craft like that in which they were placed, although the natives, habituated to them, were able to keep the sea in very rough weather in these little craft, which, to an English eye, appeared no safer than

THE FOUR GODS
SEE PAGE 250.

cockle-shells. The boys rowed with all their strength in the direction in which the island lay, but before they reached it sharp puffs of wind struck the water and the steerage of the canoe became extremely difficult. Presently, however, they heard the sound of a dull roar, and knew that this was caused by the slow heaving swell, of which they were already sensible, breaking upon a beach. Ten minutes later they were close to the shore. Had it been daylight they would have coasted round the island to search for a convenient spot for landing, but the wind was already rising so fast that they deemed it better to risk breaking up their canoe than to run the hazard of being longer upon the sea. Waiting, therefore, for a wave, they sped forward with all their strength. There was a crash, and then they all leaped out together, and seizing the canoe, ran her up on the beach before the next wave arrived.

I fear she has knocked a great hole in her bottom," Reuben said.

"Never mind," Ned replied. "We shall be able to make a shift to mend it. The great point now is to drag it up so high among the bushes that it will not be noticed in the morning by any natives who may happen to be about. Until this storm is over, at any rate, we have got to shelter here."

The canoe, laden as she still was with provisions, was too heavy to drag up; but the boys, emptying her out, lifted her on their shoulders and carried her inland, until at a distance of some sixty or seventy yards they entered a grove of cocoanut trees. Here they laid her down, and made two journeys back to the beach to fetch up their provisions, and then took refuge in the grove thankful that they had escaped on shore in time, for scarcely had they landed when the hurricane which had been brewing burst with terrific force. Seas of immense height came rolling in upon the shore. The trees of the grove waved to and fro before it, and shook the heavy nuts down with such force that the boys were glad to leave it and to lie down on the open beach, rather than to run the risk of having their skulls fractured by these missiles from above. The sound of the wind deadened their voices, and even by shouting they could not make themselves heard. Now and then, above the din of the storm, was heard the crush of some falling tree, and even as they lay they were sometimes almost lifted from the ground by the force of the wind.

For twenty-four hours the hurricane continued, and then cleared as suddenly as it had commenced. The lads crept back to the grove, refreshed themselves with the contents of two or three cocoas apiece, and then, lying down under the canoe, which they had taken the precaution of turning bottom upwards, enjoyed a peaceful sleep till morning.

CHAPTER XX

A Portuguese Settlement

The day broke bright and sunny. The first care of the boys was to examine their canoe, and they found, as they had feared, that a huge hole had been made in her bottom by the crash against the rocks on landing. They looked for some time with rueful countenances at it, and then, as usual, turned to Ned to ask him what he thought had best be done.

"There can be no doubt," he said, "that the natives make a sort of glue out of some trees or shrubs growing in these islands, and we shall have to endeavor to discover the tree from which they obtain it. We can, of course, easily pull off the bark from some tree which will do to cover the hole. The great point is to find some substance which will make it water-tight."

The grove was a very large one, and appeared to extend along the whole coast. Seaward, it was formed entirely of cocoa-trees, but inland a large number of other trees were mingled with the palms. All day the boys attempted to find some semblance of gum oozing from these trees. With sharp pieces of shell they made incisions in the bark of each variety that they met with to see if any fluid exuded which might be useful for this purpose, but in vain.

"If we can kill some animal or other," Ned said, we might boil down its sinews and skin and make glue, as Tom and myself did, to mend our bows with, among the Indians on the pampas. But even then I question whether the glue would stand the action of the water.

As to their subsistence they had no uneasiness. Besides the cocoas, fruit of all sorts abounded. In the woods parrots and other birds flew screaming among the branches at their approach, and although at present they had no means of shooting or snaring these creatures, they agreed that it would be easy to construct bows and arrows should their stay be prolonged. This, however, they shrank from doing as long as any possible method of escape presented itself. Were it absolutely necessary, they agreed that they could burn down at tree and construct a fresh canoe; but they were by no means sanguine as to their boat-building capabilities, and were reluctant to give up the idea of continuing their voyage in their present craft as long as a possibility of so doing remained. So they passed four days; but succeeded in finding no gum or other substance which appeared likely to suit their purpose.

"I should think," Reuben said one day, "that it would be possible to make the canoe so buoyant that she would not sink, even if filled with water."

"How would you do that?" Tom asked. "There are many light woods, no doubt, among the trees that we see, but they would have to remain a long time to dry to be light enough to be of any use."

"I was thinking," Reuben said, "that we might use cocoanuts. There are immense quantities upon the trees, and the ground is covered with them from the effects of the late gale. If we strip off the whole of the outside husk and then make holes in the little eyes at the top and let out the milk, using young ones in which the flesh has not formed, and cutting sticks to fit tightly into the holes, they would support a considerable weight in the water. I should think that if we treated several hundred nuts in this way, put them in the bottom of the canoe, and keep them in their places by a sort of net which we might easily make from the fibres of the cocoas, the boat would be buoyant enough to carry us."

The idea struck all as being feasible, and Reuben was much congratulated upon his inventive powers. Without delay they set to work to carry out the plan. A piece of thin bark was first taken, and by means of a long thorn used as a needle, was sewn over the hole in the canoe with the fibres of the cocoa. Then a

large pile of nuts was collected, and the boys set to work at the
task of emptying them of their contents. It took them some
hours' work to make and fit the pegs. Another two days were
spent in manufacturing a net to stretch across the boat above
them. The nuts were then placed in the boat, the net put into
shape, and choosing a calm night for their trial—for they feared
during the daytime to show themselves beyond the margin of
the forest—they placed it in the water, and paddled a short distance out.

They found that their anticipations were justified, and that
the flotation of the cocoas was amply sufficient to keep the boat
afloat. She was, of course, far lower in the water than she had
before been, and her pace was greatly deteriorated. This, however, they had expected, and returning to the shore they
watched for the next night. Then, taking in a load of provisions,
they started at once upon their way. It was weary work now, for
the water-logged canoe was a very different boat to the light
bark which had yielded so easily to their strokes. Fortunately,
however, they met with no misadventure. The weather continued calm. They were unseen, or at least not followed, from any
of the islands that they passed on their way. But it was ten days
after their final start before a large island, which they all recognized as Ternate, was seen rising above the water.

"Easy all," Ned said. "We may be thankful indeed that we
have arrived safely in sight of the island. But now that we are
close, and there is no fear of tempests, had we not better talk
over whether, after all, we shall land at Ternate?"

"Not land at Ternate?" the others exclaimed, in consternation;
for, indeed, the work during the last few days had been very
heavy, and they were rejoicing at the thought of an end to their
labors. "Why, we thought it was arranged all along we should
stop at Ternate."

"Yes, but we arranged that because at Ternate alone there
seemed a certainty of a welcome. But, as you know, Tidore only
lies twelve miles away from Ternate, and from the position we
are now in it will not be more than five or six miles farther. You
see when we were there the king was preparing for a war with

the Portuguese in Tidore, and he would certainly expect us to assist him, and probably to lead his fighting men."

"But we should have no objection to that," Reuben said.

"Not in the least," Ned replied. "But you see if we are ever to get back to England it must be through the Portuguese. Their ships alone are to be found in these seas, and were we to join the King of Ternate in an attack upon them, whether successful or not, we could never hope to be received in Portuguese ships, and should probably, indeed, be taken to Goa, and perhaps burned there as heretics, if we were to seek an asylum on board. What do you think?"

Viewed in this light it certainly appeared more prudent to go to Tidore, and after some little discussion the boat's head was turned more to the west, and the lads continued their weary work in paddling the water-logged canoe. So slowly did she move that it was late at night before they approached the island. They determined not to land till morning, as they might be mistaken for natives and attacked. They, therefore, lay down in the canoe and went to sleep, when within about a mile of the island; and the next morning paddled along its shore until they saw some canoes hauled up together with an English boat and supposed that they were at the principal landing-place of the island.

On either side of the landing-place the cliffs rose steeply up at a short distance from the beach. But at this point a sort of natural gap existed, up which the road ascended into the interior of the island. There were several natives moving about on the beach as the boys approached, and one of these was seen at once to start at a run up the road. The lads had carefully removed all vestige of the paint from their faces and hands, and having put on their doublets, concealed the strange appearance presented before by their white shirts. No resistance was opposed to their landing; but the natives motioned to them that they must not advance inland until a messenger returned from the governor. The boys were only too glad to throw themselves down full length on th soft sand of the beach, and to dry their clothes in the sun, as for ten days they had been constantly wet, and were stiff and tired.

Presently a native came down at a run, and announced that the governor was at hand. Rising to their feet and making the best show they could in their faded garments, the lads soon saw a Portuguese gentleman attended by four soldiers coming down the road between the cliffs.

"Who are you?" he asked in Portuguese as he reached them, "and whence come you?"

"We are Englishmen," Ned said in Spanish. "We belong to the ship of Captain Drake, which passed by here in its voyage of circumnavigation. By an accident we in the canoe were separated from the ship and left behind. We have come to seek your hospitality and protection."

"We heard of an English vessel at Ternate," the governor said, sternly, "some weeks since, and heard also that its captain was making an alliance with the king there against us."

"It was not so," Ned said. "The admiral stopped there for a few days to obtain supplies such as he needed; but we are not here either to make alliances or to trade. Captain Drake on starting intended to voyage round the the coast of America, and to return, if possible, by the north. After coasting up the western shores of that continent he found that it would be impossible to pass round the north, as the coast extended so rapidly toward the north of Asia. He, therefore, started to return by the Cape, and on his way passed through these islands. Had it been part of his plan to make alliances with the King of Ternate or any other potentate he would have stopped and done so, and would have given his armed assistance to the king. But his object was simply to return as quickly as possible. Had there been any alliance made, we should naturally have made for Ternate instead of this island. But as we have no relations with the king, and seek only means of returning to Europe, we preferred, of course, to come here, where we know that we should find Christians, and, we hoped, friends."

There was palpable truth in what Ned said, and the governor, unbending, expressed his readiness to receive and help them. He then asked a few more questions about the manner in which they had become separated from their friends, and seeing no advantage in concealing the truth, and thinking perhaps that it would be well, if an opportunity should offer, that the governor should send a vessel to search among the islands near where the wreck took place, and see if any of the crew had sought a refuge there, they told him frankly all the circumstances under which they had left the *Golden Hind*.

"It would be sad indeed," said the Portuguese, "if so grand an expedition under so noble a commander should have been wrecked after accomplishing such a work. We in these parts are not friendly to any European meddling. His Holiness the pope granted us all discoveries on this side of the Cape, and we would fain trade in peace and quiet without interference. But we can admire the great deeds and enterprise of your countrymen, and indeed," he said, smiling—for the Portuguese are as a rule a very small race—and looking at the bulk of the four young men, which was indeed, almost gigantic by the side of himself and his soldiers, "I am scarcely surprised, now I see you, at the almost legendary deeds which I hear that your countrymen have performed on the Spanish Main. But now, follow me to my castle, and I will there provide you with proper appliances. What position did you hold in the ship?"

"We are gentlemen of Devonshire," Ned said, "and bore a share in the enterprise, sailing as gentlemen adventurers under Captain Drake. I myself held the rank of third officer in the ship."

"Then, senors," the Portuguese said, bowing, "I am happy to place myself and my house at your disposal. It may be that you will be able to render me services which will far more than repay any slight inconvenience or trouble to which I may be put, for we hear that the King of Ternate is preparing a formidable expedition against us, and as my garrison is a very small one and the natives are not to be relied upon to fight against those of the other island, the addition of four such experienced soldiers as yourself will, in no slight degree, strengthen us."

The boys replied that their swords were at the service of their host; and, well content with the turn things had taken, they proceeded with him up the road into the interior of the island.

Upon gaining the higher land they were surprised at the aspect of the island. In place of the almost unbroken forest which they had beheld in other spots at which they had landed, here was fair cultivated land. Large groves of spice trees grew here and there, and the natives were working in the fields with the regularity of Europeans. The Portuguese method of cultivating the islands which they took differed widely from that of the English. Their first step was to compel the natives to embrace Christianity; their second to make of them docile and obedient laborers, raising spice and other products for which they received in payment calico, beads, and European goods.

The castle, which stood in the centre of a small plain, was built of stone roughly hewn and was of no strength which would have resisted any European attack, but was well calculated for the purpose for which it was designed. It consisted of a pleasant house standing in an inclosure, round which was a wall some fifteen feet in height, with a platform running behind it to enable its garrison to shoot over the top. A ditch of some ten feet in depth and fifteen feet wide surrounded it, so that without scaling-ladders to ascend the walls or cannon to batter holes in them, the place could be well held against any attack that the natives might make upon it. The garrison was not a formidable one, consisting only of some thirty Portuguese soldiers, whose appearance did not speak much for the discipline maintained. Their uniforms were worn and rusty in the extreme. They were slovenly in appearance, and wore a look of discontent and hopelessness. A large portion of them, indeed, had been criminals, and had been offered the choice of death or of serving for ten years, which generally meant for life, in the eastern seas. Ned judged that no great reliance could be placed upon this army of scarecrows in the event of an attack of a serious character.

"My men would scarcely show to advantage at home," the governor said, noting the glance of surprise with which the boys had viewed them. "But in a country like this, with such great heat and no real occasion for more than appearances, it is hopeless to expect them to keep up the smartness which would at home be necessary. The natives are very docile and quiet and give us no trouble whatever, and were it not for interference from Ternate, where the people are of a much more warlike nature, the guard which I have would be ample for any purposes. I am expecting a vessel which calls here about once in a six months, very shortly, and anticipate that she will bring me some twenty more soldiers for whom I wrote to the viceroy at Goa when she last called here."

"What is your latest news from Ternate?" Ned asked.

"I have no direct news," he said. "What we know we gather from the natives, who, by means of canoes and fishing-boats, are often in communication with those of the opposite island. They tell me that great preparations are being made, that several of the largest sized canoes have been built, and that they believe when it is full moon, which is generally the era at which they commence their adventures, there will be a descent upon this island."

"Then you have seven days in which to prepare," Ned said. "Have you been doing anything to enable you to receive them hotly?"

"I have not," the governor said. "But now that you gentlemen have come I doubt not that your experience in warfare will enable you to advise me as to what steps I had better take. I stand at present alone here. The officer who, under me, commanded the garrison, died two months since, and I myself, who was brought up in a civil rather than a military capacity, am, I own to you, strange altogether to these matters."

Ned expressed the willingness of himself and his friends to do all in their power to advise and assist the governor; and with many mutual compliments they now entered the house, where a goodly room was assigned to them; some natives told off as their servants; and the governor at once set two native seamsters to work to manufacture garments of a proper cut for them from materials which he had in a storehouse for trading with the neighboring chiefs, who, like all savages, were greatly given to finery. Thus by the end of the week the boys were able once more to make a show which would have passed muster in a European capital. At the governor's request they had at once proceeded to drill the soldiers, Ned and Gerald taking each the command of a company of fifteen men, as they understood Spanish and could readily make themselves understood in Portuguese; whereas Tom and Reuben knew but little of the Spanish tongue.

"I think," Tom said, the first morning to the governor, after the friends had discussed the prospect together, "it would be well to throw up some protection at the top of the road leading from the shore. I should order some large trees to be cut down and dragged by a strong force of natives to the spot, and there so arranged that their branches will point downward and form a *chevaux de frise* in the hollow way, leaving until the last moment a passage between them, but having at hand a number of young saplings to fill up the gap. There are, I suppose, other places at which the enemy could land?"

"Oh, yes!" the governor said. "On the other side of the island the land slopes gradually down to the shore, and indeed it is only for a few miles at this point that the cliffs rise so abruptly that they could not be ascended. Yet even here there are many points which a native could easily scale, although we in our accoutrements would find it impossible."

While Ned and Gerald drilled their men with great assiduity, astonishing the Portuguese soldiers with their energy and authoritative manner, Tom and Reuben occupied themselves in superintending the felling of the trees, and their carriage, by means of a large number of natives, to the top of the road. Preparations were also made for blocking up the lower windows of the house, so that in case of the enemy succeeding in carrying the outer wall a stout resistance could be made within. Large piles of provisions were stored in the building, and great jars of water placed there.

"Are you sure," Ned asked the governor one evening, "of the natives here? for I own that there appears to me to be a sullen defiance in their manner, and I should not be surprised to see them turn upon us immediately those from the other island arrive. If they did so, of course our position at the top of the road would be untenable, as they would take us in the rear. However, if they do so, I doubt not that we shall be able to cut our way back to the castle without difficulty. I think that it would be in any case advisable to leave at least ten men to hold the castle, while the rest of us oppose the landing."

There were in store four small culverins and several light wall-pieces. Two of the culverins were placed on the cliff, one at each side of the path, so as to command the landing. Two others were placed on the roof of the castle, which was flat and terraced. The wall-pieces were also cleaned and placed in position at the corners of the walls, and the boys, having seen that the musketoons and arquebuses of the garrison were in excellent order and ready for service, felt that all had been done that was possible to prepare for an attack.

The day before the full moon a sentinel was placed at the cliff with orders to bring word instantly to the castle in case any craft were seen coming from Ternate, the distance from the cliff to the house being about a mile. A short time after daybreak next morning the sentry arrived at full speed, saying that a great fleet of canoes was visible. Hurrying to the spot with the governor, the lads made out that the approaching flotilla consisted of eighteen great war-canoes, each of which, crowded as it was, might contain a hundred men; and in addition to these were a large number of smaller craft. The invading force, therefore, would considerably exceed two thousand men. Reuben had the command of a gun at one side, Tom at the other, and these now loaded and sighted their pieces so as to pour a volley of case-shot into the canoes when they arrived within a quarter of a mile from shore.

The canoes came along in a dense body, as close together as they could paddle, their rowers filling the air with defiant yells. When they reached the spot upon which the guns had been trained Tom fired his piece, and its roar was answered by wild screams and yells from the crowded fleet. Reuben followed suit, and the destruction wrought by the guns was at once manifest. Three of the great canoes were broken to pieces, and their occupants swimming in the water climbed into the others, among which also a great many men had been wounded. The effect of this reception upon the valor of the natives was very speedy. Without a moment's delay they backed off, and were soon seen making out of range of the guns, like a troop of wild fowl scattered by the shot of a fowler.

"They have a horror of cannon," the governor said, exultingly, as he witnessed their departure. "If we had a few more pieces I should have no fear of the result."

The dispersal of the canoes continued only until they thought that they were out of range; for although the lads now sent several round shot at them, these did not produce any effect, the canoes being but small objects to hit at a distance when on the move, and the culverins being old pieces, and but little adapted for accurate shooting.

The fleet were soon seen to gather again, and after a little pause they started in a body as before along the coast.

"They are going to make a landing elsewhere," Ned said, "and we shall have to meet them in the open. It is a pity that we have no beasts of burden to which to harness our pieces; for as these are only ships' guns it is impossible for us to drag them at a speed which would enable us to oppose their landing. Where are all the natives?"

At the first alarm a large body of the islanders had assembled upon the cliff, but in the excitement of watching the approaching enemy their movements had not been noticed. It was now seen that the whole of them had left the spot, and not a single native was in sight.

"I think," Ned said, "we had better fall back and take up a position near the house, and repel their attack with the assistance of the guns mounted there. With muskets only we should not have much chance of preventing their landing, and indeed they will row much faster along the coast than we could run to keep up with them."

The governor agreed in the justice of Ned's view, and the whole force were now ordered to fall back toward the castle. As they proceeded they saw large bodies of the natives. These, however, kept at a distance; but their exultant shouts showed that they must be considered to have gone over to the enemy.

"I will make you pay for this," the governor said, stamping his foot and shaking his fist angrily in their direction. "Each man shall have to furnish double the amount of spice for half the amount of calico for the next five years. Ungrateful dogs! when we have done so much for them!"

Ned could scarcely help smiling to himself at the thought of the many benefits which the Portuguese had bestowed upon these unfortunate islanders, whom they had reduced from a state of happy freedom to one which, whatever it might be called, was but little short of slavery.

It was late in the evening before great numbers of the enemy were seen approaching, and these, swelled as they were by the population of the island, appeared a formidable body indeed by the side of the handful of white men who were drawn up to defend the place. The enemy, numerous as he was, appeared indisposed to commence a fight at once, but began, to the fierce indignation of the governor, to cut down the groves of spice-trees and to build great fires with them.

"I don't think that they will attack until to-morrow," Ned said, "and it would be well, therefore, to withdraw within the walls, to plant sentries, and to allow the men to rest. We shall want all our strength when the battle begins."

"Do you think," the governor asked, when they were seated in his room, and had finished the repast which had been prepared, "that it will be well to sally out to meet them in the open? Thirty white men ought to be able to defeat almost any number of these naked savages."

"If we had horses I should say yes," Ned said, "because then by our speed we could make up for our lack of numbers, and, wheeling about, could charge through and through them. But they are so light and active in comparison to ourselves that we should find it difficult, if not impossible, to bring them to a hand-to-hand conflict. We have, indeed, the advantage of our musketoons; but I observed at Ternate that many of the men have muskets, and the sound of firearms would therefore in no way alarm them. With their bows and arrows they can shoot more steadily at short distances than we can, and we should be overwhelmed with a cloud of missiles, while unable to bring to bear the strength of our arms and the keenness of our swords against their clubs and rough spears. I think that we could hold the house for a year against them; but if we lost many men in a fight outside it might go hard with us afterwards."

When morning dawned the garrison beheld to their dismay that the Indians had in the night erected a battery at a quarter of a mile in front of the gate, and that in this they had placed the culverins left on the cliff, and a score of the small pieces carried in their war-canoes.

"This is the work of the two white men we saw at Ternate," Gerald exclaimed. "No Indian could have built a battery according to this fashion."

As soon as it was fairly light the enemies' fire opened, and was answered by the culverins on the roof of the house. The latter were much more quickly and better directed than those of the Indians, but many of the balls of the latter crashed through the great gates.

"Shall we make a sortie?" the governor asked Ned.

"I think that we had better wait for nightfall," he replied. "In passing across this open ground we should lose many men from the cannon shots, and with so small a force remaining, might not be able to resist the on-rush of so great numbers. Let us prepare, however, to prop up the gates should they fall, and tonight we will silence their guns."

At nightfall the gates, although sorely bruised and battered and pierced in many places, still stood, being shored up with beams from behind. At ten o'clock twenty of the garrison were let down by ropes at the back of the castle for Ned thought that scouts might be lurking near the gates to give notice of any sortie. With great precaution and in perfect silence they made a way round, and were within a hundred yards of the battery before their approach was discovered. Then, headed by the governor, who was a valiant man by nature, and the four English, they ran at great speed forward, and were inside the battery before the enemy could gather to resist them. The battle was indeed a hard one, for the Indians with their clubs fought valorously.

Reuben and Tom, having been furnished with hammer and long nails, proceeded to spike the guns, which they did with great quickness, their doings being covered alike by their friends and by darkness. When they had finished their task they gave the signal, and the Portuguese, being sorely pressed, fell back fighting strongly to the castle, where the gates were opened to receive them. In this sortie they lost eight men. The next morning at dawn the natives, being gathered in large numbers, came on to the assault uttering loud and fierce cries. The cannon on the roof, which were under the charge of Tom and Reuben, at once opened fire upon them, while the soldiers upon the walls shot briskly with their musketoons. The natives, however, appeared determined to succeed, and firing a cloud of arrows pushed forward toward the gate. Among them were borne, each by some thirty natives, long trees, and this party, surrounded by the main body, proceeded rapidly toward the gate, which, damaged as it was, they hoped easily to overthrow.

The fire of the two culverins was, however, so deadly, and the concentrated discharge of the musketoons upon them as they advanced so fatal, that after trying several times to approach close to the gate, the natives dropped the great logs and fled.

CHAPTER XXI

Wholesale Conversion

That day and the three which followed passed without adventure. The natives were seen ravaging the fields, destroying the plantations, and doing terrible damage, to the intense exasperation of the Portuguese governor. But they did not show any signs of an intention to attack the castle.

"I believe," Ned said, on the fourth day, "that they have determined to starve us out. They must know that, however large our stock of provisions, they will not last for ever, and indeed they will have learned from the men who bore them in something of the amount of stock which we have. It will last, you say, for two months, which would be little enough were it not that we are expecting the ship you spoke of. If that comes shortly we shall, with the additional force which it is bringing, and the crew, who will no doubt aid, be able to attack them in the open. But were it not for that our position would be a bad one."

"I fear," Tom said, "that even when the ship arrives evil may come of it."

"How is that, Tom?" Ned asked.

"The captain will know nothing of what is passing on shore, and if he lands his men incautiously upon the beach, and advances in this direction, the natives will fall upon them, and, taking them by surprise, cut them to pieces, and our last hope will then be gone."

"But we might sally out and effect a diversion," Reuben said.

"Yes," Tom replied; "but, unfortunately, we should not know of the arrival of the ship until all is over."

It was clear to all that Tom's view was the correct one, and that the position was much more serious than they had anticipated. For some time the governor and the four young men looked at each other blankly. The destruction of the reinforcements, which would be followed no doubt by the capture of the ship by the war-canoes and the massacre of all on board, would indeed be fatal to their hopes. After what they had seen of the determination with which the enemy had come up to attack the gate, they were sure that they would fight valiantly outside. The question of sallying forth was again discussed, and all were of opinion that, unequal as the fight would be, it were better to attempt to defeat the enemy than to remain quiet and allow them to triumph over the coming reinforcements.

"Upon what day do you think the ship will arrive?" Ned said, after considerable thought.

"I cannot say to a day," the governor replied; "but she should be here this week. There is no exact time, because she has to touch at several other islands. She leaves Goa always on a certain day; but she takes many weeks on her voyage even if the wind be favorable. She might have been here a week since. She may not be here for another fortnight. But unless something unforeseen has occurred she should be here by that time, for the winds are steady in these regions and the rate of sailing regular."

"The one chance it appears to me," Ned said, after thinking for some time, "is to give them warning of what is happening here."

"But how is that to be done?" asked the governor.

"The only possible plan," Ned said, "would be for one of us— and I should be ready to accept the duty, knowing more perhaps of the ways of natives than the others—to steal forth from the castle, to make for the shore, and to lie concealed among the woods until the vessel is in sight. If then I could find a canoe, to seize it and paddle off to the ship; if not, to swim."

The other lads eagerly volunteered to undertake the work; but Ned insisted that he was better suited to it not only from his knowledge of the natives, but from his superior powers in swimming."

"I may have," he said, "to keep myself up in the water for a long time, and perhaps to swim for my life if the natives see me. It is even desirable, above all things, that whosoever undertakes the work should be a good swimmer, and although you have long ago given up calling me 'the otter,' I do not suppose that my powers in the water have diminished."

After long consultation, it was agreed that this plan offered more chances of success than any other.

"It would be most desirable," Gerald said, "that we should have some notice here of the ship being in sight, in order that we might sally out and lend a hand to our friends on their arrival. I will, therefore, if you will allow me, go with Ned, and when the ship is in sight I will make my way back here while he goes off to the vessel."

"But it will be impossible," Ned said, "to make your way back here in the daytime. I can steal out at night; but to return unnoticed would be difficult indeed."

"But when you see the ship, Ned, and get on board, you might warn them to delay their landing until the next morning, and in the night I might enter here with the news, and we might sally out at daybreak."

This plan appeared to offer more advantages than any other, and it was agreed at last that the two lads should, having darkened their skins and put on Indian dress, steal out that night from the castle and make for the shore. Tom and Reuben regretted much that they could not take part in the enterprise; but the governor assured them that even were it desirable that four should undertake the mission, they could not be spared, since their presence would be greatly needed in the castle should the natives, before the arrival of the ship, make an attack upon it.

That night Ned and Gerald, according to the arrangement, stole out from the castle. Their skins had been darkened from head to foot. Round their waists they wore short petticoats, reaching to their knees, of native stuff. They had sandals on their feet, for, as Ned said, if they were seen close by the natives they were sure to be detected in any case, and sandals would not show at a short distance, while they would enable them to run at full speed, which they certainly could not do barefooted. They took with them a bag of provisions, and each carried a sword. Reuben had pressed upon them to take pistols also; but Ned said, that if cut off and detected, pistols would be of no use, as nothing but running would carry them through, while should a pistol be fired inadvertently it would call such a number of assailants upon them that their escape would be impossible. A thrust with a sword did its work silently, and just as well as a pistol bullet.

The natives apparently had no fear of any attempt at a sally from the castle, for there was nothing like a watch set round it, although near the entrance a few men were stationed to give warning should the garrison sally out to make a sudden attack upon the invaders. The natives were, for the most part, scattered about in small parties, and once or twice the lads nearly fell in with these; but by dint of keeping their ears and eyes open they steered through the dangers, and arrived safely upon the coast at a point two miles to the west of the landing-place.

Here the cliff had nearly sloped away, the height being only some twenty or thirty feet above the water, and being practicable in many cases for descent; while behind lay a large wood in which concealment was easy, except in the case of an organized search, of which they had no fear whatever. The next morning they made along the shore as far as the point where the native war-canoes had been pulled up, in hopes of finding some canoe small enough for Ned to use for rowing off to the ship. But none of them rowed less than twelve or fourteen paddles, and so cumbrous a boat as this would be overtaken in a very short time should it be seen making out from shore. Ned therefore determined to swim out, especially as they observed that a watch was kept both day and night near the canoes. Five days passed in concealment. The cocoanuts afforded them both food and drink. Occasionally they heard the boom of the culverins at the castle, and knew that the natives were showing within range; but as these shots were only heard at times, they were assured that no persistent attack was being made.

It was late in the afternoon of the fifth day that the lads

observed a sail in the distance. It was indeed so far away that, as the light was fading, they could not say with absolute certainty that it was the longed-for ship. They both felt convinced, however, that they had seen a sail, and watched intently as night darkened for some sign of its passage. It was four hours later when they saw passing along at a distance of about half a mile a light on the ocean which could be no other than that on board a ship.

"Now is the time," Ned said. "I will keep along the shore under the cliff until I get nearly to the landing and will then strike out. Do you make for the castle, and tell them that the ship has arrived, and that we will attack to-morrow, but not at daybreak, as we proposed, but at noon."

As Ned proceeded on his way along the shore he saw suddenly blaze up far ahead at the landing-place a small bonfire.

"Ah!" he muttered to himself. "The natives have seen the ship too, and are following the usual custom here of making a fire to show them where to land. I trust that they will not fall into the snare."

When, however, he had reached within a quarter of a mile of the landing he saw a small boat come suddenly within its range of light, and two white men step out of it. They were received apparently with much respect by the natives assembled there, and at once advanced up the road, while the boat, putting off, disappeared in the darkness.

"They will be murdered," Ned said to himself, "before they have gone a hundred yards. The natives were crafty enough to allow them to land without hindrance in order that no suspicion might arise among those on board ship."

In the stillness of the night he thought that he heard a distant cry. But he was not sure that his ears had not deceived him. Far out he could see a faint light, and knowing that this marked the place where the ship was moored he prepared to strike out for it. It was a long swim and further than he had expected, for in the darkness the captain, unable to see the land, had prudently anchored at a considerable distance from it. Even, however, had it been several times as far Ned could have swum the distance without difficulty; but the whole way he could not forget that those seas swarmed with sharks, and that any moment he might have to encounter one of those hideous monsters. He had left his sword behind him, but carried a dagger, and, as he swam, kept his eyes in all directions in order that he should not be attacked unprepared. The ocean was, however, fortunately, at that time, deserted by these beasts; or if they were in the neighborhood, the quiet, steady, noiseless stroke of the swimmer did not reach their ears. As he neared the ship his heart rose, and he sang out blithely, "Ship ahoy!"

"Hullo!" was the reply. "Where are you? I cannot see your boat."

"I am swimming," Ned answered. "Throw me a rope to climb up the side. I have a message from the governor for the captain of the ship."

A minute later Ned stood upon the deck of the Portuguese vessel, the soldiers and sailors looking on wonderingly at him, his body being white, but his face still colored by the preparation.

The captain himself soon appeared.

"I am the bearer of a message to you, senor, from the governor," Ned said. "It is here in this hollow reed. He gives you but few particulars, but I believe tells you that you may place every confidence in me, and that I have detailed instructions from him."

The captain split open the little reed which Ned handed to him, and taking out a paper coiled within it, opened it, and by the light of a lantern read: "We are in a very critical position, and it will need at once courage and prudence to come out of it. I have sent my friend Don Eduardo Hearne, an English gentleman of repute, to warn you against the danger which threatens, and to advise you on your further proceedings. He will give you all particulars."

The captain invited Ned to follow him to his cabin, and calling in the officers, asked for an explanation of this singular visit. Ned briefly entered into an account of the landing of the natives of Ternate, and of the present situation, and the captain rejoiced

THE MESSAGE FROM THE GOVERNOR
SEE PAGE 273.

at the escape which he had had from falling into an ambuscade; this he would assuredly have done had he landed the troops in the morning as he had intended, and marched them inland, fearing no danger, and unprepared for attack.

Ned explained that the plan was that the troops on board the ship should land and fight their way into the interior, and that simultaneously the garrison should sally out and attack the natives in the rear, and fight their way toward each other, until they effected a junction. They could then retire into the castle, where their future plans could be arranged.

"I have, however," Ned said, "ventured to modify that plan, and have sent word to the governor that we shall not attack until noon, instead of landing at daybreak, as before arranged. We have been examining the position where the canoes are lying. They are all hauled up on the beach in a compact body. It is in a quiet creek whose mouth you would sail past without suspecting its existence. I cannot say, of course, the depth of water, but these creeks are generally deep, and I should think that there would be enough water for the ship to float. At any rate, should you not like to venture this, your pinnace might row in, carrying a gun in her bow, and might play havoc among the canoes. Or, better still, if you could send two boat-loads of men there tonight and could manage to land and destroy a portion of the canoes and launch and tow out the others, I think that we should have a fair chance of getting peace. The natives would be terrified at the loss of their canoes, and would be likely to make any terms which would ensure their return to their island."

The captain at once agreed to the proposition. The three boats of the ship were lowered, and the sailors and soldiers took their places, only two or three being left on board ship, as there was no fear whatever of an attack from the shore during the night. Ned took his place in the leading boat of the captain, and acted as guide. They coasted along at a short distance from the land, until Ned told them to cease rowing.

"We must," he said, "be close to the spot now; but it is needful that one boat should go forward and find the exact entrance to the creek."

Rowing very quietly, the boat in which he was advanced until within a few yards of the shore, and then proceeded quietly along for a distance of a few hundred yards, when the black line of shore disappeared, and a streak of water was seen stretching inland. Quietly they rowed back to the other two boats, and the three advancing, entered the creek together. Before starting, each officer had been assigned his work. The crew of one of the boats, consisting principally of soldiers, were to land, to advance a short distance inland and to repulse any attacks that the natives might make upon them. Another party were to stave in all the small canoes, and this done, they were to assist the third boat's crew in launching the war-canoes into the water.

As they approached the spot they were hailed in the Indian tongue by some one on shore. No reply was given, and the hail was repeated louder. Then, as the boats rowed rapidly up to the place where the canoes were hauled up, a shrill yell of alarm was given, which was re-echoed in several directions near, and could be heard growing fainter and fainter as it was caught up by men inland.

The moment the boats touched the shore the men leaped out. The soldiers advanced, and took up the position assigned to them to defend the working parties, while the rest set to vigorously to carry out their portion of the work. The war-canoes were heavy, and each required the efforts of the whole of the crew to launch her into the water. It was therefore a work of considerable time to get fifteen of them afloat, and long ere this had been done the natives, called together by the alarm, were flocking down in great numbers. They were, however, in entire ignorance as to the number of their assailants, and the fire which the soldiers opened with their arquebuses checked them in their advance. Feeling sure that their canoes were being destroyed, they filled the air with yells of lamentation and rage, discharging such volleys of arrows at random in the direction of the Portuguese, that a great number of these were wounded. Indeed, the natives pressed on with such audacity that a considerable portion of the workers had to go forward to assist the soldiers in holding them at bay.

At last, however, the whole of the canoes were in the water, and every other boat disabled. The canoes were tied together, five abreast, and one of the boats towed these out of the harbor, while the crews of the others remained keeping the natives at bay, for it was felt that if the whole were to embark at once while still encumbered with the canoes they would be able to get out of the creek but slowly, and would for the most part be destroyed by the arrows of the natives.

When the boat had towed the canoes well out to sea it cast them adrift and returned up the creek. Then, covered by the muskets of the soldiers, the others took their places in good order and regularity until at last all were in the boats. The soldiers were ordered to stand up and to keep up a steady fire upon the shore, while the sailors laid to with a hearty good-will. The natives rushed down to the shore in great numbers, and although many of them must have fallen under the fire of the soldiers, they yet waded into the water in their anxiety to seize the boats, and poured large numbers of arrows into them. When the three boats gained the open sea there were few indeed of the Portuguese who had not received wounds more or less severe by the arrows, and several had been killed in addition to others who had fallen on shore. The soldiers had suffered much less severely than the sailors, for although they had been more hotly engaged, their breast-pieces and steel caps had protected them, and they were principally wounded in the limbs.

The canoes were now picked up, and with these in low the party returned to the ship. Here their wounds were dressed by a priest who accompanied the vessel in her voyages, landing at the different stations and ministering to the garrisons of the islands. He had some knowledge of the healing art, and poured soothing oils into the wounds inflicted by the arrows. The men were much alarmed lest these arrows should be poisoned, but Ned assured them that none of those who had been wounded during the attacks on shore had died from the effects, and that, although it was the custom in many of these islands to use poisoned weapons, the people of Ternate at least did not practice this barbarous usage.

Morning was just breaking as the party gained the ship, and the captain was glad that Ned had postponed the landing until mid-day, as it gave the tired men time to rest and prepare themselves for fresh labors. As soon as the shore could be seen it was evident that the destruction and carrying off of the canoes had created an immense impression. The cliff was lined with natives, whose gesticulations as they saw their canoes fastened to the stern of the whip were wild and vehement.

A little before noon the boats were hauled up alongside, the soldiers took their places in them with loaded arquebuses, and as many sailors as could be spared also entered to assist in their advance. The ship carried several pieces of artillery, and these were loaded so as to open fire before the landing was effected, in order to clear the shore of the enemy. This was soon accomplished, and the natives who had assembled on the beach were seen streaming up the road through the cliff. This was the most dangerous part that the advancing party would have to traverse, as they would be exposed to a heavy fire from those standing above them on both flanks. They would have suffered indeed very severely had not the captain turned his guns upon the masses gathered on the high ground, and, by one or two lucky shots plumped into the middle of them, created such an effect that the fire of arrows kept up upon the troops as they advanced was wild and confused. Several of the sailors were severely wounded, but the soldiers, well sheltered by their mail, pressed on and gained the level ground, their blood being fired as they went, by the spectacle of the dead bodies of their first officer and supercargo, who had landed the night before.

Here the natives were assembled in great force, and as they were now out of sight of those on board ship the guns could no longer render assistance to the little party. These showed a good front as the masses of the enemy approached them, and charged boldly at them. The natives, however, maddened by the loss of their canoes, and feeling that their only hope was in annihilating their enemies, came on with such force, wielding heavy clubs, that the array of the Portuguese was broken, and in a short time each was fighting desperately for himself. Several had been stricken down, and although large numbers of the natives had been killed it was plain that the victory would in a few minutes be decided, when suddenly a great shout was heard, and a volley of musketry was poured into the rear of the natives. The hard-pressed whites gave a cheer, for they knew that assistance had arrived from the castle. The natives, whose attention had been directed to the attack in front, were taken completely by surprise, and as both the parties of whites simultaneously charged, large numbers were unable to escape, and, were cut down, while the rest fled precipitately from the spot.

Very hearty were the congratulations of the Portuguese as the forces came together. Gerald had safely reached the castle after some narrow escapes, he, having fallen among some sleeping natives, had been attacked and forced to trust to his speed.

After a short consultation it was decided to press the enemy, and to leave them no time to recover from the demoralization caused by the loss of their boats and the junction of the two parties of white men. The forces were, therefore, divided into two equal parts, and these started in different directions. Clump after clump of trees was searched, and the enemy driven from them. At first some resistance was made; but gradually the natives became completely panic-stricken and fled without striking a blow.

Until nightfall the two parties continued to hunt and shoot down a large number of the natives. Then they returned to the castle. They now had a consultation as to the terms which they should grant the natives, for they had no doubt that victory had declared itself finally in their favor. Some were for continuing the strife until the enemy were exterminated; but the governor of the island was opposed to this.

"In the first place," he said, "mixed up with the Ternate people are all the natives of this island, and to exterminate them would be to leave us without labor and to ruin the island. In the next place, the havoc which has been already wrought in our plantations is such that it will take years to repair, and the longer this fighting goes on the more complete will be the destruction. I think, then, that we should grant them the easiest terms possible. They will be only too glad to escape and to get back to their own land, and will be long before they invade us again."

"I think," the officer who had arrived with the reinforcements of soldiers said, "it would be well, senor, if you were to consult with the priest who is on board. He is a man who has the ear of the council at Goa. He was but recently arrived, and knows but little of the natives; but he is full of zeal, and it would be well, I think, were we to make an arrangement of which he would perfectly approve, so that his report when he reached Goa should be altogether favorable."

The governor agreed to this proposal, and decided to send a party down to the shore in the morning to bring the priest up to the castle.

Early in the morning a large crowd of natives were seen at a short distance. In their hands they held boughs of trees, and waved them to express their desire to enter into negotiations. The governor, however, fired two or three shots over their heads as a signal to them to keep farther away, as their advances would not be received. Then, while a party went down to the shore to fetch the priest, he again sallied out and drove the natives before him.

When the holy father arrived another council was held, and he was informed that the people were ready to treat, and asked what in his opinion should be the terms imposed upon them. He heard the arguments of the governor in favor of allowing them to return to their island; but he said, "In my opinion it is essential above all things that they should be forced to accept Christianity."

At this the Englishmen, and indeed the two Portuguese officers, could with difficulty repress a smile; but the governor at once saw that a wholesale conversion of this sort would do him much good with the authorities at Goa, and he therefore willingly fell into the priest's views.

The next morning the natives again appeared with their green boughs, and the governor, with the officer, the priest, and a body of ten soldiers, went out to meet them. The King of Ternate advanced and bowed himself submissively to the ground and expressed his submission, and craved for pardon and for permission to return with his people to Ternate, promising solemnly that never again would they meddle with the Portuguese settlement.

The governor, who spoke the language fluently, having been there for some years, uttered an harangue reproaching him with his folly and wickedness in wantonly declaring war against the Portuguese. He pointed to the destroyed plantations, and asked if any punishment could be too great for the ruin caused. The king and his councillors offered to pay large tributes annually of spice and other products until the ruined plantations were again in bearing.

"This will not repay us for the losses we have suffered, and for the evil spirit which you have introduced into this island. We have, however," the governor said, "only your interests at heart, and therefore we have decided to pardon you, and to allow you to return to your island, upon the condition that you and all your people embrace Christianity, and pay such a tribute as we may impose."

The king had no understanding of the meaning of what was proposed to him, and the governor said that he and his people were, in the morning, to assemble before the castle, and that the holy father, who had been sent on purpose to turn them from the wickedness of their ways, would then explain the doctrines of Christianity to them; that if they accepted and believed what he said, pardon would be theirs; if not, they would be hunted down until all were destroyed.

Next morning the assembly took place in front of the castle gate. The King of Ternate, surrounded by all his principal councillors and warriors, took his place, while the fighting men stood around him. The priest mounted on the platform of the wall, the governor standing beside him to interpret. The Englishmen, much amused at the ceremony, stood at a short distance off. They did not wish to be recognized by any of the people of Ternate, as it was possible that some English vessels might again come into these seas, and they did not desire that the pleasant remembrance of the visit of the *Golden Hind* should be obliter-

ated by the sight of some of its crew in alliance with the
Portuguese.

The priest began an elaborate explanation of the Christian religion, which he continued for the space of two hours, to the surprise and astonishment of the natives, who could not, of course,
comprehend a single word that he said. Then he paused, and
turning to the governor said, "Will you translate this for the benefit of these benighted heathens?"

"I fear," said the governor, "that it will be impossible for me
to do full justice to your eloquent words, and, indeed, that these
poor wretches would scarcely take in so much learning and wisdom all at once; but in a few words I will give them the sense of
what you have been telling them."

Then, lifting up his voice, he addressed the king.

"There is only one God. These idols of yours are helpless and
useless. We have brought ashore those from your war canoes,
which my men will now proceed to burn, and you will see that
your gods will be unable to help themselves. Indeed, they are
not gods, and have no power. God is good and hates wickedness.
All men are wicked. Therefore He would hate all men; but He
has sent His Son down, and for His sake pardons all who believe
in Him. Now, if you believe in him as I tell you, you will be pardoned both by us and by God. If you do not believe, we shall kill
you all and you will be punished eternally. Now you have the
choice what to do."

The matter thus pithily put did not require much consideration. After a short consultation between the chiefs, the king demanded what ceremonies would have to be gone through to become Christians, and was informed by the governor that the
only ceremony would be that he would have to declare himself
a Christian; that the priest would make upon him the sign of a
cross with his finger, and would sprinkle him with water; and
that, when this was done, he would be a Christian.

Much relieved to find that the entry into this new religion was
so easy, the king and his people at once agreed to accept
Christianity. The governor informed them that the priest
thought that they were hardly yet prepared, but that on the

morrow the ceremony should take place after a further explanation. The next day a great altar was erected outside the walls of the castle, gay with banners and waxlights. Before this the King of Ternate and his people assembled, the gunners on the walls standing with lighted matches by their cannon in case of trouble. The priest then made another long oration, which was again briefly and emphatically translated by the governor. The king and all his people then knelt, and according to the instruction of the priest made the sign of the cross. The priest then went along between the lines of the people sprinkling them with holy water, and this being done the ceremony was declared complete, and the King of Ternate and his people were received into the bosom of the Church. Then, escorted by the soldiers, they were taken down to the sea-shore. The two white men were permitted to depart with them. The governor had at first insisted that these should be put to death. They pleaded, however, that they had acted under force, and Ned interceding for them their lives were granted on the condition that they should, on reaching Ternate, at once embark for some other island, and never return to Ternate. The canoes were brought alongside, and there being now no fear of any attempt at resistance, as the entire body of invaders had given up their arms, they were allowed to enter the canoes and to paddle away to their own island, with numbers greatly diminished from those which had landed to the attack of Tidore a week before.

The governor and the priest were alike delighted at the termination of the war, the former because he was really anxious for the good of the colony which had been intrusted to him, and believed that it would now progress peaceably and without disturbance. He believed, too, that his successful resistance to so large a body of enemies would insure him the approval of the viceroy at Goa, and that the report of the priest would also obtain for him the valuable protection and patronage of the ecclesiastics, whose power in the eastern seas was even greater than it was at home.

Tidore was the furthest of the Portuguese settlements, and the ship, having now made her round, was to return direct to

Goa. The priest hesitated whether to remain or to return in her. He had made it one of the conditions of peace with Ternate that a missionary should be received there, a place of worship erected, and that he should be allowed to open schools and to teach the tenets of his religion to all, and he hesitated whether he would himself at once take up that post, or whether he would report the matter at Goa, where perhaps it might be decided to send a priest who had acquired something of the language of the Southern Seas. He finally decided upon the latter course.

The governor furnished the lads with letters recommending them most warmly to the viceroy, and stating the great services which they had rendered to him in the defence of the island, saying, indeed, that had it not been for their prudence and valor it was probable that the natives would have succeeded in destroying the small body of Portuguese and in massacring the reinforcement landed from the vessel. The priest also, while viewing the young men with the natural horror of a Portuguese ecclesiastic for heretics, was yet impressed with the services that they had rendered, and considered their own shortcomings to be in a great measure atoned for by the wholesale conversion which had to some extent been effected by their means.

Bidding a hearty adieu to the governor, they took their places on board ship and sailed for Goa. It was a six weeks' voyage; but the vessel was well furnished with provisions, and after their hardships the boys greatly enjoyed the rest and tranquillity on board. In due time they found themselves lying off the mouth of the river up which, at a short distance from its mouth, the capital of Portuguese India was situated.

CHAPTER XXII

Home

The captain, who was accompanied by the priest, rowed up the river to report the arrival of the ship and the events of his voyage to the authorities, and to place in their hands the letter of the governor of Tidore. Twenty-four hours later the captain returned with orders for the ship to sail up the river, and that on their arrival the young Englishmen were to be landed and conducted to the presence of the viceroy himself.

The young adventurers, much as they had travelled, were greatly struck with the appearance of Goa. It was, indeed, a city of palaces, most solidly built of stone, and possessing an amount of magnificence and luxury which surpassed anything they had ever seen. In the streets a few Portuguese magnificently dressed and escorted by guards moved among a throng of gaily attired natives, whose slight figures, upright carriage, and intelligent faces struck the boys as most pleasing after their experience of the islanders of the South Seas. The immense variety of turbans and head-gear greatly astonished them, as well as the magnificence of the dresses of some of those who appeared to be men of importance and who were attended by a retinue of armed followers.

The young men were escorted by two officers of the viceroy, who had come on board ship as soon as she dropped anchor, to conduct them to his presence. At the sight of these officials the natives hastily cleared the way, and made every demonstration of respect as the party passed through them. The vice-regal palace was a magnificent building, surpassing any edifice the

boys had ever seen, and they were still more struck by the luxury of the interior. They were led through several vestibules,
until at last they arrived in a large chamber. At a table here the
viceroy was seated, while around him were a large number of
the councillors and leading men of the place. The viceroy rose
as the young men advanced and bowed profoundly.

"You are, I hear, Englishmen, and I am told, but I can scarcely
believe it, that you belong to the ship of the Captain Drake
whose exploits in the West Indies against the Spaniards have
made him so famous. But how, belonging to him, you came to
be cast on an island in the South Seas is more than we are able
to understand."

No news of the expedition had reached the Portuguese, and
the surprise of the viceroy was only natural.

"The *Golden Hind,* sir, the vessel in which we were gentlemen adventurers, rounded Cape Horn, sailed up the American
coast, and then, keeping west, crossed through the islands, and
has, we trust, long since rounded the Cape of Good Hope and
arrived in England, having circumnavigated the globe."

An expression of surprise broke from the assembled
Portuguese. But a frown passed over the face of the viceroy.

"What was the object of your captain in visiting these seas?"
he asked. "They are the property of Portugal, and without the
permission of his majesty no ship of any other nation may pass
through our waters."

"I can assure you," Ned said, "that there was no object either
of conquest or of trade on the part of our admiral in visiting
these seas. When he rounded the Cape his object was to discover, if possible, a passage round the northern coast of America
back to England. But when we went north we found the cold
was great, and that the land stretched away so that it would join
with Asia to the north. Being convinced, then, that no passage
could be obtained in that way, he sailed for England round the
Cape of Good Hope, fearing the dangers of a passage round the
Horn, by which he lost on our passage out two of his ships, and
was well nigh wrecked himself. He only abode in the islands of

the South Seas for a few days to get provisions and water, and then sailed straight for home."

Assured by this explanation the viceroy now begged the boys to sit down, and he and his council listened with admiration and astonishment to the records of the expedition, and especially to the passage from America of two of the young men before him. the depredations which had been committed upon the Spaniards excited no indignation among the Portuguese, for these nations were rivals, and although they did not put their contentions to the test of the sword, each was glad enough to hear of any misfortune befalling the other.

The viceroy now assured the young men that he was proud to welcome the members of so gallant a crew as that of the great English navigator. "England and Portugal," he said, "did not clash, and were always natural allies. He trusted they would always remain so, and in the meantime he should be glad to treat the boys with all honor, and to forward them home by the first ship which might be sailing." Apartments were now assigned to them in the palace, and here they were delighted to find a stock of clothes suited for them.

For the next fortnight they passed a pleasant time at Goa. They were the objects of much attention on the part of the Portuguese, and all vied in the attempt to make their stay pleasant to them. They found that the town of Goa occupied but a small space, and that it was strongly fortified, and the Portuguese made no attempt to conceal their very high estimate of the fighting power of the natives. One young officer, who was specially told off to accompany the lads, and who spoke Spanish fluently, was particularly frank in his description of the state of affairs.

"All these gaily dressed natives that one sees in the streets are, I suppose, Christians?" Ned asked.

"No, indeed," the other said, surprised. "What should make you think so?"

Ned replied that in America he had found that the Spaniards insisted on all the natives at once embracing Christianity on pain of death.

"The Spaniards," the young Portuguese said, "are lords and masters there. The natives are weak and timid, and able to offer no resistance whatever. That is very far from being our position here. We are, I can assure you, only here on sufferance. You can have no idea of the power of some of these native sovereigns of India. The Mahrattas who live beyond the mountains you see on the horizon could pour down such hosts of armed men, that if they combined against us no resistance that we could offer would be likely to be successful. And yet they are but one among a score of warlike people. So long as we do not attempt to proselytize, and are content to appear as merchants and traders, no general feeling exists against our residence here. But I can assure you that if it became known in India that we were forcing the natives to accept Christianity, the footing which we have obtained here would be speedily lost. These people have regular armies. They may not indeed be trained as are ours at home; but, individually, they are very brave. They have artillery of heavy calibre. In the South Seas, as you know, we´ endeavor to convert the heathen. The people there are degraded savages by the side of these Indians. But we do not adopt the strong methods which the Spaniards have done. We have in Portugal a good deal of your English freedom of opinion, and the Inquisition has never gained any firm footing amongst us."

Upon one occasion the boys had the satisfaction of seeing a grand Indian durbar, for the chief, on the corner of whose territory the Portuguese had built their town with his permission, came in to see the viceroy. The boys were surprised at the magnificence of his cavalcade, in which elephants, camels, and other animals took part, and in which the trappings and appointments were gorgeous indeed; while the dresses of the chiefs absolutely shone with jewels. The attendants, however, made but a poor show according to European ideas.

There was at this time in European armies no attempt at regular uniform, but there was a certain resemblance between the attire and arms of the men who fought side by side. When upon the march regularity and order were maintained, and the men kept together in step. Nothing of this kind was apparent among the troops who accompanied the Indian chief. They marched along by the side of the elephants, and in groups ahead and in rear of them, in a confused disorder; and it seemed to the lads that a mere handful of European troops would rout such a rabble as this. They said as much to their Portuguese friend; but he told them that the people on the coast could scarcely be considered as a fair sample of those who dwelt in the hill country behind. "The climate here," he said, "is much more relaxing. Vegetation is extremely abundant, and all the necessities of life can be obtained in the easiest manner. Consequently the people here are enervated, and cannot be compared to the horsemen of the plains. The seat of the Indian power lies at Agra and Delhi—sometimes one and sometimes the other. The emperors there can take the field with two hundred thousand men if necessary, and even these, with all their power, have difficulty in maintaining their authority throughout India. You may judge, therefore, of the power of the various territorial chiefs."

A fortnight later, to their great delight, the lads heard that a vessel would start in three days for Lisbon. She was taking home a large cargo of spice and articles of Indian manufacture, and a number of invalided soldiers. She was said to be a slow sailer, but as no other was likely to start for some months the lads did not hesitate to avail themselves of the offer of the viceroy. At parting he presented them each with a sword set with diamonds, and also purses of money in token of his appreciation of the valor displayed by them in the defence of Tidore.

"It is," the viceroy said, "an honor to us to honor the members of the greatest marine expedition which has yet been made. We Portuguese may boast that we have been among the foremost in maritime discovery, and we can therefore the more admire the feats of your valiant Captain Drake."

The ship, the *Maria Pia,* was a large one, far greater, indeed, than the *Golden Hind,* and the boys felt that in a floating castle of this description their voyage ought to be a safe and pleasant one. The captain had received instructions to do all in his power to make the voyage agreeable to them. A handsome cabin had been placed at their disposal, and their position on board was altogether an honorable one.

The result justified their expectations. The voyage, although long, passed without incident. The *Maria Pia* experienced fine weather round the Cape, and, catching the trade-winds, made her course northward, and arrived off the mouth of the Tagus without accident or adventure of any kind.

Sailing up the river, she fired a salute with her guns, which was answered by those of the fort at the entrance. The news had been signalled to the capital of the arrival of a ship from the Indies, and officials boarded her as soon as she cast anchor. The captain at once went on shore and reported to the minister of the Indies the news which he had brought from Goa, and gave an account of his voyage. He delivered a letter from the viceroy, stating that he had given a passage to four English gentlemen, who had formed part of Captain Drake's equipage, and who had rendered very great services in defeating an attack upon the island of Tidore by the people of Ternate, of which matters, the viceroy added, the gentlemen would themselves give a full account. The minister at once sent on board an official to request the young men to land, and upon their so doing he received them with great courtesy, and gave a grand banquet the next day, at which the British minister was present.

The lads were delighted upon landing to receive the news that the *Golden Hind* had arrived safely in England four months before, and that all Europe was ringing with the great feat which she had accomplished. The lads found that they were received by the distinguished company which met them at the table of the minister with much honor and respect, and this was heightened upon their giving a detailed account of the adventures which had befallen them since leaving England. The British minister offered them a passage to England in one of the Queen's ships; and having provided them amply with money, they were enabled to make a good appearance, and to enter with zest into the round of festivities of which they were made the objects during their stay. They were presented to the king, who received them most graciously, and presented each with a sword of honor.

Three weeks later they sailed up the Thames, and upon landing in London at once inquired for the residence of Captain Drake. This they had no difficulty in discovering, as he was the hero of the hour. It was with great pleasure that they were received by the commander. He expressed but little surprise at seeing them, for, as he told them, he made sure that sooner or later they would arrive, and had given orders that upon the division of the great sums which had been gained by the *Golden Hind* on her voyage their shares should be scrupulously set aside.

"You had twice before," he said to Ned, "appeared after we had all given you up as dead, and I could not believe that the four of you together could all have succumbed. We got off the reef the next day, shifting her cargo all upon one side and hoisting some sail, so that the wind bore her down, her keel lifted from the reef upon which she had fastened, and without damage she went into deep water. We spent four days in looking for you. We landed at the island to which you had been directed, and searched it thoroughly. We then went to an island further to the south, and spent three days in cruising round its shores. We landed and captured some natives, but could not learn from them that they had seen any traces of you whatever. Most on board conceived that the canoe must have upset, and that you must have been drowned; but I never believed this, and felt convinced that from some unknown reason you had been unable to return to the ship, but that sooner or later you would arrive. From that point all went well with us. We had a rapid voyage down to the Cape, and coasting along it at a short distance. The weather was fair, and we turned our head north without loss of time; and so, by the help of Providence and a fair wind we made our course to England, where our gracious sovereign has been pleased to express her approval of our doings. I told her something of your journey across the south of the American continent, and she was pleased to express her sorrow at the loss of such gallant and promising gentlemen. I am sure that her majesty will receive with pleasure the news of your return. Now tell me all that has happened since I last saw you."

Ned recited the history of their adventures, and Captain Francis approved of the course which they had taken in making for Tidore instead of Ternate. He was greatly amused at their experiences as South Sea deities, and said that henceforth, let them be lost where they would, or for as long as they might be, he would never again feel any uneasiness as to their fate. He invited them to take up their abode with him while they stayed in London; and although they were eager to return to Devonshire, he told them that he thought they ought to wait until he had communicated with the Queen, and had seen whether she would wish to see the gentlemen in whom she had kindly expressed interest.

Captain Drake had received the honor of knighthood from the Queen's hand on his return from his voyage, and was now Sir Francis Drake, and was for the time the popular idol of the people, whose national pride was deeply gratified at the feat of circumnavigation, now for the first time performed by one of their countrymen.

Captain Drake despatched a letter to her majesty at Westminster, and the following day a royal messenger arrived with an order that he should bring the four gentlemen adventurers with him, and present them to her majesty. The young men felt not a little awed at the thought of being received by Queen Elizabeth. But upon their presentation by Sir Francis, the Queen received them with so much condescension and grace that their fears were speedily removed.

"I thought," she said, to Captain Drake, "that I should see four huge and bearded paladins. You told me indeed that they were young, but I had not pictured to myself that they were still beardless striplings, although in point of size they do credit to their native country. I love to listen to tales of adventure," she continued, "and beg that you will now recite to me the story of those portions of your voyage and journeyings of which I have not heard from the lips of Sir Francis."

Then modestly Ned recited the story of their journey across

America, and afterwards took up the narrative at the point when they left the ship, and her majesty was pleased to laugh hugely at the story of their masquerading as gods. When they had finished she invited them to a banquet to be given at Greenwich on the following day, gave them her hand to kiss, and presented each with a diamond ring in token of her royal favor.

The following day they went down in the barge of Sir Francis Drake, which formed part of the grand *cortége* which accompanied her majesty on her water passage to Greenwich. There a royal banquet was held with much splendor and display, after which a masque, prepared by those ingenious authors Mr. Beaumont and Mr. Fletcher, was enacted before her.

Three days later they embarked upon a country ship bound for Plymouth, and after a rough tossing in the Channel, landed there. They were received with much honor by the mayor and dignitaries of Plymouth, for Sir Francis had already written down, giving a brief account of their adventures and of the marks of esteem which the Queen had been pleased to bestow upon them; and Plymouth, as the representative of the county of Devon, rejoicing in giving a hearty welcome to her sons who had brought so much credit upon them.

After a stay of a few hours the lads separated, Tom and Reuben each starting for their respective homes, while Ned, who had no family of his own, accompanied Gerald, in whose home he was looked upon almost as a son, and where the welcome which awaited him was as cordial as that given to Gerald. The share of each of the adventurers in the *Golden Hind* was a very large one, and Ned purchased a nice little property and settled down upon it, having had enough of the dangers of the seas, and resolving no more to leave his native country unless his duty to his Queen should demand his services.

That time was not long in arriving, for toward the end of 1586 all Europe rang with the preparations which Philip of Spain was making to invade England. The Devonshire gentlemen who had fought on the Spanish Main, and who but lightly esteemed Spanish valor at sea, at first scoffed at the news, but soon no doubt could be entertained. Early in 1587 Sir Francis Drake wrote to his friends who had fought under him that her majesty had honored him with a commission to beat up the Spanish coast, and invited them to accompany him. The four friends hastened with many others to obey the summons, and on joining him at Plymouth he was pleased to appoint each to the command of a ship. Some weeks were spent in earnest preparation, and in March a fleet of thirty vessels set forth, full manned and equipped. Accustomed as the young men were to see great Spanish ships taken by single boats, and a whole fleet submissive before one ship, it seemed to them that with such an armament they could destroy the whole navies of Spain, and even then that little glory would be divided between each vessel. Upon the 18th of April the fleet was off Cadiz, and Sir Francis made the signal for the captains of the fleet to go on board the flagship. There he unfolded to them his plan of forcing the entrance to the port, and destroying the Spanish fleet gathered there. Cadiz was one of the strongest places of Spain, and the enterprise would to most men have seemed a desperate one. But to men who had fought in the Spanish Main it seemed but a light thing. As they left the admiral's cabin, Ned invited his three friends to dine on board his ship, the *Sovereign,* and a right merry gathering it was, as they talked over their past adventures, and marvelled to find themselves each commanding a ship about to attack the fleet of Spain in its own harbor.

Upon the following day the fleet sailed boldly toward the port of Cadiz, where the people could scarce believe that the British intended to force the entrance to the fort. When they saw that such was indeed their purpose they opened fire with all their batteries, great and small. The English ships sailed on, unheeding their reception, and delivering their broadsides as they neared the port. Although they had been in many fights this was the first great battle at which the friends had been present, and the roar and din of the combat, the sound of their own guns and of those of the enemy, the crash and rending of wood, and the cheers of the sailors in no little surprised them. The Spanish gunners in their haste shot but badly, and with Sir Francis Drake's ship leading the way the fleet forced the entrance into the port. As they entered they were saluted by the cannon of the Spanish vessels within, but without more ado they lay these aboard. So mightily were the Spaniards amazed by the valor and boldness of the English that they fought but feebly, jumping over for the most part or making their way in their boats to shore. Then Sir Francis caused fire to be applied to the Spanish ships, and thirty great war-vessels were destroyed before the eyes of the townspeople, while the English fleet sailed triumphantly away. Then following the line of coast as far as St. Vincent the admiral captured and burned a hundred other ships, and destroyed four great land forts. Looking into the Tagus, the King of Portugal having been forced by Spain to aid her, Captain Drake captured the *St. Philip*, the largest ship of their navy, which was, to the gratification of the sailors, laden with a precious cargo. After these exploits the fleet returned to England in triumph, having for the time crippled the forces of Spain. Philip, however, redoubled his preparations, the fleets of Naples and Sicily, of Venice and Genoa, were added to those of Spain, the dockyards worked night and day, and by the end of the year all was in readiness.

In England men had not been idle. A great army was raised of people of every rank and condition, Catholics as well as Protestants uniting in the defence of the country; while in every port round, the din of preparation was heard. The army was destined to combat the thirty thousand Spanish soldiers commanded by the Duke of Parma in the Netherlands, where a fleet of transports had been prepared to bring them across when the great armada should have cleared the sea of English ships. By dint of great efforts 191 English ships of various sizes, these mostly being small merchantmen—mere pigmies in comparison with the great Spanish galleons—were collected, while the Dutch despatched sixty others to aid in the struggle against Spain. On the 29th of May the Spanish armada sailed from the Tagus, but being delayed by a storm it was not till the 19th of June that its advance was first signalled by the lookout near Plymouth.

Then from every hill throughout England beacon-fires blazed

to carry the tidings, and every Englishman betook himself to his arms and prepared to repel the invaders. Instead, however, of attempting to land at once, as had been expected, the Spanish fleet kept up channel, the orders of the king being that it should make first for Flanders, there form junction with the fleet of the Duke of Parma, and so effect a landing upon the English coast. As the great fleet, numbering a hundred and thirty large war-vessels, and extending in the form of a crescent nine miles in length from horn to horn, sailed up channel, the spectacle, although terrible, was magnificent indeed.

The ships at Plymouth at once slipped anchor and set out in pursuit. Sir Francis Drake led, and close by him were the vessels commanded by the four friends. Paltry indeed did the squadron appear by the side of the great fleet, but from every port as they passed along came reinforcements, until in numbers they equalled those of the great ships of Spain. These reinforcements were commanded by Admirals Hawkins, Frobisher, and other gallant seaman, while Lord Howard, lord high-admiral of England, was in chief command. There was no general action attempted, for the floating Spanish castles could have ridden over the light ships of England; but each commander fell upon the enemy like dogs upon the flank of an array of lions. Sir Francis threw himself into the centre of the Spanish lines, followed by many other English ships, and thus separated several of the great galleons from their consorts, and then fell to work battering them.

The Spaniards fought valiantly, but at a disadvantage, for the smaller ships of the English were so quickly handled that they were able to take up positions to rake their enemy without exposing themselves to the broadsides, which would have sunk them. When at last they had crippled their foes they would either close upon them and carry them by boarding, or, leaving them helpless wrecks upon the water, would hoist all sail and again overtake the Spanish fleet.

The battle continued day and night for five days with scarce an intermission; the various English admirals sometimes attacking all together, sometimes separately. The same tactics over prevailed, the Spaniards sailing on and striving to keep in a compact body, the English hovering round them, cutting off every ship which lagged behind, breaking the ranks of the enemy, and separating vessels from their consorts. Hard was it to say that in that long struggle one man showed more valor than another, but the deeds of the ships commanded by the Devonshire gentlemen were second to none. On the 27th their ships were signalled to sail to join those assembled near Dunkirk, to check the progress of the Duke of Parma's fleet. They reached the English fleet in time and soon the Spaniards were seen approaching. They kept in a compact mass which the English ships could not break. For a while the fight went badly, and then a number of fire-ships were launched at the Spaniards. Seized with panic these at once scattered, and the English falling upon them a series of desperate conflicts ensued, ending almost always in the capture or destruction of the enemy. The Duke of Medina Sidonia, who commanded the main Spanish fleet, sailed north intending to coast round the north of Scotland and so return to Spain. The English ships followed for a while, but were, from the shortness of the supplies which had been placed on board, forced to put into harbor; and a great storm scattering the Spanish fleet and wrecking many, only 60 vessels, and these with their crews disabled by hardship and fatigue, ever returned to Spain.

As a consequence of their gallantry in these battles, and upon the urgent recommendations of Sir Francis Drake, her majesty was pleased to bestow the honor of knighthood upon each of the four young Devonshire gentlemen, as upon many other brave captains.

After this they went no more to sea, nor took any part in the disastrous expedition which Admirals Drake and Hawkins together made to the Spanish Main, when the brave Sir Francis lost his life from fever and disappointment.

Soon after their return from the defeat of the armada Sir Edward Hearne married the only sister of his friend Gerald, and lived with her happily to a green old age. The friendship between the four friends never diminished, but rather increased as they grew in years, and many marriages took place between their children and grandchildren.

Four times a year, upon the occasion of special events in their lives, great family gatherings were held at the house of one or other. Sir Gerald generally held festival on the anniversary of the defeat of the Spanish attack on the forest fortress in Porto Rico; Tom upon that of his escape from the prison of the Inquisition; Reuben generally celebrated the day when in the character of a South Sea idol he aided to defeat the hostile islanders; while Ned kept up the anniversary of their return to England. As to the victory over the armada, they always had to draw lots as to the house in which that great event should be celebrated. Upon all these occasions stories were told at great length, and their children, grandchildren, and great-grandchildren, for all lived to see these growing up, were never tired of listening to tales of the Spanish Main.

THE END